THE LUCKY STARMAN

THE LUCKY STARMAN

COLIN ALEXANDER

A LEIF THE LUCKY NOVEL

www.affictionado.com

For my family

PROLOGUE

I shouldn't write this story. I don't really want to, and I wasn't going to. Of course, this isn't the first time I've done things I shouldn't, didn't want to, and wasn't going to do. I spent seven years in the army, after all, from 2055 to 2062, and much of that was in combat. But I've been out of the service for a while, somewhere around nine years of my awake time and close to two centuries by the calendar on Earth. That's long enough for me to learn to do what I want to do—certain special situations excepted, naturally.

I don't actually *have* to write this. It's not as though I'm planning a memoir or hoping to achieve literary immortality as a diarist.

However, if I don't tell this story, it won't be fair to some people I care about. Their stories will go untold, and that matters to me. Starfolk don't form strong attachments to others, but somehow, I did. I seem to be stuck with my feelings. I'll never be able to look at the stars the same way again, anyway.

I guess I do need to write this. So, I've put it all down, including the parts where I don't look too good. I'll let you be the judge.

We all have our ghosts.

Leif Grettison

EARTH
AD 2251, EFOR

PART I

Though the mills of God grind slowly,
Yet they grind exceeding small;
Though with patience he stands waiting,
With exactness grinds he all.

Henry Wadsworth Longfellow, "Retribution" (1846)

CHAPTER ONE

"Leif, we have a problem."

I heard Charley's voice as if from a great distance. The post-hib blur was a dense fog in my mind. I recognized the words but could not grasp their meaning. In my defense, I hadn't even sat up in the hibernation unit yet; its bath was still draining.

I wrenched off the mask and cannula and removed the port from my arm. Then I sat up with a profound groan. Nearly four and a half years' hibernating did more than blur the brain. Every muscle was stiff. I was surprised my joints didn't squeak. Multiyear hib did not get better with repetition. I blinked and tried to bring Charley's face into focus. Dr. Charles Osborne, I told myself. Our ship's physician. He was supposed to be with me when I came out of hib. He had dark brown skin on a kindly round face, short black hair, and a closely cropped beard.

"Leif, we have a problem," he repeated. "Yang needs you on the bridge."

Why did there always have to be a problem? Why couldn't someone say, *Leif, life is great, and the world is beautiful. Why don't you come share it?* But, no, that's not the way my life goes.

I groaned again and managed to say, "What?"

Charley shook his head. "I don't know. Look, I'm sorry I didn't get your equipment off first. I'm, I don't know, worried. Here's your OJ. Yang asked you to skip the gym. She really wants you on the bridge as soon as you can get there."

That bit penetrated the blur. Yong had woken me early on the flight to High Noon, the very first starshot, when the ship's computer tried to abort the mission after a hib failure. What was it this time?

I downed the orange juice with sugar in one fast chug. Having come out of four previous multiyear hib stretches on starflights, I had learned that the best way to return to the status of a functional human was to follow a carefully escalating workout routine in the gym. It felt awful while I was doing it, but it worked. There would be a good reason if Yang Yong wanted me to skip it. And the good reason would be something bad. Count on it.

I blinked again. "Can I at least get dressed and grab a couple of protein bars from the caf?" I did manage to get the croak out of my voice.

"I'm sure," Charley said. "Just grab 'em and go to the bridge."

"I'm on it," I said. "Where's the famous laxative pack?"

Charley had that in his other hand. The constipation from hib on an interstellar flight would not, in fact, kill you, but there were times I wished it would.

Once Charley left, I pulled myself out of the unit and stood up, shivering. My muscles shook trying to hold me upright. At least I'd done this often enough to know what would hurt most and how to manage it. The biggest problem was the knee that had been surgically rebuilt after I was wounded on Mindanao back in 2062. That was why I had left the Rangers and the service, and with each long hib, it got harder and harder to return it to normal.

No help for that. I settled for cursing long and loud while I toweled off. Then I pulled on the ship's polo shirt with its NASA emblem over the left breast and my name, Grettison, embroidered below it. The starshot emblem of a gloved hand clutching a star above STARSHOT XV was stitched over the right breast. Ship pants, ankle socks, and ship boots completed the outfit. We were obviously decelerating at one gee because my weight felt normal, so I didn't need the SureGrip soles for the Stick-Strips on the deck.

I pulled open the privacy screen around my unit and stepped out onto the hib deck. All the other units I could see were off. My adrenals squeezed immediately and I felt a sense of panic. Then my mind pulled its memories through the post-hib blur. Of course nearly all the units were empty and off. We had put the colonists down on the planet called Heaven, meaning only seven of us were on the *Dauntless* for the return to Earth.

I did a set of breathing exercises and got my heart rate and blood pressure under control. It wouldn't do for me to have a stroke before I heard Yong's problem. Maybe afterward, if it was bad enough.

With my legs wobbling under me, I took the lift to the deck where the caf was and grabbed energy bars. I took the time to eat one of them and chug another sugared orange juice. I needed to get to the bridge, but I also needed to not fall on my face when I got there.

When I entered the bridge, two energy bars swallowed and two more in my pocket, one of the chairs swiveled around. Yang Yong, pilot-in-command of the *Dauntless*, stood to greet me. She was a petite and slender woman with high cheekbones and brown hair cropped as short as mine. Small, yes, but there was nothing soft or delicate about her. She'd been a crack attack plane pilot for China's People's Liberation Army Air Force during the Troubles, which meant we had been on opposite sides of the fighting. Opposite sides, hell. She had damn near killed me on Mindanao when she bombed my platoon's position the day the world almost ended.

Fortunately, our relationship had evolved from there. We were now two sides of the same coin and had decided to spend our lives flying through the universe together. It's not that either one of us ever used the L-word, but we knew what we meant to each other.

She did not smile at me. She did not even give me her tight little grin. I knew her well enough to tell that she was tense, though no one else would see any difference in the way she held herself.

If Yang Yong was tense, something was very, very wrong.

"What's the problem?" I asked.

"I don't know. We are not receiving anything."

"Nothing?" I tried to wrap my mind around that and let my hand drop from the pocket with the energy bars. They could wait.

"Nothing," she repeated. "We are inside the orbit of Pluto, and there is no signal from the International Space Commission. I have sent transmissions to Earthbase, NASA, and CNSA. We have received no response, and enough time has elapsed for a reply to reach us. Before you ask, I have checked over our equipment. It is fine. The solar system is silent."

CHAPTER TWO

We sat for a while in front of the screens and control panels, Yong on the left, in the seat reserved for the pilot-in-command, and me on the right, in the seat the copilot would take if awake and on the bridge. If we had one. I was trying to process what Yong had told me through my poor hib-blurred mind.

"Our equipment is okay," I repeated for the third, or possibly fourth, time. "Nothing in the receiving or transmitting units got vaporized while we were running at near cee."

"Yes. They work perfectly. I have checked the system. Twice." Yong's voice was calm. She was being very patient with me. I think that made it even scarier.

"But you said we've received nothing. You're saying there's been no attempt to communicate with us, although the ISC must have detected *our* signals. We're not even picking up a transponder response to our bea-con signal."

"Correct." Yong stayed calm and patient.

"And you've sent messages"—I held up three fingers—"not just to the ISC but also NASA and your CNSA in China. No reply."

"Not only those," Yong said. "I have also sent to Roscosmos, GSY Station, Lunar Base, and Artemis City on Mars. I am also broadcasting on random frequencies on the off chance the frequencies have been changed since we left, as unlikely as that might be."

"Is it possible we abandoned space? Totally? And forgot there was still a ship out here?" I stared at the starfield on the fore screen, unable to keep disbelief out of my voice.

"I am not picking up anything in the system," Yong said. "No miscellaneous transmissions. No vids. No radio. Our equipment isn't su-persensitive, but we should be able to pick up some of it."

My mind had shied away from the one explanation for all of this, but now I was forced back to it. I gagged on the words. "Is it possible . . . is it possible we actually blew ourselves up?"

"It is possible." Yong's voice acquired an edge and she turned away from the panels to look at me. "We knew when we left that the Powers were rearming, were rebuilding their militaries."

I remembered. Both Yong and I had been asked to join that effort by our respective armed forces. We had declined and gone back to the stars. Could there have been a repeat of the Troubles, that ten-year stretch of fighting from 2052 to 2062?

"Could it have gone beyond where the Troubles stopped? We used to say it was luck that we stopped right at the brink in 2062." It was melo-dramatic to whisper on a bridge where only Yong was present, but that is what I did.

"It is possible that there was a full-scale war, and we must consider it." Her voice had gone hard. Her eyes were hard too. "It is the most likely explanation."

"Okay." Think of it as a training exercise, I told myself. "What do we do?"

"That's what I want to talk to you about, Leif Soldier Boy," Yong said. "Flight decisions are mine to make, but I think we need to plan for multi-ple scenarios: at the station, with our crew, and possibly on the ground. I need your thoughts."

"You don't want to make decisions based on thoughts coming out of a blurred brain. I'll be better in a day or so. Maybe the rest of the crew can stay in hib until we can go through the options carefully and with clear minds."

"My thought as well," she said briskly. "We do not have a copilot anyway."

Right. Jorge Olivares had been our copilot on the trip out, but he and our junior doc, Song Jing, had elected to stay on the planet named Heaven. On the panels in front of us, Jorge's handprinted LAWS OF COMPUTER SYSTEMS, a mocking set of three laws about all computer systems being hacked, were still taped where he'd left them on the flight out. Thoughts of Jorge and Jing filled my mind, along with thoughts of Penny and Hiep, two of the colonists I had become very fond of before we left the Heaven settlement.

"I wonder how they're doing." I knew my slip the instant the words were out of my mouth.

"Seventy-six years EFOR, Earth Frame of Reference," Yong said before I could take it back. "Basically, the same as their frame of reference."

Right. We had traveled seventy-six light-years back from Heaven with our fusion ramjet pushing the *Dauntless* to near cee, the speed of light. Inside the ship, in the Ship Frame of Reference—SFOR—about four and a half years had passed. On Earth and Heaven, seventy-six years had gone by. The friends we had left on Heaven had lived their lives, grown old, and died. Their children—not even born when we left—had grown old, and some of them would have died too. Their grandchildren would be reaching middle age. Meanwhile, Yong and I—thanks to relativity, hib, and the drugs infused while we were in hib—were biologically still thirty-three to thirty-four. I focused on the chronometer, which was right above where Jorge had taped the paper bearing his laws. The year showed as AD 2251. I was born in 2038. The cosmos scared the shit out of me sometimes.

"Is the chronometer off?" I asked, mostly to pull myself away from thinking about friends who were dead. "We were at Heaven in 2174 EFOR, and it's seventy-six light-years."

"We spent over three months there," Yong said. "We're not at relativistic velocity the entire time, and it's a calculation. You don't want to argue with the computer, do you?"

"No." I laughed. With that, the spell of dread that time and relativity had cast was broken. "And, back to what we were saying before, it's been one hundred and fifty-three years since we left Earth. God knows what those idiots could have cooked up in that time."

"I agree," Yong said. "So here is the first decision we need to make. I can alter our trajectory so that we will fly by Mars. That will use up only a small additional amount of our antimatter fuel. We can get a look at some of the surface installations and see if we can pick up low-powered signals. What do you think?"

"I shouldn't be making decisions now."

"No choice. Now is when we need the course adjustment."

My brain didn't want to focus. I squeezed both temples with my fingers. It occurred to me that if Yong didn't think we should do this, she would never have brought it up. "Do it," I said.

"Good." She tapped at her panel and gave me a tight little grin. "From here, it's still five to six hours for a signal to get to Earth. We can wait before we try again, and we can let the others stay in hib until we know more. Would you like to join me in my quarters?"

Usually, we flipped a coin to decide whose room we used, but some decisions are easy to make, post-hib blur or no post-hib blur.

CHAPTER THREE

We were having lunch in the caf with Charley when the *Dauntless* made its flyby of Mars. Yong and I had taken to having most of our meals with Charley during the many days it took us to go from the outer stretches of the solar system to Mars. This was from, I'm sure, a sense of obligation. Don't get me wrong. Charley was a genuinely nice guy. I don't know anyone who didn't like Charley or enjoy his company, but that wasn't why we ate together.

Yong spent most of her time on the bridge. If it were not for those meals with Charley, she might have spent all her waking time there. She didn't need to. There were no changes planned for our course, the ship would record any transmissions we picked up, and even the repeated signals we sent out could have been handled by the computer. I think pilots like the sense of control that comes from being in the cockpit, even if it's mostly an illusion.

I stayed with Yong. When we weren't on the bridge, we reconditioned in the gym or went to bed in either one of our quarters. Whatever had happened in the solar system was far beyond our control. We didn't do a whole lot of talking, and when we talked, it was mostly speculation about the situation, or planning for scenarios for when we reached Earth or discussing what set of exercises to do next for which muscle group. For certain, we avoided talking about our feelings. The ghosts of wars past crowded too close for comfort to both of us, even under normal circumstances. The stress of the current situation, of *not knowing*, made it worse. It was all too easy to trigger an emotional land mine, no matter how much we denied those existed.

I just wanted to be next to Yong, preferably skin to skin. She was the only comfort I could find. I had created in my mind this fantasy universe in which we traveled the starways together until, as someone once said, the stars grew cold and the heavens dark. Whatever had happened in the solar system, though, made future star voyaging seem very unlikely. I could not escape the feeling that if God were to speak directly to me, He would say, *Leif, we have a problem.*

Needless to say, all this time we spent being a couple and brooding silently left Charley rather lonely. I did feel sorry about that and suggested eating together as a way to make up for it. That's why we were a threesome when we made our closest approach to Mars.

Charley and I were both a little surprised that Yong did not go to the bridge for our flyby. She gave me a puzzled look when I said that, pointing out that the closest approach was no different from any other point along our flight path. The tweak to our trajectory that Martian gravity would give us was known precisely and had been programmed in.

"I am not going to use the engines," she said. "We can't afford to burn the additional fuel it would take to make orbit around Mars and then leave orbit."

I did know that. To go from star to star, the *Dauntless* used a catalytic ramjet, which sucked in interstellar hydrogen, fused it to helium through a carbon–nitrogen–oxygen cycle, and spat out the helium. Ramjets didn't need to carry their own fuel. We couldn't light the fire on the ramjet, however, without reaching 6 percent cee, and to get to that velocity we needed antimatter-fueled rockets. We also needed those rockets for the final deceleration and maneuvering within a star system. We had to carry all the rocket fuel with us, and that fuel was limited.

"All we need is the images from the surface." Yong's voice had gone soft and quiet, and she wasn't looking at either one of us. "I'm not expecting much now, not after we've picked up no transmissions on our way in and no response to multiple queries. Granted, the information we have on the Martian settlements is a century and a half old, but it is hard to believe that everything would change so drastically that we could not communicate."

She stared off to her right and into space. That's not what she was actually doing. She was chipped in, her implanted chip interfaced with the ship's computer, "seeing" the displays and panels like a heads-up display superimposed on the scene in the caf. She pulled out her phone base and tapped on it to send instructions to the computer.

The screens in the caf, which had been blank, came alive with images of the Martian surface. After flipping through several, she froze one, then enlarged it. I saw buildings.

"That has to be one of the towns." I left my chair and floated, courtesy of zero gee, over to the screen on the wall. It was no different from an aerial recon photo.

"Yes. Artemis City," said Yong. "I'll enlarge further."

When she did, I could see, away from the buildings, a field of photovoltaic panels. Something did not look right. "Can you enlarge it more?"

The result was a bit pixelated, but I knew what bothered me. I would expect a field of photovoltaic panels to be rectangular or, at least, to have straight borders. The colonists on Heaven had set up such a field while we were there. But one side of this field had an irregular curve.

"It looks like a wave or a shore." I sucked in a breath and blew it out. "It's sand. The field is partially buried in sand."

"Not good," Charley said.

Yong scrolled the image so that the buildings were centered on the screen. "What do you think of that?"

In the center of the settlement was a peculiar zone. I could not see the regular outline of the buildings. What I did see were fan-shaped sprays of dark material.

"There were explosions there," I said. "If this was an after-action photo from Earth, I'd say there was a missile strike. More than one, although I guess big ground-level explosions from something else would look similar. How long ago?"

"I cannot determine that," Yong said. "The buried panels say it has been a pretty long time, although I don't know how frequent big sandstorms are in this area and how fast the sand piles up. My guess is that surrounding buildings and perhaps a partial remaining dome—which we can't be sure of from this image—have kept the sand from covering the site of the blasts. I think we can assume that no one remains alive on Mars."

"And on Earth?" Charley asked. His face had taken on an ashen hue.

"We'll find out when we make orbit there," Yong said.

"I think we should wake the other four crew members," I said. "We need to brief them on what we know. I suspect we're going to have some hard decisions to make when we reach Earth."

"Agreed," Yong said. "They'll need the time for reconditioning."

CHAPTER FOUR

The entire crew of the *Dauntless* was on the bridge when Yong took us into orbit around Earth. Dev Likhar, a dark-complexioned man with straight black hair who'd been down on the surface of Heaven with me and Yong, and Zoe Klein, a freckle-faced white woman with curly red hair, were our two nuclear engineers. Anil Jenkins, the shortest of us and a shade lighter than Dev, and Cristina Domínguez, a tall woman with an oval light tan face, were the engineers who handled Ship Systems. Along with me, Charley, and Yong, that was all of us. We were a not-so-magnificent seven as we stared in silence at the images of Earth displayed on the bridge screens.

Oh, Earth from space was as beautiful as ever. Don't get me wrong on that. The sphere was bright blue, with swirly white clouds, and green-brown continents peeking out from under those clouds, all set against jet-black space that was sprinkled with the fairy dust of stars. It was gorgeous enough to make me cry. What was bringing tears to my eyes right then, however, wasn't Earth's beauty. The night side of Earth was dark. The brilliant grid of electric lights that lit up the night and revealed the cities and towns was gone. I did see scattered splotches of rather feeble yellow. Some level of civilization was down there, lights against the dark. It had to be more than campfires, but those weren't electrified cities, for sure.

We had talked in the caf all those days from the orbit of Mars to Earth about seeing images like this. We had talked about what we saw on the Mars flyby, what those sights and the radio silence had to mean. Talk was one thing; this, on the screens, was reality. It was the difference between sparring in a gym and taking a punch in the mouth in a street fight.

Yong tapped at a control panel. The view of Earth was replaced by an aerial shot of a large coastal city. I didn't recognize the location, but it took less than a second to see there was a crater in the center of the city, surrounded by a zone of destruction.

"How long ago?" I asked.

"I can't be certain," Yong said. I saw her eyes shift to the right to read something off her projection field. "Making some assumptions about the warhead from the radiation, it happened not more than a hundred and twenty years ago and not less than fifty. The actual date doesn't matter. Not really."

I saw Cristina cross herself.

"I didn't know you were religious," I said.

"I grew up poor in Mexico City," she said. "The church raised me. I fell away at university, but when you go to the stars, it is like seeing the hand of God."

I wouldn't call myself religious in the sense of organized religion and going to church, but trust me, I prayed to God every time I went into action. Seeing that crater made me think we were going to need the hand of God.

"Where is that?" I asked.

"Shanghai." I could barely hear Yong's voice. "I grew up in Wuxi near Lake Tai. Generations of my family lived there. Maybe eighty to ninety miles from the impact point." The scene shifted to another huge city, pockmarked by a crater and a blast zone. "Beijing," she said. "At least there are three craters in Moscow." Her voice firmed a little with those words. Was it satisfaction I detected?

We had no Russians on the *Dauntless*. Would she have sounded the same speaking of Washington or New York if I were not aboard? I didn't want to ask.

"Snow cover in the Northern Hemisphere is much greater than expected for this time of year." Yong seemed to be speaking to herself. She tapped the control panel, and an image of North America swapped back and forth between the current one and one labeled 2097. "Those warheads blasted dirt into the atmosphere. Ash from firestorms in the cities added to it. Maybe volcanic eruptions as a consequence also. Surface temperatures are lower by several degrees than when we left."

So, the cure for global warming was nuclear winter. Wonderful.

"How many . . . How many people are left?" Cristina asked.

Yong's fingers danced across her panels. Numbers flashed on a screen. "Again, we cannot be sure," she said. "I am having the computer run estimates based on the amount of light in the nighttime images and apparent farmland. For what used to be the United States and Canada, you can see the outputs. Twenty to twenty-five million people. Maybe. The distribution is very uneven. Most appear located in the Midwest, upper Midwest, and a different zone in the Southeast of the old US. West of the Mississippi River, nothing except for small areas on the West Coast. Some areas in Mexico as well. Canada, nothing. I can find similar areas on other continents, but the precision is no better. Margin of error is about fifty percent overall. The computer cannot use built-up areas in the estimate, because that would count ruined cities too."

A collective gasp sounded on the bridge.

"That's less, much less than the population of the United States back in 1860," Charley said. His eyes were looking to the right, at a file he had pulled up.

"When we left, the population of the United States was almost four hundred and fifty million." Zoe's voice quavered. "If you are saying there are twenty million now, and it's at least some decades after whatever happened, then there were even fewer right after. What happened to all the people? Were they all killed in a nuclear war?"

"No," said Yong. "We can see where the missiles struck; we can count the number. There were not that many. Far fewer than the number of nuclear weapons that must have been in the arsenals. So, some of the people died in the blasts and firestorms, yes, but I think most of the people must have starved or frozen afterward, when crops failed and temperatures dropped because ash in the atmosphere blocked the sunlight, and the supply chains and the power went down."

The words cut into my mind like a knife. I remembered the history books about the Cold War, about schoolchildren taught to crawl under desks in air-raid drills. I remembered my own high school and the talk that the Troubles would spin out of control and blow us all up. It was always talk about bombs and missiles. I didn't recall fearing that we would starve to death in the dark and maybe freeze while we were doing it.

"Oh God." Zoe was crying. "We knew, going to the stars and on a voyage this long, that none of our acquaintances or relatives would be alive when we came back. I mean, none of us were tight with our families—if we even had them—and we didn't have close friends. That's who crews starships. But we assumed we were the ones going into danger, that the people we left behind would live out their lives in peace. Not that we would come back to . . . this."

Cristina had always struck me as the strong, reserved type, but she had buried her face in her hands.

"You said there are people left," Dev said. "Still quite a number. What is left of civilization? Buildings, cities, all of that?"

"That is hard to say from what we can see," Yong answered. "The old metroplexes like the Shanghai Peninsula and the Bosnywash Corridor are dead. No evidence of any activity there. There's some activity around small towns, or in what used to be open land."

She shuffled more images across the screens. "I would say that Earthbase has inhabitants. What they are doing is another question. One we cannot answer from here. But look at this."

"What is it?" Dev pointed to the image on the screen.

It was pixelated, but I could tell that it was an object and its shadow on the ground.

"It's a horse pulling a wagon," Yong said. "That's the situation down there."

CHAPTER FIVE

We reconvened in the caf a couple of hours later. The idea had been to give everyone a break from the intensity of what we'd seen on the screens on the bridge, give people a chance to pull themselves together. I'm not sure it did any good. Yong never left the bridge anyway. She sat in the pilot-in-command chair, glued to screens that carried line after line of data and images of cratered and burned cities. It was only by threatening to pull her out of the chair that I got her to leave for the caf.

The seven of us took seats around one of the tables. All the screens were off, so we were not looking at the images that we had seen on the bridge. That had been part of the idea of meeting in the caf, but it might not have been such a good one. The blank screens in a caf big enough to handle 128 colonists contributed to a sepulchral quiet that pervaded the space. I have been at funerals that were less somber. None of us said anything after we sat down, and no one was making eye contact.

Charley got a cup of coffee and came back to the table, but did nothing with it except pass it from hand to hand while staring at the zero-gee lid and drinking nipple. Dev slouched down in his seat with his neck hyperextended over the back of the chair so that he was staring at the fixtures attached to the ceiling, the ones we'd use when the starship's acceleration vector turned that into the floor. Zoe stared down at her fingers splayed out on the tabletop. Anil had both elbows an inch above the table and held his head in his hands. Cristina sat with her hands in her lap, staring at one of the blank screens. Even Yong wasn't herself. Her lips made a thin line, and little muscles at the corners of her mouth bunched. Her eyes were focused far beyond the ship's wall, and I was afraid she was seeing a scene from the Troubles.

"I will report," Yong said abruptly, breaking the silence. That served to draw all eyes to her. "Antimatter fuel for the *Dauntless* is at four percent of capacity. Fuel for the spaceplane is at three percent. As you already know, we cannot establish contact with anyone on Earth or on GSY Station in Earth orbit. There is no sign of a people-pusher from the station to take us off the *Dauntless*. On normal rations, we have food for three more weeks. We can extend that by reducing our intake. What we do have a surplus of is hib supplies. Since we were able to successfully off-load the colonists, and Jorge and Jing stayed with them, we have hib supplies for one hundred and thirty people for four years and four months, SFOR."

Dev spoke in the direction of the ceiling. "What good is that?"

Charley made a point of pulling out his phone base and tapping at it as a way of showing us that he was calculating something. "Are you implying that we should go back into hib? For just the seven of us, those supplies would last about eighty years. Are you saying we should hibernate for eighty years and bet Earth recovers?"

"I'd bet we wake in eighty years and find we're in the same shit we are now," Dev said. He had not shifted his focus from the ceiling.

"It doesn't have to be." Zoe looked up from her hands for the first time since we'd sat down. "The world went from inventing the electric light bulb to landing on the moon in, what, just about ninety years. Maybe that's the way out."

It was left to me to be the Grinch. "Sorry, that won't work," I said. Zoe looked stricken, so I had to finish. "I worked for Prof Chiang in the Hibernation Lab in Miami all those years ago. We had rodents in hib for a large proportion of their life span and they woke okay, but eighty years is damn near a full life span for us. The combination of hib and the selective telomerase activators we infuse while we're in hib holds our biological aging down to about one month for every SFOR year in hib, but people have gone four to five years max, not eighty. Even if the drugs still work fine, you know what it's like when we wake after about four and a half years.

We get away with the long starflights because once our velocity is up close to cee, the incremental SFOR time for each additional light-year is very small. If we go in and stay in here, those years are all SFOR years. Nobody has ever tried anything like that—not that I know of, anyway—and my guess is that all we would be doing is committing suicide with, maybe, a nasty death if we do wake."

I'm no rocket scientist—not any kind of a scientist; I was a lab tech—but I worked on hib and have probably gone into and come out of hib more than any other human. Unless they had improved the technology after we left for Heaven, I didn't think we could do eighty years in hib. Even if they improved the technology, we didn't have it. We had what we'd left with.

Charley wasn't ready to give it up. "We could wake every four to five years," he said. "Recondition, then go back in."

"We'll run out of food with all that awake time. Right, Cristina?" She nodded. I turned back to Charley. "That's also assuming the equipment will do fifteen to twenty cycles, and I don't know that. But even if it does, we don't have enough food."

Zoe started to cry, her tears floating away.

"What do we do now?" Dev asked.

Good question. Even before interstellar travel became possible, Hollywood had produced countless vids about a crew of star travelers who returned to Earth to find that civilization had been destroyed in a global war. We had fallen into a lousy Hollywood show. I hate postapocalyptic fiction.

I felt helpless. I *was* helpless. This wasn't one of those times when I could tell people that they needed to get some perspective, that it wasn't so bad, that we could work through the problem. Our cities had been missiled. Our civilization had been destroyed. And we were stuck in space in a starship that was almost out of fuel and food. This qualified as desperate straits.

"We do not have many choices," Yong said.

"Do we have any at all?" Charley brought his coffee up to his mouth but put it down without taking a sip. "GSY Station is supposed to send a shuttle on our return, a people-pusher, to take us off the ship and bring us into the station. That's not happening, obviously."

"We have two options, and we are not dependent on a shuttle to the station." Yong's voice came back to its usual crispness and she was erect in her seat, as if at attention. "The spaceplane has, as I said, three percent of its fuel remaining. Not much, but if we choose our landing site and calculate an unpowered descent, I believe I can take us out of orbit and manage the landing. It is quite risky but it can be done. There is a better alternative, however." She paused for an instant, so our eyes were on her as we waited for her to finish. Dev sat up straight. "We go back to the stars."

That sentence dropped like a brick into the quiet surface of a pond. All eyes remained riveted on Yong.

"That's impossible!" Dev looked at Yong. "We don't have enough antimatter fuel to even reach six percent cee and light the fire on the ramjet, much less manage our entry into a system on the other end of a flight. I *know* this."

"I know the fuel situation as well, and there is a solution." Yong stood up, anchored on the StickStrips, and faced Dev. Faced all of us. I saw her give a quick tug at the first two fingers of her left hand. "Antimatter fuel is produced at the plant at Lagrange Point Five. During the Troubles, almost two hundred years ago EFOR, it was a Chinese military installation. It was given to the ISC after the Treaties to make fuel for the starshots. It is entirely automated. Even when we left the solar system, crews only went to check on the operation at intervals. I have verified that the facility is still there; it has not been destroyed. That plant has adequate solar power, and for obvious reasons, certain functions are designed to be permanently on. I have been able to query it for a status update. Production of fuel continued until the plant's storage capacity was reached. It is there, waiting for us. As we have discussed, the *Dauntless* has adequate hib supplies, more than enough for any star voyage we will take. Awake-time food will be tight, but we can shorten the awake time and we may be able to salvage some food from GSY Station. If we decide to go to the stars, we can do it."

"You still have the same problem of landing the spaceplane with so little fuel. Same risk as on Earth," Dev said.

"Not quite," Yong replied. "The LZ at any colony will have functioning instruments and we will not need to worry about the landing area itself, or the conditions around it. There will be no possibility that air defenses will still be active and shoot down the spaceplane."

Dev's eyes opened wide. The idea of being shot down had obviously not crossed his mind. He paused and everyone else waited for him. "Okay. Say we do go back to the stars," Dev said slowly. "Where do we go? Back to Heaven?"

That thought was an electric cattle prod in my ribs. I know I stiffened. In my mind, I saw Penny and Hiep waving to us as Yong and I took off from the LZ there in the spaceplane. Our awake time since we left Heaven had been about three months. My memory of their smiles and waves was as clear as if the time from then to now had been that brief. Yet if we went back to Heaven, we might meet their great-great-grandchildren. Penny and Hiep would be long dead. Time traveler's remorse was a bitch.

"Not necessarily," said Yong.

Thank you, I thought. I would have preferred an outright rejection, but this helped to loosen the brain lock that had seized me.

"Listen for a moment." Yong was turning to look at each of us, as though to include everyone in what she said. "If the colonies have transmitted updates on their progress, the ISC office in GSY Station should have the information. We can access that. Heaven cannot have sent an update. Even if they sent a transmission when we left, the signal would have reached here only months ahead of us, and we know they did not have that capability then. We know that a ship was sent before we left to establish a colony on High Noon, and that star is only fourteen light-years away. They could have sent progress reports to the ISC. Those can tell us if it would be a good destination. And there may be other possibilities. We will need to get into the station and see if we can pull anything from the ISC offices."

"That assumes," Dev said, "that we decide to leave Earth. Forever."

Yong put her hands behind her back and came to a position of parade rest, rigid as a statue on the StickStrips. "Please understand. During the Troubles, I joined our army with great patriotic fervor. I was an eager volunteer, ready to fight even if it cost my life. I flew the missions. I dropped the bombs. I fired the missiles. I prepared the way for those who did what we see here now. I believe I share the responsibility . . . and the guilt. I need to leave."

I rose and took a few steps to stand next to Yong on the caf's StickStrips. I had my own ghosts: the people I'd killed, the ones who'd died alongside me. "I fought in the Troubles as well," I said. "I'm with Yong. Where she goes, I go."

"My heart aches for you. It really does." Charley stood and took a step toward Yong. His arms started to come up in what might have been the beginning of a hug, but nobody hugged Yang Yong. Nobody except me, and that was totally private. Charley realized this and put his arms back down, then brought them up again and crossed them over his chest. "Look, you have a right to your feelings. I'll never say otherwise. But it's different for me. I wasn't born yet when the Troubles happened. For me, the Troubles are history, not part of my life. We've seen that there are towns and cities down there with some level of civilization, not just craters. Earth is my home. I want to go home."

"You can't really go home, Charley," I said. "We have no idea what it's like now, except that it's not electrified. And don't discount temporal alienation. You won't fit. We found that out when we came back from High Noon, and Earth then was a lot closer to the one we left than this one will be."

"I get it, Leif," he said. "If this is how my journey ends, so be it. I want to stay."

"So do I," said Dev.

One by one, the remaining three took the same position.

"Yong said the spaceplane might have enough fuel to manage a landing," I said, "but there will be no fuel to return to the *Dauntless*, and I doubt we'd find any on Earth. We all go or we all stay. If we stay here, it's only one landing. We all go to the same place."

Silence descended again. It was a stark choice. Yong was in command, but this wasn't a choice made by command.

Then Dev tapped a forefinger to his lips. "Maybe it's not a binary choice. If the space elevator is still functional, we can use that. The antimatter production facility seems to have been operating, and the elevator has its own power source."

Except for one minor problem. "The elevator goes down to an artificial island in the ocean," I said. "We can't bet on a boat or serviceable plane being there to take us to land."

Dev's face froze, then relaxed in a smile. "The elevator platform has emergency escape pods. They're located below the main platform. Those should be functional. They were designed to work if all power and communication went out."

Out of the debate that followed, a plan emerged, a decision tree of sorts. Our first stop would be the antimatter production facility at L-5. Yong confirmed that we had enough fuel to get there and back to Earth even if we found nothing. If no fuel was there despite the readouts Yong had obtained, she would take the spaceplane down to Earth with everyone from the crew. If the fuel was there, we would refuel the *Dauntless*. That would give us both starflight capability and flexibility in maneuvering around Earth.

The next step after the production facility would be GSY Station. We could connect to the station network, but we could not get any communication either from people or computers. Still, it seemed reasonable to believe that there would be information, in the ISC offices if nowhere else, about where it might be safe to land on Earth and which colonies among the stars would be worth trying for. We might also be able to locate more food, and more fuel for the spaceplane.

The last step would be the space elevator. Charley and Zoe were Americans. Dev was from India, Anil from Britain, and Cristina from Mexico. Each of them wanted to land in their own country, whatever was left of it. If we could refuel the spaceplane, that could be done. Even if we could not do that, the information in our computer indicated that the escape pods at the space elevator could be programmed for individual landing spots. Once the other five were taken care of, Yong and I would take off for . . . somewhere.

If all else failed, Yong promised that we would pick the best landing place from the information we found at GSY Station and she would take everyone down in the spaceplane. I was afraid of what that last option would do to Yong's mind, and I did try to talk to her about it as soon as we were alone, back on the bridge, with her at the controls and me in the copilot seat.

"That school bombing was not your fault, Yong. One side tricked you, and the other side was using the school and the kids there as a shield. It's not your fault." She had told me about bombing a command center during the Troubles, only to discover afterward that it had been inside a school.

Her eyes narrowed. "It's not only the school. It's not any single mission, or even all of them together. I had a dream last night that I was flying a nuclear mission."

"Yong, don't do this to yourself."

"I am not doing anything." Her eyes narrowed further, the way they did when she was angry or intense. "We did this, you and I and our fellow soldiers. Without our willingness to fight, this never happens. The responsibility and guilt are real. We all have our ghosts, Soldier Boy. I deal with mine the best I can."

"Wherever you go, Flygirl, I'm going with you. Even to hell. You know that."

She smiled then and touched me lightly on one arm, although she took her hand away quickly. "I do. Let's do what we have planned."

It was an impressive set of plans, drawn up under pressure and in very little time. We had a contingency plan for whatever might happen. We had thought of everything.

Yeah, sure.

CHAPTER SIX

The antimatter production facility was at the Lagrange Point L-5. This spot in space represented one of the three angles in an equilateral triangle with the Earth and Moon. Objects at a Lagrange Point were in stable orbits; they stayed where they were relative to the Earth and Moon. This made them good locations for factories in space, especially for one involved in the large-scale production of antimatter.

My first trip with Yong to this antimatter production facility had been from the old NISS, at that time the New International Space Station. We had flown in a cramped transport ship, a four-seater. It was cramped even though we were the only occupants and not truly on speaking terms at that time. With the small rockets and limited fuel of that transport, the trip had taken two days.

The *Dauntless* had an antimatter drive that propelled us at one gee for half the distance. Then Yong flipped the ship around and used the engines to decelerate. It made for a short trip at constant gravity except for the flip-over time. Comfortable.

Until we got there.

We were closing in on the plant. Our velocity difference with the plant had dropped close to the point that Yong was going to cut the antimatter engines and nudge the *Dauntless* next to the facility with the little maneuvering thrusters. I was seated, as usual, in the copilot's chair.

Suddenly, red lights flashed on the displays in front of Yong. Her reactions were near instantaneous. Her hands played over the controls. A hard burst of acceleration drove me into my chair. Then we were weightless.

I was chipped in, and our internal channel filled with a babble of voices. Message notifications popped all over the periphery of my field. It is astonishing how much noise fewer than half a dozen humans can make.

"Silence!" Yong's voice of command cut through all the chatter. "No one speaks or sends except by my order or to report an issue."

The channel went dead quiet. The notifications and messages cleared.

"Ship systems," Yong said, "I show a hull breach. Report."

"Ye-es," Cristina's voice quaked as she spoke. "We have a puncture on deck three, the colonists' quarters. The deck is empty. Internal air locks have sealed and isolated it. Looks like a micrometeorite puncture."

"It was not a meteorite." Yong's voice was devoid of emotion. "We were attacked."

Attacked? In space? I had a vision of an alien starfighter, like in a Hollywood vid, zooming in from the depths of the galaxy. The image morphed in my mind. I saw a Chinese J-45 superstealth attack plane, low over the water off Mindanao, missiles locked on my position. I fought to clear my mind. That was nearly two centuries ago, I told myself, even while my stupid brain insisted that it was happening *now*. My vision cleared, but I found myself dripping sweat, my breath coming in rapid gasps. Thank God Yong was too busy to notice.

"Anyone injured? Report now," she said. No reports followed.

"Good. Everyone into suits. Notification to me only when you are suited. Dr. Osborne, when you are in your suit, get to the Medical Unit. Your position will be there. If anyone sustains an injury, go to the Medical Unit. Report only if you cannot reach it without assistance. Likhar, I want you on the bridge as soon as you are suited up. This channel must remain clear. Yang out for now."

Yong stood in a single graceful motion anchored by the StickStrips. Her face was as impassive as a marble statue. "Our suits are in the locker on the bridge. It looks like we're going back into action, Soldier Boy."

"Mind telling me what is attacking us out there?" I asked.

THE LUCKY STARMAN 33

"Suits first," she said. "I'll explain when Dev gets here."

Yong was pilot-in-command, and in a combat situation—which, somehow, this had become—her authority was absolute. She slipped back into a combat role as though she had never left it. Reflex kicked in. I shut up and followed orders.

We were weightless, so I was careful to stay to the StickStrips as I moved to the suit locker. We had all practiced getting into a suit in zero gee on a regular schedule—survival skills need to be kept current—but it wasn't something we did every day. Still, I was in my suit, helmet locked and air flowing, only a little behind Yong.

As soon as I had the suit on, I heard "Likhar, where are you?" on the channel.

"Getting my suit."

"Immediately." Yong's response was an order.

It took longer than Yong wanted, but Dev did appear on the bridge in his suit in what I thought was reasonable time for a civilian. I could hear him breathing hard on our open channel.

"This is the situation," Yong said. "There are multiple small objects in space here. The computer identified them as rocks or space junk. Some of them are not, however. As we approached the facility and its control module, two objects changed position and moved toward us." Yong sent images from one of the screens that showed two trajectories converging on the position of the *Dauntless*. "Both detonated, firing a burst of fléchettes at the *Dauntless*. Cameras picked up the event." She sent a brief vid clip. When I played it, I saw a sudden burst against the starfield. "The graphene supercoil structure of a starship is designed for potential impacts prior to the time the ramscoop field deploys. These objects appear to have been designed with that structure in mind. The fléchettes were deployed at high velocity but did not rely on that alone. They contained thermite or some related compound to burn through the hull. It is all cleverly designed to penetrate a ship and cause a massive decompression. Even with the design of our hull, we are at risk. External equipment, like the generator for the ramscoop, will be at greater risk. An ordinary in-system ship would likely have been destroyed. We have a hull puncture, and it could easily have been worse. The *Daredevil*, the ship that set up the Heaven settlement prior to our arrival there, would have been less than a year ahead of us returning from Heaven and we have had no sign of them in orbit, so it is possible they fell victim to these defenses."

My mind tallied up the information and I didn't like the conclusion. "We are in a fucking minefield," I said. "Who puts a fucking minefield out in space?"

"I don't know, but I agree with your assessment about what we face." Yong put her hands on her hips.

"We have lasers for space rocks," Dev said. "Can't we use those for defense and zap these things?"

"After the first one detonated, I tried that with the second," Yong said. "They are mirrored, and I think the mirror was designed with military lasers in mind. One of our lasers was damaged by reflected light."

"Maybe it's better if we give up and leave," Dev said.

"We need the fuel. And we may encounter similar, call them minefields, at GSY or the space elevator platform, or defense systems if we try to land on Earth. I have a different idea." Yong paused. "The antimatter rockets are a variant beamed-core design with ultrahigh-efficiency magnetic nozzles. The exhaust is a collimated beam of charged and uncharged pions with an exhaust velocity approximately seventy percent cee. Correct?"

"Yes, of course," Dev said. "Where are you going with this?"

"The pions decay rapidly. Refresh me on the cascade."

Dev complied, launching into a verbal avalanche about muons and gamma rays and positrons and other particles I forgot as soon as I heard them, all with associated energies and other characteristics. For all I understood, he could have been speaking Chinese.

Yong walked back to the pilot-in-command chair and drummed her suited fingers on its back. "Can we alter the angle of one or two of the nozzles independently and adjust them as we go so that I can aim the exhaust?"

"I think so," said Dev. "If you do that, it will apply an acceleration vector."

"I realize that," Yong said. "I will compensate with the thrusters and hope I do not exhaust their fuel in the process."

I didn't follow the particle physics, but I did grasp Yong's intent. The mines might be designed to account for a laser, which was photons—light, in other words. She was going to sidestep the mirror defenses built into those mines. She was going to turn the rocket exhaust into a subatomic ray gun and fry the electronics in those mines and their fléchettes with particles and gamma rays.

I always loved the Buck Rogers remakes.

CHAPTER SEVEN

Pushed by an array of our little attitude thrusters, the *Dauntless* flew ahead into the minefield, rocket nozzles pointing ahead of us. We were charging into battle ass-first.

Yong watched the screens for an alert that some rock wasn't a rock but was moving toward us. Then she had to manually adjust the aim of one of the magnetic nozzles and blast the mine. Each shot jolted us and changed our vector, which required more adjustment with the thrusters. We had no way to program the ship's computer to do this; it was all on Yong. We had four more close encounters on the way in. She hit every one of them with her first shot.

.   .   .

"Well, there it is," Dev said, "as though it were waiting for us."

It was the collection of antimatter fuel containers. They were held in four separate lattice frameworks that were in turn attached to a small transport ship. Magnified on our screen, that ship looked little different from the one Yong and I had flown here before the first starshot, when we were just a couple of hostile strangers. The crew and control modules for the production facility were there as well. Those had changed. That structure was much larger than I remembered, with additional modules attached to the cylindrical section. The conical control module, which had formed the front end of that station and where I had fought with Miles Richmond, was gone, replaced by a spherical unit. Oddly, the transport was not docked to the station. It floated quietly in space a kilometer away from the station, according to our instruments.

"Yeah, all it needs is gift wrap," I said. "How do we get it from there to our ship?"

This was antihydrogen we were talking about, stored in magnetic bottles at the near absolute zero of cold space. Fueling our ship with that and the paired containers of normal hydrogen was not going to be like the ancient days of internal combustion cars, when all you did was stick a hose from the pump into the car's tank.

"Into the ship is easy," Dev said. Naturally, a nuclear engineer would say that. "All we need to do is align the free base of one of the lattices with the fueling port on the ship. The co-bots will engage—Zoe and I can run them—and the ship will load the containers. Time consuming, but not difficult. I'm only surprised it's waiting here for us."

"I'm not," Yong said from the pilot-in-command seat. "The facility is intact and operational and it is automated. So, it will do what it was designed and programmed to do—generate antimatter fuel in the production area. Once produced, the bots will package it and transport it to the crewed station and ready it for transport. The system has stopped only because all positions in the production chain are full and no one has come to pick up any fuel."

"Then why is that transport here?" I asked. "The transports were flown here to get the fuel. That's how we did it. I would think that if the chain stopped because no one was taking fuel anymore, there would be containers at the station waiting for a ship."

Yong frowned. "That's a good question. Maybe something happened to the last crew. It is a bit of good luck, since when the lattices are coupled to the transport, they are set to load into a ship. Much simpler than having to load from an uncoupled lattice or free containers."

She tapped one of her panels and looked at the figures on a screen. "When we left the solar system, it would have taken four transports to fuel the *Dauntless*. This one is carrying enough to do it alone."

"Are you saying," I said to Yong, "that all you need to do is go over to that ship, maneuver it over here, and we're done?"

"No." Yong leaned back in her command seat. "We were attacked on our way to the facility. We are in a combat zone. I cannot predict if there will be further hostilities. Therefore, I cannot leave the bridge of the *Dauntless*." She swiveled her seat around. "You need to pilot the ship over here, Soldier Boy."

My mouth dropped open. When I got control of those muscles again, I said, "What? I don't know how to fly a spaceship!"

Dev laughed. More of a cackle, I thought. "Come on, Leif! You're always talking about how good you are self-driving cars and rovers."

I stared at his grin. He must have felt that he was getting even with me for something I had said in the past, but I had no idea what that something could be. Well, maybe I did.

"I self-drive cars and military equipment," I said. "I know how to do that. This is a *spaceship*."

"Same thing, except without wheels and add a rocket." Dev laughed again.

"Fine. I'll figure it out."

On occasion, I speak without thinking through the issue.

Yong nodded as though she expected nothing else. Quite probably, that was the exact truth. "Dev, you're going with him," she said. "We need to have direct inspection of the containers and the feeder mechanism."

From Dev's expression, I believe he would have preferred me to figure out that bit as well. What he said was, "Can't we maneuver the *Dauntless* so that we line up with the feeder on the lattice? Zoe or I can go EVA on the hull and check the feeder and containers that way."

"No. We cannot afford to use that much fuel from the attitude thrusters," Yong said. "Not after what I had to burn coming in the way we did. Even if I could, this starship is not designed for that kind of precision maneuver."

"But—"

"Enough. This is a combat environment and I am in command." Yong cut him off with a hard, cold voice. "There will be no further discussion. It only wastes time."

Dev's face showed a flash of fright. Yong could have that effect on people.

·   ·   ·

We were at the air lock by the transport and people-pusher dock, one deck below the bridge, and running through our checklists, when Dev said, "You do know that I was just joking with you before. Right?"

I have had people comment on my sense of humor. But I can take a joke, even if I can't tell one.

"Of course," I said. "Why would you think otherwise?"

"Well . . ." Dev paused while we both went completely on suit systems and finished our checklists. "You sounded serious."

I finished off the checks on the suit's jetpacks. "You think I'm sensitive?"

"No, of course not. It's just—"

"It's just that you're about to jump out of a starship with me and ride back in the rocket I'm going to pilot," I finished for him. "Make sure your tether is clamped, just in case we miss the transport. Now, let's do our jobs."

I can take a joke. Even a bad one.

I opened the lock's inner door, floated through, and attached my tether. Dev, now silent, followed me and attached his. The inner door slid closed behind us. I checked my tether again, then evacuated the air from the lock. When the door light flashed green, I opened the outer door and pushed off. Black space, liberally sprinkled with stars, was all around me. It's an awe-inspiring, stomach-churning view, but I didn't have time for it. I checked that my jetpack was, in fact, working properly, never mind the assurance of the readouts. One puff of a jet turned me and another puff stopped me. I checked six and there was the *Dauntless*, big and bold in sunlight. I spun again and saw the little transport in front of me with the frameworks that held our fuel. It was time to do this.

"Grettison, here," I said on the ship channel. "I'm good to go." I could see on the readouts that my pulse was up. That annoyed me but I was chipped out, so Yong wouldn't be able to see it, and it didn't show in my voice.

"This is Yang. You are cleared to proceed." Her pulse would be up, too, and it never, ever showed in her voice.

I fired the jetpack. The distance to the transport closed faster than I'd expected. A lot faster. True, the tether would stop me, but it would look bad. I fired the opposing jets. That stopped my flight toward the transport and actually pushed me back slowly toward the *Dauntless*. This now

looked worse than having my flight braked by the tether. I turned off the
channel and swore to myself in my helmet. When I was done, I opened
the channel again and tried to give a minimal push to the suit. These jetpacks were tricky to use. The only time I had done this before, other than
a brief training course, was when Yong and I had come to this very same
station before the first starshot and I had to blast my way in to get to Miles
Richmond. A lot had happened since then.

With some trial and error, I was able to graduate the pushes from the
jets so that I came to a stop adjacent to the transport. Percolating through
my mind was the thought that I would have to do a better job maneuvering the ship or we might have a bit of a problem. At least getting into
the ship was simple. Air locks don't have exterior locks, for obvious reasons. They are also designed to be opened by people too panicked to think
straight. The exterior door was marked by a broad black-and-white outline. A large touchpad in the shape of a hand was next to it. At the touch
of a gloved hand by the lock, the exterior door slid open. I looked for Dev
and allowed myself a tiny bit of amusement when I saw that he had gone
at an angle and was at the end of his tether, well above the transport. Yong
and I talked him through the process to reach the lock.

The transport held air, but it was cold. Not outer space cold; the ship
had been powered down to provide only enough heat to prevent damage
to its components. But way too cold for people. White rime covered every
interior surface.

"We'll have to see if it will power up and respond to commands,"
I said over our channel. "There is, obviously, still power here, but the
rest . . . we'll have to see."

"Can you chip in?" Dev asked.

"No. I don't intend to try and you shouldn't either. There's no reason
for this ship to recognize either of us by voice and eye, and any access
codes we have are a century and a half out of date. And even all the way
back in the Troubles, military systems were hardened against chip intrusion. The space here is mined, so there must have been fighting even out
here. And we don't know if this ship was used by someone's military. I
don't want to find out the hard way, by trying and having it blow up."

Dev looked suitably chastened through his faceplate. I had another
reason for not trying to chip in. A worry tickled at the back of my mind
that, perhaps, the ship's computer could do something to *me* if I chipped

in. Computer systems taking over people through their chips was a staple of Hollywood and graphic novels when I was a kid. It had also been an excuse used by neo-Luddite factions protesting against people having chips at all, but that was nothing more than fiction. That wasn't how chips worked. Not then. But what couldn't be done in 2069, or even 2097, might be possible in 2251—especially if the solar system had gone stark, raving mad and civilization had been destroyed in a war. Which seemed to have happened. I can't say the idea didn't bother me.

I set the suit cameras so that Yong could see what I was looking at. Then she started giving me directions. I was able to clean off enough frost from the instruments in front of the pilot-in-command seat that she could figure out how to fly the ship. Yong had flown one of those transports exactly once, after training for a day on a simulator. She was, however, the best pilot in the galaxy and could fly anything. Okay, that was my opinion.

"The layout looks similar to what we had," she said. "I don't think they changed much in the time between when we left and this war happened. Try this."

I pulled myself into the pilot-in-command seat and did that. She sent me instructions and I tapped and clicked. The panels and screens in front of me came alive with lights.

"That's good," she said. "Now, I don't want the main engine. Just the attitude thrusters. You have nearly one hundred percent of fuel capacity."

Again, I followed directions. Stars swung past the front viewport as the little ship turned.

"Good. Now, here is how to bring up your orientation and distance to the fuel feeder port." Then she sent me the information on how to check the alignment. "These are the thruster sets you will want in order to correct angle and distance. Play with it a bit while I watch the screens, before we do it for real."

I tried each thruster, watching how the angles, speed, and distance changed. It felt like a vid game. It felt a lot easier, in fact, than steering a smart missile to its target from the other side of a hill—and I had done that. Those missiles moved a hell of a lot faster and there was minimal reaction time. Of course, if you missed with the missile, you'd curse and maybe get chewed out. If I screwed up here, well, we were sitting in the ships that would crash.

Once I had a feel for what the attitude thrusters did, I used the cameras again to let Yong see the screens and control panels. Then I let Yong talk me through the maneuver. It was a clumsy process at best, with a lag time between when information on the transport's screens needed to be acted on and when my fingers reacted to Yong's words. If I had been chipped into the transport, it would have been quicker, but it may have been better the way we did it, because sometimes I made the wrong move. Fortunately, the transport did not need to move fast. We took our time and nudged it into the correct position and orientation.

After something like an eternity had passed, I heard Zoe's voice. "Alignment is within the margin of error. I'm opening the fuel compartment and extending the feeder tracks."

That assembly would connect to the transport's lattice holding the fuel containers and begin loading them into the *Dauntless*. Assuming the design hadn't changed in the time we had been gone. Assuming the two were still compatible.

Yong must have had the same thought. "You can extend the feeder tracks but do not couple. Repeat, do not couple. Dev, I want you to check the alignment and the actual coupling. Make certain that this will work before we start the feed process."

"It looks fine on-screen," Dev said. "If I could chip in, I could examine the actual latch structure and circuits."

"You cannot chip in," Yong said. "We've been over that. I want you outside on the lattice. Direct visual inspection."

Dev grumbled, but I think he closed off the circuit to Yong first. He was suited up anyway, so it took him only a couple of minutes to go out the lock. I waited by the control panels as he made his way down the lattice. I could hear his breathing as he went. Then I heard a sharp intake of breath.

"This is odd," he said. "There is some device at the end of the lattice on the feeder line. Not sure what it does, but I am pretty sure we can still couple and feed. There's an additional assembly next to it. Looks like I can use that to align this device so it's out of the way. I'm recording now."

A window opened in my field so that I could see what Dev was picking up with his camera. The main part of it looked like a box holding a bulb attached to a tripod that was, in turn, mounted on a plate. There was a separate handle on what looked like a lever. As his light swept over it,

I noticed something else. That assembly had been attached to the feeder system; it wasn't part of the original build.

Dev's hand reached for the lever. My subconscious put the pieces together without me thinking about it.

"It's a bomb!" I shouted. "It's booby-trapped! Don't touch it!"

My words coincided with a burst of smoke that obscured everything in the field of Dev's camera. Dev's scream filled my helmet, then stopped abruptly.

CHAPTER EIGHT

The blast must have knocked Dev off the lattice, because when he was clear of the dust, his cameras showed a spinning starfield. He was no longer tethered to the transport. I couldn't raise him on the channel. I didn't need access to his chip readouts to know that he had been killed.

Shit.

"Leif, what happened?" That was Yong.

"Booby trap. It blew when Dev grabbed part of it. Can you find him on a camera?"

"Searching." Yong went silent for a minute. "I have him. His tether was severed. Multiple suit punctures, including in the helmet. It must have blown out edged pellets, designed to defeat a self-sealing suit and be nonsurvivable. He is dead. I do not think we can retrieve his body, and I do not believe it is wise to try. Did that explosion damage the lattice or feeder?"

"I can't tell from in here. I'm thinking that was a secondary booby trap in case someone found the bomb, which is very nasty thinking on someone's part. The antipersonnel part of this might not have damaged the feeder, but there is still a bomb attached to it. Safest thing to do is I'll jetpack back and we can leave this little bomb to float on its own."

"We can't do that," Yong said. "Not if there is any chance of using this feeder. We still need the fuel. Even if we go to the production facility and find more fuel containers, there are probably other booby traps, and we might not find them. We know the booby trap here."

"What are you saying?" I asked.

"I need you to go take a look at that feeder. If it's still intact, and the bomb is still there, you're going to have to disconnect it, Soldier Boy."

I'd known she was going to say that. I would have said the same if I were in her place and someone from my squad was in mine.

By this time, even though I had not turned up the heat in the crew area of the transport, the use of the control panels and screens had generated enough heat to melt the frost on them. That created water drops across those surfaces. It looked like the ship was sweating. Some of the droplets came loose and floated through the cabin. As I prepared to go EVA and deal with the bomb, I felt like I was sweating as much as the panels. It's not really a good idea to do that in a space suit.

The ship had a tool locker behind the seats for the crew, and I ransacked that. Some of the stuff I didn't recognize and didn't trust, but I found one item that looked like a motorized metal cutter. That, I thought, could prove useful. Then I went out the lock and climbed hand over hand down the lattice.

I passed Dev's tether. It had been sliced by the projectiles from the booby trap. When I reached the end of the framework where he had been, I played a light on what was there. I saw the same assembly that we had seen from his cameras. The exception was that the handle and lever he had grabbed were gone.

"That main assembly does look like a bomb," I said, "but it's not designed to blow up somebody inspecting the feeder."

"Agree," Yong said. "It was protected by a booby trap placed for exactly that purpose. I can't be certain, but I would say that the primary assembly is designed to blast a projectile into a fuel bottle as it comes down the feeder. The ship AI puts that probability at ninety-two percent and suggests that it contains hydrogen."

Sure. The fuel bottles containing the antihydrogen weren't armored against projectiles. Blast some regular matter into one of them, especially a hydrogen canister. The initial explosion would rupture other bottles.

Hydrogen and antihydrogen would mix. As the old saying goes, a star is born. I had the chills.

"That's why this transport was left floating here with enough fuel for a starship," I said. "It's just like troops retreating after a ground action. They'll leave booby-trapped rifles, backpacks with food, all sorts of things some dumb soldier will pick up. This was a lure. God in Heaven, it got evil here."

"Someone wanted to make certain that the antimatter fuel and the production plant were not accessed. Possibly afraid of it being used to make bombs." Yong's voice rang in my helmet even though she kept her tone normal. "I would assume they did not want to destroy everything here, perhaps thinking that they would come back after a victory. How many other traps were set? The *Daredevil* may well have died around here, if not in the minefield. I wonder about other starships when they returned."

"Let me have a look at this bomb," I said. This was the devil we knew. I did not want to go looking for fuel anywhere else.

I shined my light at it from all angles. What I saw was not very helpful. I guess, in the back of my mind, I was hoping for a bright red wire labeled CUT HERE TO DISABLE. No such luck. In reality, I didn't see any wiring.

"The antipersonnel blast didn't set it off, so it's not a simple motion detector. Maybe mass, maybe mass plus motion. I bet it will pick up a fuel container going past and then it fires."

"Yes," Yong said. "And it fires a projectile. It doesn't simply explode."

That also made sense. We were in the vacuum of space. An explosion might wreck the feeder, but a projectile that penetrated the fuel container would cause the disaster we had speculated about.

"That gives us a little margin of safety," I said. "If it's not pointing right at the fuel container when it goes off, we're okay." More specifically, I would be okay.

That was when my metal cutter gave me an idea. "If I can cut the inside leg of that tripod, I can tilt the platform a little. Then we can make it fire and miss."

"Reasonable," said Yong. "Here's the AI assessment on audio."

The sultry voice of a young woman that Jorge had picked for our computer's audio interface filled my helmet. "Based on the available information, the likelihood of success is estimated at eighty-four percent."

I grimaced. Jorge was long since safely dead and buried on Heaven. I didn't need that distracting voice while I was trying to concentrate. Eighty-four percent. An estimate. Well, my gut said this was 100 percent the way to go—and my gut had been in combat, where you had one chance to get it right and no time to think. That computer was a damned civilian.

I worked around the bomb assembly to position the cutter at the leg I wanted. I wished that I could have convinced Yong that she could land on Earth and that the nightmares and flashbacks would go away. I wished I could have convinced her that the school she'd bombed in Sumatra that had been used to shield a command center, and whatever else she had done during the Troubles, had nothing to do with how the world had fucked itself up since then. I wished I could have convinced her that flying to another star wasn't a cure either. I couldn't do any of that. Anyway, we needed our last resort of getting away, if the information we found at GSY was too discouraging about conditions on Earth.

Star light, star bright, / First star I see tonight. The bedtime prayer my mom sang to me when I was little. Bad thought to have in my mind at this particular moment.

I cut the metal strut that was the leg of the tripod I had selected. Nothing happened. I braced myself against the lattice so that I could push against the assembly to move it away from the feeder track.

There was a flash at the canister. Something shot out. A vapor trail went right past the edge of the first container in the feeder line and then off into space.

I tried for a hearty "Aha!" into the comm, but it came out more like a nervous chuckle. After a moment more, I was able to say, "Okay, let's get the feeder engaged and do what needs to be done." I think I had the sangfroid back in my voice at that point.

.   .   .

Given what we had seen of the ingenuity behind the booby traps and the determination to kill people, none of us was willing to test the computer in the transport. That meant Zoe monitored the fuel transfer in the

Dauntless while I retreated to the cabin of the transport and watched the feed from that end. This was a multi-hour process. Fortunately, the cabin held air and I could manually bring the temperature up to comfortable levels. That meant I could open my helmet. I suppose I could have taken off my suit, but I wasn't that trusting. I would have liked something to eat or drink, but even with the transport as cold as it had been, I wasn't sure the food would be safe to eat. As it turned out, it didn't matter. The transport had no food or drink, yet another indication it had been placed there purely as a trap.

When the fuel transfer was complete, I opened my channel to Yong. "All we need to do is disengage the feeder lattice. I'll give this thing a little push away from the *Dauntless* and we'll say goodbye. I'll come back by jetpack."

"No, don't do that," Yong said. "We have to get into GSY Station and the space elevator station. It will be better if we keep the transport."

"You want to fly this back to the station?" I asked. "Even if this has more fuel and a better engine than the one we had in 2069, that means we need to turn the computer on. I thought we didn't want to do that."

"I don't," Yong said. "I want you to jettison the lattice and then dock the transport at the docking port on the *Dauntless*."

I was temporarily speechless. I said eventually, "That's bold," recalling the adage that there were old pilots and bold pilots but no old, bold pilots.

"I'll guide you through it," Yong said.

I guess when you have lost everything, your concept of risk changes.

Disengaging the feeder and then the lattice was simple. With Yong watching the panels and screens through my cameras, as though perched on my shoulder and whispering directions in my ear, I used the thrusters to move the transport and roughly align it with the docking port one deck below the bridge.

The docking process was also simple. In concept. The screen on the transport showed a blue circle that marked the docking target and a red circle that gave the orientation of the transport's docking module. When the circles coincided and the ship was close enough, the docking probes from both ships would extend, grapple, and then bring the transport to dock. It was a simple task for the ship's computer to jigger the thrusters just right to make that happen.

But we weren't going to turn the computer on. We were all too afraid it would be programmed to ram. I had to do the thruster jiggering myself.

"The concept is no different from using a jetpack," Yong said as I struggled to line up the transport and bring it close enough at the same time.

Yes, the concept was the same. We were in space, in zero gee. Once an object—a transport ship, for instance—is put in motion, it stays in motion until an opposing force, like another thruster, stops it. However, while zero gee means no weight, the mass of the ship is the same as always.

"If I don't apply a reverse thrust from the jetpack properly, Yong, I'll hit the ship and bounce away. If I make the same mistake with the transport, I could smash it through the docking port."

"You need to wait longer on the reverse thrust, Soldier Boy. You're stopping too far away."

"If I wait too long, the nose of this ship ends up in your lap."

"You are exaggerating. Fire forward thrusters on my mark. Do not—I repeat, do not—fire the reverse until my command."

I pushed us forward. The circles lined up. The distance shrank. And shrank. I jumped the gun again.

"You were early, Soldier Boy. But close enough."

I could feel the docking machinery grapple.

I guess close only counts in horseshoes, hand grenades, and spaceship docking.

·   ·   ·

We held a memorial service for Dev, one of those "celebration of life" things, but we couldn't find much to say that wasn't in the ship's bio file. We had flown 152 light-years together, but no one could think of an amusing anecdote to share, not even one Dev had told about himself. That was the way it was with all of us, I reflected. Starfolk—me and Yong excepted—didn't make connections. ISC had built that into the selection profiles after we returned from the first starshot and were hit with the effect of temporal alienation. Each of us was like the person a group of friends brings to a party because they sort of know them and think it would be nice for that person to make friends. Afterward, though, no one can remember what that person said or did, and no one invites them again. Starfolk were so two-dimensional we could slip between the cracks in any group of humans. That's who buys tickets on relativity's one-way time machine.

CHAPTER NINE

It was time for me to add another title to my now-impressive résumé: burglar.

That said, breaking and entering into an apparently dormant space station in orbit around Earth was not as simple as it sounds. GSY Station—named for Yuri Gagarin, Alan Shepard, and Yang Liwei—was a giant doughnut spinning in space twenty-five thousand miles, give or take a few, above the surface of our planet. When I use the word *giant*, I do mean huge. The diameter of that doughnut was officially four thousand meters, about two and a half miles across. That meant a ring of more than seven miles of corridor lined with shops, hotels, offices, and storage rooms. Getting in was not as simple as crawling through an unlatched window.

We sat around a table in the caf, most of us drinking coffee through zero-gee nipples. That had become our preferred way to plan an operation. Charley had picked a smaller table than we had used before, one that would hold only the remaining six of us around its perimeter. My view about that, though, was what it had always been in the field: I knew we were down one and I moved on from there.

"Normally, we would have several ways to enter the station," Yong said. "The simplest is at the central hub. There is a docking station with a spaceplane port, as well as ports for the type of transport ship we brought from the antimatter production facility. However, to dock a transport, the station controllers need to spin the hub counter to the rotation of the ring so that the port is at rest relative to the ship coming in. We are not arriving in normal times."

"The station has power and seems to have air pressure inside. I can tell that," Cristina said. "But there won't be anyone to manage the rotation of the hub. I can't do that from here either. Can you spin the ship with thrusters to match the station?" she asked Yong.

"I can, but I'm not going to leave the bridge. Not under these conditions."

"I'm not going to try it," I said quickly. I might have passed Yong's crash course—and that phrase did pop into my mind—in piloting a transport, but this was too big a risk.

"Another option," Cristina said. "GSY is big enough to have docking stations for transports and people-pushers along the wall of the doughnut ring. Without computer control, though, docking that way isn't as simple as it sounds." She tapped at her phone base and looked aside at her projection field. "GSY Station maintains a gravity of one gee in the ring. That's where people live and work. Or they did." She caught herself, then returned to using technical details to keep emotion out of her voice. "It does that by spinning on its axis to create centripetal force. For a ring that size, that means the rim is moving at more than thirty miles an hour. Since we are talking about a rotating ring, the port isn't moving in a straight line either."

"Over a short distance, the curve won't be noticeable. I can do it with Soldier Boy. Like before."

I was going to pilot the ship again, with Yong riding on my shoulder. Figuratively speaking.

We proceeded to plan this mission as carefully as any operation behind enemy lines that I've been on. The information about GSY Station that we had on the *Dauntless* was a century and a half old, but the station did have power, and internal maps were public access. It took a little work, but we were able to download them. They were, in fact, very similar to what we had. That gave us some assurance that the interior of GSY Station hadn't changed too much.

We had two key objectives. First were the offices of the ISC. If any single place would have information about conditions on Earth, and about which of the interstellar colonies were successful, that would be it. Colonies at the nearer stars would be more than a century old. If they were doing well, they would have beamed information back to Earth. That information would have reached Earth by now, and the colonies were unlikely to realize that sending it was a futile undertaking. I hoped—prayed might be closer the mark—that we could find that information. I worried that in her current mood, Yong would launch off into space without even a clue that we had a settlement to go to. And, yes, I was going with her, no matter where.

As for the situation on Earth, I was charier. We would probably find out what had happened and when it happened, but I doubted we would learn much about what the planet was like now. Nobody down there was transmitting anything—we would have picked it up on the *Dauntless*. But if there had been transmissions even a few years ago, that might be useful. We would also have a chance to learn whether we could refuel the spaceplane at GSY Station.

After we were done at the ISC offices, we would look for supplies. Nearly all the gear we would use for exploration, from campsite wards to ReadyMeals, had been off-loaded on Heaven. Depending on what Earth was like, backcountry gear could make the difference between life and death.

Would we find anyone on the station? Alive, that is? I didn't think so. From our assessment of the craters in Earth cities, too many years had passed for anyone who was on the station when the war occurred to still be living there. Anyone on the station who'd survived the time of the war would have tried to get down to Earth, rather than doom their children to certain death once the supplies ran out.

The plan determined our team. I was going, of course. Cristina was coming with me. She had worked on GSY Station for two years before she joined the crew of the *Dauntless*. That experience, and her position in Ship Systems, meant she would be the most capable at working with whatever station systems we found. We decided that there was no need to bring Charley. We did take a small cargo bot to carry supplies back—another reason to dock the transport instead of finding an external air lock we could jetpack over to.

I met Cristina at the ready room before the air lock to the docking port on the *Dauntless*. "Suits for this one," I said as I tapped the locker panel.

"Why? The station has power, heat, and pressure."

"Don't bet your life on what we can tell from here," I said. "Anyway, I'm not exactly an expert pilot. We can always take the suits off over there, if we don't need them."

I saw her eyes widen and her eyebrows arch up, maybe from my comment about piloting. She hesitated for an instant while her eyes searched my face. Then she pulled her shoulder-length brown hair out of its ponytail and twisted it into a tight bun that would be better in the helmet.

I turned away from her to deal with my own suit. This might be unnecessary, and it was cumbersome—especially getting into it in zero gee—but if we needed the suits and didn't have them, we would be, as the saying goes, shit out of luck. Too many missions that did not go as planned had left me cautious about preparation.

Before I got into the suit, I checked a sealed pocket in my pants for one other essential item. It was the printed selfie Yong and I had taken together in the meadow on High Noon, with the red star at the horizon behind us. That pic had traveled with my personal gear to Heaven and back, and it was going with me now. I guess I'm superstitious as well as cautious.

Once we were suited, we passed through the air lock into the transport. The interior had warmed up and dried out, so I was no longer having to read screens through ice and water. I settled into the pilot-in-command seat and opened my channel to Yong.

"Ready to go, Soldier Boy?"

"Sure thing, Flygirl."

I started to transmit vid to her of the control panels and screens in front of me. She began giving instruction. I tried to follow each command without hesitation, as though I were an extension of Yong, the same way we had managed the transport before. It was still clumsy, but we were getting better. Anyway, I liked having her whisper in my ear.

You can make of that whatever you want.

Our little transport undocked from the *Dauntless* and made the short flight to the station without incident. We had positioned the *Dauntless* so that I had a direct visual on the docking port we wanted. All I had to do was line up the docking guide with the bull's-eye on my screen, which meant that the ship's port was positioned to mate with the station's, and bring the transport to rest with the port. But we kept drifting offline.

I wasn't compensating properly for the rotation of the station; we weren't quite at rest with respect to each other. Every time Yong fed me the correction, the circuit with two humans in it was a little too slow. I needed to make the correction before Yong told me. The problem was obvious. But if I knew how to do it, I would be a pilot. There was a pattern to what we were doing, however, and after three misses, I decided to make the same adjustment but sooner. I heard a sharp intake of breath—I won't call it a gasp—from Yong when I fired the attitude thrusters on my own. The circles on my screen merged to one. A chime sounded.

The screen showed: DOCKING GUIDE ATTACHED.

From that point, the process was automatic. The station reeled us in like a fish.

"Nice going, Soldier Boy," Yong said.

"It was nothing." In my mind I gave a good laugh, but I couldn't bring myself to do it for real.

"We should leave the bot with the transport for now," Cristina said.

"Why?"

"It will automatically connect to the station's system," she said. "I want to know everything is okay first. We can come back for it if we need it for supplies."

"Now you're getting as suspicious as I am," I said.

Cristina and I unbelted and moved to the transport's air lock. The door closed behind us. *Now we find out if the station's systems are really operational*, I thought. Our outer door and the station's outer door slid open to reveal a short corridor into the station's air lock.

"What the fuck?" I stared at the door leading into the station.

Red block letters painted diagonally across the door spelled out INFECTED.

"Are you seeing this?" I asked Yong.

"Yes. I wonder if bioweapons were used."

"Good question," I said. "Still, we're in suits, so it shouldn't matter. We'll just stay in the suits. Charley can rig decontam in the air lock when we come back."

"What about the supplies?" Cristina asked. "Should we bring anything back?"

"If it's sealed and we can put it through decontam, it should be okay," I said. "But let's see what we find first." That was what we were there for, and if we didn't look, we would never know. I'd had this feeling before, when I'd busted through doors not knowing what was on the other side. "The door panel shows green," I said. "I'm going to open the inner door."

I tapped the panel. The door slid open.

Cristina screamed.

CHAPTER TEN

Automatically, my hand went to my belt for my pistol. I wasn't wearing it, but why would I? Who would wear a firearm on a space suit and take it to a space station? The floor of the locker room beyond the air lock, where people would suit up, was littered with bodies. I counted six of them, all in various stages of getting into suits.

I pulled my hand away. There was no threat. Whatever had happened to these people had happened long ago.

I moved into the room to check the bodies. They looked mummified; faces shrunk down tight over skulls. The rest of their bodies were covered with clothing or suits. I did not see any wounds, nor any sign of blood on their clothing or the floor.

"Infected. That's what someone painted on the door." Cristina had recovered from her initial shock and was also examining the bodies.

I looked down at a withered face. "Is that what happened here, do you think? They were too sick to get out, and whoever did get out painted the sign on the door?"

"If you want to take samples, I can try to analyze them in the Med Unit," Charley said on our channel. "I don't know, though, that the information is worth the risk of bringing whatever it is on the ship."

"I don't think it was infection." Cristina knelt next to one of the corpses. "The air pressure in here is one atmosphere, so that's fine. The air, though . . ." I could see the shake of her head through the helmet visor. "It's about ninety percent nitrogen; the rest is CO_2. No oxygen, no water vapor. I don't understand how that could happen from a systems perspective, but it fits what we're seeing here. They all died at the same time, or very close together. They were asphyxiated, not hit with some virus."

"Then why the sign warning us about infection?" I asked.

"No answer to that," Yong said on the channel. "Not yet. Maybe some did get their suits on and got out. If they were panicked, or hypoxic, they might not have realized what was happening. Particularly if bioweapons had been used elsewhere on the station. I would remain vigilant about that, and we will rigorously decontaminate whatever comes back to the *Dauntless*."

"Where did they go? The ones who got out, I mean?" Cristina straightened up from the body she was bent over.

"The space elevator, probably," I said. "This dock is only good for a transport like we have, or a people-pusher. Those ships can't reenter the atmosphere and land. That means the elevator system was still working when the end came up here." I paused. "Or they thought it was working. Come on. We need to find some answers."

I walked over to the door that led from the locker room to the station corridor and left the bodies of the stationers behind me. Maybe someday someone would come and give these people a decent burial in space, but that could not be our duty. In any case, I was pretty sure they weren't the only dead on GSY Station.

The panel by the door showed green and the door slid open in response to my tap. A brightly lit and completely empty hallway lay ahead of us.

"Air composition is the same on this side of the door," Cristina said. "It wasn't done only to the people in that room. The entire station must be like this."

"It's a good thing the lights are still on," I said. "Having no oxygen would be a problem if we had to find our way by torchlight."

The joke fell flat. Possibly, my timing was poor.

We walked down the hall to where it intersected the broad main corridor of GSY Station. That corridor was a circle that went the entire circumference of the station, half as far as the length of Manhattan from Battery Park at the southern tip to Spuyten Duyvil at the north end. It was a broad avenue lined with shops, restaurants, bars, hotels, and business offices. The station was a major city in orbit around Earth.

Right now, the corridor was still and vacant. The windows of all those shops, restaurants, bars, hotels, and offices stared silently at us as we walked down the corridor, a host of unseeing eyes on us. One door was open, a body half inside and half in the corridor. Over time, the door had squeezed it against the frame, then stopped because it lacked the force to chop through the body.

"That's odd," Cristina said.

"What is?" I asked.

She pointed to the door and the trapped body. "If you step into a doorway when a door is closing, it will reverse to full open. That's a failsafe, part of standard code for every building in the Major Powers for decades. I worked here, and I know it was the same on GSY. The door should never touch you."

"Maybe systems or sensors are failing over time," I said. "We should be careful and not assume everything works as it should." I considered the implications. "Obviously, we need to stay in the suits and on suit air, but we don't need pressure in the suits. That will improve our mobility. Just in case we need it."

Our downloaded schematic of the station showed the ISC offices as being only a short distance from where we entered the main corridor from the dock. We didn't need the map location to identify it. Emblazoned in gold lettering along one wall was: INTERNATIONAL SPACE COMMISSION. The letters were four feet high, and the symbol of the hand clutching a star went from floor to ceiling. Even at the last, the ISC had indulged in grandiosity. Next to that sign, the actual doorway into the offices looked like it belonged in a miniature dollhouse.

Cristina and I looked from the door to each other and back again. I didn't want to chip in, and it wasn't as though I could shoot out a lock. The telltale light by the door panel was green. I shrugged and put my hand on the door's entry panel. It slid open and remained open while we walked through. Then it slid closed behind us.

"Well, that behaved normally," I said.

"Yes. Maybe whatever happened to the air on the station forced an evacuation and killed the ones who couldn't get out, but the rest of it is just the way it was." Cristina peered at empty offices and workstations past the receptionist station by the front door. "Where do you want to look first?"

The interior was both empty and dead quiet.

"Let's try the director's office first. Their computer station is probably locked up, but we have ISC access because we're part of the *Dauntless* crew, and maybe it's still valid on an ISC computer. It would make sense that personnel access for a departing starship crew would stay in the system long term. At least in a limited area."

The director's office, with a nameplate on the door reading MICAH SMITH, was all the way at the back of the office area at the station wall. It had an actual viewport. I could see a starfield through that port. A nice touch for the boss, I thought. A few printed and framed pictures—presumably Micah and his family—sat on the desk. In the middle of the desktop, right in front of the pushed-in chair, was a phone base.

"That's strange," I said. It was strange. Nobody would evacuate and leave their phone base sitting on top of the desk. At least, that would have been the case the last time I was in the solar system.

I stepped out of Micah's office and walked down the hall to the left. There was another door with the plate DIRECTOR'S CONFERENCE ROOM next to it. The conference room was not empty.

"Oh shit," said Cristina when she looked past my shoulder through the doorway.

Six bodies occupied the room: four men, two women. All of them wore bright blue polos, and the ones I could see had the ISC symbol over their left breast. Two of the men were still in chairs at a large conference table, one facedown on the table, the other slumped back in his chair, neck hyperextended, mouth open, sightless eyes staring at the ceiling. Of the bodies that had fallen to the floor, I could make out enough of the dark skin and facial structure on one of them to match him to the picture on the desk next door.

"This is Micah." I pointed down.

"What happened to them?"

I looked at the table. Two empty bottles of wine. Six empty glasses.

"A farewell toast, I think," I said. "I'll bet they put something in the wine. Fast acting, I imagine."

"What's that?"

Cristina's question brought my head up. She was pointing at the far end of the room. A screen took up most of that wall. The screen was dark and blank, as expected, but in the middle of it, someone had taped a piece of paper. I walked over to inspect it. A handwritten note. The words had been carefully block-printed so that it was easy to read.

Greetings, explorer, we who are about to die give you fair warning. The World Cyberwar is over. It has ended because the internet is down. Completely and probably permanently. Malware, bot attacks, and electromagnetic pulses have seen to that. All logistics networks, supply chains, and power grids on Earth are down as well. We have no idea how many have died and will die because there is no electricity or access to food and water. The physical armies continue to fight, we can see that, but the nuclear strikes have ceased. The computer systems for the missiles have been corrupted as well.

The irony is that we thought we were safe here from the madness. We were wrong. All computer systems on GSY Station have been massively infected. Even our simple service bots have been weaponized in the same way that cars on Earth were turned into weapons to kill the occupants or crash into other cars, and appliance bots made to attack or explode.

Evacuations from here have stopped because there are no more ships. Even if there were, the systems of the last three were infected and caused uncontrolled dives into the atmosphere. The life-support system here has been infected and is now slowly removing oxygen from the station. Our end is near. We wish by the time this is read, all people have learned to live together in peace, although we have little hope of that.

You would do best to destroy this station utterly.

We put our names and nations below.

3 October 2137 EFOR.

Micah Smith from the United States was the first name. I wondered, for a second, what had happened to the wife and children I'd seen in the pictures on his desk. Nothing good. I knew that.

My eyes went back to that date: 2137. Thirty-nine years after we left. I thought of María Gutiérrez—Gute, to me—the nurse I'd flown transport with in Miami. She would have been in her nineties. Maybe she didn't live to see the catastrophe. But her children and grandchildren . . .

Oh God, Rissi. Beautiful, lively, ambitious Rissi. My last fling on Earth. She would have been caught in this. I thought of what Yong had said. We fought in the Troubles; did we share the responsibility for this? I wrenched my mind away from those thoughts. Wallowing in sadness did nothing for the already dead and less for those who needed to move forward. My sergeant on my first deployment had said the same thing, if a bit more colorfully.

"This all happened only thirty-nine years after we left," I said on our ship channel, putting some crispness into my tone. "We hadn't even reached Heaven when the solar system fell apart. The ruins have been sitting here for one hundred and fourteen years."

"Some of the starshots that were out, and some that went out after us, would have come back after this happened," Yong said on the channel. "We know the *Daredevil* did. Is there any sign anyone else has been in there?"

"No," I said. "There isn't much dust here to create tracks, but no indication that anything has been disturbed. Not that we are disturbing anything either."

"Could all of them have gone to the antimatter plant and been destroyed by those defenses?" Yong asked.

"It's possible," I said. "They could also have parked their starships and ridden the spaceplanes down. Or tried."

"True," Yong said. "There is no way to tell now. Finding a starship powered down and in a wider orbit would be difficult. It would take a lengthy search, and finding nothing would mean only that we found nothing, not that we proved nothing is there."

For the moment, I had no other answers. I took photos of the printed note and left the page in place.

"Let's try our access on Micah's workstation," I said. "We need to do what we came here to do."

Cristina and I went back into Micah's office, and I sat down at his desk to see what I could pull out of his system. The screen lit up when I looked at it. I was wearing a space suit. I set the visor for maximum transparency and turned on the external speakers.

"This is Leif Grettison, exoplanetary scout, Starship *Dauntless*," I said while looking directly at the screen.

"Voice and eye are recognized," said a pleasant baritone. "You may access files that you have rights to."

Indeed, I was still in the ISC system. Finding information, however, was a clumsy and protracted process. The system in this office, unlike one on a spaceship, wasn't designed to be used by someone wearing a space suit, even if the suit was depressurized. I kept hitting the wrong spot, my fingers massive in the suit gloves. To open files, I had to keep my head positioned just so; otherwise, the helmet visor interfered with the computer's ability to recognize my retina. Neither Yong nor I had Jorge's familiarity with hacking systems. On top of all of that, an electronic picture frame clipped to the computer screen kept displaying smiling images of the man who was dead in the next room. I saw Micah hugging his wife, the two of them with various combinations of three cute kids. It made me visualize him in that conference room, faced with either slow suffocation or a glass of quick poison. My mind created snapshots of his wife and kids as civilization fell apart around them. I tried to tell myself that this had happened over a century ago, that all of them would be many, many years dead by now even if there had never been another war. It was useless. In the end, I pulled the picture frame away from the bevel around his screen and placed it facedown on the desk. I turned the printed ones over too. I blamed all the delay on my clumsy fingers.

With some searching, I turned up the starshot records. "There weren't many after us," I said. "Only eight. The last one seems to have gone in 2121, sixteen years before the end."

"I wonder why they slowed down and stopped," Cristina said.

"We know the answer to that." Yong's voice was harsh in my helmet. "They poured the money back into the armies. That's what the Treaties were designed to prevent, to channel the money into space instead."

I remembered having that explained to me. "The Treaties failed in the end," I said. "We see the results."

Cristina edged closer to peer at the screen past my shoulder. "They never sent another ship to Heaven the way they said they would do. Do you think . . . Do you think the colonists managed okay anyway?"

"I hope so." I thought of the people we had left there, who would have expected a ship in three to five years. One that never arrived. I hoped they had prospered anyway. I couldn't worry about that now. It was all history, however it had gone.

"Look at the dates." Cristina's voice grew soft. "We went the farthest, we and the *Daredevil*. No ships are left to come back. We're the last of the starfolk."

"This is not accomplishing our mission." Yong's voice broke into the silence that accumulated after Cristina finished.

"Three ships went back to High Noon," I said. "One was the mission before ours, then the other two in 2099 and 2101. Let me see what I can find."

Eventually, we stumbled on a folder that held downloads of messages from star colonies. There weren't many. At only fourteen light-years away, there had been time for multiple transmissions to come in from High Noon. A settlement was growing out there; it appeared to be thriving. The time stamp on the last transmission, however, was fifty years ago. Had there been a catastrophe out there? I checked the other colonies that had sent messages. No message was more recent than fifty years back.

"Most likely, the problem is the receiver in the solar system," Yong said, "or in the station's computer system."

"Or the colonies quit sending when nothing had come from Earth for, what, about sixty years," I said.

"Maybe," Yong said. "It doesn't matter. There is enough in the system from High Noon that we can decide on that. We have been there, Leif. It's a good choice."

Her words brought up in my mind the picture of us in the meadow in Shadowland I carried in my pocket. That place was achingly beautiful. That was the first time Yong and I had . . . well, connected. Yes, I would go back there with her. I would go anywhere with her, but High Noon and Shadowland would be my pick if I had a choice.

"I still want to stay here, go down to Earth," Charley said on the channel. "I want to be where my family was, to visit their graves."

"That might not be possible," I said.

"Doesn't matter," he replied. "I'm going to try."

"I'm going to Mexico City," Cristina said. "There's something I need to do."

"What?" I asked.

She hesitated. "I'm going to a particular church there, a special one. Its full name is the Metropolitan Cathedral of the Assumption of the Most Blessed Virgin Mary into Heaven. I'm going to pray there. That matters to me. Once I've done that, I will be fine with whatever happens. If I can't get there, but I've tried, that will also be fine. I will pray for you and Yong," she said in my direction, "wherever you go. And I will pray for the souls of Micah and his family." She stared at the overturned picture frames.

Zoe and Anil reiterated their determination to return to Earth. We went ahead and tried to check in the ISC system for any information about conditions where they wanted to land. We found nothing. Far less than about the star colonies. I guess that should not have been a surprise. It was not as though the wars had just ended. The collapse of civilization in the solar system had happened in 2137. Communication systems had not functioned in over a century. Nothing in the computer system on GSY Station had any relationship to the situation on the ground. That did not change any minds either.

"Are there available stores of fuel for the spaceplane?" Yong asked.

"Give us a little more time to check," I said.

In the end, our search for additional spaceplane fuel was both discouraging and definitive. All fuel had been exhausted by the spaceplanes that had tried to return stationers to Earth. That did not change any minds either.

"All right," I said at last. "All we're doing now is wasting time and suit air. Let's check the closest storage area and see if they have Hi-Cal bars or some updated version. That way, what you can carry in your packs will last a lot longer than ReadyMeals."

CHAPTER ELEVEN

The main corridor when we came out of the ISC offices was as quiet and spooky as when we went in. That was not going to change. No one was going to pop out of a door and say hello. My mind kept veering back to the threat of weaponized bots that the note in the conference room had mentioned. What was I keeping watch for? A war-bot mounting a machine gun? Or a vacuum cleaner with an attitude?

Our next objective was only a few hundred yards down the corridor. That had been part of the plan. We were almost there when Cristina put a hand on my arm and pointed. Over a doorway was the lettering: WINDOW ON THE UNIVERSE. Underneath it, in script, was A UNIQUE DINING EXPERIENCE.

"My God," she said. "We ate there. Remember, Charley and Zoe?"

"Yes," came Charley's voice. "About a week before departure. Great food, but expensive as hell. We all joked that we didn't need to worry about the money."

I had never gone. I had spent my time with Yong on the *Dauntless.*

"It has windows in the outer wall," Cristina told me. "You can sit at a table and see the Earth and stars. It's still here. Was here. At the end, I mean."

I looked at the entrance. A set of posts had been bolted to the floor to create a barrier a person could walk through, but the spaces between the posts were narrow enough that no bot could roll through. The posts were a sloppy affair. One of them had been knocked over by an impact. A hand-lettered sign was posted next to the entry. I walked over to read it.

YES, WE HAVE FOOD, it read. And below that, DO NOT ALLOW ANY BOTS PAST THE DOOR.

"I wonder," Cristina said. She walked in front of the door and it opened. She went through. A few seconds later, I heard, "Oh no."

I hastened to reach her and saw what had stopped her. Across the interior of the restaurant, bodies were scattered on the floor. Empty glasses sat on tables.

Unbidden, the image of a New Year's Eve party popped into my head, with everyone toasting the new year at midnight. Had the people here gathered to toast their approaching death and chugged down the poison because there was no hope? How many other dead were haunting GSY Station's main corridor and side passages? How had they faced the end here, with no hope of rescue and no chance of escape? Anger? Despair? Resignation?

It didn't matter, I decided. It was history. It was over.

"C'mon. We have work to do." I gave Cristina's arm a gentle tug, and that was enough to break the spell of the dead and get her moving.

The supply store did not have posts in front of it. Past a utilitarian reception area was a warehouse with floor-to-ceiling racks for boxes and goods. Many of the racks were empty. I tried a computer screen at the end of one row, but it would not recognize my voice and eye.

"Can't tell how this is organized," I said. "We're going to have to go through it and check by eye."

"Got it," Cristina said. "I'll start at that end." She pointed to the far end of the area and walked in that direction.

The racks and shelves in front of me contained hardware of various kinds. It was all coded, but I couldn't make any sense of the letters and numbers. I had to break open some of the boxes to be sure, which was problematic in a suit. All that mattered was that none of it looked like food. Check quickly and move on.

The silence was shattered by a squeal of tires on decking.

"Leif! Help!" Cristina's shout was followed by a crash and then the sound of her pain.

I ran toward where she had gone to look, her agony filling my helmet and the channel. The scene I found was surreal. A loader-hauler bot—essentially a motorized pallet—had rammed Cristina and driven her into the stack of shelves at the back wall, pinning her in place. The bar at the front of the bot had hit her at mid-thigh and below the level of a shelf. The bot spun its wheels as it tried to drive *through* Cristina into the stack of shelves.

How do you stop a homicidal pile of metal, plastic, and circuitry? A firearm could have put a bullet through the motor or its circuit boards, but I was unarmed. I ran to the back of the thing and jumped into its cargo area. It paid no attention to me. There had to be wiring from its battery to the engine and the boards with its chips, but nothing was visible. This was not the time to find a serial number and look up a circuit diagram. This bot model might not have existed when we left, anyway, so it wouldn't be in our computer for me to access.

Cristina was crying and trying to pull free. Her left leg had a bend in the middle, where legs don't bend. It was broken.

Well, in order to know where it's going and what it's doing, a bot needs a camera array. It's not an eyeball, but the function is the same. I pulled myself to the front of the bot and looked down over the edge of the pallet. Three small conical housings. My belt had a tool designed to adjust or remove a jetpack. All I cared about was that it was hard. I smashed the tool into each of the bot's cameras. The bot lurched backward. I almost lost the tool as I scrambled for a handhold.

Released from the pressure against the stack of shelves, Cristina collapsed to the floor. The bot started to turn in a circle. Of course! It had cameras on each side. Once it registered her again, it would likely try to run her over. I found more camera eyes. Smashed them. Once I had ruined all of them, the thing simply kept turning in a circle in the space in front of the shelving.

Jesus! I was sweating in my suit. This was what the note meant about weaponized bots. Someone had fed malware into its tiny brain, programming it to visit random mayhem on humans. What had it been like on this station? What had it been like on Earth?

Hell, probably. But I had no time to think about it.

"My leg, Leif. Oh my God, my leg. Don't leave me here, Leif. Don't leave me!"

"I'm not leaving you. Don't give that a thought. We're leaving together." I wouldn't leave her. I would get her back to the ship or die trying. That's the way it worked on a battlefield, and the station had become a battlefield. The problem was, how? We couldn't chip in to the *Dauntless*, but I didn't need her chip's report on her condition to see that her leg was broken. Mid-thigh. That meant the femur. Shit. The station had one gee in the inhabited areas. There was no possibility she could put any weight on it. I was afraid she was going to pass out.

The first thing I had to do was reduce the fracture. Busted bones could have jagged edges. If I didn't get it reduced, something might get sliced when I moved her, like a blood vessel or nerve. The problem was that I couldn't see what I was doing. I couldn't tell if it was a compound fracture, where one end of the broken bone comes out through the skin. The suit covered everything, and I couldn't take her suit off.

I had to try, though. No choice about that. Sometimes all you can do is the best you can do, and that has to be good enough. From where the angle was in her leg, I guessed the break's location. I said a quick silent prayer and put traction on the leg from below. Cristina gasped. The leg straightened, stayed straight. If I'd had the medikit, I could have shot some pain med through the suit and counted on its self-sealing properties, but I had nothing to give her.

A nearby shelf held a bunch of plastic rods. Whatever their original purpose, I could use them as a splint to keep the leg in place. The general-purpose pack on the suits held duct tape.

I pulled out the roll of tape and brandished it. "I have no idea where they came up with the name, but it holds anything. I think God uses duct tape to keep the stars up in the sky."

"It's not funny, Leif." Her voice was soft. "Just do this, please."

I had thought it would be good to lighten the mood. I guess not. I put the rods around the break and swaddled it with tape.

"Okay," I said. "We just need to get you back to the *Dauntless*."

I started to wish we had brought the bot from the transport, then was glad we hadn't. I didn't want to find out what would happen when it linked to the station's systems. I chopped off those thoughts. They were a waste of time and focus.

"I saw some tarps down that other row," she said. "If you put one on the floor, I can roll onto it and you can drag me."

"Not going to work," I said. "We have too far to go. Also, I don't want you on the ground if we run into another crazed bot. You won't be able to get out of the way." I gave the problem no more than a second's thought. "I'll carry you. Fireman's carry. I'll hoist you up in front and over my shoulder."

"Leif, I'm five-ten. How are you going to do that all the way back to the dock?"

"I've done it in combat, carrying a guy in the platoon who was bigger than you." I was going to be tired as hell by the end, but I *had* done it and I was *going* to do it.

However, I had not done it wearing a space suit. What I discovered was that when I had her up over my shoulder, her weight pressed down on one side of my suit's life-support pack.

"This isn't going to work," I said. "The connections aren't designed for this kind of load, and it's asymmetric. I can think of several ways this could end badly."

I put Cristina down again, stepped around the bot that was still going in circles, and raced around looking at shelves for inspiration. I found some coils that looked like the netting that hung in the spaceplane bay of a starship. I unwound one of them and found it was longer and wider than I wanted. I had nothing to cut it with. It was flexible and pliable, however, and I could fold it.

With a few minutes' work, I had her up on my back, the cabling looped under her butt to make a seat. From there, the netting crossed between her chest and my suit's pack, then looped over my shoulder. I secured the netting in front of me. It wasn't perfect—the loose ends dragged on the deck—but it would hold her while leaving my hands free, and it didn't put pressure on my life-support pack.

"You can hold my shoulders or the netting," I told her. "Just don't grab the life-support pack."

"I'm okay," Cristina said, although her voice didn't sound it. "I'll do it like you say. And I will say a special prayer for you when I reach the Cathedral."

I wondered if Charley could get Cristina's bone to heal fast enough for her to go to Mexico City, but I figured that could be a discussion for another time. I prayed he wouldn't comment on the channel at that moment, and my prayer was answered. "Let's concentrate on getting you there first," was all I said.

I looked at the partially filled shelves around us with regret. We could not look for the Hi-Cal supplements. Even if we found them, we would have no way to carry more than the few I could stuff into a suit pouch. The ones who landed on Earth would have to manage with whatever Ready-Meals they could carry in a pack.

I made sure Cristina was settled on my back as comfortably as possible for both of us and then headed out of the storeroom. I fell into an easy trot down the main corridor, my eyes trying to pick up any movement that could be a bot. Jogging while carrying someone and a pack is not the easiest thing. It was part of my training with the Rangers, so I could do it for a quarter of a mile. That was about as far as we were from the transport dock. However, when I did it in the service, I hadn't been wearing a space suit. And I hadn't done it since the docs had rebuilt my knee after the battle outside Camp Schwarzkopf. The doc had told me afterward that I wouldn't be able to meet standards on that knee, and that was why I hadn't renewed my enlistment contract. We were going to find out how good a job the army doc had done.

By the time we were halfway there, the knee was on fire. My run turned into a wobble, and I imagined I could feel the knee grind every time my foot hit the ground under our combined weight. Each jolt from my uneven gait brought gasps of pain from Cristina. Had even a malware-infected floor-cleaning bot happened on us, it could have punched our tickets to the next world without difficulty.

The glowing sign indicating the side corridor to the transport ship dock was as welcome as any signal I've seen. The air lock brought a problem I hadn't foreseen, though. The way Cristina was strapped onto my back, her head didn't clear the frame of the door. If I bent over, her weight squashed the life-support pack and set off multiple red lights on my readouts. She had to get off me. We managed to fit into the air lock side by side, with Cristina hopping on one leg and me holding her, but the entry on the transport past the lock wasn't that wide.

Finally, I had Cristina lie down on her back in the air lock. I sealed it against the station and waited for the green on the ship side. I triggered the door, then got down on my hands and knees over her. She clasped her hands behind my helmet and I crawled, dragging her under me, into the transport.

I collapsed on top of her, faceplate to faceplate. She looked like she had passed out at the end. I fumbled with my helmet, got the fasteners loose, opened it, and took a deep breath of stale ship air. It was wonderful.

It was a relief to separate from the dock at GSY Station and fire the thrusters to back us away into space. I could see the station again through the transport's viewport—at least, I could see part of the huge ring. It would stay there, maybe forever, spinning in space, a monument to its dead and humanity's capacity for evil.

CHAPTER TWELVE

As much as I wanted to take Cristina back to the *Dauntless* as fast as possible, docking a spacecraft is not something you rush. I had now docked the transport twice—and I do get better with practice—but that did not make me a rocket man. With Yong's guidance, I slowly and gingerly eased the transport back into the dock at the *Dauntless*.

We were in zero gee, so I could float Cristina through the lock. Charley and Zoe, anchored on the StickStrips, met us on the other side with a stretcher. We fastened Cristina into it and went straight to the Med Unit.

Charley's face was grim when he turned away from the screen of the imager to face me and Zoe. He didn't say anything, and I didn't need him to. I could see the screen myself past his shoulder. He walked to the head of the bed Cristina lay on.

"It's broken in two places. That means three pieces of bone that have to heal together. You must have surgery. There's no other way this heals. I'll put a titanium rod down the center to line everything up and give it strength, and I'll put some pins into the bone to help hold all of it in place. We can do it here, and there really is no choice. Do you understand what I'm saying?"

Cristina nodded. "You do what you have to do." She managed a little smile. "I don't have a party to go to tonight."

"Good." Charley fastened the bed's diagnostic lead over Cristina's head to give the best communication with her chip. "Chip in now. That will help. Then I'll give you some med to make you drowsy. I'll have to put you out for the procedure."

Once that was done, he had the surgi-bot come to the bedside and set up the sterilizing field that would give us a serviceable operating room. Charley initiated the programming and self-diagnostics on the surgi-bot. With a tilt of his head and shoulders, he indicated that Zoe and I should step out.

He joined us a couple of minutes later in the outer section of the Med Unit. "Leif, I need to speak with you."

Zoe took that as her cue to leave. When she was gone, Charley stepped close to me, although no one else was around.

"We actually do have the rod and pins that we'll need," he said. "I'm sure they're in the stores because orthopedic injuries on explorations—well, you plan for that. However, I've never done this procedure, never mind in zero gee. It's not something any ship's doc would have done. If there were any other option, I wouldn't do it." He paused. "If I didn't have the surgi-bot, I don't think it would be possible. I don't have Jing anymore, though, and I need a second person. I need you to assist."

I looked him in the eyes, saw both worry and determination. "I'm with you. I'll scrub in. You tell me what to do and I'll do it."

Even with the surgi-bot, it took us five hours to put Cristina's leg back together. We did it, though. I could see the bone perfectly lined up, its nice, new titanium rod hidden down the center of the shaft. Pins and plates held the pieces in place. They would remain permanently. It looked every bit as good in the imager. Cristina's chip reported that she was in good shape. Charley closed up the deep part of the surgical wound and then the surgi-bot did a quick stitch at the skin layer. Cristina would have a long, thin scar, but that would be the only external evidence.

We walked into the outer section of the Med Unit and pulled off our masks. Charley let out a huge sigh. He had half-moons of sweat under each arm.

"You were magnificent," I told him. "How about we go down to the caf? I'll buy you a cup of coffee."

He shook his head. "I messaged Yang. We need to talk."

It wasn't just him and Yong who needed to talk. An all-crew notification popped up on my field as soon as he finished speaking. Yong wanted all of us on the bridge.

·   ·   ·

The bridge had undergone a metamorphosis from the last time I was there. All the screens were subdivided, and red-rimmed threat windows showed the space on all sides of the *Dauntless*. Those windows identified every object our instruments could pick up and labeled each one with mass, velocity vector, and distance. GSY Station occupied a window all its own, some areas highlighted in red, others in yellow or blue. That window showed the station as if it were a target—not that we had any weapons, beyond the exhaust from the antimatter rocket nozzles. The bridge had been transformed into a battle station.

Zoe and Anil were next to Yong, who sat in the pilot-in-command chair, waiting for us. One look at her face and I saw her as she used to be when she was wearing her uniform.

"I wanted all of us together for this," Yong said. "Charley, you messaged me about Cristina's surgery. About her recovery."

At a nod from Yong, Charley looked from face to face around the group. "Healing from that kind of injury and surgery is prolonged," he said. His voice was hesitant, as if reluctant to tell us the medical situation. "Not less than three months. Could be six or even more. Being in zero gee won't help the bone get ready to bear weight. It's likely to make full healing even more prolonged."

Anil paled. "We don't have that long to wait. Not even three months. Our food won't last. Even if some of us go into hib, some have to take care of Cristina."

"Wait. Wait a sec," I said. "We can go back to the station. We still have the pistols. I'll go armed. It's not like there are war-bots over there." I would have preferred one of the M8 rifles we'd left with the colony on Heaven, but they were long gone. Given the situation on the station, I wasn't going to worry about a bullet hole letting out air.

Yong wasn't having it. "You don't know what is there. Not in reality. The two of you were on the station only a short time, and we have one seriously wounded. We cannot afford to lose you."

I think Yong was allowing her personal feelings into the argument. Not that you could tell from her voice, and not that I was arguing. GSY Station had the feel of a haunted mansion in a Gothic horror vid.

"Then what are you proposing?" Charley asked.

"Can she make a starflight in hib?" Yong asked Charley.

I saw Charley's face go blank. "I don't know," he said. "Leif, I've looked in the personnel records. You've spent more time in hib labs than anybody. What do you think?"

"I was a lab tech, not a doc or a scientist." I've noticed people forget the difference when they expect me to have a miraculous answer. "Would the drugs that block aging in hib also block healing? I don't know."

Charley threw his hands in the air, then slapped them down against his thighs. "There might be some experimental data on bone healing in hib, but I can't imagine there's a record of a human doing it on a starflight. No way we'll find out more than that. I mean, I can get an assessment from the AI, but it won't be based on data. It'll be a guess coming out of a computer."

"Cristina didn't want to make another starflight," Zoe said. "She wanted to go home to Mexico City."

"We cannot wait the length of time it will take her to heal, and we don't know if she can heal in hib," Yong said. "She cannot take a landing from one of the elevator escape pods without being fully healed. And unless we can refuel the spaceplane, which seems unlikely now, the only other way we can put her down in Mexico City is if all of us go to Mexico City. Even if we do that, she will be helpless on the ground. We know nothing about the conditions there. Please think about what you are saying before you say it."

Zoe turned red and swallowed hard. She looked away from Yong as she spoke. "She should still have a say in what happens to her. That's the only right thing to do. You can't just make those decisions for her."

I don't think I have ever seen a face colder than Yong's at that moment. Her eyes narrowed to thin slits. "If I need to make a decision, I will make one. Regardless of anyone's likes or feelings. However, I agree we should discuss this with her. A starflight may be as risky as anything else, and we have the time for that conversation. All of you need to understand that we may need to make difficult decisions soon, and they may need to be pragmatic and utilitarian."

"Pragmatic for you is a starflight," Zoe said. "Not for us."

Yong gave her a withering look, then ignored her. "Charley, will Cristina have a clear enough head for discussion tomorrow?"

"Probably," Charley said. "I'll let you know when she wakes."

. . .

The next morning came much sooner than I expected, in the form of an alarm to my phone that woke me before 6:00 A.M. ship time. I sat up in bed and rubbed my head. I was alone. Yong hadn't wanted to leave the bridge; she might have slept in her chair. I looked at the alarm flashing at the periphery of my vision and it opened. Charley wanted me in the Med Unit. Immediately.

I could see there was trouble the moment I walked through the door. Charley was at Cristina's bedside. An oxygen mask covered her nose and mouth.

"She was asking for you," Charley said. "Just understand, she's not making a lot of sense."

I walked to the bedside and did not like what I saw. Cristina was breathing very fast and straining at it. I could see the muscles and veins at her neck stand out.

Her eyes darted toward me and she grabbed my wrist. "Leif, we need to get out of this hotel. Take me to the Metropolitan Cathedral. I want to pray at the altar of forgiveness. We need to be forgiven. Will you come with me?"

"Sure, Cristina. But we can't go right now. You hurt your leg. Remember?"

"Did I? Yes, it does hurt. Maybe I should rest a little. You'll take me there later today? I need to go today."

"I'll take you, Cristina. Just rest now." I held her hand.

She closed her eyes.

"What happened?" I asked Charley.

"Look at this." He pulled up her top and I could see a rash across her chest. Lots of tiny discrete red dots. They were flat and didn't blanch when I pressed one. I saw them also under the arm next to me.

"I don't need the readouts or the damn computer," Charley said. "She's had fat emboli. Little globules of fat. They can get in the blood from fractures of big bones, or maybe I caused it the way I put that rod in. It's my fault."

"Stop that, Charley. You did the best you could with the situation you had. And you just said it happens with this kind of fracture. More important, what do we do now?"

"Oxygen," Charley said. "Which I'm doing. I can try putting her on a ventilator. But this isn't an ICU, and I'm not an intensivist."

"Do what you can." I put a hand on his shoulder. "It's not your fault."

I didn't think Cristina would be going to the Metropolitan Cathedral.

.   .   .

Cristina lasted another two hours. Ventilator or no ventilator, oxygen wasn't getting from her lungs to her bloodstream. Charley was ashen as he shut down the equipment after her heart stopped for good.

Zoe and Anil were standing in the Med Unit when I walked out with Charley. A mist filled the air from tears that had been shed. The tears floated in zero gee until the air-handling system swept them up. No one spoke. It was more by silent consensus than any actual decision that we trooped down to the caf, sat at a table, and stared at one another.

The caf door opened behind us, and Yong walked through on the StickStrips. She looked as haggard as the rest of us. She launched from the doorway, floated to a nearby chair, grabbed the back, and pulled herself into the seat.

"There are no evident threats," she said, as if to explain why she was not on the bridge.

"I think we should assume everything we see is a threat," I said. "Nothing might be coming at us, but I would assume that anything and everything, especially if it has electronics, is a threat."

"What did they do?" Zoe asked. "Booby-trap everything they could put their hands on? Kill people at random? What kind of people do that?"

"Ones who can find ways to justify it to themselves," I answered.

"Yeah." Charley's voice lacked any emotion. "Leif, when I looked at the records about hib experience, I saw you were called Leif the Lucky. Why?"

I winced at that. "That last attack during the Troubles at Schwarz-kopf. I was the only one in the platoon left alive."

"Oh." He stared at me, his eyes flat. "I was hoping your luck rubbed off on people around you, but it sounds like the opposite."

I wasn't interested in talking about luck—not mine, not anyone else's. An oppressive silence descended on the caf, as suffocating as a pillow squashed over your face.

"Now what?" Zoe's voice was small even amid the silence. She picked at the skin around her fingernails, not looking at any of us. "Are we going to die one by one? Is that all there is left for us?"

"No," Charley said. "We should go down to Earth now. Forget trying to find more fuel for the spaceplane. Let's go to the elevator. Take the escape pods."

"You would trust them?" Zoe raised her head and looked at him. "After what's happened, you would trust anything here?"

"No," Charley said again. "I don't trust anything. And you know, even if we all agreed on going to one place, do I trust going down in a spaceplane that doesn't have enough fuel? But Yang thinks she can land it? No offense, Pilot Yang, but I don't." Charley was getting heated. "I just think it's time to *do* what we're going to do, and what happens is what happens. I just don't care anymore."

"Charley," I said, "what happened to Cristina wasn't your fault."

"I didn't say it was!" Charley's hand slammed down on the tabletop and he glared at me. "What I said was it's time to move on. We're not going to find some miraculous answer to our problems amid the shit that's been left floating around."

"All right," said Yong, and it was immediately quiet again. "I will move the *Dauntless* over to the space elevator station. Leif will ferry you over there, unless any of you changes your mind and wants to fly with us. Check the escape pods. If they are not operational, I will keep my promise and attempt to land all of us in the spaceplane. If that is what we must do, I will try for Earthbase in Kansas. Three of you are American, we all speak English, and, honestly, I cannot tell that anyplace else would be better. Are we agreed?"

CHAPTER THIRTEEN

We gave Cristina a solemn burial in space before we did anything else. After that, it was a very short trip from GSY Station to the space elevator. The two were, essentially, in the same orbit around Earth, approximately twenty-five thousand miles above the surface. It is a little odd to say that the elevator station was in orbit, because it was tethered to the planet by a long woven nanotube cable that ran down to an artificial island in the Atlantic Ocean. The crawlers ran up and down the cable like a subway train, taking people and goods from the surface to orbit and vice versa. At least, they used to.

We said brief and embarrassing goodbyes on the bridge. We were strangers who had been thrown together on a voyage and were now going our separate ways. I gave Charley a quick hug and we exchanged pats on our backs. Zoe moved apart and stared at the screen with an image of Denver, or the ruin of Denver. Anil looked at the deck. It was, frankly, a relief to start moving.

From what we could tell on the bridge of the *Dauntless*, the elevator station had normal air pressure. After our experience on GSY Station, however, none of us were willing to bet that it was breathable. We went in full space suits. We had plenty of cold-weather clothing on board that the colonists on Heaven, with its broiling climate, had not wanted. Charley,

Zoe, and Anil wore layers under their suits. The chronometer read September 13, but the Northern Hemisphere was chilly from the temperature readings we had on our screens.

Anil divided up ReadyMeals, and anything else nonperishable, into equal shares for the three going down to Earth. The amounts seemed small, and they really were. They were limited by what an individual could carry and what we figured would fit in an escape pod. The remainder would stay on the *Dauntless*. I thought it would be enough to get me and Yong to High Noon, if we spent maximum time in hib and went on half-daily rations.

Before we went to the dock, I went to get my pistol and belted it to my suit. If I saw something I wanted to shoot, I intended to do it. I didn't care if I put a hole in the elevator station wall.

I undocked the transport from the *Dauntless* and flipped it around. A short burst from the thrusters was all we needed to cover the distance to the elevator station. There was no conversation inside the transport. We were in our suits, of course, but there was no talk on the ship channel, not even any messages. The realization had sunk in that this was *it*. We might not have been the closest of friends, or even the tightest of teams, but we were about to go our separate ways forever. Once those escape pods left the station, there would be no going back. I wondered if I was the only one with no misgivings about my choice.

I lined up the transport for docking at the elevator station and waited for Yong to come on the channel.

"Brief hold where you are," she said. "Some odd readings on the screens. I want to check and correct."

I thought I could do the docking by myself this time. Had I been alone, I would have responded with a request to do that. However, I wasn't going to do it with three passengers on board.

Whatever was bothering Yong on the *Dauntless* must have cleared up quickly. She came back on the channel and guided me through the docking maneuver. I was pleased to note that she found nothing to correct.

I led them through the air lock into the station with its WELCOME TO THE MILES RICHMOND SPACE ELEVATOR sign. I thought back to crazy Miles. It was a little ironic, how he—quite unintentionally—had started the boom in space exploration, and how it was now ending at this platform.

I was relieved to see an empty platform ahead of us. Specifically, I was glad to see no bodies. Our instruments claimed that the air was a normal nitrogen–oxygen mix and had normal pressure, but I told the others to keep their helmets sealed and suit air on. No one argued.

I avoided the entrance to the ISC offices—all we might find in there would be bodies—and followed the signs to the emergency escape capsules. Those proved to be on a deck below the crawler platform. We found a control station there, next to a half dozen tubes. Each of those tubes held a capsule, like a round chambered in a rifle. Red paint daubed on each of the ones we could see read SAFE. That was something, I thought.

The mechanism was pretty basic. We had all the information in the database on the *Dauntless* from when we left, and I doubted thirty-nine years would have brought radical changes.

"These capsules are single-occupant," I said as a rehash of what they should have read over before we came. "They're basically heat shields, seat, and parachutes." We walked over to the nearest tube and examined the capsule, as the real thing was always different from a picture on a screen or field. "Climb in through that hatch." I pointed. "You'll find a personal just-in-case-everything-goes-to-shit parachute. Strap that on and belt into the seat."

"We've got this," Charley said. "We enter our destinations on Earth on the screen in the capsule. The computer controls the ejection velocity and fins when we hit atmosphere. You don't need to do it for us from the panel. Then we hit Launch and that's it."

Zoe and Anil repeated all the information back as well. Everything else was automatic. The system would spit the capsule out of the tube like a peashooter opposite to the direction of Earth's and the station's rotation, with the adjustments to the velocity and direction for the intended target. From there, the capsule would fall to Earth, much like one of the first manned missions nearly three hundred years ago.

"The computer will deploy a drogue chute at twenty-one thousand feet and the main chutes at ten thousand," I said. "There is an independent altimeter to strap to your wrist, and manual controls so you can do this all yourself, but you're not going to do that."

"No," said Charley. "That's ridiculous."

"Agreed. Understand that you are going to land with some force. It's going to rattle your joints. Have any of you ever skydived?"

I got three headshakes. "Well, this should be easier. You'll have the seat and the capsule to help take the shock. You'll be okay."

Power for the elevator station came from solar panels on an asteroid that had been linked to it as a counterweight. That ought to be functioning perfectly well, and all the panels at the control station were on. I found the capsule hatch controls and tapped for tubes 1 through 3. A sucking sound in triplicate came as the hatches separated from their seals and swung up to reveal the capsule interiors.

"The system is operational," I said on the ship channel. "We are go for escape capsule launches."

"Good," Yong said. "I am having some issues again on the bridge. I would prefer to have you back here sooner rather than later."

I didn't like the sound of that. Yong could look a full-fledged disaster in the face and call it an "issue."

I turned away from the control panels and walked back to the tubes where the three of them stood. "Okay, folks, it's go time. If you want to change your mind, come back with me. Otherwise, strap in for launch."

None of them said anything. They turned to the row of capsules and climbed in. It took some doing to fit their packs in and secure them, because the personal chute had to be secured to their backs and they also had the life-support packs from the suits. Screens at the control station next to me lit up with destinations: Tulsa for Charley. Denver for Zoe. Hampshire, England, for Anil. The hatches swung closed.

"You are go for launch," I said, probably unnecessarily. Oddly, I felt choked up.

"Goodbye to all of you," Charley said. "It has been my pleasure to know you and work with you. Godspeed to wherever you are going, and good luck when you get there."

Zoe and Anil echoed his words. Yong and I responded with our own final goodbyes. Then the three capsules shot down their tubes on their way to Earth.

"Leif, you should get back here," Yong said.

The main screen at the control panel showed THREE ESCAPE CAPSULES LAUNCHED with a letter and number code for each one. As I turned to go, the perimeter of the screen flashed red.

"Wait," I said to Yong. "Something is wrong."

I looked helplessly at the screens and controls. Red on the main screen meant trouble, but I didn't know how to manipulate the system to figure out what was happening.

ATMOSPHERE REENTRY came up next to each of the capsule codes on the main screen. Then, HEAT SHIELD JETTISONED began to flash next to each one.

"What?" I screamed that into the comm channel. "They just reentered! Why would they jettison the heat shields now?"

"The systems must have been infected, corrupted," Yong said. "They are going to burn up on reentry."

"Booby traps! Again! And painted to make you think they're okay. Goddamn!" I stared at the screen, jaws clenched, as though I could will the capsules back to the platform. I could not believe the casual malevolence of what had been done.

REENTRY FAILURE. CAPSULE DESTROYED. The words displayed next to each capsule code.

"They're gone," I said. "Oh my God."

"Leif, get back here. I have a problem."

That galvanized me. I turned away from the control boards and their message of death and headed for the access to the upper platform, where the docking port was.

"What's wrong, Yong?"

"I'm not certain. The ship's engine fired to decelerate the *Dauntless*. That would take the ship out of orbit and into the atmosphere. I have overridden it manually."

"How does that happen? Ships don't just *do* things like that." I was afraid that I knew the answer even as I said the words.

"The *Dauntless* must be infected with malware," Yong said. "The computer is trying to crash the ship. I have manual control now."

"How is this possible? How could we have been infected?"

"When we downloaded the layout of GSY Station, I believe," Yong said. "If I allow the systems on automatic, this programming in the computer takes over."

I reached the main crawler platform. "I can handle the undock and docking," I said. "You focus on the ship."

"You should wait, Leif," she said. "Stay there. This malware is trying to take control."

"Then get out of there, Yong! Take the spaceplane! We'll rendezvous and then try to land."

"No." That was a flat, hard no. "It keeps trying to subvert my control. If I do not continuously impose manual control, it will take over. I see what the programming is trying to do. It intends a controlled descent, so the ship does not burn up, and then a crash into the surface. It is targeting one of the remaining areas with significant population. This is a starship fully loaded with antimatter fuel. I cannot permit this. I will not permit this."

"What are you going to do?" I was right by the docking lock. Framed in a window port, I could see the cylinder of the *Dauntless*, tiny against the stars, blue light flaring from its rear.

"I am taking the ship away from the planet. I will prevent this programming from causing the disaster its creators intended. Leif, I I—"

"Unauthorized transmission detected," said the sultry voice Jorge had given the ship's computer. "Shutting down all comm channels."

"No!" I screamed. "No! No! No!" I knew what she had been about to say.

I braced my hands on the port and stared out into space. I couldn't see the *Dauntless* any longer. I couldn't see the blue flare from the engines. Then, suddenly, a new star bloomed in the sky.

"No! Yong, I love you! I love you! Goddammit, I love you! Come back!"

I screamed myself hoarse into the uncaring silence of a dead comm channel and empty space. I screamed out the words that were too late, and ended with a sob and in tears.

CHAPTER FOURTEEN

I don't know how long I stood there, transfixed by a port window that showed nothing but stars. Yong had blown up the ship in a last-ditch move to prevent the computer from murdering God knows how many people by crashing it on Earth. Or the computer had blown up the ship because Yong was blocking its maneuver. I stared at empty space long enough that my suit oxygen was moving toward redline. I didn't care. Not really. I will admit that the thought in my head was to undock the transport, open its hatch, and vent my suit to space.

I didn't do that. It wasn't a conscious decision; it's simply not the way I'm built. I came to terms long ago with the idea of dying, and in my agony on the space elevator platform, I wanted to die. However, I wanted to die fighting. I wanted to die doing something. What I wanted . . .

I wanted to line up all the sanctimonious, patriotic, and blind leaders who had foisted this evil on humanity and break each one of their necks. I wanted to give them weapons and see them try to stop me from killing them. I wanted Yong back.

At some point, I pulled myself away from the port and walked back to the access to the escape capsule level. I won't say I was thinking. I will say I wasn't going to sit there until my air ran out. It came down to who I was and what my training was. If this Ranger was going down, this Ranger was going down while trying to do something.

But what? Well, when a starship returns to Earth, the pilot reports to Earthbase to complete their mission. That's what Yong would have done under normal circumstances. That's what I was going to do. I was going to complete our mission.

I stopped. How was I going to do anything? The situation was about as bleak as it could get. I had lost the woman I loved. The only one I had ever loved or ever would love, and I hadn't said the three words that would have made it real. Not until it was too late. I deserved to fry in hell for that. I was probably going to do that pretty soon. I was on a space elevator platform twenty-five thousand miles above the surface of the Earth. I had no food, and the air in my suit was running out. I had a transport rocket, but the only place I could go with that was the haunted booby trap of GSY Station. I had no way down to Earth because the escape capsules marked SAFE weren't.

I didn't care.

On the level below the crawler platform, I looked at the control boards by the tubes. Everything on the panels was green. Sure. Three new capsules had moved up into tubes 1, 2, and 3. All were marked SAFE. Sure.

I didn't care.

I tapped the main control board, and the hatch on one of the capsules swung up. I pulled on the personal chute, settled into the seat, and adjusted the straps. Then I looked at the screens and the controls in the capsule.

IF LAUNCHED WITHOUT ENGAGING COMPUTER DESTINATION CONTROL, THIS CAPSULE WILL LAND IN THE VICINITY OF STRATTANVILLE, PENNSYLVANIA. PLEASE TURN ON COMPUTER CONTROL AND GUIDANCE AND ENTER A TARGET FOR LANDING.

"Fuck you," I said to the screen.

Then I shut the computer off. With the screen blank and most of the panels dark, I looked at what was left. I had manual controls for the parachutes and an emergency eject. I also had an altimeter that went with the harness for my last-ditch personal chute. And, yes, the Launch button glowed bright green.

Okay. I had no idea what, if anything, was left of Strattanville, Pennsylvania. It didn't really matter. I was as likely to burn up going down or land with a splat. I didn't care. I was doing something. I was completing our mission.

As I thought about completing our mission, the idea burst into my mind that maybe, just possibly, Yong had escaped the ship in the space-plane. If she had, she would land at Earthbase. Yes, she could have done that. Yong could do anything. I told myself she would be at Earthbase waiting for me. I needed to reach her there.

I shut the hatch.

I hit the Launch button. Acceleration smashed me against the back of the seat as the capsule was shot out of its tube. I fell to Earth. Forever.

I've done HALO jumps—high altitude, low opening—where I jumped out of the airplane at around twenty-five thousand feet and opened the parachute at three thousand. Here, I was being ejected from the space elevator platform at twenty-five thousand *miles*. I hoped that with the computer shut off, whatever malware had jettisoned the heat shields on the other capsules would be inoperable. That meant I would need to release the parachutes manually, based on watching the altitude.

I could feel warmth through the capsule as the heat shield took the brunt of the reentry friction. If it failed, I would die fast enough not to notice. When the altimeter told me I was below ten miles, I figured I was not going out in a burst of flame. At twenty-one thousand feet, I hit the release on the drogue chute. A sharp jerk told me it had worked. I released the main chutes at ten thousand feet. Those seemed to work as well. Maybe I could ride the capsule all the way down. The problem with that was that I wanted some say in where I landed. I hit the emergency eject.

There was a bang and a flash and I was sitting in midair, with the pieces of the capsule around me and being flung away by the gusting air. I saw mountains and what I thought was farmland through breaks in the clouds below me. I was falling away from the mountain region, which was fine with me. I let my free fall continue until I was down to three thousand feet. The ground below looked reasonably promising. I pulled the rip cord.

With an abrupt jerk, the chute opened. I was floating through blue sky toward green land below. I hit hard, harder than I wanted to, and felt pain shoot through my knee. I rolled and tumbled, and eventually came to a stop facedown on a grassy slope.

I shook my head, glad of the helmet's visor between my nose and the ground. Then I pushed myself to a sitting position and opened the helmet. I stared at an overcast sky with patches of blue and felt the chill wind on my face.

Welcome home.

Sort of.

PART II

But not even at the present day are the cities of our country inhabited as formerly; deserted and dismantled, they lie neglected until now, because, although wars with foreigners have ceased, domestic wars continue.

Gildas, "De Excidio Britanniae; or The Ruin of Britain" (6th century AD)

CHAPTER FIFTEEN

It took me a little while to get organized. I wasn't thinking, only moving based on my training. Some part of my hindbrain took over, decided I had missed the drop zone, was behind enemy lines, the mission was fubared, and I needed to survive. Any higher part of my brain was anesthetized.

I gathered up the parachute. I had no means to bury it. Hiding it under rocks was a possibility, but I thought the fabric might prove useful. So, with folding and tying, I worked out a way to carry it. The suit I simply took off and left on the hillside. It was cold once I was out of it—chillier than any mid-September day had a right to be—but those suits were not designed for hiking cross-country. The boots, which I could detach from the suit and had to keep, were bad enough. The SureGrip soles were great for zero gee when you needed to use StickStrips. They would not work so well marching across rough terrain. At least the dirt and mud I'd hit on landing covered most of the bright blue of those soles.

That left me in my ship pants and short-sleeved polo, definitely the wrong gear for the weather. Otherwise, I had my phone base, which did not connect to anything, and my pistol with three spare clips. It wasn't much, but I figured I would warm up once I started hiking. Oh, I had one more item, the most important of all. In my sealed pants pocket, I still had the printed pic of me and Yong on High Noon. Nothing else mattered.

The phone base did have some utility. I had taken pictures of the area as I was coming down, and I could display them on my field. A place that I estimated to be a handful of miles away looked like a farm. The nearest thing to a town—one that looked like people still lived in it—was much farther. I had no food, but I could shoot something or scrounge edibles in the wild. Still, the farm seemed like the best bet for my primary target.

I oriented myself and got moving. I wanted to get whatever use I could from the phone base before it ran out of power.

The land around me was lightly wooded, more brush than trees in many places. The trees themselves weren't tall. Some of them were dead, with bare branches. The pines were solid green, as were the trees with leaves on them. It felt cold for green leaves, but they change color by the length of daylight, not the temperature. The up and down of the low hills was murder on my knee. The hills also blocked my view of the surroundings, although I could use my phone base and chip to stay on course.

I was about halfway to my goal when shots rang out from beyond the rise in front of me. It was a bunch of individual shots—too many for a single hunter, but not a volley and certainly not an automatic weapon. I drew my pistol, cursed my knee, and moved toward the sound of the gunfire. I wanted to see who was shooting before they saw me.

When I cleared the crest and found an opening in the brush, the scene below me was macabre. The ground was open between the downslope I perched on and another treed slope across from me. An old road, partly covered in grass and weeds, ran down the middle of the open ground. On my side of the road, less than a hundred yards away, was a group of six laughing men with their horses nearby at a guardrail. They wore long leather dusters and knit caps. Four of them carried rifles. Those were nothing like the M8s I had used; they looked like old lever-action rifles. One of the other two held a pistol, also of an old design. Three bodies lay on the ground in puddles of blood, gunshot wounds evident. The last of the men in dusters had a small figure in his grasp, a girl, judging by her long braid. His arm was across her throat, her arms futilely trying to pull it away. The other men were taking turns pummeling the shit out of a man who wore a stitched-together fur robe.

I worked closer and reached a good viewpoint in time to catch a glimpse of the man's face. It was a bloody, pulped, swollen mess. He fell at that moment. The man with the pistol holstered it, then kicked the fallen man three times in the groin. After he finished kicking, I saw the man snap his fingers. Three of the others fired their rifles into the man on the ground. The body jerked at the impact of the shots, did not move again. The man who had snapped his fingers pointed at the girl and started to undo the front of his pants. I knew what was coming next.

I didn't know who the gunmen were. I didn't know the people they'd killed, or why. I had no idea who the girl was. I *did* know whose side I was on.

I sighted on the man who now grabbed the girl's pants. It was a long shot for a pistol, but not too far for me. My first bullet hit the man with his hand on her pants and snapped his head to one side. A gout of blood flew out of his cap. At the shot, the others spun around, weapons ready, searching for the source of the shot on the hillside. These were no casual predators. I could tell that from their reactions. They were accustomed to gunfights. It didn't matter. They hadn't been looking my way when I fired; they hadn't seen the muzzle flash from my pistol. I had no mercy for them. I fired four times in quick succession. Four men fell. The one holding the girl tried to use her as a shield. I shot him through his screaming mouth, the bullet going out the back of his head. None of them got off a shot at me.

I worked my way down the rest of the slope to the open ground, each time my weight landed on that knee sending a jolt of pain up to my head. The rusted remnants of the guardrail at the side of the road held me up until I could swing my leg over it. While I made my slow progress to her, the girl neither bolted nor froze. Instead, she knelt by the body of the man who had held her, searching under his duster. When she straightened up, she held a pistol in one hand and a dagger with a blade the length of her forearm in the other. Given the size of her hand compared to the pistol, she didn't hold it entirely steady, but she did keep it trained on me. I made a point of stopping to holster mine. Then I trudged the rest of the way to her.

"You stop!" she cried with more force than I thought could come out of that thin body. "You stop or I'll kill you or make you kill me!" Her English was strange, the word *you* little more than *y'*.

I held up empty hands, palms toward her. I gestured at the bodies on the ground. "I think I just saved you. Why would I hurt you?"

"You're a man. What more reason you need?" She bared her teeth and clenched them together.

"How do I convince you I'm not going to hurt you?"

"Shoot yourself. If you're dead, I'm sure."

This relationship was not off to a good start. True, my relationship with Yong hadn't started much better. The ache that came with that thought made me not care if the girl shot me. The weight of the pistol made her hand waver from side to side.

"You might want to grip that with both hands," I said. "If you're going to shoot me, I'd prefer it be a good shot."

"You're stupid! Or crazy!"

"Maybe both. It's been said before. Now, I'm coming the rest of the way." I limped ahead to close the distance.

She didn't shoot. She didn't lower the pistol either. I stopped with the barrel an inch or so from my stomach. At that point, I could have taken it away—no guarantee, but a high likelihood of success. However, there was the knife in her other hand. That was held expertly. We examined each other from close range.

The girl in front of me was thin to the point of skin and bones. Her homespun trousers were at least two sizes too large. A knotted rope at her waist cinched them tight so they didn't fall down. Holes had been worn through the fabric and revealed a pair of knobby knees. Long hair, dark brown in color, was pulled into a braid that hung over her left shoulder. Pieces of leaf stuck in the hair. Her face was a shade lighter than her hair, with a straight, pointed nose and thin lips pressed bloodless in an attempt to look fierce. Droplets of blood from the man I shot first had sprayed her forehead and clotted there. Her right cheek was discolored with a large yellow-and-greenish bruise. That hadn't come from today's incident; I figured it for a week old. Her eyes—

My gaze stuck there. Those irises were a smooth, polished jade green, a color that contrasted sharply with the brown of her face and hands. I'd seen eyes that color before, when I was on Earth in 2097. I had thought it artificial then. That wasn't possible now.

"What're you staring at?"

"Your eyes."

"What about my eyes?" she demanded. "I'm an indie. Most of us have these eyes."

I had no idea what she meant by that.

"What about you?" she asked. "Dumb-looking boots. And what about that shirt? Stupidest shirt I've ever seen, and you must be an even stupider man to wear it. No woman to make you anything better?"

Yes, this relationship was progressing very well.

"My name is Leif. What's yours?"

"Elvy."

"How did you get that bruise?" I pointed at her cheek.

"It's nothing. I've been beat much worse."

She didn't say anything else, nor did she change her stance. The weight of the pistol was getting to be too much for her hand, though. The barrel sagged down to point at my foot. A howl echoed through the woods around us. It was answered by two others.

"We should get out of here," I said. "Keep the pistol and the knife. You have my word I will protect you, not hurt you."

"You don't have a word till I know you," Elvy said. "And I know how to live in the wild. Better than you, I bet. Why're you limping? Fall down a hill?"

"An old battle," I said softly. "A long, long time ago. How old are you?"

"Twelve."

By size, I'd have taken her for ten. She pulled a cord from a pocket and used that to make loops that hung the pistol and knife from her rope belt. When I saw her start to tie up the weapons, I turned my attention to the dead to see what I could salvage. Three of the horses had broken free and bolted when I shot the men in the dusters, but the other three were still tied to the old guardrail. I was not going to turn down a ride to where I was going. Even better, the saddle packs might have food. I'll never be mistaken for a broncobuster, but one of the horses let me close enough to stroke his face. Soon, I was able to pat his neck and grab the reins. That relationship showed more promise than the one with Elvy. The horse didn't comment on my polo shirt.

Whatever I felt about Elvy's thoughts about my shirt, I was cold in short sleeves. I checked the fallen men. One of them was big enough that his duster would fit me. I'd shot him through the left chest, so there was a bullet hole and plenty of blood. The bullet must still have been in the body, because the back of the coat was intact. I stripped it off him and rubbed the coat against the ground until the liquid was gone. Then I pulled it on. It gave me good protection against the wind and the chill, and as long as the bullet hole wasn't matched by one in me, I didn't care about blood or smell.

One of the men had a roughly stitched pack. Each of them had a pistol holstered at their belt. I gathered the pistols and whatever ammunition the dead men had and dumped all of it in the pack. Those pistols were rather basic. They loaded with a magazine in the grip and fired as a semiautomatic, but they looked susceptible to jamming. The rifles were lever-action ones and would fire a single shot at a time. All had seen much use and little cleaning. I lashed the rifles to one of the horses.

The people these men had killed were dressed like Elvy: homespun trousers and shirt with stitched-together skins over the top. Their weapons were bow and arrow and knife. Unlike Elvy, the three men and one woman had white skin, but they all shared the same green eyes. I heard footsteps on the ground next to me as I checked the last body, twisted to look over my shoulder, and saw Elvy looking down at the corpse I was examining.

"How were you with these people?" I asked. "They don't look like your family."

"Family is where you find it. Even you must know that." She shrugged. "The band did tallies; knew we didn't have enough food. Gipson"—she pointed at the body of the man I had seen brutalized before he was shot—"he said there were farms this way. Figured I'd be useful to some woman. I didn't want to go. Didn't have a choice." She shrugged again.

I straightened up. Her face turned up to look at me. "This doesn't bother you?" I asked. "The killing? The bodies?"

"Course not. Indies travel to the east. Bodies all over the old areas—bones and skeletons, anyway. Used to be bodies. Poke into any old building, you probably find one. Dead is dead. A child knows that."

I had the impression she thought she was talking to a child, and not a terribly bright one at that. I slapped my hands against the side of the duster I had appropriated.

"All right. You said this person leading your group was headed for some nearby farms. There's one not too far from here, and this"—I stamped my foot on cracked pavement—"what used to be a road, goes that way. I'm headed there also. With the horses, we can make it there before dark. We can ride together that far."

I brought the horses over, figuring we would each ride one and I would lead the other by a rope. Elvy shied away and I saw fright on her face for the first time.

"You've never been on a horse?"

She shook her head.

Would wonders never cease? My experience with horses, my sole experience, came from a time during Central Asia II when my platoon ended up with several of the animals after an action left us holding a ranch. I remembered Petey and Jamal laughing themselves silly as I was thrown time after time. I learned to ride just to spite them, because neither of them would try. I wasn't telling all of that to Elvy. I only said to copy me as I put a foot in the stirrup and swung up. She didn't move.

"Scared?" Then I realized the stirrups were very high for a small girl. I held out a hand. "I'll help you up."

"You're a shit, talking to me that way!" She coiled like a compressed spring and launched herself into the air, aiming for the saddle. She landed against it, got her arms across it. The startled horse bucked. Elvy held on for dear life and pulled herself up. Somehow, she managed to avoid sticking either the horse or herself with the knife at her belt. The horse bucked again but did not dislodge her. Slowly, she pulled herself forward until her butt was in the saddle and the horse had settled down. Her knuckles were white from her grip on the reins. Then she did the first thing in the period of our acquaintance that was typical of a twelve-year-old. She stuck her tongue out at me.

＊ ＊ ＊

Fortunately, it was only a few hours' ride to the outlying farm I had spotted at the tail of my descent. I say fortunate because, while my knee was glad I wasn't hoofing it, and even though I looked good getting into the saddle, I had never ridden horseback for any distance. It didn't take long before the muscles in my thighs and butt were screaming. I couldn't complain, because I wasn't going to do that in front of Elvy. A glance at her face told me that she was at least as miserable as I was.

Our route was as short and easy as I could make it. I think I would have found my way perfectly well on my own, but the image in the phone base I had taken from the air and could pull up on my field meant no wrong turns or need to check landmarks. I could see that Elvy was impressed when we rode through the last screen of trees, and the fields and buildings came into view just as I said they would.

The fact that I was concerned about impressing this twelve-year-old is a separate matter.

As we closed in on the farm buildings, I could see that the house was made partly of logs and partly of unpainted wood planking. The roof was steeply pitched and covered with chunks of shingles that must have been salvaged from elsewhere and nailed in place. Smoke curled up from a chimney at one end. I could see a barn behind the house, at least one shed, and some chicken coops. The barn leaned a bit to one side but did not appear in danger of falling down. A boy of four or five was playing in the dirt before the door to the house. He looked up at the horses, let out a wail, and ran inside.

A moment later, a tall, thin woman came out the door. She wore baggy black pants with a tunic for a top, and she carried a rifle. I was going to yell out a greeting, was going to give her a wave of my hand, but first I had to bring the horse to a stop. I never got to do any of those things, because she brought the rifle up, leveled it, and fired.

Thank God she was a lousy shot! I didn't think it was intended as a warning. I swung a leg over the horse to dismount and went for my pistol simultaneously. I jump out of choppers and airplanes ready to fight; I don't leap into action from horseback—and my boots were designed for spaceships, not stirrups. My foot caught in the stirrup and my knee wrenched. Instead of landing with my weapon ready and the horse between me and the shooter, I sprawled across the ground.

What saved me was Elvy. She slid off her horse while the woman was trying to shoot me and ran straight at her, waving her arms.

"Don't shoot him! Don't shoot him! He saved me!"

The woman's rifle shifted to point at Elvy. The girl came to a stop less than ten yards in front of the barrel. She was breathing heavily but showed no sign of being afraid. I took the opportunity of the riflewoman having her attention on Elvy to regain my feet. I did not go for my pistol, not with Elvy right in front of the rifle.

"I say he's good!" Elvy shouted. "He killed the raiders who killed the indies I was with. I say it!"

The rifle shifted back to me. "A lone Athenian raider who saves a feral child. Explain this to me."

I wasn't sure how to explain it, because I had no idea what she was talking about.

"Feral child?" was what I came up with.

"She has feral eyes, idiot," the woman snapped. "If you travel in Pennsie borderlands, you'd have to be blind or stupid not to know that."

"Six men killed the people she was traveling with," I said. "I killed them. I don't know anything about feral eyes or raiders or borderlands, but if we can talk and not shoot, I can explain."

A quick pump of the lever action had her rifle ready to fire again, but she did not pull the trigger. Her eyes moved to Elvy. "Late in the year for ferals to be traveling to the farms for work. What were they expecting?"

I could see Elvy's eyes go wide, white around the green. She began to back away. "I can live in the wild. I should be there, not here. I'm going to the woods. I am nothing but a horrible little girl who should be in the woods by herself." I saw her start to shake as she backed away, and her voice rose to a scream. "Gipson and the others, their idea was to find a farm, rob it, kill the family, take the food. That's what they were going to do. They took me from the band because they said some woman would take a little girl and they could get in close that way, and the band sent me away because no one even likes me. I said I wouldn't do it and they beat me, which is where this came from." She pointed at her bruised face. "They said if I didn't do it, they'd break my face so bad I couldn't talk. Then they'd show me to some woman who'd take pity and it would happen the same as they wanted. Then the riders came and killed Gipson and the others and then he killed them and saved me and that's the truth and I'm going to the woods and starve by myself."

"Stay where you are," the woman said. "You could have lied to me. Why didn't you?"

"I don't know," Elvy said. "I didn't want to. I'm a horrible little girl and you should shoot me." Her face twisted in agony, the corners of her mouth pulled down, her nostrils flared. Any thought I had that her words were a ploy for sympathy vanished.

"I'm not going to shoot a child," the woman said. "I thank you for telling the truth. Can I now have the truth from a raider who killed the other raiders?"

A laugh sounded from off to my right. "Look at that raider coat he's wearing, Ma! If he was in it when it got that bullet hole, I don't think he'd be standing there!" A figure stood up from behind a woodpile with a rifle leveled at me. I took him for a teenage boy. He had a broad pale face with freckles under curly light brown hair, with the beginnings of a beard on his cheeks. Loose homespun pants were held up by suspenders.

I tried to make sense of the situation. The woman holding the rifle had brown skin, a shade darker than Elvy's. She had high cheekbones on a narrow face with a thin, straight nose and light-brown eyes. Her hair was straight, went halfway down her back, and was black with a few strands of silver. Wind gusts blew it around below a band of white lace. The contrast with the boy who had called her Ma could not have been greater.

"I took the coat off one of the men I killed," I said. "I'm a traveler from far away. I don't know what's happening here." Far away in both distance and time, I thought. I wondered how that explanation would be received.

"Believe him!" Elvy said. "You should see the stupid shirt he's got under that coat!"

The woman came to a decision. "Drop your weapons on the ground. All of them. Then take the coat off and drop it on the ground with the weapons, so I can see there's nothing under it. Step away there"—she waggled the rifle as a gesture—"and my son will pick them up. Yours too," she said to Elvy.

I did as she instructed. Then both she and the boy stared at my ISC polo and she pointed the rifle at the ground.

"Welcome to my house and please come inside," the woman said. "Both of you. My name is Charity Blessed Montgomery."

CHAPTER SIXTEEN

The interior of the farmhouse was warm, if a bit smoky. It was snug, too, with the ceiling only a few inches above my head. What seemed like a whole roomful of children watched with a mixture of curiosity and anxiety as Elvy and I came through the door. After counting, I realized they numbered only five.

A fire crackled over several logs in an open hearth at one end of the main room. On the packed earthen floor in front of the hearth stood a stout wooden table with benches on each side. A woodburning stove sat against a wall a few feet from the end of the table, adding to the heat inside. Dishes and utensils were visible in an open cabinet next to the stove. Closer to the entrance, but still within the warming radius of the fire and the stove, were a spinning wheel and small loom. Three straight-backed chairs and a rocker occupied the other side of the room. Two doors led to the rear. One of them was open, and I could see a row of beds with heavy covers.

Charity and her son put their rifles and our weapons on a rack nailed to the wall. Two other rifles and, incongruously, a banjo were already in the rack. A battered speller was open on the floor next to the rocker.

Charity offered me one of the chairs. When I sat down, she took the rocker. Then she introduced her family by pointing as she spoke.

"My eldest"—she indicated the freckled teenager—"is No Nonsense Johnson. He is sixteen now and keeps the name of his first family." There followed Courtesy Always, a pale, blond girl of ten who was Elvy's size; Amazing Grace, a boy of eight; Doubting Thomas, the five-year-old boy I had seen in the yard; Measure Carefully, a girl of four; and Renounce Pride, a boy of three. Amazing Grace, Doubting Thomas, and Measure Carefully all resembled Charity in skin and hair, but Renounce Pride had nearly black skin and tightly curled black hair. None of them had Elvy's eyes of bright, polished jade.

Charity folded her hands in her lap and addressed me as though she were making a formal speech. "Make Peace Montgomery, my man in both law and fact, was killed last spring in a skirmish with raiders when he went to help farmers a day's ride south of here. I have managed the farm by myself since, although No Nonsense is a great help, and the other children do their work as they are capable. We distill our own alcohol, and that powers an engine to help with plowing and harvest, and there are ferals who take work in spring and summer. Not this late in the year, however, as I have said." She glanced at Elvy.

Elvy nodded. "I'm Elvy," she said.

"Feral name and feral eyes," said Courtesy.

The look that passed between the two girls was challenging in both directions.

I looked from one to another, at features and colors that did not fit together. "I don't understand," I said. "These are your children, as you say, but I—" I knew I was going to stammer over words that would have been impolite in the extreme when I was growing up, but I went ahead anyway. "I don't see how. I mean there's no resemblance with some of them. To each other or to you."

"Family is where you find it," Charity said. The same words Elvy had used. "The Twelve Saints preached that, and we, like most, follow the church. I will never turn away a child who finds us. If she wishes to stay and be part of this family, Elvy will be my eldest daughter, as you have not claimed her, nor she you. I can feed her and I have no prejudice against ferals. You do not need to go to the woods, child," she said to Elvy, "and I do not blame you for the crimes that band might have planned."

Elvy took a solid minute to study each of the children, her eyes longest on Courtesy. "I will stay, Ma." She took a seat on one of the benches with her back in front of the fire. "He doesn't understand simple things." She pointed at me. "I think something is wrong." She tapped her head.

"Maybe it's time for him to speak," Charity said. "The family has been introduced; we should give him his time. I, for one, do not think there is anything wrong with his head."

I was surprised it had taken this long. I would have been dying of curiosity if an oddly dressed stranger appeared on my isolated farm. I guessed their introduction was a ritual formality that had to come first.

"My name is Leif Grettison. My shirt, which Elvy finds so amusing, is the uniform from the starship *Dauntless*, a ship that flies between the stars. We left Earth one hundred and fifty-three years ago and met disaster on our return. I'm the only one who survived. Our base is—was—in Kansas, and if I can return there, I am going to do so."

A long silence followed my little speech, broken only by the occasional snap from the burning logs.

"You're a starman? A real starman?" The words shot out of eight-year-old Amazing Grace. "That means you're from before!"

He rushed to my chair and leaped onto my lap, knees on top of my thighs, supporting himself with his hands against my chest. He thrust his face at mine so I had to pull my head back to avoid bumping noses. I could feel his breath across my face. All I could see was his eyes, boring into mine.

"I don't see anything in his eyes," he said.

"I'm not surprised." No Nonsense grabbed the child by the back of his shirt and pants, lifted him off me, and deposited him on the floor. "Stories say red numbers would flash in the eyes of people from before because of what they used all the time," he said to me. "Maybe those are just stories, or maybe you're not from before. Why should we believe you're from before, and a starman at that?"

Charity broke in before I could start an answer. "I have letters and numbers, and I work to teach you, No Nonsense, and the other children. Elvy, you do not, do you?"

Elvy froze, saw Courtesy stare at her, then gave a minimal shake of her head.

Charity's focus was on No Nonsense. "Look at that shirt. His name is stitched under the symbol on his left breast. Now look at the symbol on the right. Stories say the Saints used that, or something like it. There are letters under that symbol. Read them to us, No Nonsense."

The boy came close to me and peered at the lettering under the symbol of the space-suited hand clutching a star over my right breast. He sounded out the word slowly as he read it, saying the letters at the end. "Starshot XV."

"The *X* and *V* are very old-style numbers," I said. "They stand for fifteen. We were the fifteenth mission to the stars. I was also on the first."

"When were you born?" Elvy asked.

"2038."

"Saints from the stars," Charity said. "Before the Tribulation and the Die-off. Long before."

"Then you used electronics," No Nonsense said. "You must have had electronics. Do you have any?"

The only thing I had was my phone base in its little pocket on my belt. I wasn't sure what reception it was going to get, but I drew it out. The screen lit up in response to my thumb. Its battery was almost drained and it would never be charged again.

No Nonsense backed away from me so fast, he tripped over his own feet and landed on his ass. The other children shrank into a far corner. Even Charity got out of her rocker and put a little more space between her and me. The exception was Elvy. She walked over next to me and looked down at the phone base, her bright green eyes alive with curiosity.

"This is what destroyed the world?" Elvy asked.

"Not that. Not that one." Charity's voice was unsteady. "But things like it. Electronics. *Computers.*" She said the last as though it was a filthy word and she wanted the taste out of her mouth.

"I'm sorry," I said. "I'll put it away. It really won't do anything."

"No," said Charity. "If you would like friendship or family here, that needs to be destroyed. And even if you choose to leave instead, I will advise you not to let anyone know of it. Most folk are not . . . understanding."

I made a quick decision. The phone base was of no use to me anyway. Once the battery ran out, it would be nothing more than a brick of plastic and silicon. I held it out. "Here. Take it. Whatever you want to do."

No Nonsense backed away on the floor. Charity didn't move. It was Elvy who plucked it from my hand.

"For a man, you are so scared, big brother," she said to No Nonsense. "It didn't burn him—Leif, he said his name is—and it's not going to burn me. What do we do with it?" She flourished it like a prize.

"Take it out back," Charity said. "Destroy it and bury it."

Charity lit a lantern and then she, No Nonsense, Elvy, and I walked around to the back of the farmhouse, where coops stood and chickens clucked. Dusk had fallen while we talked inside. No Nonsense walked to the barn and returned with a pickax. Elvy put the phone base on the ground. No Nonsense lifted the pickax up over his head and brought it down with a mighty swing that drove the point through the phone base's screen. A notification popped up on my field that read: PHONE CONNECTION LOST. No Nonsense got a shovel, dug a hole, and buried the remains of the phone base.

"Is there anything else?" Charity asked.

I decided not to mention the chip implanted in my head.

·   ·   ·

We trooped back into the farmhouse after the impromptu ceremonial destruction and burial of my evil electronics—that is, my phone base. Before I reached the door, a punch like a small rock hit me in the ribs. I looked down and saw Elvy's intense face.

"Listen." Her voice was a soft hiss. "I know you don't know what you're doin'. Ma is goin' to give you something to eat because you're a guest. Don't finish it. Leave some."

"Why would I insult her like that?"

"You are stupid. If you finish everything, it means you're still hungry, that she didn't give her guest enough food. She'll keep giving you more even if it's everything she has, because you can't leave a guest hungry."

Indeed, as soon as we were back inside, Charity busied herself putting some slices of meat and what looked like yogurt into a bowl. She set that for me on the table. The meat was tough; it had been dried. The yogurt was a bit sour and reminded me of the skyr I'd had as a child during vacations in Iceland. It was all delicious. I made a point of leaving a piece of meat and said I was full. Charity smiled and told Amazing Grace to clean up. I looked over and saw Elvy nodding approval.

Then Charity went out through one of the doors leading to the back of the house. She returned with a jug plugged by a stopper. She distributed mugs from her cabinet to me, No Nonsense, and Elvy, keeping one for herself. She pulled the stopper out and filled the mugs with an amber liquid.

"To family and triumph over tribulation." Charity raised her mug and took a long drink.

I essayed a swallow. It was hard cider.

I don't drink alcohol, but the reason for that was the alcoholic mess my father made of himself. Abstinence was, for me, a choice rather than a necessity, but I could not see explaining that to the people watching me. I drank. As soon as I did, No Nonsense and Elvy did as well, and Charity finished her mug.

"This is good," Elvy said.

"Don't get used to it, Daughter," Charity said. She did lean back in her rocker, though, the first time I had seen her relax. "Much has been said, and it's reasonable now for me to give some explanations. We say family is where you find it because that has been the way since the wars and the Three Years' Winter we call the Tribulation. In the Great Die-off that came with that winter, there were many children left without parents. There were men and women with no partners and with no children. Where they could come together, they did. That's how any of them lived through those times. The Saints preached that, and those who wanted to live followed their words. That is how families are made. Certainly, two grown people may marry and, if a man and a woman, make their own children. I have three from Make Peace. But for others, family is where you find it. Life was not that way before, was it, Leif?"

"No."

"I thought not, from your confusion, although I wouldn't have known it without you being here. So, Elvy is now my daughter because a child should have a ma and she has come here and is willing to stay. I would also say to you, Leif Grettison, if I have your name right, that I think children should also have a pa, or a second ma, and, speaking for me, a house should have a man as well as a woman, and a bed should have both. Make Peace is long gone and dead is dead." She smiled at me.

If Elvy had taken a hot poker from the fire and stuck me in the back, I would not have sat up any straighter. The offer Charity was making was as obvious as it was a surprise—at least to me. None of the children aged eight or older appeared surprised; they were leaning forward to hear an answer. I do have to say that Charity was very attractive when she smiled and loosened up the steel that made her spine.

I couldn't come up with words. I looked at Charity, but it was Yong who was in my mind's eye.

Elvy took the opportunity of my silence to giggle and act like a twelve-year-old again. One who had been slurping hard cider. "If he stays in your bed, I want to watch!"

No Nonsense roared out a laugh. "Uncivilized feral child! In a proper family, children are only allowed . . . to listen!"

The heat I felt in my cheeks was not from the fireplace. I was sure I was bright red. Charity and all the kids were laughing. That child, Elvy, was going to be the death of me.

I needed to say something, and I had to do it quickly. I came up with the truth.

"The woman I love died on our way here. She died in space, preventing a disaster. Died a hero. I can't . . ." As I spoke, in my head, where no one could see, my mind fought with itself to preserve a glimmer that Yong had, against all odds, gotten away from the *Dauntless* in the spaceplane and flown to Earthbase. I had to stop for a moment, because I couldn't breathe. They waited for me. "I have a picture. It's printed. I'll show it to you, but no one touches it. Agreed? No one."

Carefully, I took out the pic of me and Yong on High Noon. I held it so they could see it in the firelight. "We were on a planet around another star. That's why the grass and the light look strange."

Courtesy came over and leaned close. "She's pretty. Her eyes are strange. Can she see with them?"

"Mayor Guo in Eastview has eyes like that," Charity said. "I've met other people who do too. They see just like you and me. It's only the shape that's different, and that means nothing." She paused. "She was pretty. Was she a good woman, Leif? A good cook and handy with weapons? Able to take revenge if need be?"

I thought about Charity's definition of a good woman. I had no idea if Yong could cook. For the rest of it, though, I had no question. "She was the best," I said. I could feel a fullness in my eyes.

"I am sorry," Charity said. "I loved Make Peace as well. Enough that he was my man-in-law, and three of the children in this family are his.

Dead is dead, however. We must do what we must do so the living do not become dead as well."

I managed to get out "I need some time."

I was saved from dwelling on my feelings by Courtesy, who burst out with, "If he's a real starman, does that mean he's my lucky starman?"

"It means he's *my* lucky starman," said Elvy. "I knew as soon as I saw that special shirt."

I had a different recollection of Elvy's impression of my polo, but I let that pass. "What's this about me being a lucky starman? Never mind whose. What do you mean?"

"You wouldn't know, would you?" Charity leaned back in her rocker and smiled again, a soft smile, a curl of her lips and a dimple in her cheek. "In so many stories, a starman brings luck—that's why people talk about having a lucky starman. It's in a rhyme we sing to little children when we put them to bed."

"I know it all!" shouted Courtesy.

"So do I," said Elvy right away.

"No, you don't," Courtesy shot back. "Ferals don't know anything."

"We're indies, which means independent. And I know lots more than you do."

"No, you don't. You don't have letters; you can't read. And you have feral eyes."

Elvy tensed. If she launched at the younger girl, there would be more than hair-pulling.

Charity saw it too. "Cool down, both of you. You can both sing it together for Starman Leif, because it is time to go to bed. And if one of you tries to do it louder than the other, it'll be my hand you'll be feeling."

Jade-green eyes and pale blue ones glared at each other. Military lasers sent less heat than those stares. Then both girls said, "Got it," and turned to me.

Starlight, starbright
First star I see tonight
I wish to live, I wish I might
I wish to eat, without a fight
A lucky starman's kiss,

Make my wish true tonight.

This was what people used for a nursery rhyme to put kids to bed? And what did a starman have to do with it? I must have looked blank.

"The men and women who went to the stars before the Tribulation, they were lucky," Charity said. "Some of them have come back from time to time, like the Saints did, and the stories say they bring a little bit of their luck with them. That's what we tell the children."

"It is true, isn't it?" Elvy, Courtesy, and Amazing all asked together.

I paused to think about the answer I was going to give. Whatever luck I had never seemed to do anyone else any good. Was this going to be like telling a child there was no Santa Claus?

"If I'm lucky, I'll give it all to you," I said. Then I made a show of pointing at Elvy and Courtesy in succession. "But it's split equally. Among all of you. Understood?"

A ring of smiles told me I'd gotten it right.

Charity ushered the children except for No Nonsense to the back room, where several beds waited. Elvy didn't have one, naturally, so Charity told her she would sleep with Courtesy.

"You're sisters now," Charity said. "You need to be good sisters and not fighting sisters."

"Your ma is right," I said. "A starman's kiss is ruined if you fight. The luck is lost. I might as well go out and kiss a horse."

The two of them exchanged wary looks, then clasped hands, gave a shake, and climbed into the bed. Charity sang the little rhyme again once all the young ones were under covers. She had a lovely voice. When she finished, I went from bed to bed and placed a little kiss on each forehead. Smiles followed the kisses. Who knew that would make me feel good?

.   .   .

"That should hold matters for this night," Charity whispered to me when we left the room.

It should only be so easy to bring peace on Earth. I wished that I genuinely had luck and could transfer it with a kiss. I would have given every last drop.

When we stepped out of the room, I thought I could see a faint image in the dark beyond the flames in the hearth. In the back of my mind, I heard Yong say, *You did good, Soldier Boy.*

After that, I went to sleep in the barn.

CHAPTER SEVENTEEN

The barn was drafty, but it was warm enough with the horses, cows, pigs, and goats I could hear and smell; the hay I was in; and a horse blanket I borrowed. I couldn't fall asleep, though. My thoughts chased each other through my head in useless circles. I thought about war, nuclear war, cyberwar. We had thought it was over after the Troubles, that we had been lucky, that we were okay. I could see how wrong we had been, how naïve. Were we condemned to fight one war after another until the last two surviving humans beat each other to death with rocks? I thought about getting up and going outside. It would be cold out there now, but I could sit alone in the quiet and think. But I stayed in the barn, staring up at the dark void below the rough wood ceiling. If I went outside, I might see stars. I did not want to see stars.

Thinking of stars made my muscles tense. I was mad at myself, mostly, for not having gone back to the *Dauntless* the instant Yong said the ship was acting up. I probably wouldn't have been able to do anything except die with her, but that would have been okay. I should have died with her.

I was mad at Yong too. She should have taken the spaceplane and gotten away. I had told her to do that. She had chosen to stay—maybe she had wanted to die in expiation of sins that weren't hers. But why had she chosen to leave me in this miserable world without her? This world was not our fault!

I caught myself and stopped that train of thought. My rage at Yong was wrong in so many ways. I couldn't allow myself to feel that. I did what I had learned in years of combat. I shut off and locked away the emotions I neither wanted nor could afford.

Unfortunately, making myself numb did not turn off my mind. For me, less than a year of awake time had passed since Rissi picked me up at the Boston hotel—since I met Yong at Earthbase, took her hand, and then flew to Heaven with her on the *Dauntless*. It was all fresh in my mind, ready for conversation over coffee in the morning. But in real life, it was all history.

Every person I had ever known before today was dead. Some died in peace; others perished in the cataclysm of the wars and their aftermath. My crewmates had been killed when we returned to the solar system. They were all gone. Despite the family in a house not more than thirty yards away who would welcome me, I was as alone as a person could be.

My world was gone. The stars were gone. Yong was gone. All gone forever, while I was still here. Alive on the outside and dead inside.

. . .

I must have fallen asleep at some point, because I woke up to find a large black cat looking down at me. Making no value judgments, I was too big to be a rat, so maybe the cat was only curious about what animal had invaded its barn. I sat up and the cat gave an aggrieved meow and leaped away. I stood up to brush off the hay that clung to my clothing and almost fell down.

My knee had swollen up to the size of a grapefruit. The fluid that filled it felt like a mixture of maple syrup and gravel. There wasn't much I could do for it—other than curse—since my medikit was gone with the *Dauntless*. Maybe the army doc hadn't done such a good job after all. I hobbled to the house like an elderly man. Even though I had been born 213 years ago, I wasn't that old.

Life isn't fair. It's not as though that was a new revelation.

Inside the house, Charity was seated at the table with Doubting Thomas, the book I had seen on the floor the previous evening now open under the boy's nose. As Charity pointed at a page, Doubting Thomas sounded out letters and words. Intent on her teaching, Charity did not notice me come in. Near the loom, I saw Courtesy and Elvy seated and knitting. Courtesy was fast and precise. Her needles clicked in a blur and her work seemed to grow as I watched. Elvy, to be kind, was trying but obviously struggling. Courtesy kept looking over at Elvy's work and whispering. I'm sure she was pointing out flaws. In fact, once I saw her stop her own knitting and point at Elvy's. I could see how that might end.

Amazing Grace came in while I was watching the two girls, a wire basket that held a few eggs in one hand. At his "This is what there is, Ma," Charity turned and saw me. She closed the book and shooed Doubting Thomas away from the table. I glanced at the book's cover, which showed a poor-quality image of a boy and a girl, each clad in dark green fatigues. Printed above the picture was a title, MY FIRST READER: THE ARMY IS THE STATE AND THE STATE IS THE ARMY. Oh my God.

"Where did you get that?" I asked.

"The church gives them out," she said. She must have picked up on my expression, because she added, "The children need to learn their letters, and there's no school out here. If there were, they'd probably use the same anyway. That's what there is." She slapped her hands together as if brushing them clean. "Would you like something to eat?"

Before I could answer, she'd put a plate of food under my nose. The plate had a faded rose printed in its center with the words BERNIE'S DINER around the rose. It was the kind of cheap plastic I remembered that would—and obviously did—last through the apocalypse. It held several slices of the dried meat, an egg that must have come from one of the coops, a cut apple with honey on it, and more of the skyr. That's when I discovered the worst thing about life in postapocalyptic America.

No coffee!

I should have figured this out in advance. Even when I was growing up, and the climate in North America was heating up, there were only a few areas in the southern US or California where people tried to grow coffee. A touch of nuclear war had ended that. Charity gave me a sort of tea, brewed from pine needles and spruce. I would never wake up again.

I'm sure Charity had other work to attend to, but she made a point to sit across the table from me and ask how I was. The lines of care on her face smoothed out and she looked younger. In the morning light, I could see how bright her eyes were and how pretty her face really was.

"Well enough, considering what's happened," I said. "Although, if I were smaller, I think the cat in your barn might have considered me for a meal."

"Oh, you have met King Solomon!" Charity clapped her hands together. "He's a good mouser, and they're worth their weight—more than that, even—in solids."

"Solids?"

Charity's eyebrows pulled together in puzzlement. "I can see I'll have to explain every other word to you. Solids are solid dollars, real metal. Not like before, when people put their money in those *computers* and all of it vanished. A good cat is expensive and a sign of a successful farm. It means we don't need to trap the mice to eat them ourselves."

I wish to eat, without a fight. The line from the rhyme ran through my head. I was confused. My position on the *Dauntless* had been exoplanetary scout, someone who explored strange, unknown worlds. That's what Earth had become. I had a million questions to ask. Some were more important than others.

"Yesterday, the men I killed . . . the men who killed the, ah, ferals Elvy was with. Who were they? You referred to Athenian raiders, which means nothing to me. Are there more of them, and is that coat I took off one of them like a uniform?" I should have asked this last night, but events had spun out of my control emotionally. Getting back to something quasi-military was easy, and it was important.

Charity frowned and lines etched back into her forehead. "They call themselves Randolph's Raiders. They claim to be Athenian soldiers, and Athens is the state to the south. I'm not sure what that part of the old country was called, but I think the name of the city was Athens even then. They claim that all this land to the north and east belongs to Athens." She gave a bitter laugh. "What they are is nothing more than robbers and murderers. There's no real border out here, only people who see good land and set up farms and a town here and there.

"The last three years, though, these raiders have been riding up. They burn out places and kill families. We all fight back, best we can. That's how Make Peace died. New Terra sends soldiers south to strike back at them, and the people there probably say all the same things about us. I've never heard of a group of them up this far east and north of Eastview before, and I'm not happy to hear it." She shook her head. "Your killing them was a blessing for us, and I'll hope they don't send another group this way. My farm is farthest east, I think. I don't think anyone will settle much farther than this because you get into lots of lime."

Elvy had obviously heard part of our conversation because she came over to the table while we were talking. "Indies go all the way east to the ocean. We witched the woods so everyone else gets limed and stays out."

Charity regarded her for a moment. "I know if you have feral eyes, you don't get limed. Whether it's witchery or not, who knows? Now, you have knitting to work on with Courtesy or, if you prefer, the chicken coops need to be shoveled."

The conversation paused until Elvy considered the options and decided knitting was the lesser of two evils. From the corner of my eye, I could see both girls pretending to work with the wool. Their real focus was us, and I doubt the transmission receivers of the *Dauntless* had been as sensitive as those ears.

"Forget about ferals and Lyme for a minute," I said, having given up on the idea of a private conversation. I thought I knew what they were referring to when they said *lime*, but I figured I could worry about that later. "What is this New Terra you mentioned?"

"That's the state here," she said. "New Terra controls the land west to the Mississippi and north as far as anyone lives."

New Terra? Pretentious name, I thought, but that didn't matter at the moment. "And west of the Mississippi?" I asked.

"Nothing," Charity said. We call those the Empty Lands. No one lives there; no one survived there. Oh, people are crossing the river now to farm, same as we came here. Folks would go south, too, except for the Athenians."

"Are you safe here?" Quite suddenly, the idea of Charity and a houseful of kids being in a disputed borderland bothered me.

"No one is safe anywhere," Charity replied. "And where would we go if we left here? The world is not kind, and it's least kind to a family without a house and holding of their own. It's not like when Make Peace and I came here to settle. But we have weapons and know how to use them, and that will be proof against any band of thieves. Armies are not coming through here. Athens will strike farther west, at the heart of New Terra. That's where the next war will be."

"War?" My voice went up an octave, along with my eyebrows. "Are you telling me that, after wars that nearly wiped out humanity, people are going to war again? What reason could there possibly be?"

Charity shrugged. "Does there need to be a reason? There are always wars. There were to the north of us when Make Peace and I chose to move to the east, outside the state, to have a farm and live in peace. There is no peace. I've learned that. If you go into Eastview, which is the nearest town and west of here, you can ask the marshal or the preacher. Either one will talk your ear off about it, I'm sure. Last night you said you were trying to reach your base in some place called Kansas. In the stories, starmen come from a place called Earthbase. Is that it? Where is it?"

"Yes, that's it. Earthbase is west, across the Mississippi."

"And why do you need to go there?"

In the light of day, and after having shown the picture last night, I couldn't say Yong would be there waiting for me—even if the thought had been popping into my mind with horrifying regularity. "I need to report to them about our mission to a star, to a colony there," I told her.

"Do you realize," Charity said, "that even if there is anyone there at all, no one will care or even know about this mission of yours?"

"Yeah." I nodded. "But I need to complete my mission. That's what I do. Besides, there's nothing else left for me to do."

"Hnnh." Her face went stern, furrows making a V between her eyes. "If you need something to do, see what No Nonsense is doing outside. You may be able to help him."

I can take a hint.

.   .   .

I found No Nonsense pacing back and forth in front of a small shed that occupied the space between the chicken coops and the barn. Muttering to himself, he went to the door once, put his hand on it, then pulled away and stuck his hands in his pockets.

"What's up?" I asked. "Is that where we store the zombies?"

He looked blank and I sighed.

"Okay," I said. "I guess some things are out of fashion. Tell you what. I'll give you a hand with whatever is in there and you give me some information."

No Nonsense had the look of someone who wasn't sure he was making a good deal, but said yes.

"Where do your names come from? I've never heard people named the way you are."

He broke into a smile and aimed a gobbet of spit at the door before he answered. "Names are two words, most of the time," he said. "I think the Saints started it. Some saying about putting in a good word or two. You could ask the preacher about that. I mean, some folks have names from the Bible because the church uses the old holy books, and then some still have old-time names, although lots of people think that's unlucky, because any part of before is unlucky. But most of us have two words. They're supposed to say something about you—or, since your first ma gives them to you, what she thinks about you." He sighed then. "I sure don't know what my first ma was thinking when she named me. She cursed me."

"That I don't understand," I said. "What's wrong with No Nonsense?"

"Oh, that's fine." He hunched his shoulders. "That's why it's a bad joke. When you get to know someone, when you're friends, you tell them they can just use your first word. What are you going to call me? No? I mean, what happens when I get a girl? When we want to be . . . close? What's she going to say? 'Oh, No? No, No, No?' I mean, what was my first ma thinking when she did this? It's not fair."

I tried not to laugh. "Maybe she was making a statement about your father."

He folded his arms over his chest and glared at me, but his attempt at being stern quickly dissolved in a chuckle. "Leif, you may be a starman, but you're an ass anyway."

"You're not the first to say it. What do we need to do in there?" I pointed at the shed.

"That *thing* isn't running right," he said. "We had trouble during the harvest, and Ma doesn't want to let it sit."

When he didn't elaborate, I yanked the door open and took a peek inside. The *thing* was a version of a tractor. Judging by the other implements in the shed, it could pull a plow or a small harvester. It was obviously key to the amount of land Charity could manage, especially with only herself and No Nonsense for heavy tasks.

The thing had an internal combustion engine that ran on alcohol. I remembered Charity's comment about that the previous night. It wasn't a sophisticated engine. It didn't have a starter; it had a crank, and for sure, it had no computer controls. From No Nonsense's comment, we were going to have to take the engine apart and tinker with it.

I was familiar with the way a basic engine worked. The US Army had used internal combustion engines in some vehicles during the Troubles. Plenty of places where the fighting happened had never gone electric. You could find gasoline, but forget charging stations. Our vehicles had plenty of electronics, but I had seen something like this one in a village in Central Asia. That one had used a gasoline–alcohol mix, but the mechanics were basically the same. It wouldn't be too hard even with the limited tools Charity had. I got to work.

No Nonsense stood and watched me from a distance of about six feet. I offered to show him what I was doing, but he shook his head.

"I've never liked that thing," he said. "I always say a prayer before I touch it. Don't you?"

"You mean so I don't fuck it up?" I laughed. "I understand how it works. It's not that complicated. We'll have this done and back together and running perfect. Promise."

"That's not what I meant."

I gave him a puzzled look.

"It has wires in it," he said, his eyes serious. "There's electricity. Aren't you afraid the wires will get into you, take you over? People tell stories like that. What can happen if you're not careful."

I wiped grease from my hands with a rag to give myself a minute to think about my reply. "You're thinking of old stuff like computer chips." I remembered my own wild thoughts when Dev and I had boarded that transport, about an implanted chip being hacked to take over a person, and decided No Nonsense deserved some respect. "These are nothing but dumb wires. Can't do anything more than give a spark or a signal. It's okay. Nothing bad can happen."

At that, No Nonsense did come closer so that he could see better, and he let me show him what I was doing with the parts. He wouldn't put his hands anyplace where he couldn't see exactly what they were touching, however.

While we were working out in the shed, the younger children were working at a variety of chores. On an isolated farm, the most important parts of the daily work—and I was sure it was nearly ceaseless—probably had to do with food management and clothing. Almost all the clothing I'd seen had been made by hand, a process that required spinning and either knitting or weaving on the loom. Since clothes wore out regularly, there was always something to be done. Courtesy had clearly learned the techniques young and was good at them. Elvy—well, from the little I had seen, if Elvy knitted a sweater, its best use would probably be as a fish net. I was sure that as soon as I left the house, Courtesy had returned to commenting on Elvy's mistakes.

I had just finished with the reassembly and was trying to get my hands clean when I heard a shout. A streak in boots and homespun shot past the open door of the shed. No Nonsense and I went out to investigate and saw Charity come around the house and stride to the barn. She did not look pleased.

She stopped at the barn door. "Elvy, don't think you're going to hide in there until I forget about this. You come inside and apologize, or I'm going to take my boot and put it where it will do some good."

I exchanged looks with No Nonsense and we ambled over to the barn door to see what was going to happen. By the time we reached it, a head was poking up from the hay stacked at the back wall.

"She earned it," Elvy said.

"I don't care," Charity answered.

After a moment's standoff, Elvy climbed out of the hay, stalks protruding from her clothes and hair. I noticed her right hand was sooty and wondered what that could mean. With her head down, she walked to the house in front of Charity, a prisoner headed to the gallows. My curiosity piqued, I went along.

Inside, Courtesy was crying and trying to clean soot from her mouth and tongue. Her efforts seemed mostly to spread it more around her face.

"She said I was a fuckin' dumb feral and ferals are dumber than worms," Elvy said, getting her defense in first. "If she's gonna have a dirty mouth, it might as well be dirty."

I saw a small pan of ash from the fireplace that had been placed near the spinning wheel. Elvy had planned her action. I liked Elvy.

"She'll apologize for what she said after you apologize for what you did," Charity said. "Two wrongs do not make a right."

Apologies were made and hands shaken, but I knew this was the end of a round, not the end of the fight. Charity gave me a wink that told me she knew it as well.

Elvy was sent to shovel the coops and then work outdoors. That was fine with her, and from the little I knew of how she had lived, I wasn't surprised. Charity asked me to do an assortment of things in and around the barn and keep an eye on Elvy while I was out there. She was good with the animals and careful collecting eggs. A small orchard of apple trees stood beyond the buildings—the obvious source of the apple on my plate earlier. Elvy climbed one to get an apple to eat while she worked and then tossed one to me. She was also talented in setting up snares and traps. When I looked them over, she claimed she could shoot game with a bow and arrow. As Charity didn't have those, I couldn't tell if it was true or braggadocio.

One of the snares caught a rabbit in the late afternoon. Elvy gave a shout of triumph when she checked it. She gave a quick twist and snap with her hands, then hoisted her prize aloft. She made sure to find Courtesy and skin and clean it in front of her.

"Want to lick the blood off my finger, Courtesy?" Elvy asked.

Naturally, she extended the middle one.

I managed to keep my chuckle to myself. Elvy was my kind of kid.

CHAPTER EIGHTTEEN

In the evening, I left the family and retired to the barn again, but it was even worse than the previous night. I could not fall asleep. I could close my eyes, but I couldn't turn off my brain. My mind seemed determined to play every moment of the all-too-brief awake time I had spent with Yong. I saw her in her dress uniform the day we met, when the look in her eyes meant death. I heard her voice over the comm the last time I would ever hear her. I remembered everything in between and loved her at each memory.

I sat up on the hay, with King Solomon watching me, and tried to convince myself Yong was alive and at Earthbase. I wound up doing the opposite. If Yong had escaped in the spaceplane, she would have been on the comm channel to me. I would have seen a notification on my field. I would have seen the flare of the spaceplane engines and its streak in the atmosphere on reentry. I'm not the type to live in fantasyland, but the truth was bitter bile in my mouth.

It was all my fault. If only I had told her that I loved her, if only I had spoken the three words, *I love you*, it might have changed the decision she made at the end. If I had said *I love you*, she would have wanted to escape on the spaceplane. She would have insisted I return earlier, and together the two of us would have escaped. A real man would have said *I love you* instead of making up euphemisms and excuses in his own mind. If only I had done that, everything would be different. It was all my fault.

If only . . .

I opened my eyes and saw sunlight filtering through the barn, catching motes of dust in its beams. King Solomon was licking my ear, trying to decide whether it was a snack. I sat up and the cat gave me a piece of his mind before retreating across the hay. A series of repetitive impacts came from outside the barn.

I pushed the door open and saw Charity near the chicken coops, chopping wood. She raised the ax high enough to arch her back and brought it down hard and fast, splitting a log with one stroke. Despite the chill air, I could see sweat on her face.

I limped over. "Would you like me to give you a hand with that?" I asked.

She stopped, let the ax dangle from her left hand, and wiped her forehead with her right. "You think I can't split my own wood?"

"I didn't say that."

"Not in so many words." She grinned. "I have other work for No Nonsense this morning. You, being a starman from before—and, I'm sure, used to your electronics and comforts—I'm afraid you'd chop your leg clean off. Then I'd have to use up one of my logs, plus spend my morning carving you a peg leg to walk around on. It's much simpler to do it myself."

"I know how to use an ax!" Cold or no cold, I felt the blush in my cheeks.

Charity started to laugh, then stilled when I didn't join in. "Leif, I'm sure you do. I was joking. You need to find your sense of humor."

Maybe I did. "Sorry," I said. "I guess I don't have much of one this morning."

Her eyes searched my face. "I'm the one who's sorry. It's too soon and too hard still. I know."

My eyes met hers. "You know what I've been thinking all night." She nodded. "How do I . . . How do you get over it?"

Charity sighed. She slammed the ax-head into the stump she had used for a base and wiped her hands on her pants. "I don't think you ever 'get over it.' But you do have to let it go. Otherwise, the feeling spoils, and that spoils everything else."

I shifted my stance. I wasn't used to having conversations like this. "How long . . . I mean, how long were you and Make Peace married?"

"Oh." Her eyes shifted and focused off in the distance. "I was eighteen and he was twenty," she said. "That's twelve years ago now. But we lived on nearby farms, so I'd known him since I was little. Thought he was a perfect beast most of my childhood." She smiled. "That changed after a town fair at the harvest."

"Did you come here because your families didn't approve?"

I saw her focus come back to me. "No, no. Nothing like that. He was a younger son and I'm a younger daughter. Neither of us would inherit any land, and where we lived, there's no open land left. Even the ruins that can be cleared for farms have been. We had just married when the territorial senator announced he was raising a new unit."

"I don't understand," I said.

"No, you probably wouldn't," she said. "I'm sure it's different. Senators raise army units from the people in their territories. The more units a senator can raise, and the bigger the units, the more prestige and power in the senate and influence with the president. So raising new ones is important. If you own a farm or have an essential job, like making guns, you're exempt, but otherwise you have to go if you're called. We hear that from the preacher from the time we first go to church. After all, the army is the state and the state is the army. So, we came here." Her eyes misted. "I lost my first child as a baby from a fever, and then I had a miscarriage. We told the preacher we would take any child that found us. That's how Courtesy came, when she was four. I don't know what happened to her. She would never talk about it. Anyway, like I told you, your story before doesn't matter. The preacher brought us Renounce just before Make Peace . . . left."

"I'm sorry."

"Don't be." She slapped her hands together. "You have to let it go, like I said. You can stay as an uncle in this family, if you want. The children seem to like you."

I wondered if she would say King Solomon seemed to like me also. "I don't know that I can 'let it go' just yet," I said. "I have a mission to complete."

Charity looked disappointed, but all she did was shrug. "Okay. I need to see that those children are at their chores. Elvy will have all outside work today. The more I can keep her and Courtesy apart, the longer they'll live, and she can't knit or weave for shit. She's bright, though. I'll see to reading and numbers for her, but I can keep an eye on her when she's doing that. You watch her when she's outside."

"Yes, ma'am," I said.

Whatever plans I might make for going to Earthbase, my knee reminded me with each step that I wouldn't be doing that for a while. Since I was going to have an interlude, I was happy to help Charity. I had survived seven years of deployments in the army; I could survive a houseful of kids. And I did like looking at Charity, even if looking was all I ever intended to do.

Amid her various chores, Elvy showed off to me her knowledge about finding edible bugs, which was a topic I was acquainted with. I wondered why she was so set on that, since Charity had been clear she had enough food. Maybe it was an ingrained habit from her previous life. She put together quite a collection.

I was back among the apple trees, listening to Elvy hold forth on which bugs were crunchiest when cooked, when I thought I heard a noise coming from beyond the front of the house. Hoofbeats? I chilled and ran for the house, shouting over my shoulder for Elvy to stay where she was. Were there more raiders than just the gang I had killed? I thought I was hearing only one horse, but I was better at picking up the sounds of tanks than horses. I went in the back door and grabbed a rifle from the gun rack. Yes, Charity kept the family weapons loaded. I pushed past Courtesy, who was peeking out the front door, in time to see a rider rein their horse in and leap to the ground in one smooth move.

This was no raider. The rider was a Black woman with skin that almost matched the glossy black hair wound tightly against her head. Closely fitted leather covered her from boot tops to collar. She had two pistols and a large knife at her belt, and a rifle in a case was attached to the saddle. She was yelling out, "Are you all right?" even before her boots hit the ground.

Charity had a rifle, but it was pointed at the ground. I relaxed. Somewhat. My rifle was still at the ready.

"We are fine," Charity said. "Is something wrong?"

"I happened to find bodies not too far from here on one of the before-roads," she panted. "Four ferals and six raiders. All shot. Dead maybe two days. I wanted to warn you. I can't tell if there are more raiders. There were tracks leading this way."

"You just *happened* to find them," I said. "In the middle of nowhere, you happened to come across the bodies?"

Her eyes shifted to me as though she had noticed me for the first time. "I was out hunting for other families. Bodies attract carrion-eaters."

"Six is all there were," I said. "They killed the other four. I killed them, so I know."

She studied me from head to foot. "And how did *you* just happen to find six raiders in the middle of nowhere and kill them by yourself?"

"I took a detour on my way back from the stars."

"Not very funny. Are you the pa here now?"

"No."

At that, her eyes narrowed, and her face said I had been weighed in the balance and found wanting. She turned toward Charity. "Are you safe here?" she asked. "Would you be safer if I shot him?" She tensed. Her hands were fractions of an inch from the grips of her pistols.

I hadn't moved my rifle—yet—but if she tried to draw those pistols, she would have no chance. I knew that, even if she didn't, but I didn't want it to end that way.

"I'm moving slowly," I said, and then aimed my rifle down at the ground. I took two steps and handed the weapon to Charity and turned back to the woman, showing her my empty hands. "Better?"

"Everything is okay," Charity said. Her face looked nervous, and she seemed to have trouble getting the words out. "Tonya, is it?" The woman nodded. "I do remember you coming by before. This is Leif. He did what he said. There was a child the raiders had taken. He saved her and brought her here. She is staying, and maybe he is staying. Will you stay and eat with us? I have enough food."

If a heavily armed person with their hands next to a pair of pistols can look embarrassed, Tonya managed that. "No, no. I won't put a hole in your food. It's . . . I know your farm is here with little children, and I saw the raiders, and there's no one else to help. And then I saw him here. I feared—" She stopped and swallowed. "I have hunting to do and need to go. I have people waiting on what I'll bring."

"Wait a moment!" Courtesy cried out from the door. She dashed into the house and emerged a couple of minutes later with a small sack. She ran to Tonya and held out the sack. "Take some apples. I will always have apples for you!"

Tonya smiled, which I hadn't thought she could do. Then she bent down and brushed some loose blond hair off Courtesy's forehead. "Thank you. You're Courtesy, right?" Courtesy nodded, her tongue locked up for the first time I had seen. "I do remember. You be well."

Tonya put the apples into a saddle pack and swung up onto her horse. A moment later, she was headed away from the farm and into the trees at a brisk canter.

"What was that all about?" I asked.

Charity shook her head. "Maybe nothing more than she said. We first saw her in the late fall a year ago, and she came again, once, in the spring. She rides up and asks if we're okay. Then she trades some work for a meal. She's never asked to stay. There are people like that, who go from one place to another." She gave me a hard look.

"I think Tonya's a hero," Courtesy announced. "She's a girl with guns who rides in the wild, and she's not afraid. Not of raiders or even ferals."

I thought Tonya was a cipher. But in a world that was itself a puzzle, where it was not completely unknown, I didn't think decoding her was a priority.

.   .   .

The reason for Elvy's insect hunting came out in the evening, when cooked bugs materialized in Courtesy's dinner. Courtesy had a mouthful of the creamy skyr before she realized what was in it. Her eyes bugged out. She gagged. The food came back out of her mouth and landed in her lap. Some of the skyr came out her nose.

"What's wrong, Courtesy?" Elvy said. "Don't you like the crunch?"

Elvy reached over and plucked one by a leg from the meal on Courtesy's plate. It was a stinkbug. Elvy popped it in her mouth and made a show of chewing so we could all hear the crunch. She favored Courtesy with a beatific smile. Courtesy gagged again.

Charity was trying to be mad, but she had a mouthful of food herself and was having trouble stifling a laugh. When she was able to swallow, she said, "All right, you two. One of the sheep got a leg trapped between two rocks and I had to slaughter it. I've already dealt with preserving most of the food, but we need to make the bloodbread. If we don't do it this evening, it will be spoiled. You're old enough to do this, Courtesy. I'll show you how to take the blood, mix in some moss I have, a bit of flour and fat, and cook it in pockets."

"I know how to sew the pockets out of the sheep stomach," Elvy said.

"Then you can show your younger sister how to do it," Charity told her. "While I watch. That's assuming you can stop giggling and keep your mind on what you're doing."

I liked Charity and Elvy. That feeling came through the numbness inside.

CHAPTER NINETEEN

The little farm and its family quickly settled back into a routine. Charity knew every detail, every task and chore that had to be done, and she parceled them out with great efficiency. She would have made a terrific platoon sergeant.

The swelling in my knee did not begin to subside for a week. Charity was quick to offer some home remedies, but I declined those. I gimped around, cursed the army doc, and tried to ignore it. I was still in no condition to head west. I knew it, and Charity didn't bring it up.

I had to do something about my clothing. The weather was too cool for me to continue walking around in an ISC starshot mission polo—and besides, I didn't like the way it made the children stare. I was bigger than Make Peace had been, but his homespun shirts were loose enough that I could wear them. I kept the cargo pants from my ship uniform, as Make Peace's pants were badly worn and way too small. Charity told me I would be able to replace them with some wool twill when I went into Eastview. The arrangement allowed me to keep the picture of Yong in its sealed pocket.

I did not become part of the family—and had no intention of ever doing anything like that—but I was happy to do my share of the work. As with the engine, most of that work was outdoors or mechanical. To compensate for what I ate out of Charity's stores, I did as much farm-work as I could. That meant spending a lot of the time with No Nonsense, which gave me a chance to ask him about his story.

"I came here when I was ten," he said. "My first family had a farm a few days' ride south. A gang of raiders lost a fight with some of our troops—we had an army detachment out here then. They went running, but our farm was in the way they were going. They burned it and killed everyone they could catch. Didn't catch me."

I told him I was sorry about his family.

"Dead is dead," he said. "It happens. I keep the last name, though, even if that's not so usual. I want to always remember them."

We were fixing some fencing at the time, and he paused in his nailing of a plank to a post. "Elvy told us that story about how you killed the raiders so fast they couldn't even get off a shot, and how you shot that last one even though he was holding her in front of him. She's told it half a dozen times already."

I didn't know any of that.

No Nonsense shook his head. "I wish I could do something like that. I'm a good-enough shot with a rifle, but that shooting you did . . . I'd love to kill a whole gang of those bastards." He was staring at the fence post as though it were a raider he was going to shoot.

"Vengeance isn't all people say it is," I said. "It doesn't bring anyone back. It only leaves more people dead, and more people looking to do more killing."

He shrugged. "I might feel better. Not that I'm ever likely to get the chance."

We went back to repairing the fence. After the next board was in place, he said, "Of course, I never figured I'd be in a family with someone with feral eyes. Those are witch eyes, you know. Spirits of the people who died in the old Bosnywash live in those eyes. That's why they're so green, you know."

I didn't know that.

"It's true. That's why Ma wants Elvy to learn to shoot. She thinks those eyes can witch a bullet to hit its target. The preacher says that sort of thing isn't true, but maybe Ma knows better. We don't go to the church in town that much." He hammered in another nail. "Even if it's not true,

Elvy's a good sister. Even if she does silly shit all the time. She should learn."

When we finished with the section of fence that needed work, No Nonsense arched his back to stretch out, then rubbed his back above his hips. "I'd say I'm getting too old for this, but you wouldn't take that too well, would you?"

"No."

He laughed. "Well, at least we've got most of the outdoor work done ahead of the snow, and that's good. Something you should be thinking about as soon as your leg is better, if you're really planning to move on."

I hadn't thought about snow. I was used to people worrying about how hot it would be. "When do you see snow here?"

"Anytime after the start of October," No Nonsense said. "Old folks say they remember snow in August, but that's probably horseshit. They always like to talk about how tough it was when they were young."

I'm not sure if that was supposed to be an opening for me to say something about when I was young, which for sure he wouldn't believe, but my mind went elsewhere. If what used to be Western Pennsylvania had snow in early October, what could I expect if I was trying to reach Kansas? On a horse?

I asked myself if I meant to do that. I didn't get an answer.

For the first time, I wondered if I would be spending the winter bantering with No Nonsense and hearing Elvy retell the tale of my prowess with a pistol. And seeing Yong standing there every time I looked at Charity.

·   ·   ·

In the evening, after the plates, utensils, and any remaining scraps of food were cleared, one of the children would add logs to the fire so the house would stay warm through the night. Charity liked to play the banjo and sing. The children would join in a pleasant, off-key jumble. After a few songs, one of them would ask for a story, and then Charity would ease into her rocker with the three-year-old while the others took chairs or sat on the floor. I qualified as a big kid and had a chair.

I tried to remember if my mom had told me bedtime stories when I was a kid, and I couldn't. All I can remember, from the time I could read by myself, was reading in bed, either with an e-reader or on the projection field from the glasses we used then.

Some of Charity's stories were about the Saints of the Apocalypse. They were twelve men and women who appeared miraculously during the Great Die-off, when conditions were awful. Food was scarce, the sun was usually hidden, even the summer was chilly, and diseases were rampant. The Twelve claimed—and it was believed—that they were starfolk; it was only later they were called saints. These saints preached about forming families, the way Charity had told me, and said that anything printed should be saved and cherished because whatever had been in the cursed computers was gone forever. They told people that surviving the Tribulation meant God had selected them to go to Heaven.

The Saints went through plenty of their own tribulations, it seemed, mostly at the hands of people who saw God differently. In Charity's stories, they all died. Violently. That was how they became saints. I could believe they were starfolk. I wondered what the name of their ship had been.

Charity also told fairy tales, and would quiz the kids about each one. One night, she told a story about a princess who'd been locked up by a wicked witch, in a castle that had only one entrance, guarded by servants of the witch. The witch told the princess that the only way she could get out would be for a prince to come rescue her. However, the harvest failed in that land and all the people outside starved. When no one brought the guards food, they ran away and left the door open. Unfortunately, the princess was too afraid to try the door. She kept waiting for the prince, who never came, so she starved to death too.

"Who knows what the story means?" Charity asked.

"I do," Elvy said right away. "It means if you sit on your ass waiting to be saved, you're doomed. You better figure out how to save yourself." She grew a wicked smile then. "That takes brains. If you have brains in your head, they turn your hair dark. If there's no brains there, the hair stays light yellow. Right, Courtesy?"

"Bricks and stones will hide the bones before your words can hurt me. Bricks and stones will hide the bones before your words can hurt me." Courtesy chanted the words like a mantra.

"Blond head, empty head. Blond head wets the bed," Elvy sang back.

Courtesy screamed and fists flew. Another apology followed.

Peace lasted until the morning. Elvy found a large spider and held it cupped in her hands, waiting for the moment she could slip it down the back of Courtesy's shirt. Shrieks, screams, and fists flew again. This time it ended with Charity's hand slamming into Elvy's rear.

Elvy demonstrated a talent for practical jokes that extended beyond her internecine warfare with Courtesy, and this became as much a part of the routine as Charity's stories. I would pull on a boot and find a rock in it, or once, something that squished. The laces to one of No Nonsense's boots would go missing. Eight-year-old Amazing found worms in his hair. Only Charity and the little ones were exempt from Elvy's pranks. The source of the gag was always obvious, since her giggles would follow the oaths or screams. The abject, if not heartfelt, apology would follow, her eyes to the floor. In my opinion, Charity had increasing difficulty in not smiling as she came up with one punishment after another. It was the same every day with Elvy, and it always ended the same way. Not that she ever cried.

No matter what happened, at the end of each day they would all troop off to bed, receive their lucky starman's kiss, and quiet would reign. For that night.

Even as my knee started to improve, I still vacillated about making a decision on what I was going to do. The routine of family life had a lulling effect, even if it wasn't my family.

·   ·   ·

It was the day of the spider down the shirt that I was woken in the middle of the night in the barn. I'm a very light sleeper, and movement around me in the dark will bring me awake fast. Someone had entered the barn. I didn't move at first, just listened. A rustling sound came from the hay at the back wall. The barn door was closed. This wasn't a loose animal. I walked over and checked the hay. Moonlight through a window showed me the source of the disturbance. Elvy was curled up in a tight ball, arms around knees and head on her knees. I could hear her sobs.

"What's wrong?" I asked.

A shake of her head.

"Do you miss where you came from? Is there a family there?"

"No!"

It has been well established that I'm no good at the empathy thing, but this was a twelve-year-old kid. "C'mon, Elvy, I can't help if you don't talk."

More sobs. "I had a dream. Ma got tired of my fighting with Courtesy. You all got tired of me. I had to leave. Go back where I came from. I don't ever want to go there again! I was just a horrible little girl who had to go live in the woods by herself. Just like they said. I had nowhere to go!"

I tried to keep my voice soft. "Where does this 'horrible little girl' bullshit come from?"

"Everyone says that. It's true." She choked on the words. "I should go into the woods by myself."

"Nobody says that here," I said. "I don't want you saying it, or thinking it, anymore. It was bad for you where you were?"

Vigorous nods followed. "I was always the one who got beat. I talk too much. I said what I thought, not what they wanted to hear. There was only one really old woman who told me I was special, and she taught me everything. I called her Great-auntie, but she died. Nobody liked me after that. Ma Charity is the only one since who's ever been good to me. Well, and you too. But she still won't want to keep me. Or you. Nobody does. Not indies either. That's why they made me go with Gipson to come here."

A light went on in my head. "So, all your shit, it's like a test. You're going to be such a pain in the ass that even Charity will get rid of you, and that will prove that you're right, that nobody wants you. Is that it?"

I had enough moonlight to see her face. It was misery. I didn't need her to say anything in order to know the answer.

"Not happening," I said. "Charity will never let go of you."

And I'm an expert on women and children.

I put a hand on her shoulder. "Look, Elvy, Charity will never throw you out. It won't happen. But even if it did, you'll always have a place with me. Okay?"

"What if you go back to the stars? You won't take me with you."

"I don't think anyone's going back to the stars," I said. "Maybe not ever. But if I did, I'd make a stargirl out of you."

And suddenly, she grabbed my hand with astonishing strength. Through crying, I heard, "Promise?"

I guess I stopped being completely dead inside. "I promise." I stroked her wet, tearstained cheek. I think that was the right thing to do.

She sniffled.

"We all have our ghosts, Elvy." I could hear Yong saying the words to me. "We deal with them as they come. And sometimes, we need help."

"Even you?" Another sniffle.

"Yeah. Even me."

．　　　．　　　．

A week after the day of the spider, Charity came to find me, rifle in hand, a pistol tucked into her belt, and Elvy in tow. The girl's appearance had changed drastically in the time since she had run into the barn in the middle of the night. She had sewn patches over the holes at her knees so that her pants looked somewhat whole. Her shirt was clean. Her face was scrubbed, with only a dark purple streak below her eye remaining from that bruise. She had pulled her hair out of the braid, combed it free of the dirt and leaf fragments that always festooned it, and brushed it until it shone. It hung loose, long, and straight, down her back. She now practiced letters and words from *My First Reader* every morning. Those odd but lively green eyes were the same. As was her penchant for tricks when you weren't looking.

Charity pulled two bales of hay out of the barn and stacked them against the nearest fence. Then she found a square piece of wood, put it on top of one bale, and leaned it against the other. With a piece of charcoal, she drew three roughly concentric circles on the wood.

Charity paced off a distance of about fifty yards. From there, she raised the rifle and fired five shots, one right after the other. I won't say Charity would have qualified as a sharpshooter, but all her shots at least hit the wood target. She was more accurate than I expected.

"I missed on purpose with that shot the day you showed up," she said with a smile. "I saw there was a child with you."

That might be the case. Of course, the surge of adrenaline that comes with shooting at someone for real in combat can also spoil your aim.

"No Nonsense told me that he spoke to you about teaching Elvy to shoot. I would like you to do it." She favored me with a broader smile. "Twelve years is old enough to be able to use a firearm."

I considered how to do this. It wasn't going to work like army basic training, that was for sure. I had spent time examining the rifles and pistols I'd collected from the raiders, and the ones at the farm seemed to be of the same type. After all, I had a professional interest in weaponry. The rifle Charity handed me was a near twin of the famous Winchester 1873 model. It was a lever-action rifle with a tubular magazine that would hold eleven bullets. It could be fired very rapidly and, if it, in fact, resembled the old Winchester, might be very accurate. A die stamp on the metal read ATHENS ARMORY. I opened it up and showed Elvy how the lever action took a bullet from the magazine to firing position. Then I showed her how to clean the rifle and watched her do it.

Next, I went to the pistol. That took a ten-bullet cartridge in the grip and looked like a copy of an end-nineteenth-century Mauser or Luger. I showed Elvy how to snap the clip in and remove it, and explained how the trigger action brought the bullet up and fired it. Then I had her clean that weapon.

"You have to keep your weapons clean," I said. "A dirty weapon will jam, and it's a law of nature that they always jam when you need them the most. In a fight, a jammed pistol is no better than a rock."

I watched as she was cleaning them and saw her hair spill across her shoulders. "One other thing," I said. "You should tie your hair back the way Charity does. The last thing you want is for a gust of wind to blow hair across your eyes when you're aiming at someone."

Jade-green eyes in an earnest face fastened on mine. "I will tie my hair back like Ma does," she said. "Only I don't have a piece of lace yet, so I can't do it just like her. When I get one, I will."

That's when the light went on in my brain. The bright, clean face every day, the hair brushed to smooth and shining: Elvy was turning herself into a miniature Charity. And why not? Charity was industrious, resourceful, and skilled at managing the operation of her farm and family. She was a strict disciplinarian, but still loving to all the children. She was very attractive and smiled at me a lot.

Shut up, Leif.

I knew where that line of thought was going, and I wouldn't allow it. It would be a betrayal. Oddly, the emotions I feared having seemed to have been amputated. Before Yong, if a beautiful woman like Charity had paid attention to me, I would have been at full boil. Now I was afraid that if I touched her, I wouldn't feel anything. I was more shut down than I had been after the worst of the fighting in the Troubles. What was wrong with me?

I cleared my mind and told Elvy it was time to learn to shoot. I took each of the weapons and modeled the stance and aiming. I fired three rounds from each, dead center on the target with all of them.

Maybe I was showing off.

Then I handed Elvy the pistol. Immediately, I could see a problem. A pistol is harder to learn than a long gun to begin with. This pistol was heavy and the grip was large. Elvy was a strong kid, but her hands were small.

"Always aim low on a person," I told her. "The kick from the shot will bring the weapon up, and you'll still be on target for the next shot." The two-handed grip I showed her helped, but not enough. The pistol wavered. Her shot hit the field somewhere beyond the fence, and the recoil took it so far offline that a second shot needed to be completely reaimed.

"Let's move to the rifle," I said. "That's your best bet."

The Winchester is fairly short for a rifle. She was able to hold it steady. Elvy fired. The recoil slammed the butt into her shoulder, and she went backward two steps. She fired again. I could see her bite her lip and rub her shoulder furtively. When she saw me look at her shoulder, she glared at me. I decided to ignore it.

I marked off a shorter distance. "Come up to here and try it again."

She fired shots in quick succession this time, and she did hit the target. I was rewarded with a huge smile.

"Can I practice some more?" she asked.

I loved that smile.

CHAPTER TWENTY

A few days after I taught Elvy how to shoot, Charity announced that she had a list of supplies she needed from town and some goods to sell.

"I've reworked a pair of Make Peace's pants so you can wear them," she said, holding them up for inspection. "Anybody looks at the stitching on what you're wearing, it will cause talk you might prefer to avoid. This way, you won't attract attention, which I would suggest until you decide what you want to do. I sewed a pocket that will hold your picture. I've seen you never let it away from you. Make Peace had a pair of boots made once that were too big. He couldn't wear them, but you can." She handed the pants and boots to me and folded her arms across her chest. "Take your gun. Almost everybody will have one. New Terran law doesn't hold out here, which is good and bad. If you're still thinking of going west, you can ask about it in town." She turned away from me.

Not long after that speech, I was on the buckboard of a horse-drawn wagon with No Nonsense, headed toward the town of Eastview. The farm was about forty miles outside town, which meant one night camped out, as the horse couldn't do more than twenty-five miles in one day. I bounced on my seat and watched the countryside barely shift as we moved along at what I estimated to be about two and a half miles an hour. Riding a catalytic fusion-powered ramjet to the stars, this was not.

I might have been bored with the actual travel, but I was happy enough with the trip. My knee had at last shrunk down to normal size again and let me move around with almost no pain. Going to town would give me a chance to speak with the town marshal, who might be able to give me information on the road west, at least as far as the next town, where I could repeat the process.

That was if I did decide to go, and my mind was equivocating on that. I had avoided making a decision by telling myself that it had to wait until I had more information. I also had a secret mission in mind.

Charity had insisted on giving me money for the trip, despite my protestations that I didn't need to be paid for work I had done on the farm. I also had some items from the raiders' saddlebags that she thought I could sell in town. My secret mission was to buy some lace so that Elvy could tie her hair back exactly the way Charity did. I think I spent more time thinking about how Elvy's face would look when I brought out the lace than I did about the journey I might take to Earthbase.

"The man you need to see is named Hezekiah Dobbins." No Nonsense's voice broke into my daydreams on the second day. "He's been the marshal in Eastview since the summer before this one and is supposed to enforce the law. Well, not much law that I've ever seen, but maybe nobody cares about that. He'll have an office in the town square, where the church is. It's a good place for it. You can go find the marshal to have him take care of a problem and then go pray that he does what he's paid for. Anyway, the marshal wears a metal star—you'll see it—so he's called the starman. I never thought about it before, but now I guess it's a joke. Like one of yours."

I didn't laugh. "No Nonsense, you've told me this three times since we stopped for the night yesterday. You don't sound too happy."

No Nonsense stared at the reins resting in his hands. "I guess I'm not." He hesitated, then blurted out, "I want to have adventures, like you did. I mean, I know I'm not going to the stars, but I want to see what's in the world. But you're the one who'll go off again, and the most I'll do is drive this wagon between the farm and the town."

"Adventure is overrated," I said. "It's mostly an opportunity to die violently in a strange place."

"Then why are you going?"

It took me a while to answer. Why was I going? Why did I need to reach Earthbase? I was past telling myself that Yong would have escaped in the spaceplane and would be waiting for me there. That fantasy was gone. Jouncing on a wagon, watching a horse's tail, I knew it had been delusional. Was I doing this as a duty, completing the mission? Yong's mission and my mission. *Our* mission. That's what I had told Charity, what I kept telling myself. "I need to complete the mission," I said at last. "Until I get there and report what we did, even if there's no one there to report to, the mission isn't complete. That's what people like me do. Complete the mission." That had been drilled into me until it was like a mantra, but I sounded like I was trying to talk myself into it.

"That's dumb," No Nonsense said. "Ma likes you."

"Your mother *needs* you."

"Boys grow up. A man's gotta do things." The wagon rolled over a bump in the road and we both bounced up and down on the board. "Gotta do more than this," he said. "Give me a reason why I should stay on the farm while you're going west."

"I told you—"

"I know what you told me. And I know about your mission. You just said it again, although I haven't seen you do anything about it, and you've had plenty of time." His voice sharpened. "I don't even think you want to go."

I stared into his set face, trying to tell him that he was wrong.

No Nonsense shook his head and looked away. "Let's forget it. Talking about it won't change anything. The town's just around this hill anyway."

Eastview did not impress me. The town had a single long street that was a street only by virtue of the ground being pounded flat and hard between two rows of buildings. Those buildings were made of a hodgepodge of materials. Most of them had a concrete base, or foundation. On top of that were rows of brick seemingly taken from other places, as parts of the brick didn't match even within the same wall. Unpainted wooden boards made up the rest of the walls. As I looked closer, I saw that even the bases of the buildings were broken pieces of concrete, the joints filled with mortar. A wooden walkway fronted the buildings, and there were railings to tie up horses. The only sign of paint anywhere along that street was on written signs that advertised businesses.

One sign, painted on the side of the first building, advertised nothing but an ominous tone:

TO HELL WITH THE FUTURE,
WE'RE DOOMED BY OUR PAST,
MAY GOD IN HIS MERCY,
BE KIND AT THE LAST.

"A wonderful way to greet people coming into town," I said.

"What? That sign?" No Nonsense turned to look at it as though he hadn't ever paid attention to it. "People write that in lots of places. They started doing it during the Die-off, I think. It's just words."

I was willing to bet those words meant something, or had, but No Nonsense didn't know and wasn't interested.

Regardless of the sign and appearances, the town was busy. People crowded the boardwalk and competed for space in the street with horses and wagons. Other people leaned on storefronts, intent on conversations, while more people went in or out of doors. At the far end of the street, I could see an opening into a town square. A whitewashed building I took for a church stood directly across from where the street entered the square.

No Nonsense tied up the horse in front of a shop whose sign identified it as HONEST MAN WATSON'S GROCERY AND DRIED GOODS. The proprietor bustled over to greet No Nonsense, and the negotiation over what we were selling and buying went at a rapid-fire pace. It was obvious that No Nonsense was practiced at this and had a good rapport with the owner. He didn't need me.

There was a shop for hunting supplies next door, and I went in there with a couple of knives I had taken from the raiders. The design was similar to a Bowie knife. I wasn't impressed with the quality; however, Charity had said that anyone could see from the blade markings that they were raider's knives, and people would pay for that. Apparently, that was the case. I came out of that store with a good handful of coins all stamped as whole, or fractions of, solid dollars. They jingled. I stuffed them in a pocket with the money I had from Charity.

I met No Nonsense back on the boardwalk as he and the shop owner finished loading items into the wagon. He put one hand on my arm. "Do you play poker?" he asked.

When I was in the service, it was impossible to be in the US Army without playing poker. I said, "I used to, when I was younger."

"Well, if you want, after you're done with the marshal, come find me at Al's Bar. There's usually a game there. We can't get back before tomorrow anyway, so Ma doesn't have to know. You can join if you want."

I assured him that I would and warned him that drink and poker end in a hangover with empty pockets. Then we went separate ways. My first stop was a dress shop, where I bought the lace for Elvy. I knew it wouldn't stay snow white for very long, but it was a good match for Charity's. That kid's face was going to light up like, well, electric light used to. I winced at the thought and tucked the lace in the pocket next to Yong's picture. It was time to find Marshal Dobbins.

.   .   .

The marshal's office was where No Nonsense said it would be, in between a large stable and the whitewashed building that was, in fact, a church. A paper notice had been nailed to the door, just below the words MARSHAL'S OFFICE. It read: *No Marshal in Eastview anymore. If you want Hezekiah Dobbins, find him at his business, the Golden Ass.*

The Golden Ass was on the other side of the church, which I found interesting because the establishment was obviously a brothel. I pulled the door open and went inside. The front room was a bar, like almost any neighborhood bar you might walk into. On either side of that room, a staircase led up to a second-floor balcony, beyond which I could see three hallways leading to the back of the building. Rooms on those halls would be where the primary business was conducted.

The bar was quiet, almost deserted. Two women and a man occupied separate tables in front of the actual bar. From the way they were dressed and the way they watched me walk by, I was sure they were evaluating me as a potential customer. I did my best to ignore them. The bartender came over as I reached the bar.

"What am I pouring?" he asked.

"Nothing. I don't drink."

Eyebrows went up and the bearded face scowled.

"I need to see Hezekiah Dobbins. For a different kind of intercourse than he usually traffics in." I smiled at the man.

From the bartender's expression, he didn't get the pun. Yes, I suppose my sense of humor leaves something to be desired.

He tapped a forefinger against the bar. I fished in my pocket, pulled out a solid dollar coin, and placed it next to his finger. His expression didn't change. All that shifted was his finger, now wagging up at him. I added another coin. He grunted, swept them off the bar, and disappeared through a door in the back.

Maybe five minutes later the bartender returned, accompanied by another man. This one was shorter than me by several inches. He had a clean-shaven face, with a permanent case of windburn on his fair skin, and thinning gray hair. A good-quality jacket made of leather came to his waist, covering but not concealing the pistol holstered there.

"We'll sit over there," the man said.

Before I could step that way, the bartender put a hand on the older man's arm. "You know that *he* is likely to be here soon. I told you I'd heard he was going to come over."

"I won't be long," the gray-haired man said, "and this man is paying for my time." He gestured for me to sit. "I understand you don't drink, but you should buy one anyway. And my man, Jake here, will expect a tip."

I paid for both and followed him to the table. Jake had a beer in place almost as soon as I sat down. I pushed that over in front of the other seat. This conversation was becoming expensive, and it hadn't even started.

"You're Hezekiah Dobbins?" I asked.

He nodded. "And you? And what do you want of a peaceful businessman?"

"Leif Grettison. I'm interested in the road west, and what I'm hearing about the possibility of fighting out that way. I'm also interested in why you quit being marshal." If there was a connection, it might mean fighting was close by, or expected to be.

"Where are you from, to be asking that? It's an odd name you give. Plus, I've never heard anyone sound like you, and I traveled a lot when I was younger."

I remembered wishing for a day when someone would hear my name and not immediately associate it with me killing Miles Richmond. I should be careful what I wish for. "Far away," was all I said.

Watery blue eyes searched my face for a moment. "Y'know, my beer is actually quite good. If you're not having it, I will." He took a long swallow. "First, about me bein' starman here. The reason is less why I quit than why I took it in the first place. It pays a salary, of course, but I don't need the money. I've got a good business here. But it's the starman's job to keep the law here and keep the peace." He took another swallow. "God-damn farmers and riders and ditchdiggers, all without a brain in their heads. They all get drunk, and play cards, and carry guns, and not much hesitation about shooting those guns. What's the point of having a nice business and making a good income if you're just gonna end your life get-ting in the middle of someone else's argument? I thought being starman might solve a problem of mine, but all it did was get me in everyone else's. So I quit. And there you have it."

"I don't have it," I said. "Not quite yet. I'm going west. Even if you're not marshal anymore, what do I need to know about the road? Is there fighting?"

When Dobbins pushed his chair away, I fished in my pocket and put another solid on the table. Half out of his chair, he looked down at the coin and reseated himself.

"And then you ask about fighting and the road west." He sighed, then swallowed the rest of the beer in one gulp, following that with a belch. "I'll make a long story short. Been riders coming up from the south for years now. Claim they're Athens soldiers, and that all this Old Pennsie land to the east and south is disputed territory. Disputed by who? Only ferals to the east of us. This was open land for us to settle. Excuse for brigandage, if you ask me. But that's here.

"New Terra's armies have been fighting to the north and farther west the past several years. That's pretty much done. But there's rumor now that armies from Athens are moving up to the west of here, and ours will be sent to stop them. Yet one more Formation War, I'll bet. That'll tear up everything out to the Empty Lands across the Mississippi. We've got a military governor for this area now, Zebulon Mendenhall. Well, we've always had one, but he doesn't have an army. Not yet. The marshal in a town heads the militia. Good respectable position, but if there's raiders to fight or an army to form, the militia has to be in it." Hezekiah smoothed his hair down with both hands. "You can see how the situation was getting for me. I sent a letter to Zeb that I was done bein' a starman. I closed the office. Can't say the town is any worse now than before. Does that answer your question, Leif from far away? And I'll throw in some free advice. If you're going to take any road to the west, you stay to the north. Fighting is bad for business, and it's worse for living to an old age."

Earthbase, whatever might be there now, would be west and somewhat south. Right where I was being told not to go. What was driving me there, beyond nowhere else to go and nothing else to do?

That was when the door to the street banged open and a man about my bio age strode in. Stomped in, might be more accurate. He wore a clean blue shirt and gray wool pants with no holes. The leather holster that held his pistol showed plenty of wear, however. I could see Hezekiah stiffen.

"Did he pay you to lure me out front with your stupid questions?" Hezekiah's voice was little more than a whisper.

"No. Who is he? The bartender warned you someone was coming."

"Yes." Hezekiah moved the beer mug with one hand while he slid his other hand to the edge of the table. "I should learn not to take every coin in front of me."

The younger man crossed the room to our table, planted himself in front of it, and fixed Hezekiah with a baleful glare. "Constant Prudence Abernathy," he announced, "is here to collect the money you owe me. Are you going to pay me, Dobbins?"

Holding his upper body rigid, Hezekiah began to slide his right hand over the edge of the table.

"If that hand comes off the table, I'm gonna draw," Constant Prudence said. "If I draw, I shoot."

The hand stopped moving. Its fingers twitched on the table.

"Do you owe him money?" I asked Hezekiah.

"It was a misunderstanding," Hezekiah said to both of us.

"Then the bullet I put up your ass will be misunderstood!" Constant Prudence swayed a little. I would bet he had been drinking before he came to the Golden Ass. How much? One of the two women in the front room had acquired a customer in the time since I had come in. He was wearing a pistol on his belt. Jake was motionless behind the bar, but I would bet he had a firearm there. Four armed men in a not-very-large room. All it would take was one of them to go for his weapon. There were no phones. Even if there were, there were no cops to call. Hezekiah had been the nearest thing to a cop. I did not want to be in the line of fire. I tried to shift my chair away from Hezekiah. That made Constant Prudence notice me.

"Hey, Pretty Face," he called out. "Do you have an *understanding* with Dobbins here? Is he gonna pay you to kiss the boys who like that? Nice lips you got for that," he said to me. "Do you like him, Dobbins?"

Whoever named Constant Prudence should have been arrested for breaking the law on truth in advertising.

"Excuse me?" I said, and stood up.

Sometimes I leap before I look.

Constant Prudence closed the gap between us. His hand had not gone to his holster. Yet. I took one large step toward him and leaped. Literally.

My left leg came around with a roundhouse kick at his ribs. Still in the air, I twisted and threw a right roundhouse kick at his head. Somehow, the bastard blocked both of them. I landed on one foot. Spun. My right leg hooked around and the sole of my boot smashed across his right ear. His head snapped sideways and he dropped like a sack of potatoes.

I had my hands up and they were empty. No one had drawn a weapon. It had happened that fast.

I turned back to Hezekiah. "Do you owe him money?"

Hezekiah was staring at me. So was everyone else. I repeated my question.

"I suppose it could be construed that way," Hezekiah said.

Constant was on the ground, waggling his head as if to see if it was still attached and trying to get up on his hands and knees.

"When he can tell you where he is and do some arithmetic, pay the man," I said. "Everybody sitting here," I pointed around the room with my left hand, "you see him do it. Understand?" By that time, my right hand was about an inch from my pistol grip.

Everyone nodded.

All I wanted to do at that moment was get out of town and go away before I did something else stupid. I wanted to get No Nonsense, go back to the farm, give Elvy her lace, and leave for Earthbase. Where was No Nonsense? Oh, playing poker. In a bar. Where, probably, everyone was armed. Shit.

Without another word, I turned my back on all of them and left.

CHAPTER TWENTY ONE

It didn't take me long to find Al's Bar on the town's only street. It was a narrow storefront of weathered and unpainted boards, with a couple of grimy windows almost as opaque as the wood. I must have walked past it on my way to the marshal's office without noticing the small sign, AL'S, above the door. I pushed it open and let it slam closed behind me.

At a round table near the fireplace, six men were seated and playing cards. One of them was No Nonsense. From the few coins in front of him, he wasn't doing very well. In fact, he lost another hand as I walked up and flung his cards on the table with a curse. No Nonsense didn't have much of a poker face. The floor, a combination of wooden planking and old plywood, creaked as I approached.

"Come on, No Nonsense," I said. "We need to get going, and it would be better to do it while you still have some money left."

"No!" he said. "I can get it back. I just need a couple more hands. The cards have been getting better. They're going to break for me. I can't go home down this much."

"Truer words were never spoken." A man across the table from No Nonsense, with his back to the wall, chuckled after he spoke. He wore a linen jacket over a shirt that had once been white. I was sure there was a pistol under there somewhere. He looked over to me. "Why don't you join us for a few hands while he makes back his losses? We can make space."

"Spent my money buying some lace," I said.

"That's okay," the man said. "People put up all sorts of things at a table, from a gun to a leather jacket. Show us the lace and we'll tell you what you can put it up for."

I saw nods from the other people.

"No, thanks," I said. "I bought it for a girl."

"Suit yourself," the man said. "I'm sure she appreciates your discretion."

That brought general laughter, which I ignored. I gestured to No Nonsense that we should go.

"I'm still in," No Nonsense said. "Deal."

What is it about sixteen-year-old boys that makes them so stubborn? I folded my arms across my chest. I could be just as stubborn. If he was going to play, I was going to stand there and watch him.

Poker has always been an interesting game, dating back to its invention in the early nineteenth century. Our chip-and-phone civilization added another dimension to it. People with sharp eyes and good memories always counted cards as a way to improve their odds of winning hands. Chip and phone gave that ability to anyone, unless they were too dumb—or drunk—to pay attention. Naturally, that capability gave rise to apps that could detect if someone was doing it, or block you from using your chip. No one I played with would join a game unless everyone allowed those apps to link. There were plenty of other ways to cheat, too, and those spawned apps that tracked hand movements and popped up notifications if a player's movements met the parameters for marking, or bottom dealing, or other nefarious activity. I'd had a full suite of those apps when I was in the army, but I lost them when my chip was removed when I was discharged. The chip Earthbase had given me had only a few basic apps for poker. I'd left those in when I deleted all the crap apps, because poker ones didn't bother me. I didn't have a phone base anymore, but I didn't need one for this. All games had a "phones off" rule. Obviously. So the apps were only eye to chip to field. Notifications popped up as the guy across from No Nonsense was dealing.

"Fold your hand, No Nonsense," I said. "We're leaving."

"What? No!"

"Yes," I said. "He's feeling the edge of the deck for marks, and he just dealt himself one from the bottom."

That brought the game to a stop and everyone to their feet.

"Accusing me of cheating is a serious thing," the man said, staring me down. He was a lean man, a little under my height, with a nose and chin that jutted forward aggressively.

"I just said what I saw. Maybe you just did it this one time because you wanted his money before he left. I don't know."

I also didn't know if any of the others were in cahoots with that guy, so I was trying to keep an eye on all of them while I grabbed No Nonsense by the arm to pull him away. All I wanted was to be out of there. I wanted to be out of that town. I wanted to be off the planet.

The cheat got up, sidled next to me, and bumped into me while I tugged at No Nonsense. I didn't like that. Not at all. Visions of a knife in the ribs danced through my mind. I shoved him backward. His knees caught on the edge of a chair and he sat down heavily.

The snap of a lever and a round being chambered caught my attention and everyone else's. The barkeep had a rifle at the ready.

"Nobody draws in my place," he said. "Settle it outside if you want."

"We're leaving," I said.

I yanked at No Nonsense, who seemed to finally wake up to what was going on. He followed me out the door. I was hoping we could walk away, hoping that the others at the table would have an issue with the cheat, hoping that they were not in on fleecing a naïve young man. That hope lasted for maybe twenty yards up the road.

"Hey, you!"

Yes, the card sharp had come out of the bar. None of the others at the table seemed to have bothered him, so maybe they did know that hand was to take the last of No Nonsense's money. I stayed silent and backed down the street so that I could keep an eye on him. People were moving out of the way, and I wasn't going to bet against a bullet in the back if I turned around.

"He owes me money for that last hand!"

"I don't think so," I said. Under my breath, I told No Nonsense to keep moving.

"Then maybe you'd like to buy this back!" Suddenly, he was holding up white lace in his left hand. The lace I'd bought for Elvy. With it, he had my pic with Yong. The asshole had picked my pocket, but he hadn't gotten my money pocket. He'd gotten the lace and my pic.

This was a bad Western vid.

I know I took a step back toward him then. My hand *might* have brushed my holster as I did.

When I did that, he waved the lace with one hand to draw my eyes, then reached under his jacket with the other hand. With that move, right after he waved the lace, I was sure he was going for a weapon. I dived at an angle, rolled, and drew my pistol as I came up to a kneeling position. I fired twice. I had no idea if he got off a shot. He crumpled.

I walked back down the street to where he lay. One entry wound in the left chest, one between the eyes, and the back of his head blown off. He had pulled a pistol from under his jacket; it was still in his hand. People were already grouped around the body. One of them picked up the lace, brushed off the dirt from the street, and handed it to me. No one had touched the pic, which was facedown. I put both back in my pocket and looked down at my handiwork. Now what?

So much for not attracting attention.

It occurred to me, after I had walked down the street and looked at the body, that what I should have done as soon as I shot the man was run to a horse, any horse, and ride away before the locals woke up from the shock of a duel to the death. But what, precisely, would I do after that? Be an outlaw in the wild? Anyway, I wasn't going to leave my pic, and I wanted Elvy's lace back.

It occurred to me, after I had retrieved them and looked at the body, that I should have burst through the growing ring of people around me, run for a horse, and ridden away with a wild fusillade behind me. And then do what? Complete my mission? That idea wasn't motivating me right then. The only people I knew in this world were Charity and her children.

The result was that I stood there looking at the body, and at No Nonsense looking at the body, while the crowd swelled to the point that I doubt I could have gotten away even if I wanted to. Eventually a short, trim man with Yong's eyes and a clean-shaven face stepped in front of me. He reached out toward me with one hand, but the hand stopped well short of me. After all, I was still holding the pistol.

"I'm Mayor Guo Fair Measure," he said. "Can we speak? Not here. Not in the street."

That was how I ended up in the marshal's office with Mayor Guo, Hezekiah, Constant Prudence, and No Nonsense. The office was small and spartan, and could have used a dusting. The fireplace was empty and cold. The furniture consisted of a crude wooden desk that had been nailed together but not finished, and two chairs. In the back of the office was a door with bars for the top half and an old-fashioned lock. Since there were only two chairs, the five of us stood.

"I'd like to understand who you are and where you come from," Guo said. "We haven't seen you in Eastview before."

"He showed up at my family's farm from the east," No Nonsense said while I was figuring out how to answer. "His right knee is limed for sure; I've seen it swollen. But he does good work."

"If he's lived in the Old Pennsie lands, that would fit," Guo said. "He's obviously not a feral. But I wasn't asking you." He looked back to me. "Got a name I can use?"

"Leif. Leif Grettison. No Nonsense is mostly right. I've lived, well, in a lot of places. I'm older than I look. Can I ask what we're doing here?"

"We have a problem here," Guo said. Before I could react, he added, "You could be the solution. You settled an argument between two partners, Constant and Hezekiah, that I expected would end in bloodshed."

Partners? I looked over at Constant Prudence. The red blotch across the side of his face where my boot had connected was already swelling and was going to blossom into a gorgeous bruise. I wouldn't be surprised if he had a concussion, but he looked focused enough.

"He didn't draw his gun," Constant said. "Took me down like there was nothing to it, and I don't know another man who can do that."

"And the man in the street?" I asked. I figured I might as well get this over with. "What are you going to do about that? He was cheating at cards." As if that was going to matter.

Guo shrugged. "I can't simply say dead is dead. Not as mayor, which means I'm also the judge and there needs to be some law in this town. Which there isn't much of since Hezekiah abandoned this office."

"That's not fair!" Hezekiah burst in. "I said I'd do it, but these idiots who come into town only want to get drunk and you can't reason with them, and I'm not about to get my head blown off for no thanks, and then *you*"—he pointed a finger at Constant—"did not understand a simple agreement and threatened to kill me."

"Enough." Guo held up his hand. "That disagreement was settled. I do not want to hear it again. Shorn of all the talk and justification, the fact is that this office is vacant. This town is too big not to have someone wearing the star and keeping the peace." Guo turned back to me. "As for Jeremiah, if you say he was cheating at cards, he probably was. I would say he started the fight in the street, and what he got for it was two kill shots and no other damage done. If you were the marshal, we would all say a job well done. So, will you take the job?"

"Excuse me?"

"I said, will you be marshal of Eastview? It's a paying job." Guo pulled a tinny five-pointed star that could have been a children's toy out of his jacket.

I was having a little trouble processing the turn of events, but being made marshal did sound like a good option compared to alternatives Guo might come up with if I turned him down. Like being hanged. I nodded my agreement.

"Good." Guo held out the star to me. "Now you're a starman. That means you also captain the militia. Constant Prudence is one of the militiamen. He'll introduce you to the rest. In addition to being mayor and judge, I also put out the town newsfeed. I'll have a special edition for you. And I will send word to the military governor, General Mendenhall. The raiders in this area are a concern of his, and he'll want to meet you. Congratulations."

.   .   .

Once we tidied up a few formalities, I rode home with No Nonsense—and godammit if I didn't think of it as riding home. I had to tell myself that we were riding back to *the farm*, but I couldn't keep it that way in my mind.

Elvy squealed with joy when I gave her the lace. She put it on at once, and she did look like a miniature Charity. After one look in the mirror, she ran back and grabbed me in a tight hug.

I froze.

My hands were in the air and six inches from her shoulders. This was actually the first time in my life a child had run up to me and hugged me.

Charity saw my discomfort immediately. "You better let go of him, Elvy. I don't think Leif knows what to do with children. Yet."

All the kids made a fuss over that ridiculous tin star. I felt like a caricature out of an old vid, but none of them had ever seen a vid, or even knew what they were. The star was a symbol that meant something to them.

Charity smiled at me and put a hot meal on the table next to the fire. She managed to rest her hand on mine after she put the plate down.

"Do you understand what you've gotten yourself into?" she asked.

I recalled my old squad mate, Petey, asking me the same question when I was promoted to sergeant. "Sure. Of course I do." That was the same answer I had given Petey, and it was just as true—not—as it had been then. "I'll figure it out as I go," I said with more honesty.

"I suppose this means you'll be spending a lot of your time in Eastview," she said.

I agreed.

"Although . . ." She paused with her hand still on mine, smiling down at me. "That also means you won't be heading west. Not anytime soon."

I agreed again. I wanted to take her hand in mine; I wanted to do more than that, but somehow, I couldn't. I couldn't move.

She gave my hand a little pat. Then she stepped back from the bench. "I'll be honest. That first night you were here and I asked you to stay, I was just being practical. Now, though, I think I'd enjoy it. I think you would too. So, you make sure you find time to get out here," she said. "The children will be looking for you."

They wouldn't be the only ones. The fire crackled. The heat on my back eased the kinks left over from sitting on that buckboard mile after mile. I had to admit it. I was happy.

The instant that word formed in my mind, I thought I should apologize to Yong.

Except I could hear her say, *Don't be stupid, Soldier Boy.* I could hear her accented English in my mind, exactly as I had heard it for real. I could see her tight little grin. What was Yong telling me to do? Feeling happy would mean letting go of Yong. I couldn't let go. It had only been a month.

I wanted Yong back. That wasn't Charity's fault. It wasn't the kids' fault. I didn't want . . . I wanted . . . I don't know what I wanted. I was usually an expert at avoiding or shutting down my feelings, but here they kept bubbling up.

My eyes misted. I wasn't going to cry in front of Charity and the kids. I shouldn't feel happy. But I did.

What was I going to do? The concept of going to Earthbase and saying *mission accomplished* sounded nonsensical even in my mind. I wasn't sure it had ever been anything more than a placeholder, a way to cover a void in a mind that couldn't deal with lack of purpose and duty. If reaching Earthbase no longer meant anything to me, I could be sure that it didn't matter to any other living person.

But there were people who mattered. They were in that small room with a dirt floor. They were talking with one another and laughing. They were playing on the floor. They were waiting to see what Leif was going to do.

CHAPTER TWENTY TWO

What Leif did was go back to town and take the job. It wasn't as though I thought it through, considered my options, balanced the pros and cons, and made a decision. I wasn't making decisions. I was a small boat on a lake, and nobody was rowing. Wherever the wind blew, I went.

The deal I received in Eastview wasn't bad. With what Guo would pay me, I could eat in town, so I didn't have to feel guilty about eating Charity's food. Being in town also took care of a different kind of guilt, one that came when I found my eyes following Charity as she moved from chore to chore. The stable next door to the marshal's office took care of my horse. Guo had left the key to the marshal's office—an actual metal key—with the owner of the stable. He let me in, gave me the key, and showed me a room up the stairs from the office that was mine to use.

It wasn't much: a bed to sleep in, a chest at the foot of the bed for clothes, and a small fireplace that provided enough heat to keep the water in the washbasin from freezing. Heavy blankets came with the bed and made up for the fireplace. I don't know when the room had last been cleaned; Hezekiah hadn't used it, so it was probably in the state the previous occupant had left it. That included dirty boot prints on the floor. I also found bloodstains on the bedding that made me think that occupant's tenure had ended badly. When night came, I looked at the linen and shrugged. I rolled into the bed and pulled up the blanket. I've slept in far worse places.

· · ·

"Soldier Boy, I've made it to the spaceplane. No fuel, but I can bring it down at Earthbase. Land the transport there and meet me."

"Yong, I can't land the transport on Earth!"

"Yes, you can. I'll talk you through it. If you can do it, I'll meet you at Earthbase."

I tried. I really tried. I turned the crank until I was drenched in sweat, but the rocket engine wouldn't start. I ran to Charity's barn, got two of the horses, and hitched them to the transport. I whipped them as hard as I could with a length of metal that had come off a lattice framework. That did it. They pulled the transport free of the space elevator station. But we didn't go to Earth. The horses pulled the transport out to the Dauntless. I could see, where the sun shone on the hull, that the spaceplane bay was still closed.

"Yong, what's wrong? The bay isn't open!"

"It's okay, Soldier Boy. If you can meet me at Earthbase, it will be okay. Leif, I l—"

· · ·

I woke with a start my first morning in the room over the marshal's office. My dream evaporated, but I still remembered what Yong was going to say. I fought to keep that in my mind as I blinked at the ceiling. Had I dreamed that Yong was alive at Earthbase? Was my subconscious trying to tell me something? I pushed the thought away. I could not—would not—deal with that.

I sat up and shivered. It was freezing. My immediate reaction was to pull on any extra clothes I hadn't worn to bed, then wrap the blankets over my shoulders. The icy floor made me wish I had slept with my boots on. Thank God someone had left wood in the room. Once I had a fire going, my stomach asserted itself. It wanted breakfast. Except I hadn't been paid yet.

The only food I could find was a loaf of bread that Hezekiah had donated. It sat on my desk in the office, a cold, hard block. Eating that would be like sucking on a crumbly icicle. I banged the bread against the wooden desktop. If I needed a hammer, the loaf might come in handy. Other than the sound of my own breathing, the office was cold, empty, and silent.

What was I going to do now? I missed Charity and the kids. I missed Elvy's unnerving eyes and her impish pranks. I missed working outside with No Nonsense. For the first time since my mom had died, I missed a family.

Maybe I should go out and meet some of the people whose safety I was now responsible for. Well, sort of responsible for. I didn't know how much the town depended on the marshal to do anything. They seemed to have been doing okay with a CLOSED sign hanging on the office door.

I stepped outside, into an empty street. A light snow had started to fall. That made the temperature feel even colder. Had I ever complained about feeling hot and sweaty? To my left was the whitewashed church. I walked to the front of it and examined the sign painted on a board nailed to two posts in front of the steps. CHURCH OF ALL SAINTS OF THE APOC- ALYPSE. Charity had told stories about those saints, but I hadn't thought of them as real saints or ever heard of a church by that name. Probably the preacher was an important person in the town. Maybe meeting him would be a good idea. Maybe he had breakfast available.

I walked up four snow-covered steps and opened the door. An echo greeted me. The interior was spartan. Rows of rough wooden benches faced a whitewashed podium. The interior walls were painted white but had no other decoration beyond the words painted in black on the wall behind the podium: BE KIND AT THE LAST. Windows on each side leaked cold air. I saw no religious symbols anywhere.

A door opened at the back of the building, past the podium, and a young man came out. He was about my height but lacked any of my build. His unlined pink face was clean shaven, an aquiline nose being its most prominent feature. A mostly white linen shirt hung loosely from his shoulders, and a pair of wool twill pants was pulled tight around a waist too narrow for his height. The cold in the building must not have both- ered him. He stopped when he saw me, gave me an appraising glance, and then walked over.

"Good morning," he said. "I'm Preacher Be Kind Blanchette. You are obviously our new starman. I've heard about you. What can I do for you?"

Honestly, my first thought was breakfast, but I suppressed that. "I'm Leif Grettison." I extended my hand. "I wanted to say hello because I'm new here." After he shook my hand with his nearly skeletal one, showing more strength than I expected, I decided to ask a question and see what happened. "Can you tell me about this church? I've never heard of it."

That backed him up a step. "It's the same church everywhere," he said slowly. "How would you not have heard of it?"

"Maybe I'm your lucky starman—and not just because I'm the marshal."

His eyes fastened on mine and I knew what he was looking for. I let him stare for a while. I knew he wouldn't see any flashing red numbers, only my blue Icelandic-Irish eyes.

"Perhaps," he said at last. "You certainly don't have feral eyes—although, in truth, those are found mostly to the east and north. Plenty of ferals in the wild elsewhere who look perfectly normal." He shrugged. "It doesn't matter. No one will care."

That wasn't what I expected to hear. "You mean people won't care where I'm from or how I got here? You're not even curious?"

"No, not as long as you take care of yourself and don't cause trouble. Why should anyone care? Everyone came from somewhere, or their parents did, or their grandparents did, and no one really knows anything more than a few generations back. It's not something to be curious about, because there are no answers. If you did come back from the stars, you are probably wishing you had stayed there. Maybe you don't know anything."

"What should I know about the church?"

Be Kind laughed. "Men and women used to live well." His tone said he was warming up for a sermon, one he had given many times before. "They were warm all the time and had plenty of food. But God tempted men and women with electronics. And they were weak and took the electronics and made computers. And they poured all their knowledge and all their thinking into those computers until they couldn't even talk to each other without them. And then God made men and women go to war, and He brought the Three Years' Winter. The computers died in those wars, and all the men and women were helpless. We call that the Tribulation. They didn't know how to do anything; they had no memory of anything, and they died. That was the Great Die-off. The Twelve Saints of the Apocalypse arose simultaneously in the places where men and women still lived. They came back from the stars and preached about families and easing suffering, and told men and women to save whatever knowledge was actually printed. They told men and women that surviving the Die-off meant that God had selected them to go to Heaven at the last. That they should forget about the electronics, and that if they lived only with what they had left, God would reward them. Mobs killed the Saints because those mobs craved what they had lost and the old churches screamed for the mobs to do it. But then the mobs died as well." He stopped, took a breath, and focused on me. "Now you've heard it. The church is our church now, the only church, and it carries on the work of its saints." He looked me in the eyes again. "People come from nowhere with no story they will tell. It doesn't matter. The church will help them find a family if it can. Did you truly come back from the stars?"

I didn't want to play games and I didn't care if he believed me. "Yes."

He let out a long breath. "Are there . . . more?"

"No. I'm the only one left of our crew."

"That may be just as well. At least, for reapocalyptics." I thought he was going to say more about that, but he caught himself. "I hope you bring luck, the way we tell the children. But, please, do not think to bring back anything else. One Tribulation is quite enough. We're better off now."

"I bring nothing else," I said. "I have nothing else."

He took my hands in his. "Be welcome," he said.

"Thank you. And what about that phrase?" I pointed at the words painted on the wall. "What does it mean?"

The preacher did not turn away from me. "That's from the Prayer of the Hungry and the Cold," he said. "It goes back to the Tribulation, and it means that God will set the world right at the end, before he takes us to Heaven."

"Did you change your name to match, or do all preachers take that name?"

"No, no." Be Kind laughed. "Honestly, my ma gave me these words. I think she knew I was always meant to be a preacher."

With the awkward part of the conversation out of the way, my stomach reasserted itself. I asked about breakfast.

Be Kind smiled. "Al will usually have a hot breakfast for the one who will shepherd him to Heaven when the time comes. I'm sure he can manage a helping for the one who will stop his bar from being shot up until it is time to go to Heaven."

He retreated to his back room and returned wearing a long woolen coat. Then he took my arm and walked me out into the snowy morning. As we crossed the square, our footprints filling as we made them, I watched the snow gather on his curly black hair and wondered. I couldn't tell if Be Kind thought me mad, a liar, or, truthfully, back from the stars. He said he didn't care and I was ready to believe him. He saw his job as taking care of strays and helping where he could. It struck me that what he described was what a church ought to do, but I couldn't remember hearing of any that actually did. I wondered how that connected to *My First Reader*, which I'd seen at the farm, and to what Charity had said. Out loud, I wondered how many came to his church.

"Most who live close enough come one day or another," Be Kind said. "I tell them the story of the Tribulation and the Die-off. I tell them to preserve whatever printed knowledge they find and care for their families. I always tell them they have been selected to go to Heaven; they only need wait for God to say it is time. It gives people comfort to hear this and it costs them nothing, so they come. They may get drunk afterward and shoot each other, but for the time they are with me, they feel good. What more can I do?"

I couldn't think of anything. I studied the buildings we walked past, the mismatched concrete blocks from older structures and the wooden beams with steel fastenings that had nothing to do with the buildings the beams were in.

"The building materials for the town have been salvaged," I said. "This stuff has all been taken from old buildings somewhere else. Why don't people just use the old buildings? The ones built with concrete or brick would probably still be in good shape, probably better than these."

He shuddered, and the cold had not bothered him to this point. "Who would want to?" The expression on his face made me think he was doubting my sanity. "Those buildings are where all the people from before died. Who would want to live with all the electronics around them? Even though all the computers and electronics are dead, the buildings are still full of wires. We find the wires and other . . . things when we take the building materials. Now, the ferals will live anywhere. They'll use the old buildings for shelter where they range, but they are little better than animals. And you will also find animals in the old buildings. And the ones here with feral eyes . . . they do good work on farms in the summer, but they can be dangerous. People say those eyes are signs of witchcraft, that they do black magic." He tried to laugh but it didn't work. "The Church says it's because even though God selected them, they tried to make old computers work again and it burned their eyes green. That's why God condemned them to wander in the woods. That story is as likely to be true as any other."

Fortunately, we were in front of Al's at that point, because I did not want to continue a conversation about people with feral eyes. Elvy might be an imp of Hades at times, but she was *my* imp of Hades. The thought struck me like a slap.

"Please go in."

My mind whirled back from the excursion it had taken and I realized where I was. I was standing in front of an open door leading into Al's. Be Kind was holding it for me. I stepped through and the warmth of a roaring fire hit my face. My body relaxed under the layers of clothing I was wearing.

"Morning, Preacher." A tall man walked over from where he had been wiping down the bar. He dried his hands with the rag he had been using. "Your usual today?"

"Yes, please," Be Kind said. "And, Al, if you have a portion available for our starman—who may really be a lucky starman—I'm sure he would appreciate it."

Al grinned, a lopsided grin superimposed on a lopsided face. "I saw what he did. Do you mean he expects to be lucky enough to live until he can find someone else to take the job?"

"I'm planning on it," I said. "In the meantime, I can be appreciative."

"Hah!" Al threw the rag back so it draped over his shoulder. "Take your table, Preacher. I'll have the cook put it together. And"—he gestured at me—"you're not a houseguest here, you're doin' a job. I'm fine if you finish it."

Be Kind's table proved to be a small, unsteady square of wood on four legs at one corner of the fireplace. The heat was enough to cook a goose, but I didn't care. I gratefully shed my coat and he did the same.

I thought about the way Al had emphasized that I could finish everything in my meal. It occurred to me that everyone I saw was thin. Rail thin. The Troubles—to the extent they had ever done any good—had taken some of the starch out of the American diet, but I had still grown up accustomed to being surrounded by fully fleshed figures. Not here. I thought about the customs around food, the way stories incorporated starvation. Nuclear winter was, apparently, also a cure for obesity.

The interior of the bar was as empty as I think it ever got. Aside from one man drinking unsteadily at the bar, we were the only people in the place.

Al was back almost as soon as I was settled in my chair. He put a plate with two boiled eggs, a mound of something that looked like hash, and a thick slice of bread, burned black and smeared with a preserve, in front of each of us. I didn't care what it looked like. I tore into mine. It was delicious.

While I was licking the crumbs off my fingers, Mayor Guo walked in. He proved this was not a fortuitous event by heading directly over to our table and dragging a chair to sit with us. For three, the table was a tight fit.

"I was told you came into town," Guo said. "I stopped by to say thank you and wish you well."

It occurred to me that the two of them probably knew more about everyone's affairs than anyone else. That could be useful. "Can either of you tell me the real story of the argument between Constant and Hezekiah?"

"Certainly." It was Guo who answered. "Everyone in town knows. Except you. Constant is Hezekiah's business partner, in a manner of speaking. Hezekiah's original whorehouse was as much tents as it was a house, and it burned down a couple of years ago. Constant gave him money to help him build a new one."

"Which, as you can see, he put next to the church," Be Kind interrupted. "Now, you can argue about the location—and I do, for all the good it does me—but Hezekiah claimed that after a heavy dose of God, men and women need to relax, and that he is an upright man. At least, that is what he claims women tell him. I wouldn't know."

Guo put a hand up to stop Be Kind's tangent about the whorehouse. "The nub of the problem is that Constant said the money was a loan and that Hezekiah owed him a percent of the take until it was paid back. Hezekiah says it was a gift—"

"To relieve the stress caused by my preaching!" The words exploded from Be Kind, and he partially rose out of the chair. "As if I and the Saints could possibly be at fault. And so it went, with Hezekiah doing his best to avoid Constant, and me, perhaps, wishing for another fire—although too worried that a fire would not spare the church to do more than make the occasional wish. And that only when the noise from next door interrupted my preaching."

"That's the way it went until you showed up," Guo finished.

"I'm surprised the two of them hadn't shot each other before I got here."

"There are reasons they didn't." Guo's broad smile revealed a few missing teeth. "If Hezekiah ever drew his gun and fired, the only thing he'd likely hit is his foot. He just wanted to be marshal because he thought Constant would have to stop nagging him for his money. I agreed to have him because there was no one else. Constant, well, he's a damn good shot, but there's no way he would shoot Hezekiah. If he did, the whorehouse would close down and Constant would never get his money. Not to mention that the town would lynch him, because Constant can't run a whorehouse. I don't think he has that kind of urge. But, yeah, eventually something would have happened, and the day you came might have been when. Then it would be my problem, with Hezekiah's customers and Constant's family."

"The one who would be happy is me," Be Kind said, "and with my luck, I'd wake up one morning and find a village worth of ferals camping there."

"Nobody likes the ferals, do they?" I asked.

"No. Probably not even their mothers," Be Kind said. "They're dirty, lice-ridden, and ignorant. No reverence for the God who selected them, and they haunt the ruined places."

I did not want to have another conversation about ferals. I changed the topic. "So, what is it that you want me to do, Mayor Guo?"

"Please, call me Fair," he said.

Good name for a mayor and banker, I thought. "Okay, Fair, what am I doing? What are the rules here, the laws?"

Guo shrugged. "It's simple. Stop the fights, or end them if they've already started. This town is not in organized territory. No senator and no government. We have a military governor, but that's more to do with armies. There's no lawbook you need to learn. Just stop the fights so that people in town can do their business, play cards, get drunk, and screw around without getting killed. It's a very simple job."

CHAPTER TWENTY THREE

I had my first job test late that afternoon. I was back at Al's, leaning against the bar and talking to Al—okay, he was gossiping and I was encouraging it, thinking I might get dinner out of it. Someone, I didn't recognize who, shoved the door open and yelled, "Hey, starman, they're shooting at Cold Sober!"

"It's a bar near the end of the street," Al said in answer to my puzzled expression. "Not as nice as mine. Take this too." He pulled a rifle from under his bar. "I won't put dinner out until I see if you come back."

"Thanks." I took the rifle and ran out into the street.

The direction of Cold Sober was obvious from a string of gunshots. The shooting stopped, however, before I reached the door. I could see someone lying in the doorway, legs outside and moving, one of them bloody. I flattened myself against the boardwalk and crept forward, chest to the ground, to see what had happened.

Inside, half a dozen patrons were on the floor, crouched under tables and apparently fine. Two men were still on their feet and unmarked. They were both trying to reload. They had clearly blazed away at each other from a distance of about ten feet, emptied their clips, and put bullets into the walls, the bar, a mirror, and the windows, but not into each other. Now one of them was trying to put a clip in but kept missing the slot in the grip.

The other had the clip backward as he was trying to jam it in. Fear and adrenaline can ruin your aim, open your sphincters, and mess with your coordination. My opportunity wasn't going to get any better.

I jumped up and ran at the closer of the two. He turned at the sound of my boots on the floor, but still couldn't find the opening with the clip. A rifle isn't a bō staff, but it can serve as one. I whipped the barrel of Al's rifle down on top of his head and he dropped. That gave the second man warning I was there, but all he managed to do was look at me open-mouthed before I slammed the stock of the rifle against the side of his head and then hit him across the other side with the barrel. He fell, as did some teeth separately.

I enlisted a few men who had been under tables, and they dragged the two of them to Guo's office, where he could hand out penalties, such as paying for the mess. They both woke up on the way, and I'm sure they had concussions. We took the man bleeding in the doorway to the town's doc.

Yes, it was a simple job. As the days passed, I spent most of my time making rounds of the town, around the little square and up and down the street, sticking my nose into every door and trying to gauge if a personal interaction was reaching a boiling point. Alcohol, of course, lowers the boiling point of humans and was a factor in almost every confrontation that I saw. Add to that the fact that everyone, and I do mean everyone, carried at least one semiautomatic pistol with a ten-bullet magazine in the grip, and we had a recipe for random violence. Fortunately, as in the incident at Cold Sober, most of the people couldn't aim for shit even when they were sober. What Guo wanted was for me to keep uninvolved people, like the guy in the doorway, from getting hurt. The prevailing opinion was that if an argument ended in a shooting, dead was dead, but nobody else should be injured.

I took to making my rounds with a rifle in addition to my pistol, but I used it mostly the way I had at Cold Sober. Folks didn't want me shooting either. Frankly, what kept the shooting under control wasn't so much my zealous peacekeeping as the fact that ammunition was expensive and in limited supply. Folks worried about that. So did I. I had only a couple of clips left for the pistol I had brought from the *Dauntless*. When they were gone, I would be reduced to the same crappy current-day weapons as everybody else.

My best source of information for what was happening in East-view, from who was broke and in danger of starving to who was screwing whom—literally and figuratively—turned out to be the same as my best source of food: Big Al Kowalski of Al's. It made sense that people would speak more freely in front of a barkeep than the mayor or the preacher. Al was a rawboned man with thick ropes for muscles along his forearms and a face God had punished over the years, which was never quite shaved. He would greet me when I strolled in early in the morning with a hearty *I see you're still alive, Leif!* and a hot plate of whatever the cook was making. Then he would pull up a chair to where I was sitting and tell me about trouble coming, or fun bits of gossip. I came to forgive him for the lack of coffee.

Al was also happy to put out meals for me during the day. As he pointed out, having me sitting in his bar was a deterrent to fights starting and an assurance of a quick response if one did. It was worth the space I occupied and the food I ate. Plenty of people filtered through Al's in the course of a day. That gave me another way to find out what was going on. The advantage of gathering information in Al's was that having a drink or two or three under their belts often increased their candor.

I even saw Tonya there once, the woman who had ridden to Charity's farm. I braced for trouble when she came in, because she had that kind of look about her, but she sat by herself and nursed a single beer for a while. When I looked her way, I saw her eyes on me—and that was more than once—but she didn't say anything, nor did she approach me. Then I looked over and she was gone. I caught Al's eye, but he only shrugged, brought me another weak tea, and said, "Hey, I can see you're still alive."

After a few days of having my survival remarked upon, I held off attacking the breakfast and asked the obvious question: "Why are you and all these other people here, if there's no law and it's so dangerous?"

Al laughed and let me see that he was missing about half his teeth. "Better no law than bad law," he said. "These open lands have no law because they're not part of any senator's territory. Stays like that, for now, anyway, because a senator gets to raise army units from their territory. So, if one of the senators can add this land to their territory, they get richer from more taxes and more powerful because of more men and women for army units they patronize. The others won't want that. To make new senators—well, that's somebody else with army units, and they would join one of the senate factions and it's the same problem. It won't last this way, of course. Nothing ever does, and we'll get some law eventually. But that'll just be some senator deciding who gets shot. Government's like an upside-down man with his head in the sand. Can't see what's really going on, and there's an asshole on top."

Al laughed at his own joke. So did I.

"Sounds like other governments I know of," I said. "But how did Guo get to be mayor? Did he just say he was?"

Al laughed again. His breath could have used a mint. "General Mendenhall appointed him. The general's about as much law as there is. He was a real hero, I guess, in the wars up north years ago. Then he, or his patrons in the senate, got screwed playing power in New Terra, but he was too big a hero to kill, so they sent him out here. They've taken most of his soldiers for fighting in the northwest and to guard against Athens to the south, so he doesn't have much left. You'll see when he comes to talk to you about your militia." Al shrugged. That seemed to be his general-purpose gesture. "New Terra is like that, all about money and power and couldn't give a shit about anything else. People get tired of it, they move out. There's plenty of empty land. Just sweep the bones out of the way."

I let the fire crackle by itself for a minute, but Al didn't get up. "New Terra is a city?" I asked. "Why do they call it that?"

Al's eyes widened the way they did when I asked a question he found particularly dumb. "It grew up near a before-city with that name. That one was called Terra something, I'm not sure what. Hote, maybe. Who knows what a 'hote' was. They just call it New Terra. For all the good they do, we could call it New Bullshit, but the president and the senators wouldn't like it. Nor the preacher. The church and the government always go to bed together, but we're the ones who get screwed. Be Kind is a decent man, but the church is the state, just like the army. Keep that in mind."

When he said that, I remembered *My First Reader: The Army Is the State and the State Is the Army*. Charity had said the church gave them out.

I was going to ask Al about it, although I wasn't sure he could read, but a creak of the door at that moment heralded the arrival of Be Kind Blanchette for his breakfast. Al scraped his chair back and went to greet the preacher. My lesson in current affairs had ended.

·   ·   ·

What Al had said about New Terra bothered me for the rest of the day and ruined my sleep. It compounded what I had heard from Charity. I was so done with armies and wars and people who thought patriotism was defined by killing those who looked different or spoke a different language or had a different symbol on a shoulder patch. I was done with it. Would never do it again. Be Kind's church had sounded good when we first spoke, but if this was all one military-religious state, maybe I should pack a saddlebag and head west.

But if I did that, I wouldn't be able to go back to the farm, even though I hadn't actually done that yet either. I would miss Charity's smile and Elvy's antics. I would miss the little ones trying to jump on my lap. I would even miss Courtesy fighting with Elvy. I didn't want to give up all of that, even if I didn't know what I should do about it. I tossed and turned in that cold room. Finally, with pale light showing through the dirt on the window, I decided I should give Be Kind an opportunity to explain what he did for the state, and why.

·   ·   ·

My chance for that conversation with Be Kind came the very next day. Water was leaking through his ceiling and he had sized me up as the sort who could fix whatever was broken. In return, he offered to share his chicken soup. Yes, he had diagnosed me pretty well.

That put me atop a twenty-foot ladder at the back of the church, above where his room was located. Along with a hammer and some nails, I had a batch of old shingles salvaged from some other building in a burlap bag that swung from a nail in the ladder. Be Kind stood below me in the snow to brace the ladder. The chances of the ladder breaking or of Be Kind losing his grip seemed about equal.

The problem was pretty obvious once I got up there. For some reason, whoever had painted the church stopped a couple of feet below the roof. Woodpeckers had stayed away from the white paint but left the unpainted boards under the eaves looking like they'd been sprayed with bullets by a machine gun. That left plenty of entry points for rain and snowmelt from the roof. I managed to nail shingles over the holes, then converted the burlap sack into an open sheet and nailed that across as much of the unpainted wood as I could, forming a netting to deter further assault by the birds. Somehow, I accomplished this without falling off the ladder.

As promised, Be Kind ushered me into his room behind the pulpit for soup. His room was as spartan as a jail cell. It held a bed with a thin blanket, a fireplace with the soup kettle, a rough table with two chairs, and a chest for clothes. He didn't even have a rug on the floor. Bowls and spoons came from a smaller chest he pulled out from under the bed.

After a mouthful of what proved to be chicken-flavored hot water, I regarded him across the tiny table. He was slurping up the liquid as though it were really soup.

"I keep hearing the line that the army is the state and the state is the army, and I'm also hearing that your church works for both. With all that's happened, if your job is to help people, tell me why you're doing that."

Be Kind stopped with his spoon almost in his mouth. He looked at me over it, then put it back in his bowl and pushed his chair away from the table.

"You make it sound like we're nothing more than a tool for the senate and the army," he said.

"Aren't you?"

He looked hurt. He folded his hands in his lap and stared at them. "Why would you say something like that?"

"Oh, come on. I've seen that reader you give out to families. I've heard that you tell people to support the state and join new army units, along with the good stuff about families and print. You're talking to someone who's been in an army, who's seen war, and I see the mess that's left. Why?"

"You don't understand."

"Tell me what I don't understand."

Be Kind's Adam's apple bobbed up and down as though something had stuck in his throat. "The church is poor," he said. "I would not call my furnishings luxurious." He waved a hand around at his room, and I was not going to disagree with his assessment. "We do ask for donations, but most people have little enough as it is. And, since we assure them they have been selected for Heaven, why should they give up what they can't afford? The state supports the church. How can we refuse doing it . . . favors in return? We're not like the damned reapocalyptics."

I was going to retort that, willing or not, a tool was still a tool, but his last sentence caught my attention. "Reapocalyptics. I heard you use that term before. What does it mean?"

"That's the other church," he said, still looking at his lap.

"Wait a minute. I thought there was only one church."

"That's true," he said. "I mean, it's all the Church of All Saints of the Apocalypse. Maybe it would be better to say there is another part. A small one. Who are incorrect, to be polite."

I wondered if I was now going to hear about a religious schism. Was there nothing humans could not only do wrong but do wrong again when given a second chance? "Why don't you tell me the difference, and why it matters?"

"I told you God sent the Tribulation and then the Twelve Saints, who were starfolk, to tell the survivors that they and their descendants had been selected to go to Heaven." I nodded. "Well, the reapocalyptics have invented a whole mythology. They say the Tribulation was only a taste of what is to come. That God will send another, final, Tribulation, and that one will be heralded by the return of another twelve starmen and women. But this time they will come at the head of an army. When that happens, God will select his chosen few. He will take those to Heaven while the rest of us go to Hell. You can see how they use that."

I shook my head. "No. I don't."

"It's simple," Be Kind said. "If you still don't know whether you'll be selected to go to Heaven, and the church suggests you should make a donation, what are you going to do? And it's more than that. They will sell you a Selection Ticket. These remove bad deeds or thoughts from your record before God makes the selections for Heaven. You can see how it goes. The reapocalyptics are rich. We need to do something about this. I know General Mendenhall would do something, if the state only gave him the means."

My soup had gone cold. It wasn't worth eating even when it was hot. I said something vaguely polite and left for my office to wait for the next drunken brawl. At least it was understandable when drunks got into a fight.

·　　·　　·

That night, I sat on the bed in the cold room over the office and didn't bother to start a fire. I brooded over what Be Kind had told me. I brooded over the state, and the army, and the church. I brooded over my feelings about Charity. I fell asleep on top of the blanket and dreamed again about

Yong telling me that if I landed the transport at Earthbase, she would be there.

The window was still dark when I woke, as frozen as I ever had been coming out of hib. I sat up and almost decided to take my pay, buy supplies, get my horse out of the stable, and ride west. Almost. I got as far as standing up. Then my brain started churning and I sat back down. If I did survive to reach Earthbase, Yong wouldn't be there. And once I saw that, she would be gone and lost to me forever. I wouldn't even be able to dream that she was still alive.

I stewed on that, then decided I would let the army and the state and the church and the town go to hell. I would ride back to the farm. But my mind said that if I joined Charity's family, that was another way of saying Yong was dead.

I had to stay here. If I kept to myself and didn't go to Kansas to put it to the test, I could still dream she was alive. It was easier to stay where I was and be marshal of Eastview. I wouldn't have to change anything, and I wouldn't have to deal with my feelings.

My thinking was a bit messed up.

My stomach decided what I was going to do that morning. I got dressed and went to Al's for breakfast and to hear him comment on my being alive. I was that. Sort of.

·   ·   ·

Guo Fair Measure, in his role as the town's newsman, did keep his promise to publish a special newsfeed announcing my appointment. The day after I had my chat with Be Kind about New Terra, Guo came down to my office to hand me a copy. It was one big piece of paper, printed on both sides in smudgy black ink. In large font at the top of page 1 was the headline, LEIF GRETTISON APPOINTED EASTVIEW'S MARSHAL. There followed a description of how I had wiped out a squad of raiders near the town. It was mostly fiction, with one grain of truth about saving Elvy. Then came a lengthy, fulsome section on my fights in town. Yes, indeed, it sounded like a superhero had come to clean up Eastview. The town, as it said, now had a real starman.

I stared at the thing, and not only for the overblown prose. Newsfeeds downloaded to your phone and were displayed on your field, or you read them on a screen. Even as far back as the 2040s, when I was a kid, I could not recall having seen one on paper.

"Can't you read the letters?" Guo asked after I had stared at it for a while and turned it front to back a couple of times.

"Yeah," I said. "The ink is smudged in a couple of places, but I can make it out."

He gave me an odd look that said he had been questioning my literacy more than the quality of his print run. "Constant will pull your militia together so you can meet them," he said. Then he took the sheet back and walked out of my office.

Al had said there was a general who wanted to talk to me about the militia. Even if I didn't care about any general, the militia was supposed to protect the town. Since I was staying, I supposed it would be a good idea if I knew who they were.

CHAPTER TWENTY FOUR

It took another week before Constant was able to bring my entire militia unit together. I wondered what would happen if we had an emergency. They met me at my office—all six of them.

First impressions are often lasting. Mine were not very favorable. Two of them were women, Tonya Spurling and Pride Goeth García, and they, at least, had windburned faces and hands that spoke of hard work. Tonya was the same woman in the leathers I had seen that day at the farm, and then at Al's. Those brown eyes of hers were milder than I remembered, and they checked me from head to boots. But all she said was, "I've heard about you, and I've watched you around town."

Watched me around town? I remembered her eyes on me when she was sitting in Al's, but that was the only time I recalled having seen her.

Pride Goeth was, by contrast, several shades lighter, with a loose ponytail, wool pants, and three layers of homespun shirts against the cold. The three men with Constant were less impressive. I didn't think they ever went outside. One of them, Ethan Wyandotte, worked as a teller for Guo. He didn't reach Tonya's five and a half feet. Although I doubted he was older than thirty-five, his hair had receded to a thin brown fringe and his face perpetually wore a worried frown. James McSorely was our town barber. Judging from his face and mustache, I would do my own shaving.

Render Praise Martin was only a couple of years older than No Nonsense. He was an assistant at the dry goods store.

After we exchanged names and occupations—Tonya and Pride Goeth were vague about that—I stood there and wondered what to do with them. I wondered, as well, what they were thinking of me, the guy with the play-action star pinned to his shirt.

I could hear Petey whispering in my ear. *Sarge*, Petey would say, *"we're not seriously goin' forward with this bunch of FNGs, are we?*

I didn't want to hear what Yong would say.

Constant broke the still life. "Maybe we should go do some shooting. We all saw Leif gun down Jeremiah, but maybe we should show him what we can do."

"All well and good," said Tonya, her eyes hardening when she looked at Constant, "but we need to go easy on the ammo. It's not like this stuff rains down from the clouds."

"Yeah," said Ethan. "And no drinking until we're done shooting. You remember what happened the last time."

Tonya was smiling, though it didn't touch those eyes. "You don't want to have to ask Guo to pay for the damages again."

Ethan colored to the top of his bald head. "No."

I didn't know what had happened, and I didn't want to ask. I did want to see if this troop of mine could hit the proverbial side of the barn. When they were sober.

I thought Constant would set up a target in the square, but I was wrong. All of them had horses tied up outside my office and the church. At a signal from Constant, they mounted up and waited for me to get my horse from the stable. Then we rode off up the street and out of town.

We went about half an hour west, until we came to a stretch that was fairly clear of brush and trees. This meant an old roadway was there—a sign I had learned to recognize, even if I couldn't see pavement. The snow had vanished from areas in direct sun, and I could see patches of asphalt through the dirt and dried grass. Along the roadside were low irregular mounds, mostly covered with brush. Occasional posts or fragments of brick wall stuck out of these, indicating that they were burial mounds for old houses.

Soon enough, we came to a ruinscape. A cluster of houses, two charging stations, and a small shopping mall had occupied this place.

Now the houses, and any other structures built of wood, had collapsed into jumbles and were being swallowed by grass, bushes, and dirt. In a few more years, they would be the same as the mounds I had seen behind us. Brick structures were mostly gone as well, the brick having been scavenged for other use over the past century. The poured concrete and metal buildings that made up most of the shopping area were still there, standing up against the sky. Someone had daubed on one wall TO HELL WITH THE FUTURE, WE'RE DOOMED BY OUR PAST. Judging by how the paint was faded, the words had been there a long time. The roofs had caved in, the windows were broken, and most of the signs had fallen, but it would be many more years before nature, on its own, knocked down and covered up the remains of these buildings.

I found the sight depressing. I wondered what the remains of a city would look like. One that hadn't been nuked.

We dismounted in what had been the parking lot facing the storefronts. However we might look, the group was well armed. Each of us had at least one pistol and a rifle. The women also had long knives strapped to their belts.

"Remember," said Ethan, "be careful about ammo. We can use a maximum of one magazine per weapon."

With that reminder, our exercise began. One of them would point to a sign still clinging to the wall of a store, calling out a name and a letter. The person whose name was called had to hit the letter using either their pistol or their rifle. Whoever shot would then call the name and target for the next shooter. My spirits rose as I watched the demonstration. Their appearance might be nondescript, but they could shoot. All of them were accurate, even with the pistols, and at greater ranges than I would have expected. Tonya gave a gleeful laugh when McSorely, the barber, called her name and the period on a sign about seventy-five yards away. She put a pistol shot through the center of the period.

"All right," Constant called out after her shot, "everybody with rifles. That plastic *W* high up on the big building. All together."

Six shots rang out in quick succession and punched a line of holes in the descending front line of the *W*.

Unfortunately, the demonstration of their shooting prowess was the extent of their interest in any military exercise. *Drill* was a foreign word. I suggested we pick one of the stores and use it for an exercise in assaulting an enemy position. I received blank stares. They thought I had seen what I needed to see, and that was the end as far as they were concerned. It was cold, and most of them wanted to be back indoors. They cleaned their weapons and packed up. Constant said I should ride back with the group.

"The shooting and the shouting, that can attract attention," he said. "You never know who might be lurking around these places."

Tonya guided her horse next to mine as we left the old shopping center. "Are you going back to Charity's farm?" she asked. "Or was that just a stopping place for you?"

"I will," I said without thinking, and was surprised at the words that had popped out of my mouth. "Why is that your business?"

"Because I'm asking. Are you sleeping with her?"

"That is definitely not your business."

She looked at my face and said, "You're not. Is it that you don't like women?"

"No! I mean, yes, I like women!" This conversation was ridiculous, but I had nowhere to go to get away from it without looking even more ridiculous.

"Then why not?"

"I—" Quite suddenly, words stopped. I knew the answer and I couldn't say it. Charity was wonderful; she was sweet; she was gorgeous. But the part of my emotional system where desire lived felt like an empty bucket. I wanted Yong back. I couldn't have her, and I couldn't move on. I realized Tonya was staring at me. "There's a lot of history you don't know. Anyway, why do you care?"

She shrugged in her saddle and guided her horse ahead of mine. That nag promptly lifted its tail and dropped a steaming load in front of me.

"You're just passing through," Tonya said over her shoulder. "A rider in the night who doesn't touch anyone. Like me. I'll be by." Without any other explanation, she spurred her horse ahead and left me with the others.

Tonya wasn't my idea of a psychiatrist, not that I needed one anyway. If she wanted to be cryptic, that was fine with me. It was the militia as a fighting force that should—and did—concern me. I could hear Petey whispering in my ear again as we rode back the way we had come. *So, Sarge, what are we gonna do? Enter a target-shooting contest?*

Hollywood had made vids since forever about heroic bands of seven disparate and unlikely fighters who save some poor town from an evil oppressor. We weren't that.

·   ·   ·

Tonya stopped by my office the day after our shooting demonstration. I had a fire going in the fireplace, but she sucked the cold in with her. The coldest part of her was her eyes.

"Are you thinking of riding the circuit?" she asked.

I had been thinking of going to Al's for hot food. "What circuit?" I asked with a faint hope that the question was reasonable.

"A wide swing around the town." Impatience tinged her voice. "That will give you an idea of what the land is like around here, around the town, particularly coming into the town."

A light went on in my head. "That's what you were doing the day you came to Charity's farm. None of this 'hunting on contract' bullshit. You were scouting."

"Yeah." Her face softened a tiny bit. "I don't go all the way east and north that often. I didn't think I'd find raiders there. I've wondered what would have happened if I had come on them instead of you. Now, I didn't lie completely. I was going to hunt to take some food to the family west of Charity's place. They're not as good with food as she is."

What was obvious in her offer was that it would be useful for me to see where the town was most vulnerable to attack. I had not forgotten the raiders I'd killed either. Yes, one of the militia had picked up on what I had wanted to do after we finished target shooting. Yes, I definitely wanted to know what the perimeter of my position looked like. Especially when there were no defense lines along said perimeter. Or troops to man any such positions.

"I'd love a ride in the country in the cold," I said. My blue eyes can appear as hard as any pair of brown ones.

Tonya was back early the next morning with a packhorse loaded with supplies. She had also stopped to pick up my horse from the stable, probably to minimize the chance I would change my mind. She saw my eyes linger on the horses.

"I'm sorry," she said in a voice that wasn't sorry at all, "but I'm figuring three days with the short light at this time of year to do what we need to do. You're okay with camping in the cold, I hope."

I was starting to feel that my return to Earth was nothing more than an unending series of awakenings from hib dreams about freezing, but something in her voice told me this was a test. "I've camped wherever and whenever," I said. "If the flames of the campfire freeze, then I'll worry about it."

Tonya chuckled and her expression thawed at last. She smiled at me. Then we saddled up and she led the way out of town to the northeast. The cold turned our breath into cloud streams and did the same to the breath from the horses. It was a clear blue sky, though, and the direct sun on my body made it feel warmer than it was. The land in that direction was open. Occasional game tracks were all that marred the dusting of snow that had fallen overnight.

"Did you expect me to back out when you mentioned camping in the cold?" I asked.

"Maybe." She didn't say anything else until we had gone another half mile. "Stories are that starmen live grandly out in the stars, like we used to do here. You might be used to comfort."

"It's not an easy life for people out there," I said. "Different, but not easy, even if where I went last was hot rather than cold. And I was a soldier here before that. A long time ago."

She looked over at me from where she sat on her horse. "That's good," she said. "Fact is, when Hezekiah was the starman, he never checked around the town, never rode the circuit."

"I can believe it," I said. "I heard he only took the job because he thought he could get Constant to quit badgering him for the money."

Tonya's laugh was harsh. "Guo Fair Measure talked him into it that way. Well, that and he convinced Hezekiah that it would keep people from misbehaving in his whorehouse. He saw real fast the job brought nothing but trouble, that people expected *him* to stop the trouble. He should have known better, but it's easy to fall in the direction you're already leaning."

"What about the one before Hezekiah?" I asked. "Did that one do a better job, and what happened to them?"

"Don't know," she said. "There wasn't one for a while before Hezekiah, and hell, I've only been here about a year."

I remembered Al's comments about New Terra and the law, so I asked her.

"And there's no law out here otherwise? People are on their own?"

She brought her horse to a stop and turned its head so she faced me. "No senator from New Terra has a territory this far east," she said. "Not yet. Someday we'll have one and regret it, or maybe we won't if there's more fighting in the north, or a new war in the south, or we have winter through the summer again and we all starve. So, maybe." She did not start her horse moving again. "Why did *you* take this job?"

What do you do when your mission no longer matters to anyone in the world? What do you do when it doesn't even matter much to you anymore? What do you do when your feelings are a jumble you can't turn off?

"I had nothing better to do."

"Hnnh." She blew a cloud of steam into the air and yanked on her horse's reins so that it moved off in the direction we had been heading.

I gave mine a kick and caught up to her. "Where did you come from, Tonya, and why did you come here?"

She didn't look at me when she spoke. "From the west. Settled country, lots of people, farms, and towns around the ruins. The ma and pa of my first family, the one I was born to, they were way too free with the belt, or the stick, or whatever they could hit with. Not saying I didn't deserve a lot of it, but I wasn't gonna take it for too long. I ran when I was thirteen. I'd find a family, work for a while—I know farmwork—then I'd move on. I heard about the east somewhere, decided I wanted to go. This area's not too bad. Not that many ruins, so I guess not so many lived here before. But I want to go all the way east, to where the burned cities are. Not just ruined ones like you can see anywhere, but the ones that burned in hellfire, where you can still find a layer of ash on the ground. Or so they say. Nothing but ferals between here and there, from what I've heard. I was going to keep going from here, but then there was trouble with raiders, and people needed help, and the pay is good, so I've stayed awhile. I'll do it, though. I'll move on next summer, or the one after. I'll do it before I'm too old."

I looked at her, at the easy way she rode. "You don't look anywhere near too old."

She laughed. "I'm twenty-four now. That's old enough to do what I want. Anyway, how old do you expect I'm going to get?"

I wasn't sure how to answer that question. "Old enough for gray hair and plenty of grandchildren," I said.

"That makes you either a fool or a liar," she replied.

She gave her horse a nudge and rode ahead of me for a while.

.   .   .

We rode in a counterclockwise loop north of town. I could see scattered farm buildings as we went, barn roofs partially white with snow and smoke rising from chimneys. A column of smoke against the blue sky or above distant trees gave evidence of more houses I couldn't see. These were the sort of pastoral views I'd seen hanging in museums whenever I was dragged to one on a school field trip. The only thing that spoiled the ambience of a bucolic paradise was the detritus of a past era—my era—that intruded in many places. There was the mile marker on a pole more rust than metal that stuck up through the snow on the ground, the mound where the wind had blown clear the concrete at one corner, the plastic sign against the sky announcing the availability of a brand of doughnuts I remembered. I tried to avoid looking at them.

If a farm was close to the route we were taking, Tonya would detour to the house. She would ride up, knock on the front door, and ask whoever answered how they were doing and if they needed anything. It seemed that everyone knew her, so this had to be something she did regularly.

"Is this how people are now?" I asked, thinking it wasn't so bad. "Checking on each other, taking care of each other?"

"No." Her face said I was nuts. "I do it."

"Why? You said you're not staying here. Why do you do it if nobody else does?"

She shrugged in the saddle. "Maybe because nobody else does. Constant is from a rich family—well, what passes for rich out here. He prefers to be comfortable. Ethan won't leave that bank unless Guo tells him to. The others just don't. Maybe I like doing it. I stopped at a place once, it's not near where we're riding now, and a woman was having a baby. The baby came out okay, thankfully. I mean, I didn't know how to do anything, but I could sit with her and hold her hand and she said she appreciated that."

"Tell you what," I said. "If you know some family needs help, let me know. I'll come and do what I can." It occurred to me that I was accustomed to having medicines and equipment ready to hand, but I could, and had, taken care of battlefield injuries with only what I could improvise.

Tonya dropped back to ride with me. "You would actually do that?"

"Yeah, I would."

Her eyes narrowed, assessing me. "You may be crazier than I am. I'll take you up on it."

·   ·   ·

A couple of hours later, we came to a cluster of four old buildings. From what remained standing, I guessed at two shops and two houses. The roofs were gone, none of them had all four walls standing, and all the windows were broken.

Tonya pointed at the structures. "Do you want to play bone hunter?"

"What's that?"

She smiled. "Children's game, mostly. Each player picks an old building. You go into the building you picked and hunt for bones. Have to be people bones. Animals don't count. You get a point for each bone you find, double count if you find a whole skeleton; but to count for the bonus, the skeleton has to have all the main parts, like it can't be missing a foot or a hand."

At first, I thought she was joking. If she was, she had the best poker face in history. "Kids really do this?" I asked.

"Sure," she said. "It's a lot harder now to find them than it used to be. Sometimes, also, the bones fall apart and turn to dust if you pick them up. But they used to be all over. I remember one family I was a part of for a while, they had a very old grandpa. He used to say that when he was a kid, you could find skeletons everywhere, that nobody got a bonus for finding a whole one. It was that easy. Anywhere there was a big town from before, there would be bones everywhere you looked. I guess bones don't last forever, just like the rest of a person."

That was true. Bones would decay naturally, turn to dust. It took longer, much longer, than soft tissue, and it depended on where the bones were. Bones could remain intact for centuries—many centuries, in fact.

The idea of making a game out of finding them felt ghoulish. It drove home the scale of death that must have happened in a short time.

I told Tonya I'd pass on the game.

· · ·

We pushed on to the west even as the light dimmed. I thought we could have ridden to where I saw chimney smoke and asked to sleep in the barn, but Tonya kept going. She finally stopped at the old ruin of what might have been a farm. The remaining walls provided some shelter, and there was space enough inside for us and the horses. We cleared debris away—including what looked like a much-gnawed femur—to give ourselves flat ground for blankets. Then we took care of the horses and gathered some wood for a fire.

"You told me you took the marshal's job because you had nothing else to do, but that's not true," Tonya said. She fed sticks into the fire until it brightened our little campsite against the dark and kept the cold at bay. "You could go back to Charity's farm. She's a good woman; she's raising good kids. That could be your family too. Why don't you? And don't give me the bullshit again about history."

"I can't." I stopped and realized I was sounding like a boor. "I told you there's history you don't know. It's not bullshit." I hesitated, then told her about Yong. Once I started, it all spilled out. I told her about the dream and my thoughts and I realized, as I talked, how crazy it sounded.

Tonya had a stick in her hand, but rather than adding it to the flames, she started digging a hole in the ground. "I don't understand a lot about what you told me, about before and being in space, and the stars, but there is one thing I do know from what you told me. She's dead. You have to know that." She looked at me, and the firelight flickered in her dark irises. "She's gone."

"I do," I said. "I mean, I know it, but I can't always let myself believe it. I like to think, sometimes, maybe . . . and that's why I think sometimes if I could complete this mission . . . and that's why there're some feelings I don't seem to have . . . and that's why I don't know what to do or how to feel about Charity." I heard the words I stammered out. What could seem real and sensible as long as I kept it in my mind became ludicrous when I told it to someone else. Maybe it was time to cope with my ghosts.

"Yeah. I hope your feelings come back." Tonya's hole had turned into quite a trench. "I'd been thinking maybe you didn't really like Charity, or you didn't like having all those kids around. I thought that maybe you might be interested in . . . me."

I stared at her. Thought of signals I had missed. Thought of all the signals I had missed for so long. Would I ever understand women? Would I ever understand myself? Probably not.

"That's sweet, Tonya. I mean, I'm sorry."

"It's not sweet, goddammit!" Her eyes were fixed on the end of that stick. "It's selfish! I just thought you seem to be a decent man, you've got a job, you can shoot, and you're not bad looking. I wasn't thinking forever, just for a while, which is the way I am—not that forever is much longer than a while out here. But I guess that's not going to work with you. Is it?" She looked up at me.

My face was hotter and redder than the damn fire. "I don't think so, Tonya."

"No," she said. "It's okay. I shouldn't have said anything. You should go back to Charity, and I can't believe I'm saying that. I'll still work with you, and if you'll help when some family needs it, I'll appreciate it. And when we ride from here, I am going to show you some things you need to see." She threw the stick into the fire. "It will be a cold night in separate blankets."

It was a cold night.

·   ·   ·

When we reached a point that marked the western limit of her circuit—and there must have been landmarks familiar to her but not obvious to me—she turned her horse to the south. The surrounding land changed as we went in that direction. The change was more obvious in Tonya. Where she had ridden along for two days, at ease in her saddle, I now saw a woman on high alert. Her eyes scanned the ground ahead of her and always to the south. We no longer stopped at the farms we came upon, because the ones we saw had been destroyed. Charred walls spoke of fire. No chimney smoke rose to the sky south of Eastview. This devastation was recent, too, not a century old. She rode directly up to one of them and said, "I want you to see this," and swung off her horse in front of what had been the farmhouse. I copied her.

The destruction had been thorough. A barn had stood to the side of the house. It had been burned to the ground. Flames had taken one wall of the house and part of the roof. What remained listed badly. It would not last through the winter.

Then I saw bodies. Animals had gotten at them, and what was left was decomposing. Some of their clothing remained intact. Three small bodies behind the house. Children. One adult I saw inside the house, sheltered by the intact portion of the roof. From the clothing and the position, I thought this was a woman and she had been raped before she was killed.

"Raiders," Tonya said. "This farm is the closest to town they've hit. We didn't get a warning in Eastview when they came here. All the farms to the south have been burned out by now. Sometimes the families get away."

"And the bodies are just left where they are? Nobody's buried them?"

"Dead is dead," Tonya said.

I'd heard that expression one time too many. "Care to tell me what people mean by that? I keep hearing it, as though it's a way of saying nobody cares."

Tonya walked over to the children's bodies and stood quietly for a moment. Then she came back to me. "I keep forgetting you're a starman, a real one. We grow up with the stories from the Die-off. I'll tell you about it, but I don't want to talk here. I only wanted you to see what happens when nobody is watching. Come on." She walked back to her horse and swung into the saddle.

We rode in silence until dusk and made camp in the shelter of a concrete wall left over from the destruction of my era. When the fire was going and the horses cared for, Tonya looked at me across the flames. "Do you know the story of Hansel and Gretel?" she asked.

I blinked at the odd question. Charity had told many stories at the farm, but that hadn't been one of them. I searched my memory for vids I had seen as a child. "I think so," I said. "That's where the woodcutter decides to get rid of the children, Hansel and Gretel, to save on food. They're dumped in a forest and then they find this witch who lives in a gingerbread house and plans to eat them."

"Somewhat like that," she replied. "Maybe they told it differently long ago."

"When I grew up, you mean."

"Yeah." I saw a grin on her face, but it didn't last long.

"Why don't you tell me today's version?" I said.

So, Tonya began to speak. She had a good voice for storytelling, a lot like Charity's. I could see her with a bunch of kids around her chair, intent on every word. But maybe not this story.

In Tonya's version, Hansel and Gretel weren't brother and sister. They were very close friends of the same age. It wasn't the woodcutter and his wife who were short of food; it was the whole village. The adults of the village decided that the only way to survive was to get rid of all the children, because they ate too much and didn't do enough work. They tricked the children by telling them they had to go into the forest—like starmen and starwomen to the stars!—to a place where there was abundant food, and bring it back to the village. The forest was a dark and dangerous place, and one by one the children died. They either starved to death or were killed by wild animals. Only Hansel and Gretel were left when they stumbled on the witch's gingerbread house.

The next part of the story mostly matched what I remembered. The witch tried to fatten Hansel up for a meal and ended being tricked into the oven by Gretel, who slammed the oven door behind the witch. The big difference was that, instead of gold and jewels, they found a hoard of food in the house, a sled they could put it on, and horses to haul it all away.

"Although there was no trail through the dark forest," Tonya said, "Hansel and Gretel had no trouble finding their way, because the bodies and bones of the other children marked the path. When they returned to the village, however, they found it full of bodies and bones. The food had run out and everyone there had starved to death. 'What do we do now?' Gretel cried. Hansel looked at Gretel and said, 'Nothing here, dead is dead. This is too much to clean up.' So they took the wagon and went to another place not too far and started their own family and village. Do you get the point?"

I was thinking about how starvation was a recurring theme in stories and customs. Tonya did not wait for me to formulate an answer.

"So many people died in the Die-off, and so few were left afterward. I told you about the bone hunter game. So many bodies and so many bones. What were the people still alive going to do with all of them? Unless they were in your way, you left them. Didn't matter to the dead. Dead is dead, as we say, and that's why we say it. Today, well, if there's a family around, yes, they'll bury the person. Or sometimes they'll pay the preacher to do it."

"Are you saying that the people who died at that farm we were at, they'll be left there until even the bones are gone? Unless some kids come to play bone hunter and take them?"

"Maybe." Tonya's eyes were intent on the fire. "If someone goes out there and wants to restart that farm—it looks like good land—they'll do something to clear the place. Bury them, maybe. Pull them into the woods if that's easier. But that's it, unless there's still a family that wants to take care of them." She stopped talking for a few minutes. She poked at the fire with a stick. She had not taken her eyes from the flames. Then she said, "For me, I can tell you, I'll be left where I die. Unless I'm in the way. I suppose, at that point, why should I care? Dead is dead." The bitterness in her voice said something completely different.

Something about her words and her tone made me think of the sad little funeral we had held for Dev. I looked at Tonya, her eyes only on the fire as she fed another stick into it. She would have been perfect for starfolk. She didn't attach anywhere. Unlike me, however, she wasn't comfortable with being that way.

The next morning, we rode back into town. Neither of us spoke much on that ride.

CHAPTER TWENTY FIVE

The days slid by, one into another, until one morning I found myself scratching a line with a pencil through November 14 on the calendar desk pad that Guo's Bank of Eastview printed up. I contemplated what I had done. On this particular day, it bothered me. It used to be that I would glance at a spot to my right and see a calendar in the air. I would look at a day on the calendar and see what I was supposed to do. When one of the tasks I had listed was done, I could make it disappear from the display before my eyes. I couldn't tell what was scarier: that the memory of a chip-and-phone-generated calendar had once been normal, or that using a pencil to draw an X through a date on a piece of paper felt normal now.

I turned to the window and felt a chill that had nothing to do with the snow that covered the square in front of my office. I was *getting used* to the situation. I was becoming *comfortable.*

My job wasn't hard, if you ignored the fact that a level of risk went with it. Risk! I had been a Ranger. I'd jumped out of airplanes. Into combat. Risk is relative.

Nowadays, I walked around the town visiting and talking. I made numerous such patrols, both day and night, partly as a way to keep from thinking—because thinking brought up a witches' brew of feelings I would rather do without. I knew every adult in town on a first-name or first-word basis and could ask after their children or their business. If they had a problem, they would talk to me. All of which kept the violence and even the petty theft down, which everybody liked. I'd fired my pistol only once after the day I shot Jeremiah in the street, and that was at a guy who got drunk and started pistol-whipping his wife on the boardwalk.

That didn't mean I wasn't careful. Twice I got tips—once from Al and once from Tonya—that some farm boy awash in testosterone was going to prove how tough he was by taking me on. Tonya made a point of telling me she had tried to talk the kid out of it, while Al included his tip with the usual breakfast gossip. I was able to prepare, and they both went back to their farms without gunfire, one of them with a wet pair of pants. Tonya told me the family appreciated my discretion. Still, I never stood or sat with my back to a door. That had become a habit.

I had gone out to Charity's farm a few times. Elvy always greeted me with a hug. I even picked her up once and hugged her back. She had come to a truce with Courtesy, or more likely, the two of them kept a truce while I visited. Elvy had taken over the younger children, and I joked that we should think about promoting her to sergeant. No one understood that.

Charity was careful with food portions going into the long winter and was teaching Elvy how to figure the needs for the family and run a farm. She always had something hot and tasty for me to eat. We would sit together afterward, Charity in her rocker, and she would talk about the work on the farm and how the door was always open to me. I would often think it was time for me to walk through that door, but I never did. Charity didn't push me. I think she was fine with me leaving it at that. No Nonsense would join us and talk about his itch for adventure. I did my best to tamp that down. Those times were comfortable. Cozy.

Now, sitting in the marshal's office, I let out a sigh and watched my breath condense on the windowpane. Could I keep doing what I was doing forever? If I told myself I would do it only for the winter, what would I do when spring came? I pulled out the picture of me and Yong from its little pouch. It had become slightly creased. I should find a real frame for it, but I didn't want it away from me. I had memorized every grain of that picture, but I would still gaze at it from time to time. It's okay to cry if no one can see you do it.

I was pulled away—or saved—from my memories by the sight of a man trudging across the square toward my office. I opened the door to find Ethan, my militiaman bank teller, stomping his feet on the boardwalk outside my door. With a shapeless coat pulled over two layers of sweater and a knit hat covering his bald dome, he was almost unrecognizable. He stepped into the relative warmth of the office and pulled off his cap. The tip of his nose was red and drippy.

"Good morning, Leif!" He blew on his hands.

"Is it? If you're down here to get me this early because somebody is already out-of-control drunk, or has been shot, or both, I wouldn't say it's going to be a very good day."

He gave me a sharp look. I don't think he picked up on my humor. "You've got mail," he said, and pulled an envelope from under his coat.

I had mail. Mail was a notification that popped up on my field and opened for reading when I looked at it. This was a sealed paper envelope with MARSHAL LEIF GRETTISON, EASTVIEW in someone's actual handwriting on the front.

"It's from the army," he said. "Guo thought it shouldn't wait until you came down to the bank, so he asked me to bring it to you."

The bank also served as the town's post office. Whenever mail arrived, which was irregular, the carrier left it with Guo, and it would sit at the bank until people came to pick it up. Some farmers had an arrangement with Guo to have a rider go out and deliver their mail, but otherwise, it was held until the addressee came to town and checked. I was at the bank multiple times a day, but there had never been mail for me. After all, there wasn't anyone in the world who would send me anything.

I turned it over in my hands twice. Then I tore the flap open. Obviously, it wasn't going to open by itself.

"General Zebulon Mendenhall, commanding the Army of the Northeast, wants me to know that he will be in Eastview on the twenty-first," I said as I read the letter. "He wants to meet with me and is sending this to be sure I'm here. I wonder what this is all about?"

"Nothing, probably," said Ethan. "He's responsible for this territory; you're the new marshal. He just wants to meet you."

Based on my experience, a commanding general doesn't bother with personal meetings with the peace officer of every ramshackle town that has a seven-person militia unit. "There will be a reason," I said. "Count on it. I guess I better be in town."

.   .   .

General Zebulon Mendenhall did grace my humble office with his august presence on the morning of the twenty-first, exactly as he had said he would. I supposed that was a clue to the character of the man I was about to meet. From where I sat at my desk, I saw a group of eight heavily armed riders come across the square. I wondered if that was a desire for show on his part, or a comment about the safety of travel in our area.

They dismounted in front of the boardwalk and tied their horses to the railing. I stayed at my desk. The door opened without a knock.

The first one in was a youngish man in a long, dark gray coat of heavy wool. His face was red from the cold air. He held the door for the others, and they filed in along with the frigid outdoors.

"It is proper to stand when the general enters," the young man said when he spotted me sitting behind the desk.

There was a time when a general officer walking in on me would have brought me to attention in a nanosecond, and once at attention, I would have displayed a rigidity a marble statue would have envied. Not this time. The man in front of me wasn't even US Army. I did feel the reflex but suppressed it as I had planned. This was *my* office.

"Perhaps the general would like to have a seat so we can talk," I said. "And perhaps the rest of you can go elsewhere while we talk."

The man who had to be Mendenhall stepped forward and stopped right in front of my desk. He was an inch shorter than I was, with an erect ramrod-up-the-spine posture. A full brown beard covered most of his face and hung down below his throat. The beard was a sharp contrast with his head, which lacked any hair above his ears except for a thin fringe across the back. His eyes were the same brown as his beard, close-set to frame a long nose, and gave the sensation that he was looking through me.

Bushy eyebrows rose when he reached my desk. "Are you saying my men should wait outside in the cold?"

"No," I said. "The church is next door and is open. Depending on the length of our conversation, they may be able to say a few prayers. I'm sure they can find reasons to do that."

Mendenhall grinned all the way to crinkles at his eyes. "Of course."

He gave quick instructions to that effect. I enjoyed the expression on the face of the young man who was still holding the door open and refrigerating my office.

"We may be more comfortable standing by the fire," I said once they had left and the door had closed. I stood up at that point.

"Thank you." He walked over to the fireplace and unbuttoned his dark gray serge coat. That revealed a light gray uniform jacket and high-collared white shirt underneath. When he pulled off the overcoat, I could see small shoulder tabs without any insignia of rank.

"We do need to talk," he said when I joined him, "since I understand you are the starman here now."

"In more ways than one," I said.

That snapped his head around. His eyes locked on mine and held them.

"You won't see flashing red numbers in there," I said.

He gave a start. Then he laughed, loud enough that his men might have heard it in the church even if Be Kind was giving them one of his sermons. "I'm sorry," he said. "Yes, I've heard rumors about you. You know, we grow up with stories and prejudices and we don't even think about them when we act on them." He paused. "You are serious, though. This is not simply rumor."

"I was Staff Sergeant Leif Grettison, United States Army Rangers. Enlisted in 2055 and honorably discharged in 2062 after the fighting in the Troubles ended, if you know about that. I flew on the first starshot, the one to High Noon in 2069, and also the fifteenth in 2098." When I said it that way, I have to admit, it sounded impressive.

"I know the term, *the Troubles*, but only the name," Mendenhall said slowly. "I know nothing about specific star missions, only that there are so many stories about going to the stars and about starmen coming back that I am convinced it's all real. Please understand that we know very little, have almost no certainty, about the century or so before the Tribulation." He shrugged, then rubbed his hands in front of the fire. "You staged this. So that you could gauge my reaction. Why?"

"I've seen some interesting reactions to the words *electronics* and *computers*," I said. "A little prudence seemed like a good idea, since you're the military governor."

"With regard to those things, yes. That's why there are ruins and skeletons wherever you look. People do not forget what is always in their faces. But starmen . . . real starmen. As I said, those are stories people tell. That we did go out to the stars. That there are people who went out and who came back. The Saints claimed they were starmen and starwomen; that's what the stories and the church lore say. I'm sure it's true, even if it's been made almost into myth today. That's why we call people who wear that star"—he pointed at mine—"starmen." He sighed. "But you are not ten feet tall, you can't heal with a touch of your hand, and you probably can't right all wrongs within the sound of your voice."

"No. I'm sorry."

He chuckled. "You did say you were a soldier. And you might be real. Please convince me."

I told him my tale, much as I had at Charity's farmhouse. He listened intently. When I reached the point where I landed back on Earth, I pulled out my pistol. I slid the clip out and handed both parts to him.

Mendenhall spent some time with both the pistol and its clip. He checked the action, opened the weapon, and checked the parts. He took a little time to play with it; then he snapped everything back in place and handed it back to me.

"It's a beautiful weapon," he said, "and, yes, that makes me believe what you say. It is in perfect condition, not something pulled from a ruin. The bullets are distinctive. We cannot make anything like that today."

I holstered the pistol. "Why not?" I asked. "You make rifles and pistols, and you must have found examples of these in the ruins."

"You wonder why?" His voice sharpened. "It's the same reason I know nothing about the Troubles or the actual star missions. I don't even know who was in charge in this country when the Tribulation happened, or why the wars happened, or what truly did happen. The reason is that the people who lived then put all the information into their *computers*. I don't even really know what a computer was, beyond a machine that could somehow think, and I have no idea how people put all their information into them, but that's what they did.

"The stories tell us that they fought their wars with computers as well as armies. Again, I do not know how you can fight with computers; it's probably nothing so simple as artillery and counterbattery fire. Somehow, they used computers and other electronics to *twist* what was in the computers so the information didn't make sense, or so it would even kill people if they tried to use it. Nothing was printed then. Or if it was, they got rid of the printed books, put everything in the computers, and only printed from what was in the *computers*—so even the print was just as twisted. Do you know who George Washington was?"

The abrupt question made me look at him. His eyebrows had drawn close together and lines furrowed his forehead. Firelight glinted from his eyes.

"Of course I do," I said.

"Hnnh. You think so. We call it George's dilemma. I can show you printed books we've found that say he was a Russian agent paid to undermine the British, others that say he was a French agent paid for the same, some that the British bribed him to turn over a key fortress—and when the plot was uncovered, he framed a loyal general and fought the British to save himself. Some books claimed that he had a male lover and revolted when he was threatened with exposure, yet others that he was the son of an escaped African slave and a white woman from New York, who planned to free the slaves but was forced from office before he could. Others say that he was a white planter from Virginia who was unbelievably patriotic for a state that didn't exist. It's the same for everything from history to industry, though history is the worst. Either it was never printed, or what was printed was also twisted. What is true? When you have so many versions of history, you have no history."

"I could tell you the truth," I said.

"Maybe," he replied. "But no one would believe you. They would assume you picked a version that suited your purpose." He stroked his beard and looked into the fire. "During the Tribulation, all the computers died and everything in them vanished. When that happened, people had no knowledge of anything, unless it was in their own heads, because they had used the computers for everything. So, the people who survived the wars starved during the Three Years' Winter because they had no idea how to grow food, or move it, or find it. All the information had been in the computers. They froze when they could have had heat. They didn't know how to do anything without the goddamn computers. So they died. This will never happen again. I can promise you that."

After his voice ran down and stopped, we both stared at the flames. I thought about the colonists we had taken to Heaven, who had to learn how to do work themselves and not depend on a bot to do it for them. My mind conjured cities full of people who starved because crops failed and transportation networks stopped bringing food, and refrigeration no longer worked, and water no longer came out of a faucet. I thought about the Saints, who were starfolk, whose ship brought them back in the midst of apocalypse. They would have been from the New Golden Age, people who had been promised a future of peace and plenty. What must they have thought to find millions, billions, of people dead and dying? They had tried to help. They had done their best. Would I have done as well as they did? I felt a chill in the room the fire could not take away.

"What do you know about luck?"

Mendenhall's question jolted me out of my reverie. I had forgotten he was in the room with me. "I have an acquaintance with the concept," I said.

He grunted. "Luck is why we still have what we do have," he said. "I don't know how many people used to live here and how many died. It was millions, tens of millions, hundreds of millions. There will never be an accurate reckoning. If only a few percent of hundreds of millions of people survived the wars and the Die-off, that was still a large number of people. By luck, some of them found enough food to get through the Three Years' Winter. To be sure, they also ate the dead. Rats ate the dead, too, and then the people ate the rats. Some people heeded what the Saints preached. Of them, some were lucky enough to find libraries with old print books. Not old books that had been put into computers and then printed *from* the computers. Nobody will trust those, and for good reason. But some places had genuine old print from long ago. Of those who found genuine books, some were industrious enough to use that information to build what we have now. It will all appear old-style to you, I imagine, because no one trusts anything that is not clearly old. Before 1900, is what we usually say. And that is the answer to your question about the pistol."

"But even starting from material that old, why haven't you got the power on again? You can manufacture, you should be able to generate electricity. Even if people are scared of it, they'll get over it."

"Do you think people didn't try?" Mendenhall's voice was harsh. "All the old systems were run by computers. Dead. Parts of the plants are melted. We would have to build new ones, and there is no fuel that's easy to reach anymore. People wasted effort and starved while they did. The work has to be for food first. Food, and then weapons to secure the food. Maybe someday," his voice became wistful, "we can have it without computers . . . but not now."

I heard the intensity, the ache in his voice as he told me all of this. I could appreciate his feelings. But not the priorities. Food I could understand. But weapons as most important after food? "How is it that after all of this, we still have armies and we talk of more fighting and wars. Are humans fundamentally insane?"

Mendenhall shook his head. "Have you ever seen oil drops spattered on a hard surface?" I nodded. "Well, as I told you, people survived in some places by luck. Not many places. Most of the land was populated only by bones. Where people did survive, the population increased and spread out, like the oil will." He raised his hands and made two fists, then spread his fingers wide. Then he made circles in the air with them. "When they spread far enough, they touched each other." He brushed the fingers of one hand with those of the other. "Like oil droplets that contact each other, they merged. Do you follow me?"

I had heard counterinsurgency strategy described that way, but I didn't think that was where he was headed. While he waited for an answer, I threw another log on the fire and watched the embers fly around. Finally, I asked, "What is the point here?"

"The question is always which community will rule after they merge. The communities of survivors grew into states, made contact, and fought. Those are the Formation Wars. There are two states left east of the Mississippi, and we have each expanded so that we are now in contact. West of the Mississippi are the Empty Lands. No one survived there; I don't even think ferals live there. Maybe there are people beyond the mountains that we know are even farther west, maybe not. From the two states here, maybe one will re-create the country that used to exist."

"Why does there have to be a war? We know where that leads us."

"You mean we should talk instead of fight? Negotiate a deal?" He stroked his beard again. "When bricks and stones hide the bones."

I gave him a sharp look. "I hear that line from ten-year-old children."

"I'm sure you do. It's an old saying." He grinned at me suddenly. "Well, maybe not so old as you. There are too many bones. They are all over, even now. Nothing is going to cover them up. So, it's an expression that means . . . never."

I watched a burning log split in the middle and the ends drop to the fireplace floor. Embers flew up. "So with the world in ruins, you're telling me we'll have another war."

"Ah. After more talk than I expected, you bring me to the reason I came to speak with you. Do you have anything to drink?"

"I have water." I poured him a glass. He took it with a disbelieving smile.

"Some would say that this war will be a matter of religion."

"Excuse me?"

"Yes." The flames had grown higher as we spoke, and now firelight flickered off his smooth forehead and lit up the hollows of his eyes as he bent toward it. "The Athenians are followers of the Church of All Saints of the Apocalypse." I was sure he was still smiling as he said that.

"So what? That's the same as the church next door, and from what I've heard, it's the same church all over." I had the feeling I was being set up.

"Yes." The smile was definite now, definitely nasty. "But most Athenians are reapocalyptics. They believe we are damned and will die in the final apocalypse. So it is perfectly okay to kill us and take over our land. Most of our churches are postapocalyptics, however, and preach that the Tribulation—the only one—was final. They say we are God's chosen, who will rebuild paradise and be taken to Heaven. Since the reapocalyptic church makes money by having their faithful pay for tickets to be selected by God, they are damned. Therefore it is perfectly okay to kill them and take over their land." He chuckled. "Simple, don't you think?"

I remembered Be Kind's discussion of the reapocalyptic version of the church. "That is ridiculous!" I recalled newsfeeds before and during the Troubles, what the US, Russia, and China each told its citizens about what the others intended. All the talk about patriotism.

Mendenhall's smile broadened. "If you ask me, I would say that it is nothing more than a cover for the same impulse that has caused all the Formation Wars: the intent to kill people and take control of their land and food. I would prefer that we not be the ones killed."

I told him that I had heard much the same talk long before and was not impressed with how it had ended.

He nodded and adjusted his collar. "I am sure you are not," he said. "However, like it or not, this is the situation we have. The borders, where they exist at all, are porous—no more than broad bands of open land. Both sides claim this land, and people are settling without regard to those claims. This is a perfect setting for raiders, who are little more than brigands, no matter if they claim to be soldiers. Sooner or later, the raiders will be followed by armies. This is how the Formation Wars have gone so far."

"Are you telling me that you are bringing an army here and you want me to join it?" I had heard that line before also. "I'm not interested in rejoining an army."

"Hah!" The way that came out told me we had reached the main point of the whole visit. "There would be a commission in it, if you wanted that, but I'll not press that point. I will be frank with you, Starman Grettison." He made that sound like a rank. "You could learn the truth easily enough even if you haven't already heard it. I am not in favor with our esteemed president and his august senate, who rule this land. I have this odd idea that a government should serve its people, not its corrupt leaders. Saying so was an unwise thing to do, apparently. In consequence, I am exiled to the northeast with rank and a staff, but little more than the skeleton of an army. I have even the petty indignity of not being allowed to wear my stars, although pettiness is preferable to a firing squad.

"Our troops and the eyes of our government are farther west, where they believe the main action will be. However, this flank is vulnerable. All the raids over the years have stripped the area south and east of farms, of people who could give warning. This has been their plan, I believe. Any force coming up from the south and east of us will meet only ferals, whom they will be glad to exterminate. They will hit us where we are weak. That is what will happen, and I need enough warning to actually raise an army before we have our own personal apocalypse."

"Nice speech. What is it you are going to ask me to do?"

"I like people who are direct. This town is the farthest east and south on this frontier, so reconnaissance from here will be important. Have your militia, such as it is, out scouting. As far as they will go, south and east. As often as they will go. If the Athenians plan an invasion, as I think they will, they will bring supplies forward to a city from before called Morgantown. If you can send someone down there to scout, it would be invaluable. I can provide ammunition, extra horses, solid dollars. That will help. What I can't provide is troops. Oh, and you might encourage the talk about you being a real starman. Don't leave it to rumors. There is magic in certain words and the myths that go with them. Can we agree that you and your militia will scout for me, Starman Grettison, and not as part of an army?"

I walked away from the fireplace and leaned against the desk, which scraped across the floor under my weight. Scouting made sense, I would give him that. I had seen the handiwork of the raiders. It would protect the town, which was part of the job I had taken. It would protect Charity and her kids. And scouting was something I knew how to do. I tried to think of a trap in his proposal and couldn't. "I'm not in your army, though," I said, to reemphasize the point. "I want that clear."

He nodded and held out his hand. I shook it. "Okay, if you're going to call me Starman, what should I call you? Since I'm not in the army."

"Zeb will be fine." He drew his coat back on. "My staff will leave you the ways to request supplies and report what you find."

With that, he was out the door, another icy gust replacing him.

CHAPTER TWENTY SIX

It took me three days to assemble my intrepid mini-militia at my office so I could tell them about Zeb's requests. I might be the head of the militia, but I didn't expect to be able to give orders the way I had in my platoon. That's why I brought some beer and sliced meat from Al's and laid it across my desk like a buffet. They did appreciate the food and drink.

"If you want someone on the circuit around Eastview, I'm happy to do that," Tonya said. "This thing farther south, though, I'm not that sure where Morgantown is. I'm guessing two to three days' ride, assuming we can find it. That's a lot of supplies."

"The general said he would pay for whatever we needed," I said.

"I'm sure he did," Ethan said. "What that means is that he'll give the bank a letter asking us to extend the monies against the army's credit. We have to send back to the capital for them to make good on that, which would not be a problem except for the fact that the army sometimes doesn't. Money has a way of disappearing in places. If that happens, Guo is going to want to recover from whoever spent the money."

"Which is us," Tonya said.

"Once you go two days south of here, you're in country that was never settled, even before the raiders," Constant said. "Nobody there but ferals. If the winter gets hard early, I hear stories they eat the people they catch."

"The raiders come up that way, don't they? I don't see them being eaten before they reach us," I said.

"They're in a group, and armed," Constant said.

It went on that way for a while, but the tenor of the discussion didn't change. They would take turns watching the southern approaches to East-view. Tonya would ride farther out and stay along her circuit, but that was about it. None of them was willing to go to Morgantown, where Zeb thought an invader would set up a staging area. If he was right, we needed eyes on Morgantown.

I sat in my office and brooded after they left. I had been emphatic to Zeb that I wasn't joining any army. I had, as Yong had said, contributed enough to the disaster that had engulfed the world. I had enough blood on my hands. Except . . . if raids were going to intensify, if an army was gathering and there was no warning at all, the people here would be the first casualties. It would be my fault, if I did nothing.

I had one individual who was trained to operate on his own, behind enemy lines, and far from help. Me. I kicked my desk and the whole thing shuddered. I had never been to Morgantown. I'd never even been to West Virginia, as far as I knew. I guessed I would see what was left of it. If I thought of my horse as a chopper that would insert me where I needed to be and then extract me at the end, I could think of this as a long-range recon. I kicked the desk again. A nail fell to the floor and one leg tilted. I cursed.

I found Constant and told him to get me supplies for ten days, an extra pistol, and plenty of ammunition. I left him a lot of discretion around the supplies, because my mind thought in terms of ReadyMeals and Hi-Cal bars, not beef jerky. I told Constant that I would trust that Zeb was good for the money. If there was a problem, I figured Guo might think twice about going after me. Then I found Hezekiah and told him that, as the previous marshal, he had to be my deputy until I came back. That done, I left Constant to make the arrangements and rode out to Charity's farm.

.   .   .

I didn't want a scene. I didn't think we needed to have one. So all I said when we were together in the main room was that I would be doing some scouting south of the town and would be gone a week or two. Charity managed a good display of stoicism, or maybe she was giving up on the idea that I would stay at the farm with her. She told me to be careful and to see her when I came back.

Naturally, as this played out, Elvy butted in. She thought I should take her with me. "I can show you how to take care of yourself in the wild," she said. "I know how we indies do it."

"I know how to do that, Elvy."

She planted herself in front of me, and her green eyes bored into mine. "Well, I can show you how to find your way where you're goin'. I know how to do that."

"I've been trained to do that, Elvy. I've done it before." I reflected that I was used to having much better maps, but I had been dropped in the middle of nowhere with next to nothing and managed to find my way. It was hard to break away from that gaze, though.

Elvy was not giving up. "Well, I can help you when you fall off your horse."

I noticed she said *when* and not *if*. It was enough to bring a laugh and a smile to Charity's face, so I let it slide, because something about Charity's smile suddenly riveted me. It was as though this were the first time I had noticed that she was a beautiful woman smiling at me with warmth in her eyes. I wanted to reach out and pull her close, but I stopped myself. That would have created the scene I didn't want.

"What about me?" No Nonsense asked. "I'm a good rider and a decent shot. Two is safer than one."

"Actually, no." I shook my head. "You don't have my training or experience. And I can't see coming back here and telling your ma something happened to you." The truth was that I would need to take care of him in the wild, which would increase the risk for both of us. I was better off on my own. It was more of an effort to leave that house than I would have thought.

.   .   .

When I returned to Eastview, I found that Constant had pulled together my supplies. He had also brought an extra horse, a factor that hadn't figured into my planning.

"The horse is a loan," he said. "Hezekiah put up the money for this—so, please, please, bring the horse back."

"So, everything is all right if this horse gets back, even if I don't?"

"Exactly."

We both laughed about the horse, raising clouds of breath in the cold air. With that, I was off.

Even under a bright morning sun, the air was chilly. A thin crust atop the snow crunched under the hooves of the horses. The layers of shirts and two sweaters under my long trail coat were no match for the thermal gear I used to have, but they kept me warm enough.

The surroundings were quiet, and I felt better once I was alone. I scanned the area around me constantly, but that was an automatic action from countless patrols and recons past. The route was easy. The old roads were mostly buried, under snow if nothing else, but even without any pavement to follow, the land was level where they ran. In many places, bushes had grown over the roads, but mile markers still stuck up here and there, or the metal poles that had supported a now-fallen sign. I saw the wreck of an old car on the first day out: tires flat, metal rusted, windows broken. Next to it was an old sign hanging on its post by one bolt. It read EVACUATION ROUTE AA. There was no trace of occupants. I suspected I might find bones not too far away but had no inclination to look. What would have been the point?

As the daylight began to fade, clouds floated in from the west and I looked for a place to spend the night. The flat land along the old road was not where I wanted to camp. I did not want to be exposed to marauders, and going by a few howls I heard, not all the danger went on two feet.

A short hike along the slope to my right turned up a deep notch in the hillside. I could wedge into the rear of that. The horses would fit in the front and still have some protection. Once positioned, I tended to the horses the way No Nonsense had taught me at the farm. It didn't matter if it was fuel in the chopper, battery charge in the personnel carrier, or feed in the horse, you take care of your transportation or there won't be any. Personally, I preferred moving by helicopter, but horse and saddle were what I had.

Once I took care of them, I had a meal of beef jerky and settled in for a cold camp. The comfort of heat from a fire wasn't worth the risk of smoke curling up into the air. I pulled the long coat closed to help keep my own heat in. I had camped in colder weather than this. My thoughts drifted back to a long winter recon during Central Asia II, the beginning of what made the world I was stuck in. I knew what Yong would say about that. I drifted off to sleep imagining her voice in my ear. I dreamed I was flying back to the stars with Yong, but when she turned in the pilot-in-command seat to look at me, her eyes had irises of polished jade green.

.   .   .

I awoke stiff the next morning. I told myself that this was what happened when you got old, but even I didn't find the joke funny.

The sky above looked like a sheet of lead, and the wind had that raw, wet feel I remembered from childhood as a harbinger of snow. I had no way of telling how much might fall, though. My weather app was useless. I figured if the snow got too heavy, there would be a ruin I could shelter in and make the best of it. I saddled up and headed south, grateful that my compass app did work.

As it turned out, only light flurries fell on and off through the morning. Then the low clouds cleared enough that I could see the outlines of Pittsburgh's ruins to the west. That was, doubtless, an impossible maze. I had no intention of going into it. I was happy when the terrain hid it from view. It was as morbid as a burned-out funeral pyre.

I did find more old wrecks along the path of the road. Some of them might have run out of battery, but at the ruins of a small shopping plaza, cars seemed to have been driven into one another from all different angles. At first, it didn't make sense. These would all have been autonomous vehicles, not dependent on the skill of a human driver. That was when I remembered the malware on GSY Station and the note in the ISC offices. What if the cars had been infected and that caused the computers driving them to intentionally crash into other cars? Had the malware been that malevolent when the world fell apart at the end? Sadly, and probably, yes.

I wondered if bones were still scattered in the brush that had grown up around the site of the wrecks. They would be hidden by snow now, but more likely, time, animals, and weather in this exposed location would have disintegrated them. I dismounted next to one of the cars and peered through a broken window. A small intact skeleton sat in the rear seat. From pieces of clothing that still clung to the bones and a small doll next to the skeleton, this had been a girl. She was about the same size as Elvy.

I reached past the edges of broken glass and picked up the doll. Made of plastic, it had proved impervious to the years and the elements. Printed letters in a child's handwriting on the back of one plastic leg read *Sally's*.

Shit.

"I'm sorry, Sally." I put the doll back on the seat next to Sally so they could continue to keep each other company.

I remounted but did not leave immediately. Sally had been about Elvy's size. Had she been about the same age too? Had she been a lively kid? Had she been scared—she must have been—that day her family had tried to flee down this road? Where had they been trying to go? Nowhere had been safe. Had Sally and the others been killed in the car crashes, or had they died waiting for help that never came? Now with the dead still unburied and the world still in ruins, we were gathering forces for yet another war. Were humans, ultimately, too stupid to survive? Did I have any choice in the matter except to pick a side? I heard Yong say again, *We all have our ghosts, Soldier Boy.*

I said a short prayer for a little girl named Sally, whom I never knew. Then I rode on.

·   ·   ·

With the short days as winter approached, and the need to find shelter each night, I could see that this trip was going to take four days, not three. I wasn't too worried about the timing. I could find food if I ran short. There were signs of plenty of game in the woods, and I could eat other stuff, even if I didn't like it. The snow wasn't deep, and the horses would paw through it to find grass to supplement the feed.

Direction also wasn't a problem. In addition to the compass, my chip had *A Tourist's Map of the United States* loaded onto it as part of the original build. I had laughed at that when I first saw it, and ignored it afterward—what was the value of a 2097 tourist map to a star voyager? Even now its utility was limited, of course, because there was no system I could chip in to. And even if I had a phone, the GPS was gone, so I couldn't display my position on the map or plot a route and follow my progress. Still, it was a map and it showed the old roads. It told me that US Highway 119 crossed the Cheat River at Point Marion, the confluence of that river and the Monongahela. From there, I would be no more than ten miles north of Morgantown.

The bridge was still there, a short undistinguished span of concrete. It was clear of snow and I could see old horse droppings on the pavement. That told me the old structure would hold both me and the horses. It also told me that raiders used this route on their way north.

I would be exposed on the bridge, but the advantage of taking it compared to a search for another crossing made up my mind. I crossed quickly. After the quiet of the journey so far, the sound of the horses' hooves on the pavement was as loud as the charge of a cavalry division.

Point Marion on the other side was a deserted ruin. Shells of low brick and concrete buildings still stood against the sky. Everything else had collapsed and was covered, undistinguished mounds with snow on top marking the ruined buildings. No smoke stained the sky. Personally, I would have had sentries there, but I guess the Athenians saw no need. Nobody lived anywhere close, and no one came down the road from the north. Until me.

If I followed the Monongahela south, it would take me to Morgantown on its east bank. I kept going. It wasn't long before I saw smoke in the sky in the direction of my destination. That slowed my pace considerably. I did not want to be seen.

I came into an area that had once been a university, based on signs I saw around the buildings. Lots of buildings of brick, stone, and concrete. Those were mostly intact in the midst of a wood that had grown up around them. The fact that those massive brick structures were still there made me think people had not resettled anywhere near Morgantown. They would have scavenged the brick.

That had both an advantage and a disadvantage. The area would have few people; I would not run into some poor guy going about his daily business. The downside was that there was no civilian population to blend into. If I *was* seen, I would have a problem. I tied the horses up out of sight—I hoped—by an old stone building with an intact eight-sided tower. BE KIND AT THE LAST had been painted on one of the sides, barely visible now. It would be easy to find on my way back, even if I was in a hurry. Then I slung the rifle and headed off on foot.

My first target was the riverbank in the center of town. I could hear noise coming from that direction: banging and clanking and shouted voices. I moved cautiously toward the sounds, going from one dead building to the next. Here, so much ground was paved over or built on that no forest had grown. Brush did choke every open patch of ground, and roots were breaking up some of the pavement, but this was still a recognizable city. The old brick and concrete buildings were mostly intact, although some of the upper stories had collapsed and all the windows were broken. Piles of rubble and glass dotted the streets, partly covered by snow. I thought about working my way through the abandoned buildings and poked my head into one of the empty window frames. The floor had fallen into the basement. It was safer to creep around the buildings than to go through them.

When I eventually reached a vantage point over the river, I found the source of the noise. A barge was tied up at a crude wooden dock. Past the dock, there was a bridge across the river, or there had been. The middle of the span had fallen into the river. I wriggled through a screen of brush and lay on my stomach in the snow to watch. Teams of men were unloading sacks from the barge and putting them into wagons. It was all lift and carry, no mechanized equipment anywhere. I couldn't tell what was being loaded on the wagons, but I didn't have to.

At the stern of the barge sat a row of four artillery pieces. They looked like pieces from a history book: long, ugly tubes mounted on wheels. At a guess, I would have said they were 155 mm or 105 mm howitzers. Those things had only one purpose. And this would not be a singular barge that had arrived coincidentally with me. Not with four artillery pieces. This would be one of many coming up the river on a regular basis. Zeb was right!

However, where was this stuff going? Raiders who harassed the area around Eastview didn't bring artillery with them, and four pieces didn't make an army. So far, I hadn't seen anything in Morgantown that suggested an army was camped here. I needed more information.

CHAPTER TWENTY SEVEN

Artillery was likely to go to wherever an army was, so I decided to follow the wagons when they left the dock. I could see the road the wagons would need to follow as they moved into the built-up area, but there was too much debris between us for me to try to tag along with them. I needed to move farther into the city, then shift over to come onto the flank of their route and fall in behind.

I cleared a corner onto another street, one that looked the same as all the others. I was moving past masonry piled on top of crushed cars and across sidewalks, squinting from the broken glass glinting in the sunshine, when I had this odd sensation that I was being watched. I spun around, pistol in my hand, and saw a seated man in the midst of the mess. I damned near blew his head off, and gave away my position in the bargain, before I realized he was a statue. Curiosity got the better of me and I took a brief side trip. He was a man with a broad, silly smile, dressed in a suit that had been long out of fashion when I was born. The inscription on the base of the statute read DON KNOTTS. I had no idea who that was or why he had a statue there. At least he had survived the apocalypse and the end of the world with a smile on his face.

A loud curse and rattle of wagons pulled my attention back to my mission of finding the staging area for an invasion. A jog up one more street gave me a clear path to the route the wagons were taking. I caught up to them and fell in behind to tail them at a safe distance.

There were three wagons, each drawn by two horses, with a driver and a man armed with a rifle seated next to the driver. At the front of this short column were the artillery pieces I had seen, each pulled by a horse. I still could not see what was loaded in the wagons, just burlap sacks that could be anything. What I could pick up, though, were snippets of conversation between the driver of the last wagon and the man riding it with him.

". . . assholes just like to see us do extra work . . . could float this all the way from Fairmont to Pitt . . ."

". . . Pitt's all dead . . . goin' east . . ."

". . . all dead there . . . point is . . ."

Trying to get closer, I dislodged some loose brick, and the rifleman swung his head around. I shrank back into a convenient shadow.

". . . not have fuckin' ferals . . ."

". . . fun to kill a few . . ."

I indulged in the thought that maybe I could kill the two of them instead. For security, though, I needed to allow more space between me and the wagons. I had to give up the fantasy of killing them as well as listening to them.

What had they been talking about when one of them mentioned going east? The road they were on headed mostly northeast. I held that question for later and continued to tail them. After what I figured was three miles, I saw a half-buried sign for Morgantown Municipal Airport. An airport? Nothing was flying over planet Earth these days. Why take horse-drawn wagons and artillery to an airport?

As I got closer, I heard noise—an inchoate noise of many people—from the direction of the airport, then a rhythmic tramping sound. I looked for someplace I could get a better view and spotted a parking garage. Three stories high, it would give me what I needed. I let the wagons go on their way, which seemed to be toward the airfield, while I hustled for the up-ramp.

The scene on the first floor of the garage brought me to an abrupt halt. I gaped. "Jesus Christ." The concrete floor was covered in bones and skulls. Here and there were random piles of them. Near the entrance, the bones—leg bones, arm bones, ribs, vertebrae—had been heaped into a stack five feet high, with a skull carefully placed on top.

Mass murder. That was my first thought. I had come upon sites during the Troubles where civilians, or sometimes captured soldiers, had been executed and dumped in a ditch. But what I had seen then was ten, maybe twenty bodies at a site. I couldn't guess how many had died here.

I got control of myself and looked closer. I didn't see a whole skeleton anywhere. Not even half a skeleton. This was a macabre assembly of random bones. I saw no bullet wounds, no bones that had been burst the way they do when a high-velocity bullet hits them. These people had not been killed in the garage. They hadn't even been killed elsewhere and dumped here. They had died somewhere else, somewhere protected enough that the bones remained a century after the unburied bodies had decayed. Possibly they had been in the buildings and hangars of the airport and died there. So how did they end up in this garage?

A nightmare of what had happened blossomed in my mind. How many people had thronged to this airport looking to escape? What did they need to escape from, and where did they think they were going? I had no answers to that. Whatever they hoped for, this had been a dead end. No planes would have been flying. Yet thirst and starvation don't kill you immediately. Why did they stay here and die? Why didn't they leave?

The answer was both sad and simple. When your transportation was a battery-powered car that drove itself by connecting to the internet, and when both the power and the internet were down, you couldn't travel. It's not as though they had horses. Or could self-drive their cars. They sat and waited for help, which is what they were probably conditioned to do. And help never came. So they died. A century and more later, someone wanted to make use of the airport and tossed the bones in the garage. Bricks and stones will hide the bones. Not here. Not for a long, long time.

I was a hardened combat veteran. I had been sure I was pretty callous. No. You don't really know your emotional limits until you feel your stomach churn.

I pulled my eyes away from all the bones. I had work to do, and that did not include getting sick like some FNG. I ran up the ramp to the roof. A car was parked on flat tires by the railing on the airfield side of the structure. It was otherwise intact and gave me a good concealed location from which to survey the airport below. The airport might no longer serve air traffic, but the flat, open space where the runways had been made a good mustering ground. I saw rows of tents. Beyond them was a crowd of men and some women, some mounted and some on foot. More wagons, and more horse-drawn artillery. Flags I did not recognize accompanied them.

A column was leaving, headed east. How many? At first glance, the force looked bigger than it was. My estimate, when I worked at a count, was five to ten thousand soldiers. The foot soldiers were all carrying rifles. I had no idea, of course, if more were in the tents. I didn't know how many men and women might have gone before, or if more were still to come. Nevertheless, whatever its true dimensions, this was no raiding party heading east. This was an army.

My old tourist map said Interstate 68 was a little north of the airport, and that would take you due east. Even if the roadway was overgrown, like everything else, it would offer a flat route that cut through any rough terrain. If its bridges were still standing, it would be an ideal avenue east.

But what was east of here? A straight line would take them just north of the capital—the old capital—at Washington, DC. They couldn't be headed there. That area had been nuked and consumed in a firestorm after the blast. We had seen the remains from orbit. These people had to know that. Which meant that at some point along their route, they were going to turn.

It had to be to the north. Logically, an army on the move could have only one destination, that open eastern flank Zeb had worried about. I had to get word to Zeb.

I can run three miles in eighteen minutes, or could. But the ground between the airport and the downtown was covered with a layer of snow. The snow wasn't that deep, but it created slippery patches and hid a brick here or the base of a post there that led to stumbles. My knee reminded me very quickly that it had been badly abused on my arrival and was still not 100 percent. I wasn't managing anything close to six minutes a mile. By the time I reached the downtown area near the university, where I had left the horses, I was pushing myself as hard as I could. I wanted to be on my way out of town before dark. I was not so watchful as I should have been and probably made more noise than was wise.

I rounded the corner of a partially demolished building that had burned down, when a man stepped in front of me, pistol leveled at my chest.

"Well, look what we have here," he said. "Drop the rifle. Now!"

I dropped it and raised my hands in the air.

The man had a narrow pale face framed by a scraggly, untrimmed black beard. I could see crooked teeth when he smiled. He wore the same type of leather duster I had seen on the men I'd killed up north.

Two other men came up to stand with him.

"Not a feral, d'ya think, Vernon," said one of them, a squat man with broad shoulders, unruly black hair, and skin as dark as the old burned brick next to him.

"Not a chance, Sworn Word," said the man addressed as Vernon. "Even a brown-eyed feral wouldn't have weapons or clothes like that. We've caught a little spy. You," he said to me, "undo the belt so the gun and the knife drop. We do want to talk to you, but I'm happy to settle for killing you if you make a move I don't like."

I saw no reason to doubt him. With careful movements, I did as he told me.

"Now get your hands up again." I did what I was told. "Sworn Word," Vernon said, "get your horse from back there"—he gave a little jerk of his head—"and ride back to the lieutenant. Tell him what we got and ask if he'll wait on our troop riding north till I bring him this asshole and we can question him."

I processed that as the Black man departed. These men were part of a raider unit, and there were more of them here. They had to be using Morgantown as a forward base also, and I had the bad luck to run into this group before they left. Had I taken my time coming back from the airport, I might have missed them completely. I found a moment to wonder if they were coordinating their activities with that army or freelancing. It was an interesting question, but I had no time for it just then.

"Now, little spy," Vernon said to me, "you're going to come with us and then you're going to tell the lieutenant everything you know and everything you've been doing. If you want to live to see the sun come up again, you'll do just what I say and do a lot of talking. And trust me, spy, if it comes to killing you, I'm going to make it fun for me."

No, I thought, *that's not the way it will go. Once you two have brought me to this lieutenant and his camp, you'll have me tied up. And when the talk is done, I'll be dead.* I could see it in his eyes. They were too eager when he talked about killing.

Then he did something stupid. He stepped up to me and stuck the muzzle of his pistol into my mouth so it knocked against my teeth. "Don't think you're going to yell for help if you've got a partner. And you keep those hands up."

My hands stayed up. I couldn't say much, because the business end of the pistol was in my mouth. This was pure intimidation on his part, but it was stupid.

We've all seen the vids where the bad guy is covering our unarmed hero with a pistol, but our hero makes a lightning move so the shot misses, and before the bad guy can correct his aim, our hero is on him and takes the weapon away. Wrong. It doesn't work like that. Our hero is not faster than a speeding bullet, and the instant he moves, that gun will fire. It takes very little time to adjust the aim at point-blank range. In real life, that would be a dead hero almost every time. But there is one situation where the hero has a reasonable chance, and that is when the bad guy is dumb enough to put the pistol right up against him.

I twisted my body and pulled my head to the left while my raised left hand—which I had kept up as instructed, but not far from the pistol—went for his gun hand. I grabbed his hand and knocked the pistol offline to my right. The weapon fired, but my head was no longer in front of it. That move had taken less time than him realizing I was moving and squeezing the trigger. That's how the bad guy misses.

I got both hands on his gun hand, put him in a wristlock, and twisted so the pistol pointed up. Then I snapped his wrist back toward his elbow. Wrists aren't built to bend that far. There was a snap. He screamed. I yanked him forward and down by that wrist. His finger was still on the trigger and he fired, not realizing the pistol was pointing at him. Blew a hole in his left shoulder. Blood and tissue flew out of his back. I squeezed his finger down on the trigger. Another shot. This one hit him in the middle of his chest. His muscles went slack.

I ripped the pistol out of his dead hand. The third man was wide-eyed, hand on his pistol grip, trying to tug it from its holster. I brought the pistol up and fired twice. Two head shots. He dropped.

I straightened and took a breath. My heart was pounding, and I was glad it was still able to pound. That had been close. Well, close only counted in horseshoes, hand grenades, and docking spaceships. By the time I had gathered up my weapons, my pulse was back to normal.

I needed to get out of there. Whatever Sworn Word had been sent to tell the lieutenant, those gunshots changed everything. Someone would have heard them. People would come looking, and they would be in "shoot first" mode. Who knew how many there would be?

It seemed likely that the three of them had tied up their horses together. I went around the burned building and, indeed, two horses were there. I picked one at random and mounted it. I thought of the packhorse and supplies I had left at the eight-sided tower and dismissed the thought at once. I wasn't going to take a chance going back there. I needed to move fast. I'd have to worry about supplies later.

I headed toward the Monongahela. If I could get to the west bank, that would improve my situation considerably, but the bridge I had seen near the dock was out. At least I had not seen any sign of raiders by the river earlier. The way I had come in seemed like my best way out. I picked my way north, watching for pursuit until I cleared the built-up area.

I thought I was going to get away clean until, on a quick check to the rear, I saw movement at the edge of a building. Was I being tracked? Well, if someone was there, it was unlikely they were out to pick up a latte. I considered my options.

I had to get across the Cheat River. The easiest way was the highway bridge, the way I had come down, but the raiders obviously knew that bridge. If I was being tailed, making a run for it and galloping across the bridge with a pack of them at my back was not a recipe for reaching old age. On the other hand, trying to swim that river on a horse in freezing weather didn't sound good either. I had no idea if I could find a ford. I would be able to plan better if I knew what I was facing.

A little farther on, I came to a three-story building north of Morgantown that had a good view to the south. I tied up my stolen horse out of sight and prayed that the stairs inside hadn't rotted through. They were concrete. Thank God for small favors. Enough of the third floor was intact that I could position myself at a window to watch.

The projection field from the chip Earthbase had given me in 2097 had some magnification capabilities. It wasn't as good as a combat visor, and nowhere near single-purpose binoculars, but it was a hell of a lot better than squinting and praying. I would see them before they could see me. The Winchester I had wasn't a sniper rifle, but if there was only one tracker, or even two, I'd have a reasonable chance of taking them out and then slipping away with no one else the wiser.

It took a while, but eventually I saw a horseman pop into the cleared area past the ruins. Then another. More kept appearing. Ultimately, I counted twenty-two headed in my direction. Not great odds. Any place that I picked to make a stand, they had enough numbers to overwhelm me. I supposed I should have felt flattered that they sent twenty-two after little old me, but being flattered and then killed never did anyone any good.

Then I had a different and more disturbing thought. The trio that briefly captured me had spoken of a troop going north. Suppose the lieutenant they mentioned had, after those gunshots, decided to move out immediately? When they saw the tracks of my horse, they might figure they would run me down in the process of their mission. What was their mission? I slipped back down the stairs, retrieved my horse, and galloped north toward Point Marion.

My mind gnawed at the problem of their mission as I rode. What mission would be given to a troop of twenty-four—given that I had already killed two—raiders? That was far more than needed to terrorize farmers. The gang I'd killed when I rescued Elvy had numbered six.

Maybe they were going to split up into smaller groups to maximize the number of farms they could hit.

Or was it possible they were going to attack the town of Eastview?

To counter the raiders' mission, I had my valiant militia of six—seven including me—and they were not a standing army. Back during the Troubles, if a reserve unit was called for active duty, the commander would send a call-up notification. That would pop up on each service member's field with an alarm that overrode any privacy setting. Service members had to respond within an hour and be on the way to the assembly point within a day. My militia was only six people and they had to be fairly close to town, but it had taken Constant a week to bring them together for a shooting demonstration. I needed to disorganize the raiders and buy myself more time to pull everyone together. I needed to get inventive.

· · ·

I reached the remains of Point Marion at dusk. A horse leaves a pretty clear trail on snow-covered ground, but following it in the dark wouldn't be so easy, especially not with a crescent moon and cloud cover. I didn't go for the bridge. I took a route through town where I wouldn't leave an obvious track, then headed east and south along the Cheat River before turning back to the west. I found a spot hidden by trees and brush to observe from and settled in to watch. The horse wasn't happy with the grass it could uncover, but I couldn't do much about it at that moment. I waited for my pursuers.

The troop of raiders made camp short of the town on some relatively clear ground. They set up tents and built some fires. It would have been easier for me if they had moved into the ruins or camped among the trees and brush, but I could work with the situation they gave me. I shifted my position to be as close to them as I could while keeping to cover. I watched and waited.

Time passed. They appeared at ease. Maybe they were complacent, this close to their base at Morgantown. I hoped so. They ate their meal and retired to their bedrolls. I watched and waited in the cold dark. They set a sentry. One sentry. Clouds covered the crescent moon. I waited some more. For the sentry to get cold.

I watched him stamp his feet and blow on his hands. He took a station near a fire and held his hands out to the heat. I crawled toward him from the dark and the shadows. I didn't have good camouflage and I was dark on the snow, but he was looking into the fire. I'm sure the only thought in his mind was when he would be relieved.

I rose up behind him, clamped a hand over his mouth, and drew my knife across his throat. I cut deep, halfway through his neck. It felt like I was pulling his head off when I yanked back. Blood fountained up, pumped out by a heart that hadn't quit yet.

I let the suddenly dead weight down gently by the fire. It made no noise. Then I moved quickly. My target was the horses. I cut through tethers and hobbles as fast as I could. I don't know how many I severed—more than half, I'm sure—before a spooked horse started neighing and stomping and set off the others. A couple of well-placed slaps on rumps started horses running. Others followed. I figured there was a chance they would run all the way back to Morgantown before the raiders managed to corral them.

Like I'm more of an authority on horse behavior than I am on women and children.

Shouts and curses erupted from the men in the camp as they woke and realized what was happening. I heard a yell, "Get the horses!" Then I heard different yells as someone stumbled over the corpse of the sentry. Wild shots flashed and banged in the night. Voices yelled that they were shooting at each other.

I smiled to myself. One thing I did know was what men with guns did when they were surprised in the middle of the night. Now it was time to leave. I grabbed a large sack the size of a duffel that was on the ground nearby and ran off into the dark. When I returned to my horse, I mounted up and rode for the bridge over the Cheat at Point Marion. It would be a while before they would be able to come after me, or do anything else, and there were only twenty-one of them behind me now.

CHAPTER TWENTY EIGHT

I didn't stop until I was across the bridge over the Cheat and had put some miles on the other side between me and the river. When the horse made clear it was tired, I called a halt and found a place to hole up for what was left of the night. It had been a good night's work. With any luck, it would take them all the next day to round up all their horses and get themselves reorganized. That should give me at least a day's lead, maybe more. It was possible, needless to say, that the ones who still had their horses would leave the others and come after me immediately, but that would mean dividing their force right after being attacked at night. If they did, I would bet they wouldn't find me in the dark. I could spot them when it was light, before they detected me. Then maybe an ambush would work, if the numbers were right.

I did take a few moments after I settled down to examine the sack I had taken. It held a few nose bags with horse feed, which my animal appreciated. The other objects in it were six sticks, each about two feet long, with a heavy, sticky cloth wound around one end. I studied them for a minute before I realized what I was holding. Torches. I had found six in one pack, so doubtless the raiders had more. At the bottom was a smaller sack of burlap. The contents of that proved to be old-style pineapple grenades. I held one up and considered the implications.

Brigands didn't need grenades to burn farms and murder families. If they were carrying grenades, their target had to be Eastview. Maybe afterward they would burn some farms farther north, if they had the opportunity, but their primary target had to be the town. Despite all the people who lived there and all the guns those people had, a sudden and surprise attack, maybe at night, could set the town afire and start a human stampede. I had to concede that it could be done. If the army I'd seen turned north—and what else was it going to do?—how far would it go before someone could raise an alarm? A long way, if Eastview and the farms in the area were gone. It all made sense, if the raiders were working in conjunction with that army.

Okay, I knew what the enemy was going to do. Now, what was I going to do about it?

In another day and another war, my priority would have been to find a signal and call this in. My orders after that would have been to spot for artillery or an air strike. If neither was possible, maybe because the resources were being directed against that army, I might have been ordered to set up a series of ambush points on the long route north, take out a rider here and a couple there, all the while fading back into the brush and trees and moving on before they could catch me—I hoped. If I couldn't get a signal, that's probably what I would have done on my own. With my M8 and plenty of ammo, if those raiders rode in a tight group without scouts, I could decimate them before they knew what hit them. However, back in that other time and place, I wouldn't be facing poorly equipped men on horseback with no armor.

I cursed myself for even imagining those tech-based alternatives. I was in the here and now. I could not get a signal, because no signal existed. I couldn't call in artillery or air support, because they didn't exist either. I didn't have an M8. All I had was a replica of an old Winchester that fired one bullet at a time and a semiautomatic pistol with limited ammo. This wasn't a vid game where a lone hero takes out a force of twenty-one all by himself. If I tried the ambush idea, I wouldn't get that many before they got me. I probably wouldn't kill enough to stop the attack on the town, and I would be dead. Not only that, but there would be no warning about the raiders or that army. The only way to contact the town was to physically go and tell them.

Do something else, Leif, and maybe, stay alive.

I needed time—and I didn't know how much—between when I reached Eastview and the arrival of the raiders. I needed to enlarge the separation from what I had already created. I needed to run from them as fast as I could.

I set an alarm on my chip to wake me right before dawn. Then I tried to get a little sleep.

.   .   .

I damned near killed that horse getting back to Eastview. I rode it until it couldn't go anymore and then rested as little as I could get away with. The feed wasn't enough either. What was in the sack didn't last long, and the grass we could find was inadequate. That cut down the pace the horse could manage. It also reduced the time I could ride, since I had to allow more time to find something the horse could eat. Think of it as finding only charging stations that would give your car a 10 percent charge. With the battery always close to being drained, you would always be looking for a stop. The horse was the same; it was perpetually about drained.

I had even fewer supplies for myself than for the horse. While the area harbored plenty of game, I was unwilling to take any time to hunt. Even if I had, there was no time to clean and cook what I caught. Fortunately, I could find fallen tree limbs that had rotted out. Breaking them open yielded beetles and other insects. I could also find stinkbugs, like the ones Elvy had put into Courtesy's dinner, under piles of fallen leaves, even at this time of year. It wasn't much—and it certainly wasn't wonderful—but it was enough to keep me going. That was all I asked, to keep moving for the days this ride would take.

This didn't mean I had given up on the idea of an ambush. Not at all. What I had in mind was finding a setting near town where we could wipe out this raider unit. To the last man, was the way I was thinking. *We* being my militia, reinforced by townspeople who were more likely to own a gun than a toothbrush.

I found the perfect location a little south of Eastview. The old road I was following curved west to circumvent a low ridge. Someone had built a convenience mart and charging station on the hillside facing south, and work crews had been busy constructing a ramp and underground lines when the world ended. I was pretty sure of that because a row of what we used to call Jersey barriers stood at the base of the hill along the curve of the road. They were now mostly hidden by trees and bushes. The concrete would stop a rifle bullet. The remains of the store, a little farther upslope, would be a great spot to cover troops at the barriers. The trees and vegetation were enough to give us cover, but not thick enough to block our field of fire. If I had a dozen men and women, I could turn this spot into a death trap.

When Eastview came into sight, I let out a whoop. I had been holding this image in my mind of galloping down the street Paul Revere–style, but that wouldn't have been productive. Instead, I rode to the bank, a gaunt figure in filthy clothes, stomped past the tellers, and bashed open Guo's office door. It was a pretty good entrance.

His eyebrows went up and his mouth dropped open when I told him what was coming. "I need the militia," I said. "I need them ten minutes ago. I need a dozen people from the town, armed and willing to fight. I need you to make sure everyone else in town knows. They're all armed here. That's enough weapons in town to make those raiders pay one hell of a price if they get past us. Tell them to defend their homes and shops and have water ready."

After the first shock, Guo took it all calmly. He didn't even ask why this was happening. Maybe having a gang on the way to burn down your town was just another disaster that people accepted without questioning. "Many people will want to use the time to take their children away," he said after a moment's reflection. "Many will want to leave themselves. Having weapons does not make someone a warrior."

"Defending your home often does," I said, "but I take your point. That's why I need to start with the militia. I don't know where they are, so we need to go for them now. I'm willing to bet I've got more than a day's lead on the raiders, but I won't bet it's more than two. We can't lose time."

"I will see to it." He rang a bell—the type you pick up and shake—that was sitting on his desk.

Seconds later, Ethan was in the office. Guo explained the situation to him. The man went as white as his shirt. Whiter. He ran out without a word.

Then I sat down and wrote a letter—on paper, so help me God!—to Zeb, detailing what I had seen. I gave him my troop estimates, descriptions of the artillery, the number of tents at the airfield, even descriptions of the flags I'd seen with the units. I gave myself writer's cramp. Guo promised me he would make sure it reached Zeb as fast as possible.

Okay, Leif, I told myself, now what about the town?

I wasn't sure what to expect when I stepped out of the bank to see what was happening, but what struck me was that it looked like any other day in Eastview. That probably wasn't fair to the townspeople. I told myself that when information had to move by word of mouth, it would take time for the news to spread. I needed to recalibrate my expectations, which came from an era of instant notification.

It did take a little while for the word to spread. But when it did, people reacted. The town bubbled over like an anthill at full boil. Plenty of them reacted by leaving town. Wagons appeared on the street and people ran out to them, carrying possessions they were determined not to lose. Those wagons also filled with kids, as Guo had said would happen, from babies in baskets to preteens holding a mother or father's hand. I couldn't blame them for leaving. If I had children in Eastview, I would probably have used the time to get them out as well. I had seen people react like that from Central Asia to the Philippines during the Troubles. People didn't change. It was only a different war in a different place.

Goddammit!

.   .   .

What I needed was my militia. I took a deep breath, then brought my horse to the stables and settled into my office to wait. I kept waiting. Night fell and I still waited.

Daylight came and the militia didn't. I made my way down to Al's for breakfast, figuring that everybody would know to find me there. Al had his rifle propped against the bar and a pistol in his belt. I received both breakfast and his assurance that he would ride with me later. The only person who came to find me, however, was Hezekiah. He asked about the horse he had provided, that I had left in Morgantown.

"Look, Hezekiah," I said, "I know you would rather have the horse back than me, but look at it this way. I can protect you against the raiders. That horse can't. Right?"

A reluctant nod followed.

"Then it's a fair deal. We're even."

He didn't follow the logic, but he did leave.

I finished breakfast, still without militia. The situation was becoming concerning. I couldn't be sure exactly how far behind the raiders were. We needed to reach the position I had picked with enough time to have everyone in place and instructed in what to do. I didn't want to cut it too close. I walked out to the street as though I would find them waiting outside the door. No.

I did see movement at upper-story windows and glints off rifle barrels. Some people planned to defend their property. Those buildings might turn into fiery death traps, but if the raiders did reach the town, those weapons could take a heavy toll on them. That was good.

In front of Guo's bank, a group had collected. Al was among them, holding the rifle I had seen him pull from behind the bar when conversations got too heated. It was a motley collection of about thirty, a quarter of them women. They stood in ones and twos, in no apparent order, most with pistols, some with rifles, most leading horses. They were my volunteers.

I looked them over with a sense of satisfaction. They might have no discipline or internal cohesion, and I had no idea if any of them could shoot worth a damn, but added to me and the militia, and firing from the positions I had scouted on my way up, I thought we had a good chance of wiping out the force riding toward us.

The problem was the militia. They still weren't there. I was starting to seethe. When I was in basic, if the DI told me to do something *now*, he expected I would be doing it before his mouth closed. Okay, no phones—I sort of understood that—but this was ridiculous. Ethan; McSorely, the barber; and Render Praise, the shopkeeper's assistant, lived in town. Of course, Constant's farm was to the northwest and I had no idea where Tonya and Pride Goeth lived. When I asked Al, he told me the three who lived in town had gone to find the others. I could only hope they all showed up within a few hours and that none of them was a day's ride, or more, away. Believe it or not, I missed my phone.

I thought I was going to be pleased when I finally saw Constant running pell-mell up the street. I didn't expect the message that he had for me.

"Leif, you need to come with me," he said between panted breaths. "There's going to be a fight between Hezekiah and Be Kind down in the square."

That made me boil over. I'm sure the fury I felt showed in my face. "In case you haven't heard, Constant, I called for the militia because there's going to be a fight between us and a troop of heavily armed raiders. If we don't win, the town is gone." I won't say that I kept my voice civil.

Constant straightened up and got his breath back. "We can't let them kill each other. Besides, I don't see the other five. We have time."

Did we have time? Constant was right that the rest of the militia was still MIA. Did I want to ride out with a group of random townspeople, most of whom did not have rifles, and no militia? No. Did I want to have Hezekiah and Be Kind in a fight when the town might need to be defended? Also no. I told my volunteer posse to wait for me and the militia, and I went with Constant.

The argument between Hezekiah and Be Kind was going on in public and in the square when I arrived. Hezekiah wanted every man and woman from his bordello who had a firearm to be defending the Golden Ass. Be Kind wanted them at his church. The myopia on both sides was astonishing. They were practically nose to nose, shouting at each other. Any closer and they could kiss.

I wanted to bash their heads together. I settled for shoving my way between them and pushing them back to arm's distance from me. "What the two of you are completely missing is that your buildings are right next to each other. If one of them burns, the other one is going to catch fire also. The only way to save yourselves is to save each other."

"We don't have enough people who can handle guns to do that," Hezekiah said. "Half the town is running away. The ones who will fight are either watching their own property or going with you. And you owe me a horse."

"Forget the goddamn horse for now!"

"I need people at the windows in the church," Be Kind said. "If I can have that, he can have anyone else."

In fact, both of them thought the way to defend the buildings was to fill them with people, someone at every window. They would all go up like a funeral pyre.

"Jesus," I muttered. "I don't have forever. Get me the people here who have weapons and I'll show you where to post them."

I rushed around placing people so that they had interlocking fields of fire that mostly covered both buildings. It wasn't perfect, and they wouldn't be able to coordinate their actions. None of them had any combat experience. Still, it might make an attack costly, and it would increase their chances of survival. When I was finished, I grabbed Constant and ran back up the street from the square.

I could see something was wrong as soon as I was out of the square. The group that had gathered to ride with me was gone. The only people waiting for me in front of the bank were my militia, who had apparently managed to arrive while I was dealing with Hezekiah and Be Kind.

"What the fuck happened?" I demanded as I got close.

"I got all of us here as fast as I could," Ethan said.

"You're lucky I was coming back into town for supplies!" Tonya shouted at him. "You can't expect me to appear here with no warning."

"All right, enough about that. You're here," I said. "What happened to the rest of the people?"

"They said they had waited long enough," Ethan said. "We told them we should all wait for you, but they wouldn't wait any longer."

"Where did they go? Back to their homes? We'll have to go round up as many as we can." I was thinking of how long that was going to take, and how close the raiders might be now.

When it took time to get an answer, I knew I wasn't going to like it.

"They said they were going to ride down to where you said the raiders were coming from," Tonya said at last. "They said they would stop them before they got to the town."

"What?" This was not the time for civilians to decide to be heroes. "They haven't even seen the position I picked out. They don't know how to position themselves, or how to make this work."

Tonya shrugged. "They left. They're just going to ride until they meet up with the raiders, and then they think they'll shoot them down."

"Shit." Staff Sergeant Leif Grettison had completely lost control of the situation. "We have to ride after them. If we can reach them before they run into the raiders, maybe we can still set up that ambush."

CHAPTER TWENTY NINE

It became real clear, real fast, that we were too far behind the townspeople. We reached the position I had selected for my ambush and found it deserted. A broad trail of hoofprints in the snow leading south made it evident that the townspeople had passed it and kept riding. Whether they had failed to recognize it from my brief description—I hadn't planned on them finding it on their own—or they didn't like the concept of hiding and waiting didn't matter. They had gone on.

The question I had to answer was whether to bet that they would miss the raiders and set up the ambush with only the militia, or ride after them and hope I could catch them before they ran into the attackers. The route we were on was the logical channel to take among the hills and trees. That was why I had picked the spot for an ambush. There was no reason for the raiders to come from any other direction.

As if to validate that thinking, a series of pops like a chain of fire-crackers came from the south. The rapid stutter I was used to wasn't there, because there were no automatic weapons, but it was heavy gunfire nonetheless. The two troops had ridden into each other.

"With me," I said to my six. "We need to see what's happening. Maybe it will come out okay, but we need to stay together." I didn't get an argument.

The gunfire dwindled down to only the occasional shot before we reached the battlefield. I saw a horse coming back from the south at a walk, carrying two riders: Al in the saddle holding the reins and a woman in front, slumped back against him. The right side of her coat was drenched in blood. I halted. As they reached me, I saw others coming up the trail behind them.

"I need to get Mary to the doctor," Al said. He kept his horse moving.

"Where's Josiah?" Constant called out to the riders behind Al.

"Dead," said a man's voice.

"What happened down there?" I asked as they came closer.

They looked grim, as men and women will after they have seen combat and death, but they also looked satisfied. Whatever had happened, these people were not fleeing in defeat with an enemy in pursuit.

"We fixed the bastards." I recognized the speaker as the cook who worked for Al. "They were riding up like you said, and we got 'em. Left three of them dead in the snow. The others scattered into the hills to the east so they can run back south. Josiah's dead and Mary's pretty bad, but only a couple of other minor wounds. We did it." Triumph showed in his voice then.

"Did anyone follow them?" I asked. "How do you know they're going to run back to the south and not regroup and take another route to the town?"

"They ran when they saw how many we had. They know we've got too many for them. They know they're beat. Where else are they going?"

I hate it when people make assumptions about what their enemies are going to do. That kind of thinking loses battles and gets you killed in the end.

"You don't know what they're thinking," I said. "All we can say for sure is you drove them away for now, but we don't know where they went. Until we can be sure they're running away, set up a couple of your people to keep watch outside the town."

"What are you going to do?" he asked.

"We're going to go track them and see what they're actually doing."

. . .

The little battlefield was not too much farther south down the trail. The trees and bushes that pressed close to the sides of the old road and invaded the roadbed in places opened into a small glade. The two groups of riders had run into each other there. I didn't see anything that suggested either side had planned for a fight. The snow in the glade had been beaten down with hoofprints everywhere. It had been a melee on horseback, with firearms instead of swords. I saw the bodies of the three raiders—two in the middle of the open ground and the third to one side, his head and torso hidden in the brush, his legs sticking out. Blood stained the snow around them. Another puddle of blood marked the spot where I figured the man named Josiah had fallen, closer to where we entered the space. The towns-folk must have collected his body to take it back for burial, although I didn't recall seeing a body draped over a horse. The three raiders had been left behind for the animals.

It didn't take long to pick up the track of the remaining raiders. Eighteen horses galloping through the snow are not exactly subtle. They had headed east, as the cook had said, through a notch between two tree-covered mounds too low to call hills.

"Another one over here!" Tonya called out.

I rode over to see what she had found. It was another man in a duster, half sitting up with his back against a tree. Snow was clumped in his beard. He clutched a pistol in one hand but it lay next to his leg, pointing only at the ground. I dismounted to take a closer look.

There was a man-sized dent in the snow next to some hoofprints, about ten feet from the tree, and a track about as wide as a man from there to where he sat. Clotted and frozen blood marked both.

"Shot and fell off his horse," I said as I looked at the track. "Either he was left for dead or was at the rear and no one noticed."

I walked over to the tree, hoping he had enough spark of life left for us to get something out of him, but it was plain he was dead. No information beyond one more down and seventeen to go.

We followed the trail forward to the east, to a place where the woods thinned out. The raiders had regrouped in that spot. Tracks coming from other directions under the trees merged there, and the snow was stamped flat. Scouting around the edge of the meeting place revealed a trail made by multiple horses. The raiders had reassembled and headed off.

"They're not headed south." Tonya sounded surprised.

I wasn't surprised. "Not at all," I said. "North and a bit east."

"Do you think they're going to turn west and come at the town from that direction?" Constant asked. "You warned the others they might do that."

"There's not much else they can do from here," Tonya said. "Unless they've decided the town is too tough for them and they're going to pick off some more farms and burn them. But the way they're going, well, there're damned few farms farther east." She looked at the land and the track again. "The first farm they'll reach is Charity's." Then she looked at me.

I said, "Maybe," but my stomach dropped like a rock off a cliff. Tonya knew the land around Eastview. I had lost Yong. I was not going to lose Charity. I would not allow it. "We need to catch up to them," I said, "and when we catch them, we are going to deal with them." It took all the effort I could muster to keep my voice cold and unemotional, the way it should be in the field.

"Why only us?" asked Constant. "Why don't we go back and pick up some of the townspeople who already fought them?"

"Constant is right," said Ethan. "As it is, if we go after them, we're outnumbered more than two to one. It's almost three to one. We need to bring more people."

"Jesus! This is not a debating society!" The expression on my face made Ethan startle. That was transmitted to his horse, which shied away.

"Leif has already killed three by himself," Tonya said, "and the towns-people killed another four. These raiders aren't invincible, and people need our help."

"Yes," said Constant, "but it would still be seven riding against seventeen, and they will be on alert now."

"Dammit!" I could feel my anger and my voice rising. "There is no time to go back and get more people. If we do, by the time we get back on their trail, they will have hit one farm, maybe more." I didn't say which farm would be hit first—but, yes, that was fueling my anger. "Our job is to keep them from killing our farm families. That's what we're here for. So, listen to me! I am a starman, a real starman. You know that. But before that, I was a soldier. I fought in the wars before the apocalypse. I know what we have to do."

The four men, including Constant, seemed to be studying the ground around their horses' hooves. The two women were looking at me. None of them spoke.

"All right," I said. "If you're afraid of the odds, okay. I understand that. Go back and get help. But I'm going forward. That's all I have to say."

"You know I'm with you, Leif," said Tonya. "You're not going alone." The look she gave the men was contemptuous.

"Me too," said Pride Goeth.

One by one, the men averred that they were ready to go with us, that I had mistaken an honest discussion for their true feelings. I kept my face a mask even though I wanted to smile. No matter how times and cultures change, nothing can shame a bunch of men into doing what they need to do faster than having a couple of women lead the way.

CHAPTER THIRTY

I wanted to catch up to the raiders before we lost the light, but days are short in December, and we couldn't do it. I wanted to keep going even when night fell, but clouds had rolled in to block the moon. That made for a dark night, and the trail wound back into the trees and bushes. My combat visor, with its night vision and infrared settings, belonged to history. My chip gave me some capabilities for that on my projection field even without the phone base, but the others lacked it, and I didn't want a discussion about how I could see in the dark and they couldn't. As far as my militia were concerned, it would be far too easy to miss a turn to the west in the dark. Truth was, the capabilities of my chip in this area were limited enough. I might lose the trail also.

We ended up making camp in a place that was at least sheltered from the wind. We hadn't planned to be out overnight, so we had no tents and only the blanket apiece that each of us routinely strapped to our saddle. The small fires we were able to light did not create much warmth. We did better in that regard by huddling close to one another and sharing our body heat. We each had jerky in our saddlebags that did not need to be cooked, but although it was enough for this night, the meager amount was a reminder that we would be hungry tomorrow morning.

I took some time to scout ahead on my own, on foot, hoping against hope that our quarry had built a campfire I could see. I found nothing, however, except trees, snow, and dark ground. Either the raiders had found a protected place for their fire or they had chosen not to have one. I hated to give them credit for learning from what I had done to them outside Point Marion, but maybe they had.

We broke camp at first light and set out on the trail again. We took it slow because I was wary of *them* setting an ambush for *us*. We did not run into one, however. Neither did we see a turn back to the west toward Eastview.

The land we crossed began to look familiar to me. We had come out on the route that I took from Charity's farm to town. It wasn't a busy road at any time, because the number of farms east and north was small, but there were signs of traffic, of wagon wheels as well as hoofprints. It would be enough to tell the raiders that there were farms, that there were habitations where they could bring terror, fire, and murder.

The anger I had felt the previous day sprang up again in my heart as we rode that familiar path. Maybe the saying I'd heard so often was right. Maybe family was where you found it. Maybe they were my family now. Maybe this wasn't just another mission in a different war. This was personal. The raiders were headed for *my* farm and *my* family.

We heard shots from the direction we were heading.

"That's the Montgomery farm," Tonya said. "We'll be too late."

"I won't know I'm too late until I get there!" I yelled at her. I gave the horse a kick and it bolted forward.

Hang on, Charity, I thought. The cavalry is coming. Any cavalry I was a part of was supposed to come on choppers, not horses. That wasn't happening. We were back to old-style, now new-style. I kicked that horse harder and then kicked it again. Tonya was racing her horse along with mine. The gunfire ahead increased to a steady crackle of shots. I kicked the horse some more. I didn't know how far a horse would gallop until it dropped, but if it dropped, I was going to run from that point. The words of the nursery rhyme we sang to the kids ran through my head: *I wish to live, I wish I might.* In my mind, I heard Elvy call me her lucky starman. I kicked the horse again. I felt not only the adrenaline surge that combat gave me but also a white-hot rage. Marry that to the skills and training of an experienced Ranger, and you had a very dangerous fighting man, albeit one with low odds of survival. I didn't care about that. There were men ahead I was going to kill.

I rode into the trees atop the little rise in front of the farmhouse and took in the fight at a glance. The raiders had dismounted and taken cover in the last of the trees before the house. They were peppering it with bullets. Flashes from windows and two raider bodies flat on their faces on the way to the front door told me the family was giving a good account of itself. Fire from three weapons at the house said that it wasn't only Charity and No Nonsense shooting back. Elvy must have a rifle too.

I could see how the situation must have developed. Something—perhaps Doubting Thomas in the yard—had alerted Charity to the raiders' approach. The raiders had tried to rush the house, and two of them had been shot down. The others had backed off and taken cover. For the moment. Thank God that farmhouse was built with logs. There was no way a bullet from one of those rifles would penetrate. But this standoff wouldn't last. The odds were too uneven.

I had pulled ahead of Tonya in the last dash to the farm. I was alone riding in. I didn't care. I pulled my rifle from its sheath by the saddle and urged the horse forward, firing at the backs of the raiders as I came on. It is possible to shoot accurately from the back of a running horse, but it takes practice and I'd never done it before. All I accomplished was to alert the raiders to a threat from their rear.

Some of them shifted position and fired at me. Sitting high up on a horse made me a wonderful target. That, and horses aren't armored. I flung myself off just before a bullet nailed the horse in its head. I scrambled for cover behind some rocks and fired back. One man crumpled.

Yells and more shots heralded the arrival of my militia. I heard a scream from that direction. That didn't sound good. Still, there were three fewer raiders than there had been. Fourteen to go, said the counter in my head.

I knew the layout of the house and the farm. I knew where the windows looked out. The raiders would figure this out. They'd move to the left, where the trees and broken ground came closest to the house, so I started to move that way. As I did, I saw smoke from the corner of my eye. I focused on that, saw a bobbing flame. The torches!

I spotted three of the raiders already moving to the left, working to use the cover and the obstructed line of sight from the windows to reach either the back of the house or the barn. Stout as that farmhouse was when it came to stopping bullets, it had not been built with fields of fire in mind. Once the enemies reached the side, there was an enormous blind spot. My militia's position was farther back; I didn't think they could see the threat. If the raiders set the house ablaze, it was game over. Even if all they got was the barn and the coops, it was winter, and that would cost Charity the animals and the feed. Those structures would go up like kindling.

I got my legs under me and left my position in a bent-over run. Bullets flew around me. I felt a tug on my coat. I dropped behind a mound of snow-covered earth and felt for the spot. There was a hole in the fabric but not in me. Fine. I dashed to a large rock, took cover there, and rechecked the situation.

The smoke ahead told me the raiders were now around the side of the house. Unless one of the family came out the back, no one would be able to stop them. Except me. I saw one of them step clear of the trees and rocks to toss his torch. I was faster. My shot drilled him in the back. He arched back, away from the building, and the torch dropped harmlessly in the snow.

I couldn't see the other two. The hell with cover! I went for where I thought they would be at a dead run. I dashed around a tree and a clump of bushes and damned near ran into one of them. He whirled to confront me. I was practically on top of him. He tried to draw his pistol with his left hand, because his right had the torch. He couldn't pull the weapon out. I saw desperation on his face as he thrust the torch at me. I blocked his attack with the rifle and knocked the torch to the side. I jammed the barrel of the rifle into his stomach and pulled the trigger. Blood and guts blew out his back. I fired again, into his head, as he fell. I looked up from the body, checked side to side, saw nothing. I had no idea where the third man had gone. I ran between the house and barn, desperately searching for that last man with a torch.

A yowl and a bolt of fur alerted me. King Solomon running away. That made me run to the barn. The man was inside, at the back, setting bales of hay on fire. I yelled and aimed the rifle. As he turned at my scream, I fired. Except, I didn't. The hammer snapped down and nothing followed. The magazine was empty.

He threw the torch into the hay and went for his pistol, triumph on his face. I flung the useless rifle at him to spoil his aim and dived to the side in a roll that might buy me an extra ten seconds. I came up from the roll to a scream of rage. His pistol had jammed.

I went for my own pistol. It wasn't there. It was behind me on the floor, dislodged from the holster when I made the roll.

He gave me no chance to go for the pistol. From a sheath on his belt, he drew a long-bladed knife. He rushed straight at me and made a sweeping backhand slash at my head.

I got my right hand up and blocked his knife-hand at his wrist. Pain erupted as his wrist slammed into the bone of my forearm. I ignored it and clamped my hand on his knife-hand to keep it from rebounding free. I stepped in and drove my left forearm into his elbow, striking right above the joint. I heard a scream and a snap. His elbow bent opposite to the direction an elbow should bend. The knife fell to the floor.

I elbowed him in the chin, and he staggered. I slid my hands up, got my left hand behind the back of his head, my right on the side of his chin. I made an abrupt twist. There was an audible snap as his neck broke. He jerked and then dropped to the ground.

Flames were already dancing across the hay. I could feel the heat on my face. Every animal in a stall was screaming and bashing against the wood. My eyes searched the barn. Animals needed water. I needed water. I saw the bucket and the trough. I grabbed the bucket and threw the contents on the burning hay. I ran over to the trough, scooped the bucket full again, and threw that on the fire as well. I repeated that until the trough was empty, the hay was soaked, and the flames were dead. I dropped the bucket and bent over, hands on my knees, and took a couple of deep breaths. It felt as though I hadn't breathed from the instant I stepped into the barn.

Two blasts from a rifle sounded behind me.

I spun around. What I saw was another raider, a fourth man I had never seen move toward the back of the house. But he wasn't shooting me. The rifle he was going to use fell from his hands to the floor. He dropped to his knees. Another rifle shot exploded his head, the bullet flying through and striking the far wall to my right. He fell forward on top of his rifle. Behind him was Elvy, framed in the open barn door, rifle at her shoulder and aimed exactly as I had shown her. Her eyes of jade gleamed beyond the smoke trickling from the barrel.

.   .   .

By the time Elvy saved my life at the barn, the Battle of Charity's Farm had come to an end out front. The remaining raiders were caught between the firing from the farmhouse and the militia behind them. They broke. It's hard to blame them for that, even though they still had numerical superiority. They had no way to know if more folks would be coming. When they ran for their horses, though, they made easy targets. Only four of them got away.

I was content for them to flee. Four raiders were not enough to pose a threat to the farms or the town. Having lost almost all the men who rode north, the only likely thought in their heads would be to get back to safety. Even if I was wrong, we were in no condition to give chase.

Constant was dead. He had been shot off his horse at the outset; that was the scream I had heard. The others showed me his body when I asked.

Tonya had been hit in the groin. The others carried her and Constant's body down to the farmhouse. I don't know why they brought Constant. Sometimes, under stress, people don't think. Two of them were helping Tonya, so the other two picked up Constant in spite of the fact that he was beyond help. In fact, there was nothing I could do for Tonya either. Even if I had my medikit, I don't think I could have done anything. The bullet had found the femoral artery. It was too high up for a tourniquet, and no matter how much pressure I put on it, blood kept pumping out. She died with all of us watching, including the children.

When my useless efforts were over, I felt a wave of sadness that made it hard to stand up. She would never go all the way to the East Coast. She'd been right that she would never be gray or have grandchildren. I was staring down at her body when Courtesy came over to squat down next to her. Some of Tonya's hair had escaped one of the braids, and Courtesy brushed it back from her forehead. Then she closed Tonya's eyes with her fingers. I could see tears falling. There would be no more gifts of apples for her hero. It was Elvy who took Courtesy's hand, led her away from the bodies, and hugged her.

"Dead is dead," Charity said, but without much conviction in her words.

Elvy repeated them.

"Shit," was what I said. My hands were covered with Tonya's blood, and my sleeves were soaked with it.

"Constant has family at their farm," Ethan said. "We'll bring him back to them. No way to dig a grave now, but they will when the ground thaws."

"What about Tonya?" I asked.

Shrugs from the rest of the militia answered me.

"No family anyone knows of," Ethan said. "Never found one here, said she didn't need another one. She'd stay for a while at one farm and trade work, then move on to another."

"We can't leave her here," I said.

"We could burn her," Ethan said. "Dead is dead, and she might like that."

"No," Charity said. "Bring her back to the church. If Be Kind needs something for her to be buried in the spring, I'll take care of it."

"Good enough," Ethan said. "Are you riding back with us, Leif?"

I shook my head. "Not right away." I put a hand out to stop him from turning away. "Wait a minute before you go. I need to send a letter to General Mendenhall."

Charity found some paper and a pencil that she used to keep her books and to teach the children. I scratched out a quick note to Zeb, giving him an update that covered the raid and the action at the farm. I closed by telling him that I had done my job and it was time for him to do his. When I folded it and gave it to Ethan, I noticed the paper was liberally smeared with blood.

After the militia had tied our dead across their horses and ridden off, I turned to face Charity. I could feel my pulse thud in my neck.

"That was extraordinary, what you did," I said. "You, No Nonsense, and Elvy. You are all amazing."

"It's easy to be brave when you don't have a choice," Charity said. "We had some luck, though, and we needed it."

"It's because we have our lucky starman," Elvy said. "We wished to live, and Leif's luck made it happen."

"You have it backward." I walked over to Elvy. "You made me lucky today. Without you, I'd be dead." How do you say thank you to a twelve-year-old for saving your life with three well-placed bullets? I picked her up and gave her a kiss on her forehead. I was rewarded with a blush.

A tap on my shoulder made me turn around. Charity was right next to me, her face turned up. I put Elvy down and took Charity in my arms. I just did it. A rush of warmth and longing came out of nowhere. Her arms wrapped around me, and we came together. Our kiss was a very long one and not on the forehead. No Nonsense hooted. Elvy clapped and then the other children joined the clapping. I paid no attention to the sound effects, and I don't think Charity did either. I was too busy kissing Charity and looking into her eyes to think of anything else.

PART III

Wars do not usually result from just causes, but from pretexts.
There probably never was a just cause why men should slaughter
each other by wholesale, but there are such things as ambition,
selfishness, folly, madness, in communities as in individuals, which
become blind and bloodthirsty, not to be appeased save by havoc,
and generally by the killing of somebody else than themselves.

William Tecumseh Sherman
Speech to Michigan Military Academy, 1879

CHAPTER THIRTY ONE

Time crawled forward and pulled us slowly into 2252. That progress was nearly imperceptible. There was nothing to distinguish January from December. The cold was uniform. The snow remained on the ground, the only change being the addition of a fresh layer on some days. I marked the passage of the days on my paper calendar from Guo's bank, with a line drawn through the number of each day when it had passed. Of course, the calendar app on my chip still kept track of the days the way it always had. I could display that on my field if I wanted to, but there wasn't much point. I had little to schedule on the calendar and no way to share an appointment with anyone else anyway. I quickly got out of the habit of checking it. It was just as easy to write a note on that paper calendar in my office. My chip did make a point of announcing New Year's Day 2252 with an animated fireworks display on my field. That was more notice than I saw anyone in town give it. There were no parties, no toasts to the New Year at midnight in Al's. I did see people in town greet each other on the day with congratulations for having made it to the next year, but that was the extent of festivities.

My life went back to a quiet routine of keeping watch in the town. Yong sometimes haunted my dreams at night, while thoughts of Charity filled quiet moments in the day. I received no reply to my letters and figured that, as the winter deepened and harshened, the troops I had seen on my scouting foray had gone into winter quarters. I might have been uneasy when I thought about it, but worrying about things I couldn't control did no good. Once, in January, I rode the circuit that Tonya had shown me. I wasn't sure that it did any good. After all, riding around the area once a month would detect intruders only by chance. But I did stop by the farms as she had done and satisfied myself that nothing had changed and that people were okay. None of the other remaining militia were interested in doing it, so I did it. Call it a debt I thought I owed Tonya. I told myself that I needed to recruit more militia, but I had no inducements to offer and no one asked me about it. The truth is that one day just slipped into the next and the thought hung out in the back of my mind that the militia was something I ought to address, but I never did.

What I did look forward to was riding out to Charity's farm every ten days or so and spending a couple of days with her. People in town knew where I was going. If I was needed, someone would ride out and get me. I stuck Hezekiah with being my deputy anytime I was gone. My absence and the time to respond seemed to be within everyone's expectation. It was a far cry from having messages and notifications pop on my field with a need to deal with them instantaneously, but I got used to that also.

Charity was always glad to see me and I was glad to see her. What surprised me was that the children were glad to see me as well. They would cluster around, even if I didn't bring them anything from town, and ask what was happening in town and how I was.

There wasn't a lot of work to do around the farm in the depths of winter. The children saw to the animals. No Nonsense took care of wood and water, and Charity managed everything with control as tight as any quartermaster in history.

The family did have a new addition in January. Truth Speaks was a fourteen-year-old boy with a shock of black hair, blue eyes, and pale skin. Frankly, Truth Speaks as the name for a teenage boy made no sense. I ought to know. He turned up in town one day, claiming to have come from the southwest. He had run away from wherever he had lived, or maybe there had been raiders, or maybe he had been thrown out. His tale shifted on retelling. Be Kind took him in and told me to take him to Charity because she would always take a child who found her. She made a place for him to sleep, adjusted the food she used at each meal, and put him to work. I thought No Nonsense would have trouble with a sudden new brother near his age—a threat to his status—but that didn't happen. I think this was because No Nonsense continued to talk about heading out for adventure and fortune, and having another boy on the farm near his age made that more feasible. Truth Speaks was, in fact, a good worker and seemed happy with his new family, so maybe No Nonsense was right.

Elvy and Courtesy appeared to have reached a peace treaty. I figured that Courtesy drew the conclusion that Elvy, having put a set of bullets into the back of a raider, was first, a hero, and second, too dangerous to mess around with. For her part, Elvy was too busy mimicking Charity and appeared to have given up seeing if a particularly egregious action would get her thrown out. Maybe they both grew up, although I don't know how that works. Elvy did give up her pranks. Mostly.

What they all wanted from me, oddly enough, were stories to fill the evening hours after dinner, when it was dark and cold outside, chores were done, but it was too early to sleep. I'm not a storyteller by nature. That's not what I do. But kids ask and look at you a certain way when they ask, and what are you going to do? Turn them down? I think Charity encouraged it.

So I told them about High Noon, a strange planet with a red sun that never moved in the sky, black plants, and monsters that looked like snakes in a nightmare. I told them about Heaven, a planet where every day was as hot as the hottest summer day, but where people had built a town and farms. I told them war stories. I was careful to edit those. I don't know why I did that. These kids were growing up in a world where hunting pieces of skeletons was a child's game, and where raiders burned farms and killed families. I did it anyway. No one asked for gore.

Then, one night, Elvy broke the routine. "Tell us about the girl in the picture, Leif. The one you showed us the day this became my family."

I hesitated. My throat closed up.

Charity smiled at me. "It's okay, Leif." She settled herself in her rocker. "I would like to hear about her as well. She obviously meant a lot to you."

I sat down heavily, almost missing the chair. All of them were looking at me. Elvy and Courtesy were right in front of me, Amazing and Doubting Thomas sprawled behind them. No Nonsense sat cross-legged on the floor with Measure on his lap, and Truth was holding Renounce.

So, I told them who Yang Yong was. That she was the greatest attack plane pilot in history. That she had been pilot-in-command on humanity's first starship when it left the solar system for the stars.

They were still looking at me when I finished.

"Could we have a story about her?" Elvy asked. "Tell us a story, not just who she was."

"Please?" Courtesy asked.

I was not used to the two of them acting as a team.

I looked away from all the eyes that were fixed on me. There, at the edge of the dimness beyond the hearth and the flickering firelight, I saw Yong standing. She was in her dress uniform, but she had that tight little grin on her face.

"It's okay, Soldier Boy." I heard her say that. Possibly it was only in my mind, but I heard it.

That was when I told the story of Yong the Magnificent. Of how Fly-girl had piloted a jury-rigged dirigible halfway across the wild planet of High Noon and saved all our lives. I told them how she had speared a monster in the sea of black grass and saved my life. I finished talking when my voice broke a little. I looked at my audience. I don't think any of them had moved. They were rapt. Right in front of my chair, Elvy and Courtesy sat cross-legged on the ground, knees almost touching, chins resting on fists. I had never seen the two of them so quiet.

Charity stood up from her rocker and walked over to me. She stroked my cheek with her hand. I felt her wipe something off.

"You're crying, Leif."

"Yeah." I'm not supposed to do that, certainly not in front of other people.

"I'm sorry you lost her, Leif," Charity said. "As much as I want you here with me, and you know I do, if she were here, I would make her welcome. With you."

I clasped her hand in mine and brought it down from my face. "Thank you. I can't say dead is dead. I can't do it. It's too hard."

"I know," she said. "Let it be. We should put the children to bed."

.   .   .

A week later, at the beginning of February, General Zebulon Mendenhall rode back into my life.

CHAPTER THIRTY TWO

As before, Zeb's arrival was heralded by a rider in uniform who wanted to make certain that I would be in town on the tenth of February. I came up with a few caveats, like the earth opening up and swallowing the town on the ninth, but his face told me the humor was not appreciated. I sighed and agreed.

Zeb showed up on the tenth with a small cluster of staff, as he had before. His eyes were bright and his face wore a smile, two things I would never trust on a general officer. His staff crowded into my small marshal's office and, unlike the previous time, showed no inclination to leave. All four of them wore dark serge overcoats, and I could not see emblems of rank. They all looked young.

"It's good to see you again, Starman," Zeb said. His voice was all hearty geniality. Another thing that made me suspicious.

"Are you here to tell me that the army I detected has been disbanded, New Terra and Athens have negotiated a peace treaty, and I never have to worry about raiders again?"

"No." He had the grace to appear a bit surprised at my question.

"Then why the jovial display?"

He laughed. "I suppose that's fair," he said, "and I can give you two reasons. The first would be from the perspective of the government in

New Terra. The intelligence that you brought back makes clear what the Athenian plan is. While most of our armies are engaged to the west, they are going to send an army off into the wilderness of the northeast. Where will this army go? Not into the old states of the Northeast, or the Bosnywash Corridor. Nothing there but ash and bones and some ferals. No, once north and safely out of sight, they will swing west and come crashing through the open flank where we are now. I had worried that they would come straight up here from the south, and that the raiders were trying to eliminate people here who might give a warning, but this is even more ambitious. Had you not spotted what they are doing, we would at best have a weak force here facing south. Athens would be on our flank and in our rear before we knew what hit us. Now we can block that little scheme. From a personal perspective, you have resurrected my career, since stopping them requires an army, a real army, not one on paper. So, the Army of the Northeast has been created and I have been confirmed in command. Forty thousand men and women, it will be. Does that answer your question?"

In a way, it did. Being given forty thousand troops to command would make a general happy. However, governments did not raise armies of forty thousand without certain events following.

"How is this possible?" I asked. "I know you told me all about the Formation Wars, and how there is always fighting as the new states here expand, but the *scale* of what you are implying . . . This isn't fighting, this is a huge war. If you have forty thousand here, it will be hundreds of thousands of troops overall. We're not much more than a century removed from almost making ourselves extinct. We haven't come close to recovering from that. How does this make sense?"

Zeb's smile went away. "I can't say you're wrong. I won't say you're wrong. But the truth is"—lines deepened on his face and his eyes smoldered—"it only takes one to start a fight. That's what has happened. Either we fight back and win or we are conquered. It's that simple."

Yes, I'd been a soldier, not a diplomat. But I was frustrated. "This continent is half-empty today. More. West of the Mississippi is called the Empty Lands. Even here, the borders are mostly open land. I had to ride several days to reach what you call Athenian territory. Are you telling me that we can't figure out how to satisfy both sides without having a major war?"

"Bricks and stones," said one of the staff officers. His face wore a smirk.

"That will be enough from you," Zeb said. The smirk vanished instantly.

Zeb shook his head. "I've got no love for our self-serving senators and president back in New Terra, and I've not been as careful with my mouth as I should have been. As my staff knows." He gestured at the knot of officers occupying my office as though it were enemy territory. "The fact I've been given an army in the field tells you the government is on the verge of panic, not that it makes them sensible. The ones running Athens are even worse. You've seen what their raiders do, what that strategy was. We have to settle this the only way we can."

"Then why come here to tell me this? You knew what I would say from our first conversation. You haven't told me anything to change my opinion."

Zeb reached out and put a hand on my shoulder. "I want you on my staff, Leif. Yes, my men are veterans of the Formation Wars, but you have knowledge no one else has. That could make the difference. It would be an honor to go into battle with you."

I should have known it was coming. Maybe I did. Back to the army? Whose army? Back to war? Whose war and for what? I had declined an offer to rejoin the US Army because I was done with shooting people simply because they wore a different uniform. How could this make sense? I remembered what Yong said about how we shared the responsibility for the catastrophe here.

I didn't say all of that. What I said was no.

One of Zeb's staff gave a short chuckle. "I guess you can be a starman without having any guts."

I stepped past Zeb, and his hand fell away from my shoulder. I couldn't see myself, but from the faces of his staff, I guess they saw murder in mine.

"I don't think we've been properly introduced," I said. "I'm Staff Sergeant Leif Grettison, United States Army." I left off *Rangers* because I knew they would have no idea what that meant. They all reacted to the words *United States Army*, though. "Let me just say that I could leave the four of you dead on my floor before any of you got a weapon out."

I've been known to exaggerate on occasion, and I've been way too impulsive for my own good more times than I care to think. I had no idea what any of these four were capable of. In their eyes, though, I saw uncertainty. Maybe fright.

Having said *A*, I decided to say *B*. "Make a move and let's see."

They froze.

"That will do." Zeb's voice was hard as iron. "A dead starman does no one any good, and I've got no use for four dead staff officers." He glanced at them. "If you don't have the intelligence to stay alive, maybe I need to find some who do."

Immediate apologies came from the four of them. That cooled the temperature in the room. I said nothing, but I did turn my eyes back to Zeb.

"Look, Leif," Zeb said, "I'm not going to pretend you should have any feelings for New Terra—or me, for that matter. I never knew the world before the Tribulation. All I know is that it is a continual fight to stay alive in it now. What I will also tell you is that if my army can't stop the Athenian advance, it will be their army that comes right through here. Right through this town. Is that a reason for you to help me out?"

I digested that, and it felt like food poisoning. Could I stand by and watch Charity's farm be overrun by an invasion? Could I let it happen to the town, to Al, to Be Kind, to Mayor Guo? I had already fought the raiders. There can be reasons to go to war.

"I'll go with you, but as a civilian volunteer on your staff," I said slowly. "I'm not sure what knowledge you think I have that you need, but maybe I can help with training. I will not join you as a soldier, though, and I won't be under orders. Not from anyone. And I'll need a few days to take care of . . . things. Are we agreed?"

His staff looked surprised, but Zeb said, "Good enough." He stuck his hand out and I shook it. "We'll expect you at our camp. Take the old road that's just north of here and go west. My officers will give you a map."

The Army of the Northeast had its lucky starman. After all that had happened, I was going back to war. In the song, Johnny came marching home again. I wondered if Leif would.

CHAPTER THIRTY THREE

My trip back to the farm was unlike any pre-deployment leave I ever had. Mom was long dead, of course, before I ever went overseas. My father had called me an asshole for enlisting and said that he would have done anything to help me go to college, which I knew better than to believe. Our relationship had deteriorated to the point where, by the time I graduated Ranger school, the less we communicated, the better. I didn't have a "girl back home." The only people I cared about were in my squad and platoon.

This was different. When I told Charity what was happening—because I couldn't tell her a polite fib like I was doing some scouting—she put her hand over her mouth. Then she folded up into her rocker and cried. I had never seen Charity cry, not even in the aftermath of the raiders' attack. The younger children all clustered around her and hugged her. It was a scene that could have been a painting on the wall of a museum.

I stood in the middle of that room with all the animation of a post. I didn't know what to do. It had never mattered to anyone when I deployed, and it never mattered to anyone when, or if, I came back. I wished Yong were there to tell me how to act. Her family had cared about her. I waited in vain for her voice to say, *Soldier Boy, go do what you need to do.*

"I know you haven't said we're family," Charity said. "I know that, but I think of you that way and I don't want to lose you. Please don't do this. Please don't go."

This was, in fact, the first time I had ever had a "please don't go" conversation. I remembered María Gutiérrez from Miami telling me twenty-eight years after the fact that she had planned to say it before I left for the first starshot, but she hadn't done it when it might have mattered. This never would have happened between Yong and me.

I wanted to tell Charity I loved her. I wanted to tell all of them how much I loved them and cared about them and that's why I had to go. Those words wouldn't come out. I managed to say, "It's scaring the children to have you cry in front of them. That's not good for the children."

Like I have any idea what is good for children.

That earned me a glare from Charity and one just like it from Elvy. With the glare, Charity asked, "Why?"

"Because there is an army coming from the south that needs to be stopped and—well, the truth is, this is what I do. I've told you my stories. It was me and people like me who wrecked the world. If I can help save a little corner of it that's important to me, I'm going to do it."

Charity slumped back in the rocker as though all her bones had gone soft. "This was part of the reason Make Peace and I came east. To the frontier. To the wilderness. It took us away from the damned state. That was what you heard, 'The army is the state and the state is the army.' New Terra was always calling for men and women to fight in this place or that place. So we came here. Who would fight out here? There's nothing here. But raiders came anyway. And now this."

I ran my hands through my hair. "I don't know what I can say. When I came back from the stars the first time, people said we had peace. The fighting was over, forever. It wasn't. Maybe it never stops. All I can say is that if there is an enemy coming toward you and the kids, I'm going to stop them."

"Are you ever coming back?" Elvy's eyes were shiny.

I had no idea life could be so hard when people cared about you. Particularly kids. I tried to smile. "I'm coming back. Depend on it. I'm lucky, remember?"

Elvy and Courtesy exchanged looks that said they were both old enough to recognize bullshit when they heard it.

No Nonsense picked that moment to say, "I'm going with Leif."

"What?" Charity was not pleased.

"I'm grown," No Nonsense said. "It's time for me to be a man and go places beyond the town."

"You are not grown," Charity said. "They won't take a boy of sixteen."

"I'll lie," No Nonsense replied. His face was set, his stance determined. "Ma, you know I'm going to leave sooner or later. I can't stay here forever. I just can't. Truth Speaks is here now and he can do my work. And I know how close you've figured the food for the winter with Elvy and now Truth. This is a good time for me to go. You know that."

It was a good speech. Charity wasn't buying it. "You're still sixteen. Don't think you're going to be lying about your age with Leif there. And don't start telling me about how I've figured the food. I know I can feed all of us."

No Nonsense looked down at the earthen floor and shoved his hands in his pockets. "I'm going to go, Ma. You know I will. I want to go with your blessing, but I am going to go."

Charity stared at him for a long minute but he didn't raise his head to meet her eyes. At last, she clapped her hands on the arms of the rocker and stood up. Then she crossed over to him and gave him a kiss on his forehead.

"You have my blessing," she said. "I have known you would leave when you were old enough. I just don't want it to be now."

"Zeb's staff will need messengers," I said. "We'll need ones who are good riders. I can see that No Nonsense is assigned to us."

No Nonsense turned to me, and his face told me that wasn't the kind of assignment his imagination had conjured up. However, I had seen combat and he hadn't. I was going to see to it that he was stashed someplace safe. Relatively speaking, anyway.

.   .   .

I set out the next day with No Nonsense. The weather had cleared, bright blue sky and brilliant sunshine replacing the gray overcast we'd been having. Crystals of snow caught the light and twinkled, making the landscape around us sparkly. Scattered columns of chimney smoke, gray against the sky, rose ahead of us to mark farmhouses. For all that it was pretty, however, it was still cold. Clouds blew from our horses' nostrils and from our own.

No Nonsense was in a chatty mood from the moment Charity's farm was out of sight behind us. I suppose I understood. This was his grand adventure, his coming of age.

"It's a good omen, don't you think, Leif?" he asked me for the fifth time.

"What?" I replied to keep him from asking yet again.

"The sky," he said. "They say a blue sky with no clouds to block the sun means God is smiling on your journey. Don't you think that's good fortune?"

"No." My own mood was as dour as it could get.

"Why not?" He twisted in his saddle to look at me, but I kept my eyes straight ahead.

"Clear skies on your journey only means you're more likely to get bombed or missiled from the air. That's what old soldiers say."

The puzzled expression on the boy's face told me he had no idea what I meant. I sighed and blew out a cloud of steam in front of me. How many generations of boys had thought marching off to war was the start of some grand adventure? I ought to know. I had been one of them. For all my cynical reasons for joining up in order to pay for college, I had volunteered for the Rangers because that was an elite unit. We stood out. Other soldiers were impressed when they saw the shoulder patch and the parachutist badge. Hell, I had RLTW—Rangers Lead the Way—tattooed on my shoulder. When I graduated Ranger school, I'd had daydreams of being a hero. Then I had become a hero and discovered what a nasty business it was and how many of my buddies it left dead in horrible gory ways. Trying to tell that to No Nonsense would be useless. Same way it had been useless for me. I squinted at the northern horizon and resolved to have Zeb keep No Nonsense as a staff messenger.

"Just be glad the ground is too hard to be digging latrines," I said when he kept staring at me. I forced a laugh. That wasn't really a joke either.

·   ·   ·

We rode north as Zeb had said until we hit the relatively open area where the old highway ran and saw the signs that labeled it as Interstate 80, with another sign to Strattanville still farther to the north. There we turned west toward what had been Ohio. The paved surface of this road was still visible except where snow covered it. In a few widely separated places, large tangled masses of wrecked or dead cars blocked the road, but otherwise, it was empty. Weeds and bushes might have grown around the roadbed and into its margins, but even with that and those old cars, it was still easier to follow the old roads than ride elsewhere. Hills had been carved out in the past to let the road through, ravines were bridged by structures still—mostly—in place, and a century wasn't long enough for dense woods to have reclaimed the space. In addition, here and there, signs still stuck up from the ground, faded and bent but readable. The towns and hotels they referred to no longer existed, but I could check them against the map my chip displayed on my field so I had a good idea of our position even without GPS.

The thought of highwaymen did cross my mind, but we were armed and the weather was cold enough that any robber watching the roadway for travelers would have been insane or an idiot. It stayed cold. One night the temperature dropped sharply and I was glad to spot a farmhouse not far from the road. The family that lived there was gracious enough to give us some space in their barn for the night. When we sat down to have something to eat before rolling up in our blankets, I discovered that the beef jerky in my pack had frozen. I might as well have chewed on a stone. Sucking on a strip of beef jerky to soften it to the point it could be chewed is not my idea of dinner. At least it didn't snow on us.

If I had hoped the cold and long rides would change No Nonsense's mind about going forward—and I did—I was disappointed. He remained stupidly cheerful about the conditions, which is, I suppose, possible when you're sixteen and embarking on what you believe is a grand adventure. I resorted to telling him more of my war stories, with an emphasis now on the gory details I had avoided back at the farm.

"What part of this aren't you understanding?" I said at last. "Heroism is usually nothing more than a way to die young."

"People die young all the time," No Nonsense said.

"Dying in a battle isn't like *bang*, and you go to sleep with no mess. It's usually pretty horrific, even when it happens to the guy next to you."

"So?" No Nonsense paused a minute, and I thought he might be considering what I had said. "I could get limed, crippled, and starve in pain because no one would feed me. Raiders could come and burn the house with me in it. What's the point of doing nothing in your life and then you die anyway? Look at all the bones. They all died. Bricks and stones, Leif. Did they ever do anything? I'm going to do something before I die."

He had an answer for everything. The last thing I needed was a smart-ass teenage boy. I had been one; I didn't want to have one. I wouldn't have won an argument with sixteen-year-old me either.

CHAPTER THIRTY FOUR

On the morning of the fourth day of our journey, we rode into the outskirts of what had been Youngstown. The scenery changed as we approached the old city. I saw ruins everywhere. Buildings stuck up through the snow, some with roofs fallen in, others with parts of walls collapsed, most with windows open and gaping empty, not even a shard of glass remaining. A few seemed untouched by the passage of time, as though the people inside had only stepped out for lunch. I saw no sign, however, that any of those places were inhabited.

Smoke rising into the sky off to each side of our route showed that people did inhabit the area, even if they had not settled near the road or used the old buildings. More smoke piled up, heavy and dense, over our destination, an old manufacturing plant for cars that had been powered by internal combustion engines. Sentries challenged us at a gate in the perimeter, a structure that must have been in place when the facility was in operation. A sign next to the gate had, I assumed, once displayed the name of the place, but only a few broken pieces of plastic remained in the frame.

I stopped in front of the sentries, identified myself, and said that Zeb was expecting me.

"We were told you would come," one of the men said. He started to give me a salute, realized he shouldn't be doing that, and turned it into a hand signal to the other man, who then dashed into the grounds enclosed by the perimeter walls.

We waited there for about a half hour until a rider appeared from inside. "I will take you to General Mendenhall," he said. "Please follow me."

The facility was enormous even by the standards of my vanished world. Huge low buildings stretched away in every direction. Smoke or steam vented from many of them. Open fields surrounded the buildings and separated some of them. I was pretty sure I would find pavement under those fields if I scraped off the snow and dirt.

The rider took us to the entrance of one building whose old windows were still intact. Black plastic numerals above the door read 35. At one time, that must have meant something.

"The general is waiting for you inside," he said. "I need to tell you to leave your weapons out here. They will be safe." His demand was almost apologetic.

"Of course," I said. I left my rifle and pistol in holsters on the saddle and saw that No Nonsense did the same.

The door was metal and the hinges squealed. The floor of the corridor inside had once been polished stone. The stone was intact, but it was dirty, scuffed, and marked along its length. We found Zeb two doors down from the entrance in what had been a large conference room. The windows along the long side of the room were boarded up to keep the cold wind out. At some recent time, a small woodburning stove had been put in one corner of the room and vented through a hole in the boards over the windows. It kept the place tolerably warm. A conference table ran down the middle of the room, its faux-wood top old even when I had been young.

Zeb wore the same uniform coat I had seen him in before, with no insignia of rank and no decoration on it. Five men stood with him, four with a single star on each shoulder and the fifth wearing eagles that looked a lot like the colonel's tabs I remembered. A sixth man stood apart from the others. His shoulder tabs had a red square, an insignia I had never seen before. None of them looked particularly happy, but that last one looked like he had bitten into something both sour and unexpected. A cluster of young officers—obviously staff—stood behind them and near the far wall.

"Welcome to Camp Lords," Zeb said. "Let me introduce my key officers: Brigadiers Felix Kamper, Fourth Division; Paul Howard, Twelfth Division; Amos Jorgenson, Eighth Division; and Sanjay Chopra, Twentieth Division." His hand indicated, in turn, a tall white man with angular features, a Black man a head shorter than the first with a moon-shaped face, a man whose hair and complexion mirrored mine, and one with black hair and skin that matched Charity's. "They command my divisions, eight thousand each when we reach full strength. Then Colonel Ezra Merz commands the 401st infantry regiment and our reserve brigade when the regiment is augmented." I had been right about the eagles. Merz had a broad square face with small eyes. Like the four brigadiers, he was clean shaven. Zeb pivoted to face the last man, as though surprised to find him in the room. "Also Political Officer Jesus Fuentes, who commands no troops. He sees to it that I do not deviate from the intent of our state, which only he knows in detail."

A political officer? My estimate of the situation I had walked into changed rapidly, and not for the better. Fuentes was not physically impressive. He stood five-six with narrow shoulders. A thin black beard covered the receding chin and hollow cheeks of a pinched face. Sunken eyes blazed.

"Your tone verges on mockery, General," Fuentes said. His voice managed to be soft and respectful, yet menacing all at the same time. "You should take care in that. The senate and the president had reservations about your appointment to command this force."

Zeb smiled. "Which is why you are here and why they waited until they had no choice but to make the appointment." He extended his arm to me. "This is Starman Leif Grettison. I have told you about him."

I knew how he meant that title.

"I hope you do not really believe he will bring us victory by luck or by magic," Fuentes said. "Even if he is not a fake who has fooled you, he's nothing more than one man."

Political Officer Fuentes and I were not going to be friends.

"I am exactly who Zeb told you I was," I said. "Born two hundred fourteen years ago and first flew to the stars in 2069. I could tell you about what it's like to fly on a fusion ramjet starship and see the stars when you're traveling at the speed of light, but none of that will mean anything to you. I was trained by the US Army, though, and I fought in the US Army. Whatever else you think, you should remember that."

Following my little speech, the air in the room crackled with the same frost as outdoors. I was very glad, as I locked eyes with Fuentes and the other officers fidgeted, that I had insisted I would only be Zeb's civilian adviser and not in any chain of command. I don't have a politically correct bone in my body, and the idea of political officers makes my skin crawl. From Fuentes's face, I think he would have preferred to ask me questions after applying thumbscrews.

"I believe we should show Starman Grettison the base," Zeb said, ignoring the tension in the room. "It has millions of square feet. As though God knew we would need it. They built internal combustion cars here long ago. Tried to repurpose it, I don't know for what, and it didn't work out. It's been sitting here idle since sometime in the twenty-first century. It's still mostly intact. Right off the old west-to-east roadway we'll advance along. Not too far from the lake, and the lake is frozen hard so it's simple to concentrate supplies and troops here. We can shelter the entire army here. The best possible winter quarters we could have, ready and waiting for us to occupy it. Which is a good thing, since we were given virtually no time to prepare." I noticed he made sure to look at Fuentes when he said that. "And you gentlemen should prepare to show him the readiness of your troops."

No one asked about No Nonsense or even made any comment about him. I think they all assumed he was my aide or something like that. That was fine with me. Maybe I could keep him out of trouble despite his dreams of glory. Thankfully, he had the good sense to keep his mouth shut in that room.

The brigadiers and Merz immediately excused themselves from any tour on the grounds of other duties. Fuentes, however, remained in the room and showed no signs of leaving even with Zeb staring pointedly at him.

"I have no duties that would prevent me from accompanying you," Fuentes said. "Indeed, I believe acquainting our starman with the base should be a priority for me."

"Perhaps we all have other matters to attend to at the moment," Zeb said slowly. He turned away from Fuentes to me. "I will have someone show you and your man to quarters in the officers' building and point out the officers' mess. Tomorrow, I'll have you review some of our units. I'm curious what a very old military man thinks."

Fuentes was still standing there with Zeb when one of Zeb's young staff officers led us out. No love lost between those two. I wondered how this would play out when the army made contact with the enemy. I also wondered if Fuentes might have a set of orders that Zeb didn't know about.

· · ·

Officers' quarters occupied a building that once housed managers in individual offices. The rooms were small but private. The old furniture was all gone, replaced by a camp bed, a desk, and a chair, which took up most of the space available. Mine had a window, and the glass was still in it—although it was so caked with grime I could hardly see through it. The biggest advantage of the room was that it was warm. That was a joy beyond any reckoning. I draped my coat over the back of the chair and luxuriated in heat and no drafts.

No Nonsense had a smaller room across the hall, without a desk. He took one look and pronounced it fine. I sent him out to find food.

I turned my attention to the contents of my pack, which, admittedly, weren't much. I was accustomed to living in whatever I was wearing. I was starting to hope that the buildings would have a warm place to wash and, perhaps, to clean my clothes, when I heard footsteps at my door. If No Nonsense was back that fast, the search for food had not gone well. When I turned around, though, it wasn't No Nonsense. It was Fuentes.

He was in my room before I could ask what he wanted. At a distance of only a few feet, I could see that his uniform was different from all the others. It was fitted, had been tailored. The fabric was smoother as well.

"General Mendenhall did not appear inclined to have me listening to his conversation with you," Fuentes said. "I can understand that. In fact, I would prefer to have a separate conversation with you myself."

He seated himself in the chair at my desk and leaned back against my coat. "Mind if I have a seat?" he asked after he did it.

I shrugged. "If you want to have a close look at my eyes, you can do that too. You won't see anything. No red numbers, anyway. All you'll see is the signs of my intelligence."

Fuentes stretched his lips into a line that passed for a smile. "You're a funny man, Leif. Grettison. Maybe starman. I appreciate your humor."

None of the people I liked ever seemed to appreciate my humor. I suppose that said something about him. "Go on," I said.

"Our intrepid general has come up with a starman for his army," Fuentes said. "Maybe you are. It doesn't matter. You could have been living on some mountain on the other side of the Empty Lands and somehow wandered here, and that would be the same as coming back from the stars, as far as whatever you bring to us. As far as I am concerned, anyway." His eyes looked me up and down, as though taking inventory. "However, I am not most people. In particular, I am not the ignorant, uneducated farm boys and girls or the equally dumb boys and girls from our cities that make up this army and most of the state. They hear the church preach about the Twelve Saints who were martyred starmen. They hear the church preach that starmen come back now and then and bring us luck. That is why our dear general wants you at the front with him."

"Yeah, I'm the army's lucky charm," I said. "How do your men and women think this works? If you rub the top of my head before battle, can I grant three wishes, or do I have to kiss each one of your soldiers?"

Fuentes laughed, then coughed up some phlegm and spat on my floor. "It's good to have a sense of humor." He leaned forward in the chair, and all sense of bonhomie vanished. "To a point. I need you to understand how you are being used. Because there may come a point when you should not be used. Or be used . . . differently." He paused, as if making sure my eyes were on him. "The army is the state and the state is the army. That is why we are neither ferals scampering through the woods nor slaves of someone else's state. We are going to win the war with Athens, and as with all wars, it is one we must win. Understand, though, there are limits to the number of men and women we can have under arms. It is not like before, when the bones tell us there were limitless numbers available. The army you see here represents the last of our trained troops. To ask the senators to raise more from their districts will mean too young or too old, or those whose work we cannot spare. The president and the senate know this."

My eyes shifted from him to the spittle that adorned my floor. Why was he giving me a lecture on political structure and manpower? "What's your point? That we shouldn't be having people we need kill each other just because they come from somewhere else?"

"No." He stood up and smoothed his jacket with his hands to eliminate any wrinkles. "General Mendenhall has a long record of service in our Formation Wars. He is personally courageous and daring. He takes risks. Wonderful in a lieutenant, not so much in the man leading the army. The president and the senate cannot have him throw away this army in a gamble. I cannot have these men and women throw themselves and all their equipment away on some glorious charge because they think their general has luck at his side. That's what this review tomorrow is about. He wants the troops to see *you* standing with him so they will be more likely to follow him into some unfortunate . . . predicament."

Ah. I was Zeb's lucky charm so that the army would think Zeb was lucky, whatever orders he gave. At least, that was the slant Fuentes was giving me. I think if I could have been reduced to a rabbit's foot that Fuentes could wear around his neck, he would have preferred that to dealing with me as I was.

"If I understand, Political Officer Fuentes," I said carefully, "you are suggesting that at some point, you may want me to act differently from what General Mendenhall wants."

"I have authority directly from the president and the senate," Fuentes said. "That is independent of the usual chain of command. I will also suggest to you that I have close ties to several very important senators, and they can be very generous with rewards."

The itch I was feeling across my body had nothing to do with the fact that I had not changed clothes in days. "I think we understand each other," I said. "Now, I have sent my aide for some food and I am becoming concerned that he has eaten it all himself. I am going to try to find him, unless you are going to tell me you need an immediate application of luck somewhere right now."

"Hah." Fuentes extended his hand. "I am sure we understand each other. I only hope you will not joke when you should be serious."

I shook his hand. That seemed the best way to get him out of my room.

After Fuentes exited, I waited a length of time sufficient for him to get out of the building and then decided I was going to find No Nonsense. Failing that, I would find the food for myself. I was barely through the door when I collided with a man hurrying toward it. I took a step back to see who it was. Paul Howard, one of the brigadiers Zeb had introduced.

Howard stepped back himself and slapped his hands together. "I couldn't help but notice that Fuentes came to your room," he said. "I thought it would be best if I spoke with you."

I seemed to have been cured of my old automatic reflex of saluting an officer. I studied the man in front of me. Howard's broad face showed streaks of sweat. The building was warm, but not that warm.

"We're some distance from the building where we met," I said. "The other rooms along this corridor don't appear occupied. That would suggest the only way you 'couldn't help but notice' would be if you followed him. Correct?"

Howard drew in a sharp breath. "Can we step into your room?"

"Sure."

I led the way back through the door into my small quarters that still lacked any food. "Care to tell me what's so urgent?"

Howard worked a finger between his collar and his neck. "I'm sure Fuentes made you an offer. You don't need to say anything. Just be aware the man is poison. He is the creature of a group of senators close to the president. They do have influence, real influence, and they can make lavish gifts, but you will not like the chains that come with the gifts. There is always an afterward, you know."

"Thank you for the education in politics," I said. Howard looked more uncomfortable by the minute, and I doubted it had anything to do with the time since my last bath. Pulling up a line I had just heard, I said, "I thought the army was the state and the state was the army."

"Hah." Howard spat, so now there were two gobs on my floor. "It is more like the army is a bunch of little states and the state has a bunch of little armies," he said. "Each senator raises units from their individual territories and appoints the commanding officer. You will understand how loyalty goes. But I will tell you one more thing. I know the boys in my division. The boys and the girls. They are weary of fighting and weary of casualties. I don't want to march them to hell with them thinking they've been made lucky."

As nervous as Howard had been when he talked about Fuentes, his voice was firm and clear when he spoke about his troops. Maybe he did care about them.

"I don't claim any special luck," I said, "and for sure, I've never made anyone else lucky. I'll do what I can do to help, and I will take your advice about the political officer."

"Thank you," he said. "I will owe you for anything you can do for the troops."

He turned to go and I reached out a hand to halt him. "One final question. Should I be expecting a procession of generals at my room today?"

"No." Howard's bearing was back to what I had seen in the conference room. "Jorgenson thinks he knows everything, and Chopra will do what Jorgenson says. Kamper wouldn't care. And with that insight, I think we are now even."

After Howard had gone, I realized he had not mentioned Colonel Merz. I wondered if that meant anything, or only that generals thought solely about other generals. I didn't spend too much time worrying about it, because No Nonsense still wasn't back with the food.

It was time to find him. From the directions Zeb's staff officer had given, I was confident I could locate the right building. I walked across an open stretch from the officers' quarters—maybe an old parking lot—and then around several other buildings. I saw more buildings beyond those. They did seem to stretch out to forever. I spotted a sprawling building with a large numeral 4 painted on it, faded but still legible, as the officer had said.

I yanked open a door. The interior was big enough to hold a town. I could see remnants of old machinery on the floor and suspended from the ceiling. Woodburning stoves along the exterior walls supplied a reasonable amount of heat.

I walked around the ancient lines and robotic arms and saw wooden partitions of more recent vintage. Men filled the space, all wearing drab olive uniforms not too far removed in color from the army uniforms I had worn. They were patching uniforms, fixing boots, and playing cards. When I saw the first card game, I knew where my search would end.

In fact, it did not take too many questions to be directed to "the starman's aide." No Nonsense sat in a circle of seven, five other men and one woman, all intent on a hand of poker. None of them paid attention to me when I walked up; their focus was on their cards. This time, at least, my chip's app showed no sign of cheating. Not that fair play changed No Non-sense's result very much.

He finally noticed me when he happened to look up after tossing in his cards on a hand. Did he have the grace to look embarrassed at being caught out? No.

"Leif, can you give me a few solids for another hand?"

"You need to learn when to quit," I said. "Or you need to learn to play better."

"How can I learn without practice? The money's no good in your pocket."

I fished out a few coins and went for the food myself.

CHAPTER THIRTY FIVE

A reviewing stand that looked like a set of bleachers had been set up along the side of one of the large open fields among the buildings. The field had been mostly cleared of snow, revealing cracked asphalt pavement with the browned remains of summer grass protruding through all the cracks. Zeb's officers, their staffs, and I assembled on the stands for the review after midday had come and gone. I think Zeb's generals dragged their feet on having the troops ready, partly because the weather was so cold and partly because they didn't want to go to the trouble of putting on a show, just so the troops could see the lucky starman up there next to Zeb. If they couldn't refuse, they could avoid being prompt.

The weather also played a role. Even with the sun overhead at noon, it wasn't much warmer than it had been at daybreak. Then we had a further delay because Fuentes could not be found. He was, in fact, still in bed. God forbid, however, that anything of note took place without the political officer observing. What would happen if he overslept when we had to go into action? I was liking the whole idea of a political officer less and less.

Despite the inauspicious start, Zeb's four line divisions put on a good show. Selected units exhibited close order drill, shift from column march to line of battle, and volley fire against a line of targets that disintegrated under the combined impacts. I'm not a big fan of close order drill as a sign of combat readiness, because I've always regarded it as parade ground stuff, nothing like what troops have to do in the field. I caught myself before I said anything, however, and reconsidered. This was an army with no chips, no phones, not even a stupid old radio. The education level of the troops was probably no better than in armies a half millennium ago. What I was seeing was evidence of discipline, training, and precise execution. If they were brave, too, that might be enough. *Shut up, Leif, and be gracious*, I told myself.

I can do that.

The precision lasted until we reached Merz's Reserve Brigade. I heard snickering from the other officers the moment the order for them was given. The core of the unit was the 401st Regiment, but it was bulked up to near brigade size by virtue of pulling into the ranks every cook, clerk, and cart driver who could carry a gun. The result was a unit composed of a mix of full-time and part-time soldiers. It would be employed that way only as a last resort. This was, in fact, the unit No Nonsense would be a part of if we needed the reserve more than Zeb needed a messenger. Why were they assembled for review that way? There was no possibility this was going to be good. Zeb rounded on Merz and asked exactly that question.

"I was told that was your expectation, sir," said Merz.

Half-hidden smiles among staff and brigadiers told me even more. Then I noticed something else.

The four divisions I had already seen were not all male, but I would put the percentage at 95. Not so this reserve. One in five, at least, were women. So was the officer who stood in front of them. Unlike the other senior officers crowding the bleachers, who wore serge overcoats against the chill, she wore the same olive drab as her men and women. I decided I liked her more than any of the staff or brigadiers. The gender ratio was obvious as the unit assembled, and that started a whole new set of jokes from the officers on the reviewing stand. I heard the old one about what a woman thinks the rifle barrel is for, and it got worse from there.

I prayed this group would put on a spit-and-polish show that would shut down the various scurrilous remarks. I found myself rooting for them. It was not to be. If it had been staged deliberately as a comedy show, it would have been funny. This was not funny. Except, of course, to the officers of the other divisions, who did not burst out laughing, only because Zeb would have had to take notice. Soldiers were out of step. They turned the wrong way. The shift to line of battle was a jumble. Merz's face turned so red I think all his blood pooled there. The other officers blamed Merz. Loudly. They put the blame on having too many women. They blamed the female officer on the field. Even louder. I saw Fuentes making notes in a little notebook. He was grinning. It is not possible to take a bunch of people from noncombat roles, graft them on to an infantry regiment, and expect the whole to look very good. They didn't.

I heard more jokes about women. Two and a half centuries after we settled the question of women in combat units, I was hearing this bullshit. I had seen women in combat, and I can say they are as deadly as the men, as courageous as the men, and took pain as well as the men. I thought of Yang Yong. She would have turned any one of those pretty close order formations into sausage stuffing without even changing her tone of voice.

Zeb barked an order. I don't know whether he had tired of the display in front of him or the nasty jokes around him—probably both—but it put an end to the farce. At the order to dismiss, the troops melted away faster than ice cream at the equator. Zeb did not move from the reviewing stand. Perforce, all of us stayed there with him.

Zeb glared at his generals. "I did not find this humorous, gentlemen. Not in the least."

"I think, sir, the reserve is in need of more training," Jorgenson said.

"You can't train a crowd like that," Chopra said. "We have to never need them. And we won't, sir."

"Maybe we should have our starman train them, sir." Jorgenson picked up the thread. "Even if he can't turn them into the legendary US Army, maybe he can at least make them lucky."

"Good thought, Jorgenson," Fuentes said. He made more notes in his little book.

Jorgenson smiled even though Fuentes had given no acknowledgment of rank. Merz stood speechless and still. Might have been trying to hide in the air.

"I think that will do for now," Zeb said. I'm not sure how he kept his tone mild. "I am going to show Leif some of our equipment. Privately. You are dismissed, gentlemen."

The other officers gave salutes and *sirs* and left the stand. Fuentes alone remained with us, as he had the other day.

"I said privately," Zeb said. "I trust you understand the meaning of this word, Political Officer Fuentes?"

"Of course, General." Fuentes's lips curled into a smile that had no effect in the rest of his face or eyes. He gave an indifferent salute and left.

Zeb took the steps down from the stand at a quick pace and headed for a distant building. I hurried to catch up.

"What did you think of that?" Zeb asked.

"About a half step from insubordinate," I said.

He turned his face to me. The beard could not hide the grimness of his expression. "At the end, you mean?" He turned back in the direction he had picked and kept talking. "My very experienced generals were selected by the senate, not by me. That means, naturally, they are all politically connected back in New Terra. Each one of them is not-so-secretly hoping that Fuentes writes something back to New Terra that will result in my recall and replacement by them. They are each restrained in their provocation, however, because if one of them were to replace me, they would have to win the campaign that is coming. They do have experience and at least know how to train their troops, but none of them wants the responsibility of flinging a hastily assembled army into the wilderness against an enemy of unknown strength. Even Fuentes is careful about that. I was asking, though, about the troops. The boys and girls who must do the fighting. What did you think?"

I hesitated, thought about it, and decided he wanted the truth. "The units I saw from your four infantry divisions look okay. At least, for whatever parade ground drill will tell you. I think you know that. That reserve brigade, the way it's put together . . ." I hesitated again. "They can shoot. The volleys were ragged, but the target hits were good. The rest . . . it's not a fair comparison. They need to train together. It's not just time. It's training consistently with the same people. You can't be a cook or a clerk most of the time and then, at the snap of fingers, be part of an infantry unit. Merz needs to understand that. If he doesn't now, he needs to be made to understand it."

We had reached the entrance to the building Zeb had selected. He stopped with his hand on the door.

"Colonel Merz is overreliant on the bottle for his own training," Zeb said. "His father is, however, a senator and confidant of our president. You may consider the implication of the fact that even with that patronage, he is only a colonel and not a general."

"Why the fuck did you take this command, Zeb?"

He was quiet for a minute. His eyes searched my face. "It is an army command," he said after a short delay. "Those are few and far between. If I refused, it would be the end for me. There would never be another. I will also say that our senators and president do not believe we can lose this war out in the eastern wilderness, and I know better. There is a third reason. I like to believe that we can have a better state in the future, but that won't happen if Athens wins this war."

"Fair answer," I said.

He still did not open the door. Instead, he stroked his beard. "I wanted you on my staff because you have experience from a different time that I do think could be valuable. This will include information that I either cannot find, because it was lost in the computers, or cannot trust, because it came out of the computers. I also know that you are not tied to the senators and president in New Terra, and have a hope that you will tell me what you actually think. That said, if we put aside the original source of the comment about the reserve, would you train them? See what you can do with them? You never know what can happen once the fighting starts. If I thought there was never a chance we would need them, I wouldn't have them."

I had put myself in a box. I watched him watch me as he smoothed his beard between his fingers and thumb. How would this Colonel Merz react if I walked over and told him I was going to train his troops? From what I had just seen, would he care? If, God forbid, we ever needed that reserve, No Nonsense would be fighting with them. "You understand I was never an officer. I was a sergeant. That's as high as I went."

He nodded. "You do know something about training, though. You must."

"I do," I said. "At the small, independent-unit levels, I do."

"That will be fine."

"I'll see what I can do, Zeb."

"Good." He yanked the door open. "Have a look at what we are working with."

What I saw through the door was . . . a row of pickup trucks. Oh, they didn't look like any brand of truck I remembered, but that's what they were.

"You're motorized!" I said.

Zeb's laugh was short and mirthless. "It would be more correct to say that we have some motor transport."

He walked through the door and I followed. Once inside the massive building, I could see that while there was a large number of vehicles, it was nowhere near enough for an army the size of Zeb's. Unless there were more somewhere else.

Zeb answered that question before I asked it. "We have enough to tow most of our heavier artillery, and that is something," he said. "It spares horses and men. Plenty of tires from before we can remanufacture. However, our biggest limitation is fuel. I have no intention of waiting here for our enemy and allowing him the freedom to maneuver and pick the site of battle. I intend to advance once we are ready and force them to respond to us. There are limits to how much alcohol we can carry for the engines."

"Can you resupply? Or capture more as you advance?"

Zeb stopped by one of the trucks and rubbed his hand on the cowling over the engine. "I can't count on it," he said. "A supply line back to here would be tenuous and easily cut. In the wild, there is nothing. The ferals haven't seen an engine since the Tribulation. Even if we reach Athenian territory, I can't be sure our engines will run on whatever they have."

"Then what good are they?"

"Limited." Zeb gave the truck a pat. "We will use them as far as they will go. Then it is back to horses. We can find feed for horses." He stared at the truck, did not look at me. "However, this is anathema to Political Officer Fuentes. He insists we remain in our own territory or, at most, no farther than we would have fuel to bring these back. How does that sound to you?"

"Stupid." Whatever gifts I have, diplomacy is not one of them. "You use the equipment you have to make a battle plan work. You don't plan a battle, or a war, around taking care of some equipment."

"Yes." Zeb clapped me on the back. "Except I will tell you that the company that now makes these trucks is controlled by three key senators, and they have, I have heard, given our president a percentage." He paused, returned his gaze to the trucks. "I sometimes think that our blessedly corrupt politicians forget that God and His Saints did not order that we would win the Formation Wars in this region. New Terra has won so far because we have outfought and out-generaled the others. This war, however, is going to be bigger. There will be more men, more equipment, in these armies than in any of the previous ones because we and Athens have swallowed all the others. If we lose sight of what it takes to win wars, we could lose this one."

"Are you sure we're fighting on the right side?"

This time Zeb's laugh was hearty. "The Athenians are not better. Worse, from what I hear. And we live here. You would not want to see what they would do as conquerors. I have heard about that. Let me show you some weaponry to cheer you up."

With one hand behind my shoulder blade to urge me away from the trucks, he walked us deeper into the building. The trucks were the only motorized equipment. I didn't see any armor. That made some sense. Even if they could manufacture a tank, those wheezy alcohol motors couldn't propel them, and the fuel situation would be even worse.

I could see places on the floor where large equipment had been mounted or bolted down in the past. The nature of that machinery was unknowable; nothing was left but platforms and anchors in the floor. Once we passed that, I saw ranks of artillery pieces ahead. Most of them looked like versions of the 155 mm and 105 mm howitzers I remembered from pictures of wars before my time.

Zeb confirmed my assessment with a smile that said I had aced his history test. "Yes." He slapped the barrel of one piece. "This is a copy of the old 155-millimeter howitzer. Well, it's a reasonable copy. Ours have an effective range of four to five miles. I believe the twentieth-century ones were good out to seven miles. Still, it's effective artillery."

Crate after crate of shells spoke to the firepower that he could unleash.

"You don't have enough motorized transport, though," I said. "Even if your trucks are used for nothing but hauling artillery and shells, you don't have enough."

"I know," he said. "We will not go faster than horse-drawn teams even at the start. Of course, that's also a reason I won't be sorry about abandoning the trucks if we can keep advancing. We won't be any slower without them. It will only make Fuentes's letters back to New Terra nastier."

He also showed me crated stockpiles of small arms. Zeb loosened some covers and I got a good look at an array of lever-action and bolt-action rifles. And then I saw an area with tripod-mounted weapons with a long tubular barrel. I stared at those.

"You have machine guns."

"Yes. Limited numbers. As with everything else, we've built them from old designs, print that is old enough it can't have been printed from computer information we can't trust, and designs that can be manufactured in plants that do not need electronics. We have light machine guns as well that I can show you."

I wasn't thinking of whether the design and manufacturing information could be trusted. I was thinking of all the drill I had seen. Of what rapid-fire rifles and machine guns had done before.

"If your generals use that kind of close order maneuvering and attack dug-in lines that have machine guns, the only thing you'll need your trucks for is to carry the corpses afterward. Even against these rifles, it will be bad. Do the Athenians have the same weaponry?"

"Probably. There's no reason to believe there's any unique document in one area compared to another. Same reason the manufacturing is at similar levels. We're all working from what's left over from the country that was here before."

"Then it will be a massacre."

"Our training standard specifies close order lines." Zeb's speed had slowed down. I heard trouble in his voice even as he gave me the party line. "We have a stolen Athenian manual. It is similar. It is said that close order is the only way to maintain control over the unit, to keep men to their duty and not in search of safety. The ability to drive home an attack is worth the casualties. It worked in the earlier Formation Wars."

"Did you have machine guns then? As many men and women with these lever-action rifles?"

"No. We started manufacturing the machine guns toward the end of the last war in the north. Our enemies did not have them."

"Then it's all bullshit." That was about as diplomatic as I could be. "Surely you have old original print books that cover this. I'm talking World War I. That was 1914. You have to have some."

Zeb ran his hand over his bald top. "Anytime you bring up history, there are plenty who will argue that any book could have been printed from a computer and what's in it is corrupted, not reliable. It's not like the design of a field gun, where we can take what is in an old print, build it, and see if it works."

"I date back to those days. I date back to when all the information in computers hadn't been altered, corrupted. My instructors dated back to before they started putting all the old books into the computers and getting rid of the print." I was vehement about it.

"I'm not doubting what you say, Leif," Zeb said. "I told you why I wanted you with me, although I hadn't expected you to throw out our whole training manual." He kicked at a crate. "There is no time to have units give up what they know and learn something new, even if we could have everyone agree on what new approach we should use." Suddenly, he was close in front of me, intense eyes boring into mine. "You have that reserve. They're at best half-trained as it is. Train them however you think best. Whatever you were taught. Do that, Leif, and show me what you have. You have until late March. The weather will improve enough to move by then, and we will have all the troops and supplies we are going to get."

I met his eyes. Less than two months. With troops no one else wanted. Half of whom weren't authentic combat troops. No armor. Under a colonel who had trouble staying sober and might not want me.

"Sure," I said.

I have been told that sometimes I don't know when to keep my mouth shut.

.　　.　　.

Later, back in my room in the officers' building, I lay on my bed and stared at the ceiling. I refused to think about tactics that were out of date by the end of the nineteenth century. I didn't want to think about officers refusing to believe any history, tried to push away the knowledge I had of what machine guns do to a tightly packed mass of men.

Instead, I thought about Yong. I remembered sitting on the bridge of the *Dauntless* with her, her hand resting on mine, both of us staring at the stars on the screen. We had no need to talk at those times. No one else was around. I had been content.

I missed my Flygirl. I would miss her forever.

A thought intruded into those memories. A thought of Charity and her farmhouse full of kids. I had, maybe, in a way, possibly, a little bit, fallen in love with Charity. But what about Yong? I couldn't do the modern thing and say, *Dead is dead*. I wouldn't say that about Yong. However, Yong wasn't coming back. She wasn't waiting for me at Earthbase. I knew that. And whether I deserved to live or not, I was living in the here and now. When I went to see Charity and her kids, I felt like I was going home. I was going to war now because of how I felt about Charity. I couldn't figure out what I was supposed to do.

I didn't sleep well.

Understatement of the year.

CHAPTER THIRTY SIX

The next morning found me cranky and tired. The fact that coffee—never mind stim pills—did not exist in this postapocalyptic version of America did not help my mood. I went to the mess in search of a substitute.

"Excuse me."

I was contemplating the steam rising up from a cup of pine needle tea, which wasn't going to do anything more for my central nervous system than hot water, when the words pulled me back to the army's mess where I was standing. The speaker was a tall young woman in an officer's uniform. Her face was pitted with old acne scars that stood out on skin so dark as to be almost black. Stern brown eyes under a high forehead framed a broad nose. She had chopped her hair short, shorter than most of the men wore theirs. She looked, somehow, familiar. My eyes went to the uniform. Major.

She was waiting for me to say something, so I said, "Yes?"

"Major Leah Samuel. Colonel Merz's executive officer, 401st Regiment."

That was why she looked familiar. "Yes, I saw you with your unit yesterday."

"Yes. You and everybody else." She shifted her stance uncomfortably. "I'm sorry. How should I address you?"

That surprised me for an instant. I wasn't in uniform; I wasn't in this army. "Leif works fine."

"Thank you, Leif. I have been told you are going to provide training for my regiment, both the regulars and the augmented reserve brigade. I would like to know what you're going to do and whether this is simply going to be another opportunity for humiliation and amusement for the brigadiers."

Okay, what was I going to do? I had run out of procrastination room, and this major had every right to be pissed off.

"How much education do your troops have?"

She blinked, looked surprised. "Not much. The ones from cities might have a few years of school. Most will have their letters, although that doesn't mean they can really read and write. The farm girls and boys, not even that. Why?"

"Because." *Okay, Leif,* I thought, *what comes after because?* "Look, this isn't the US Army of 2055 when I joined. It's not even the US Army of 1955. Your people don't have the education, the weaponry, or the tech. We can still teach them how to fight effectively, though, and not get massacred by automatic weapons." I paused while I racked my brain for a way to make that true. The US Army that had trained me had been expert in combined arms and networked operations. None of that applied now. My chip was of no use. Its memory was too limited, a factor that had never been an issue when connecting to a global database took little longer than a thought. However, after I left the service and went to college, I had read extensively in military history. I guess it was a way of sorting out everything I had gone through. I had read about how the tactics I had been trained in had evolved. Maybe, I thought, we could go back to where those tactics started, blend the old—very old—with some of my training. It was worth a shot.

"The small-unit tactics the army used and I learned actually trace all the way back to the First World War," I said as I organized my thoughts. "That's the beginning of the twentieth century. The German Army back then invented a way to succeed in trench warfare, that is, when units are dug in and have machine guns. If you attack a line like that with a formation where everybody gets up and charges at the enemy in a line, all you'll end up with is a lot of corpses. People were stupid and tried it and that's what happened, time after time. So the Germans figured out a different way and trained units they called Stosstruppen to do it. They had better weapons and more variety of weapons than we have, but we'll make do. I'll change things to fit what we have today. If you'll support it and get your officers together, I'll go over the approach."

Those eyes of hers softened maybe one iota. "I'm not looking to have my girls and boys killed for no good reason. You make me believe it and you'll have my support. Don't worry about Merz. As long as he doesn't have to do any work, he won't care. There's a reason I'm the executive officer of the regiment."

An hour later, I was back in the building with the number 35, this time in a conference room packed with officers of the 401st. I was going to tell them how to train and run their unit. As I had told Zeb, I had been a sergeant, a noncommissioned officer. I had neither the training nor the education to command a unit like this. I didn't feel right telling officers their business. It didn't help that I could hear carping from the moment I entered the room.

"This is an emergency reserve. Not a line unit."

"If the cooks are going to be training all the time, who is going to cook?"

"He may be a starman, but that doesn't make him a soldier."

That last crack made me see red. Paradoxically, that may have been what I needed. I had been a soldier. Even if I didn't know anything about commanding a large unit, I knew how units were built at the level of the soldier. From the bottom up. I glared at the lot of them. These weren't US Army officers. I owed them nothing.

"All right, ladies and gentlemen," I said, "we are going to reorganize this reserve brigade of yours and we're going to do it right now. May I assume that you know your men and women well enough that when I am looking for small-unit leaders, you will know who is good, and when I want specific skills, you'll know who has them?"

That got their attention. Backs stiffened; jaws clenched. Eyes flashed. I did see nods. Not one of them said a word. If I had been looking at my face right then, I wouldn't have said anything either. Leah Samuel had the beginnings of a smile.

"Good," I said. "We're going to break this unit up. Your smallest independently maneuvering unit is four people. Call it a fire team. One of them is the team leader. Have the four of them split into two sets of buddies. See that they bunk together, eat together, and work together. Two fire teams are a squad, and get a sergeant to lead them. Squads and fire teams will train to move and fire independently."

"I don't know what you're thinking, but that won't work." That came from a man with captain's insignia and an expression that could have meant severe constipation. "You let small groups of low ranks go on their own, they'll either wander off and get lost or go hide somewhere."

"No." I left no opening for them to question me. "You listen to me. I've had all these jobs. I've performed them. In combat. I know how this works and we're going to do it. Now, this is the weapons mix I want in each squad."

I would have preferred two teams of four, each team with two riflemen, a machine gunner, and one with a grenade launcher, but it wasn't going to work that way. We didn't have enough machine guns, and the ones a trooper could carry in combat were still bulky and weighed twenty-one pounds. We didn't have grenade launchers at all. I settled for a mix of one machine gun in a squad, two with satchels of grenades and short rifles or pistols, and five with regular rifles. I hoped it would work.

When I got outside with the troops, my next goal was to teach the men and women how to move and fire. I couldn't teach everyone myself. I had to find squads with good aptitude who learned fast and make them teachers for others. Other adaptations had to follow. We had no phones. Not even a goddamn radio. Soldiers couldn't pull up a map on their combat visors and they couldn't check their positions by GPS. Night was dark. No night vision on the visor. It was back to the World War I stuff I had read about. On the good side, the people I was trying to train never had fancy equipment. You can't miss what you never had. When I showed teams how to space themselves in a wedge when they moved, and how to adapt that wedge to terrain and conditions, most of them picked it up fast. They did the same with tactics like advancing under fire.

We had a lot of room at that base, plenty of area to set up training exercises and plenty of buildings that weren't in use. After we had the squads organized and several days' worth of exercises, I walked out with Leah to a small building separated from the others. I had no idea what the original purpose of the structure was, and I didn't care.

"Put defenders in these positions." I pointed around the structure with one hand. "Set up a machine gun here. Then pick a platoon and tell them to take it. You score how they do and who would be casualties."

Leah was waiting for me to say more. When I didn't, she asked, "How do you want them to do it? What am I telling them to do?"

"Not that," I said. "You tell them what their objective is. It's their job to figure out how to reach that objective."

Now she was definitely smiling. "I think they are going to like this," she said.

Most of the teams did like it. They responded with energy and ingenuity, enough to challenge me to think up harder problems. Even better, most of the officers liked what they saw. Some were hopeless, starting with Merz, but I hoped it wouldn't matter too much. And, yes, the cooks still managed to have the food ready.

. . .

Being considered my aide and then assigned as a messenger for Zeb's staff left No Nonsense with plenty of time for training. He liked it and he did well with it. Being young and strong helped, but he also showed initiative and imagination on the tactical problems. I could see him as a team leader once he had experience under his belt, and as a squad leader after that. Thinking that way left me with mixed emotions.

No Nonsense also gave me some insight into how the soldiers viewed the training, because he would hear comments no one would make to me. The reception was positive. That didn't surprise me. Most folks respond well to being given responsibility and independence, as opposed to being treated like a replaceable cog in a machine. I knew that from my own training. The ones who abused the independence were fairly easy to spot and weed out.

Leah gave me much the same impression, but from an officer's perspective, which I appreciated. "I think this will work," she said. "The more we practice, the faster and more coordinated they are. Most of my officers are catching on, and the ones who don't—" She shrugged and didn't finish the sentence. "You've made a believer out of me, Leif. I'd do this in combat."

Still, the real test would be how the troops performed under live fire, if and when we needed them in combat. There are always some who are great in practice and simulation and then a disaster when the shit hits the fan. I'd seen that as well.

I figured we were going to get the answers to those questions when Zeb gave the order to break camp and move out in the last week of March 2252. That process took two days by itself. It wasn't simply a matter of having the troops form up and march out. It was readying the wagons, which carried everything from the army's tents and food to extra ammunition to fuel for the trucks and feed for the horses and donkeys that pulled the wagons.

The trucks groaned and creaked, towing artillery and carrying shells. There weren't enough trucks, as I had seen, so more horse-drawn wagons carried shells, and horses pulled 155 mm howitzers. There were even more horses and donkeys as replacements. The logistics of an army on the move were daunting.

At the end of all the preparation, though, the army formed itself into a massive column and marched out of Youngstown like a huge rattlesnake emerging from under a rock. The infantry divisions strode out on foot, the way infantry did even after we had mechanized. Officers and staff rode along the column on horseback, that group including one starman who hoped he was going to stay lucky. We had a force of cavalry ahead of us and on our flanks to screen us and, hopefully, find the enemy before they found us. If I ever had daydreams back when I was fighting in Central Asia or Mindanao about what going to war would be like in the twenty-third century, this was not it.

We didn't move much faster than the slithering rattlesnake I envisioned us to be, on the order of twenty to twenty-five miles a day. I'm not sure if the limiting factor was the infantry or the horse-drawn wagons. It might even have been the trucks. Pulling artillery and fully loaded, they wheezed worse than an asthmatic ready to stop breathing. I could only hope that when we found our enemy, we could drop our loads and strike the way a snake could.

Finding our enemy and bringing them to battle was, in fact, our first challenge. We headed due east initially, along the old roadway No Nonsense and I had ridden in on. Where the snow had melted away under the early spring sun, we had a broad concrete path to march along. The painted lane markers were gone, but we didn't need them.

"It's nice that this is still here and in such good shape," I said to Zeb.

"It should be," he said. "We dug into one of them years ago to see how they were put together. Eleven inches of concrete sitting on twenty-one inches of aggregates, and that on top of compacted dirt. These will still be here when God takes us all to Heaven, or when the second Tribulation comes, if you listen to the reapocalyptics."

That made sense, I supposed. I remembered reading that these highways were supposed to be good for fifty, even seventy-five years, and that was with heavy traffic on them. Based on the app my chip used, this had to be Interstate 80, and there were enough forlorn and bent road signs to confirm it.

I could track our progress the way I had before: by checking the map my app projected on my field against highway signs that still existed. The app didn't help the army, though, because I wasn't going to admit it existed. Enough people still stared into my eyes, trying to spot red numbers flashing in my pupils. The army relied on maps copied by hand from old, printed ones and then printed from the copies. Zeb charted our progress on those march by march as we moved into what they called Old Pennsie, which I remembered as Western Pennsylvania.

We halted for the day in a patch of Western Pennsylvania that was no different from every other patch of Western Pennsylvania we had passed. The terrain had more variety than Kansas—I'll admit that—but that's not saying much. The weather had warmed to the point that only patches of snow remained in shaded areas. Some of the trees and bushes had buds. The ground had turned soft, but we were able to keep to the road, where the footing was fine, except for the occasional clumped mass of old cars. Where we stopped, at the time the world had gone to hell, a truck had run off the road and into a sign supported by two metal posts. The impact had bent the sign over so that it now formed a convenient table for Zeb and his staff to spread out their maps. While we scrutinized the maps, the army made camp.

"I have said it before and I will keep saying it," Fuentes said. "I am opposed to you marching out into the unknown, with no knowledge of where the enemy is. That risks the troops and, more important, the equipment."

"That's why we have cavalry out as scouts." I could tell Zeb was weary of the argument, which had been proceeding since the day he ordered the army to march. He lifted his hat with one hand and rubbed the other over his scalp. "They are out ahead of us and to the south. We will learn where the Athenians are."

"The cavalry are too few," Fuentes persisted. "They could miss these Athenians."

"An army can't hide behind a tree," Zeb snapped. "It takes up space, it leaves tracks—particularly in this ground, as you can see from where we had to get off the road—and it is likely to advance along the old roadways for the same reason we do. And, just in case we miss the all the signs, we get information from the feral bands. We will not miss an army on the march."

"Those bands are as likely to sell us to the Athenians as give us genuine information," Jorgenson said. "Especially the ones with feral eyes. They're the worst, and the farther east we go, the more we see of them. It upsets the troops, sir. They believe the ones with feral eyes will witch the woods to lime us all."

"Do you believe in feral-eyed witches?" Zeb demanded.

"No, no. Of course not." Jorgenson took a step back, his face turning red. "Our men and women are afraid, though."

"Yet another problem with this ill-advised advance," Fuentes added.

"Fuentes, I'm surprised you didn't ask your patron in New Terra for a line commission, given your apparent expertise in operations. Or," Zeb drew the words out slowly, "would that be because you would then have to lead men in combat?"

Fuentes colored, his jaw clenched. I could hear his teeth grind from the other side of the makeshift table. He did not reply.

"It is a good time for silence," Zeb said. "Be aware that there are limits to what even a political officer can say with the army in the field. Now"—he abruptly turned back to the map—"liming is not so much a danger at this time of year, and it is more a danger in the woods than in open country. Certainly, the feral-eyed don't get it—at least I've never heard of it happening to one—but even if they have magic to protect themselves, that doesn't mean their magic affects anyone else. And we are going to turn south." He stabbed a finger at the map. "The risk is less to the south anyway, and that is where we are going. We are going south to annihilate that base the Athenians have set up. We will catch their army in the field and destroy it. That will leave their territory open to us, the same as they thought to do to us, and that will tip the war in our favor."

I edged closer to get a better look at the map, tried to compare where Zeb was pointing on his map to what I could see on my projection field. At the rate we were going, Zeb's turn south was no more than two days' march. And what then? Were the Athenians still in their base? Or were they out in the no-man's-land of Pennsylvania with us, betting that Zeb's cavalry or feral contacts wouldn't find them before they found us? All it would take was one surveillance satellite to end the guessing. But that had been a different world.

"Any questions?" Zeb asked.

There were none that were asked.

.   .   .

In fact, it was only two days' march before we passed the ruin of a town that had once been called Clearfield and picked up the sign of another one of the old interstates that headed south. We followed it. The weather was perceptibly warmer, which was good, but that forced us to stay on the roadway. The ground was soft away from the road, and our rate of march would have been cut in half. Even with keeping to the old road, it was slow going.

A day after our change of direction, a figure appeared in the distance to the south. Our whole column came to a halt because whoever this was, they were riding directly toward us. As soon as the rider spotted our lead elements, he kicked his horse to a gallop to reach us as soon as he could. Zeb and his staff spurred to the front of the column to meet him. Like an unwanted cousin, Fuentes trailed us. We were met by the generals of the other divisions as the rider pulled up, his horse lathered and shaking.

"General Mendenhall," he called out, "the enemy has broken camp and is headed northeast. They will intersect your line of march."

"They are headed northeast?" Zeb said. "You saw them yourself? How many men? How much artillery? Were you spotted?"

"No, sir, no. Not like that." The man's words were rushed. "Captain Yoshida heard it from some ferals. So we don't have counts, sir, only that they are on the move. Yoshida sent me and three others to be sure we found you as soon as possible."

"Then we still don't know what we are facing," Fuentes said.

Zeb ignored him and turned to No Nonsense. "Johnson, go get Lieutenant Hurtgen. Have him bring half a dozen scouts and a fresh mount for this man." When No Nonsense rode off, he turned back to the rider. "I'm sorry not to give you any rest, but this is critical. My compliments to Captain Yoshida, and have him use the men I'm sending with you to find the enemy and report on their progress. And do not initiate contact with them."

"Yes, sir." The man saluted.

It took very little time for Hurtgen to appear with his men. The first rider changed mounts while Zeb repeated his orders to Hurtgen. Then the little troop was off in the direction the first man had come from.

Zeb sat on his horse and watched them as they disappeared from sight. "Well, gentlemen, it appears that our enemy has crept out of his lair. With luck, he doesn't know we are here."

.   .   .

We marched south. The land folded into hills and ridges, much different from the flat ground we had left to the north. A palpable tension filled the army. An enemy was marching in our direction. A battle had moved from a possibility to a near certainty. No campfires were allowed when we camped for the night. Men and women who could write wrote letters. These were not to send but to have on their persons in case they died, when they might be collected and given to their families. The literate ones then wrote letters for their illiterate friends. All that was left was to know when the battle would happen, and where.

We passed the southern end of the remains of Altoona, keeping the ridgeline on our right that was west of the ruins and ran north to south. At that point, I saw two riders coming from the south. I was at the head of the column with Zeb when they came in, along with two of our screening cavalrymen.

"The Athenians are only a day's ride south and east," the lead rider said. "Forty thousand of them for sure. There is open ground in that direction around some town from before. Not a big one."

"Good," Zeb said. He shifted in his saddle as the other officers came up. "Jorgenson, Chopra, your divisions will have the right. When we make contact, work to the right and turn his left flank. Do not allow him to get to the south. Howard, you will have the center, Kamper, you have the left. Kamper, if you can turn his right flank and create a double envelopment,

do so, but do not allow him to turn yours. Merz, maintain the reserve behind the center."

"And if his numbers are, in fact, far superior to ours?" Fuentes asked.

"Then we will retreat, keeping an open line to the west," Zeb said.
"Perhaps, in that case, you can pray to God to send another Tribulation
into Old Pennsie. I am not going to worry about that until I see it."

With that, his generals and their staffs raced back to their units. The
army began to split up, each division moving to the position they would
take for the start of the battle tomorrow. Zeb sent most of the horse-drawn
artillery to the right with Jorgenson and Chopra and kept the trucks with
him in the center. When it came to maneuverability on ground he had not
seen, he trusted the horses more than the trucks.

The deployment was well along in the late afternoon when the crackle
of gunfire rang out from east of our position.

"Our cavalry has run into theirs," Zeb said. "Or skirmishers. It doesn't
matter. They will know we are here, but not what we plan."

He sent messengers, No Nonsense among them, to the divisions,
telling them to have their men fed and rested, and setting the time for the
next morning's advance.

CHAPTER THIRTY SEVEN

Morning dawned, clear and chilly. I rode with Zeb and his staff into the small town the scouts had mentioned. Zeb picked a block of stores to serve as his command post for the coming battle. The buildings were made of concrete and were largely intact. One store, in the middle of the block, still had its roof. It had been a small pharmacy. The shelves that once held medication were bare, but T-shirts for tourists and packaged goods from before the apocalypse filled plastic containers on shelves that still stood, littering the floor where shelving had collapsed. I saw boxes of alcohol wipes and makeup, along with discarded plastic wraps that had once held toilet paper and candy bars, including my favorite brand. Every wrapper that had once held food had been ripped open long ago and left on the floor. We swept it all aside. The place would do for a nerve center. Messengers on horseback raced to and from this point, tying the army's components together.

By midmorning, we could hear the boom of artillery from the east and northeast, where Kamper and Howard's divisions had gone. The blasts were followed by a nearly continuous crackle of rifles mixed with the stuttering of machine guns. About an hour later, gunfire and artillery chimed in from the south.

I stayed at the command center with Zeb. He looked cool, almost casual, as reports came in. I imagine I looked the same, but what my body wanted to do was grab a rifle and use it. My usual battle surge of adrenaline was washing over me, but I had nothing to do. I was Zeb's civilian adviser. For the first time in my life, I was in a battle but not in, or even close to, the fighting. Not only that, but it was also impossible for me to tell what was happening. There were no voices in in my earphones, no symbols and positions on my visor. Information came at the speed of a horse and could easily be obsolete on arrival. The information, in fact, was no better than what a man had scrawled on paper or a rider had heard and, hopefully, remembered correctly. I found it nerve-racking.

After a couple of hours of us guessing at chaos we couldn't see, No Nonsense came galloping up from the south.

"We're winning!" he shouted as he jumped from his horse. "General Jorgenson says to tell you that the enemy is falling back!"

Zeb straightened up from where he had been bent over one of the maps. His beard moved with the flicker of a smile underneath. Before he said anything, another rider was headed in. This one brought similar news from Howard in the center.

"Good news, indeed," Zeb said. Swiftly, he prepared another set of orders to go back to the frontline divisions. "Tell the generals they are not to lose contact with the Athenians as they retreat. Keep the pressure on them and we will turn this retreat into a rout." He handed folded papers to No Nonsense and another messenger standing next to him. "If Jorgenson and Chopra can get past the Athenian flank, they are to wheel east and north to cut off their retreat. We can bag the whole army. But they must understand: Under no circumstances are they to allow the enemy to escape south, back to their base. They must prevent that at all costs. Repeat that back to me and take the writing as well."

"Yes, sir!" No Nonsense shouted, and did so, letter-perfect. He was all flushed and wide-eyed enthusiasm. "I will see that this gets through!"

I don't think I ever looked like that.

This would have been so much simpler with a phone.

"I fear you are overconfident," said Fuentes. "It could be a ruse. A trick to have our men rush forward and then crush them with a counterattack from reserves we are not aware of. We need to consolidate our positions and, if we advance, do so with caution."

"Political Officer Fuentes, if there is any man who could snatch defeat from the jaws of victory, or turn wine into vinegar while it is in the mouth, it is you. If the Athenians have a second army we have yet to see, they will attack us with it whether we advance or not. We have a chance to encircle them or push them east into Bosnywash, where there is nothing to eat but ash and stone. That is how to win. If we let them re-form, we will have to do this again and without the advantage we had this morning."

"It is still a risk," Fuentes insisted. "You were not given this army to take risks for your own enjoyment of gambling. You do not know the truth of the positions ahead of us."

Zeb pursed his lips and blew out a gust of air. "Then we should ride forward and see for ourselves what is happening. You may ride with me, Political Officer Fuentes, so you can demonstrate your courage to the boys and girls up front. Leif, why don't you come with us as well?"

Fuentes hunched his shoulders at Zeb's words, and his eyes seemed to be studying a pattern in the wrappers on the floor. His "As you say, General" was very soft. I couldn't detect a trace of enthusiasm.

I saw no particular need to demonstrate my courage to anyone, but anything was better than pacing back and forth in that derelict old store. Maybe that's an exaggeration. I saddled up along with Zeb, Fuentes, and some of Zeb's staff.

We rode forward slowly while the human wreckage of battle streamed past us, headed for the aid stations and surgeons' tents at the rear. Some wounded were carried by their mates on improvised stretchers; others staggered along, bloody but under their own power, sometimes holding a hand against part of their body to try to stem the flow of their blood. I saw one man hopping, his hand on a fellow's shoulder for support because his left leg was gone below the knee, nothing there but a bloody, dripping stump. A woman walked stiffly on her own, eyes fixed on a point in the infinite distance, one side of her face and jaw shot away so I could see her tongue and remaining teeth through the hole. No medevac would be coming for any of these men and women. No combat support hospital would treat their wounds. I doubted the medics of the twenty-third century could do much more for the wounded than those of four or five hundred years before. I sat on my horse and cursed what I and all those who had lived in my time had done to our world. I heard Yong speak in my mind about our responsibility. I felt it then. I wished I had been able to fly away with her and never have to face it.

· · ·

It took time to figure out what had happened on the battlefield. The fight had taken place under blue skies and bright sun, but the whole thing could have been hidden in a fogbank for the trouble we had sorting out events.

In fact, Chopra and Jorgenson's divisions had outflanked the Athenians. However, they had adhered strictly to that part of their orders that said to prevent the Athenians from escaping to the south. They kept to the south and did not wheel north. When the Athenian commander realized his danger, he was able to withdraw to the east. That triggered a general retreat across the Athenian line. We won the field but did not roll up their flank and did not destroy their army. Casualties were not too heavy, a couple of thousand, although I feared many of the wounded would die because of the poor treatment available. I had been sure it would be worse with the dense skirmish lines these officers used, but the engagement, for all the sound and fury, had not lasted long and neither side had been dug in. Both armies were intact and able to fight another battle.

This is where geography dictated what would happen. The land in this area was folded into a series of ridges and valleys, which ran, roughly, north to south. This was inconvenient for armies that moved by horse, foot, and wagon. The old roads in the area had been laid down long before the era of superhighways. They followed the curves of the land and sought to go around ridges or find gaps in them, wherever those were located. The effect was to spread out both armies across a wider front. The divisions in the south went farther south, those in the north farther north. Neither side had enough men and women to cover the front with a continuous line of troops, and the ridges would have broken them up even if we did.

Days passed without the battle being rejoined. Only the occasional burst of gunshots as skirmishers ran into each other served as a reminder that an enemy was nearby. The Athenians continued to withdraw, seeking to find a way to bring their army back together. We continued to pursue, now as three semi-independent forces: Jorgenson and Chopra to the south, Kamper to the north, and Howard in the center where Zeb, I, and—regrettably—Fuentes rode.

The weather did not remain sunny. Whatever else had happened, this was still the northeastern part of America. The clouds rolled in. While it was too warm to snow, we got a chill rain. That washed away all the remaining snow and left mud in its place. We were away from the superhighways. The old roads were narrow asphalt, badly broken up and often covered over. Some of those damned trucks got stuck, and we had to harness teams of horses to the trucks to pull them loose. Even the horses sank into the mud, and it was only with an effort and a sucking pop that the horse could walk forward. Men and women fared little better. Our advance became a slow slog. Any chance of catching our retreating foe sank into the mud and mist along with our boots.

Nothing lasts forever. Not even misery. Five days after the battle, the rains slowed to a light drizzle as we passed through another old and desolate town. As always, the town was deserted. If any ferals—or indies, as Elvy called them—lived nearby, the armies would have scared them away. I had reached the point where I was no different from Zeb and all the rest. I paid no attention to the relics of a bygone world. TO HELL WITH THE FUTURE had been painted on a wall along one street, BE KIND AT THE LAST on another. It was all part of the landscape, like the trees and the rocks. I didn't even look at bones, if there were any still visible. Something did catch my eye in this particular dreary place, however. It was the name of the town on the side of a building: Chambersburg.

In that blink of an eye, I knew where we were. I didn't need a map—not Zeb's paper, not my chip. I knew this long chase was coming to an end. I knew it because that name meant we were coming to a place where the old roads would come together. It would be a place where the armies would coalesce and fight.

I knew it because it had all happened before.

I knew the name of that place.

Gettysburg.

CHAPTER THIRTY EIGHT

We didn't recapitulate the first battle of Gettysburg. Too many things were different. Both sides had machine guns. The artillery was far deadlier and had longer range. There were fewer troops—far fewer—on both sides, and their positions were spread over a wider area. The Athenian right was well north of the old town and dug in, blocking Kamper. Jorgenson and Chopra had at last turned north as the Athenians fell back along what had been the Taneytown Road, but the line was south of the Round Tops. Only the center was much the same, with the Athenians dug in on Cemetery Ridge. Their artillery was situated behind them, where it could fire to all parts of the battlefield.

That artillery on each side was a big part of why both armies dug in and dug in deep. It is astonishing how fast men can dig and throw up earthworks when bullets and shells are flying at them. Within a day of reaching these positions, a set of trenches appeared that would have been at home in the First World War. They lacked only the barbed wire, which neither side had brought along.

On the first day, Kamper attacked the northern lines in the morning; Jorgenson and Chopra attacked in the south in the afternoon. Both were repulsed bloodily. Even if they had coordinated the attacks the way they should have—and that's not so easy without phones or radio or even tele-graph—I don't think the outcome would have been different.

The next day, the Athenians in their turn attacked our lines to the north and south. Their attacks were better coordinated, but the results were the same: bodies in the space between the lines. On the third day, the armies traded attack and counterattack up and down the whole line. A position was taken here and there, but the attackers were always so de-pleted that counterattacks easily recaptured the positions. The day ended with the positions where they had started. The only difference was a great many men and women dead. That and wounded between the lines, who moaned and called for water or their mothers until, one by one through the night, they fell silent.

It occurred to me that if we managed to kill ourselves right down to the last man and woman, there would be no armies left in the east, and no threat of invasion, and we could call that a victory. And it would serve us all right.

The fourth day was quiet. Some desultory shooting took place up and down the lines from time to time, but there were no major attacks. Both sides were too exhausted. Zeb and his generals and all their staffs gathered at a group of cottages by a lake. The cottages had been built of stone, mostly, and some were in fair condition. I won't say they were out of range of the Athenian artillery, but it would have been extreme range, and the cottages weren't obvious amid the trees. We found one with the roof almost intact and the staff set it up as a headquarters. I was there, too, as was Political Officer Fuentes, like the ghost at the banquet. A hastily sketched map of the area with unit positions drawn on it lay on a wooden table, the center of attention.

"The problem," said Jorgenson, his uniform clean and neat, "is that your man"—he stabbed an index finger at Howard—"could not get up this ridge yesterday." He took the finger and banged it onto the map where Cemetery Ridge was marked. "If your man had the courage or the leader-ship, his troops would have overrun those positions, gotten to the artillery, and we could have driven home our attack from the south."

Howard bridled at the accusation. "If you and Chopra had done what you were supposed to days ago and cut off their retreat when you had the chance, we would not even be in this position. My division shattered itself on that hill yesterday. That position is impregnable. You know the legends."

"I know plenty of legends," Jorgenson retorted. "It's no different from George's dilemma we teach children. I can find print in New Terra saying that ridge could not be taken even by the best army of its time. But I can also show you print that says the Southern army did pierce that center and the ridge did fall. Who knows which ones are true? We know better than to believe stories from before the Tribulation. They might as well all be fake. What *is* true is that *your* men did not take the position yesterday."

"Enough." The one word from Zeb cut off the argument like a knife across the throat. "Our job is to find a way to win, not to find fault."

All four generals should have been relieved, except I don't think Zeb had anyone better to replace them with. Not to mention the politics that went with all of them.

"I do know the truth," I said. Sergeants don't break in on generals, but I was a starman and not part of the army, and I was getting sick of the carping and whining. "On July third, 1863, the South tried a frontal attack on that ridge and failed. They lost the battle. That's the history; I don't care what's in any of the books you can find today. That's not the point, though. No position is impregnable. It's a matter of finding a solution to an attack problem."

"Well, our lucky starman has spoken," Jorgenson said, his face set in a sneer. "What's your solution? To have Howard's men attack in groups of four when they won't hold together even as one unit?"

"That is not fair, Jorgenson!" Howard shouted. He leaned over the table, jabbing a finger in Jorgenson's direction. "My men cannot go up that hill again. They cannot."

"Again, enough," Zeb said. "In this, I am inclined to agree with General Howard. His division took too many losses yesterday. The only fresh unit we have is Colonel Merz's." He turned to me. "Those are the men and women you trained in your tactics, Leif. What do you think? If we send all of them, including the emergency reserve, will that be enough?"

This was not the first time I should have kept my mouth shut.

"If each squad has clear objectives and is allowed to find their own solution, and if the artillery will fire the way I tell you, and if you have troops to reduce the strong points the first wave bypasses and exploit the breach they make, yes, it can be done." I got all of that out in one sentence because I was sure someone would cut me off if I paused at any point. While I spoke, Merz's face lost whatever trace of color it had.

"Good." Zeb turned to Merz. "Bring your boys and girls up behind the lines but keep them concealed. We'll give them their objectives and let them familiarize themselves with the situation."

"No!" That came from Fuentes, who had been standing back from the table, and it startled all of us. "The only role that reserve should be taking is to screen our withdrawal, and that is what we should be doing. We cannot throw this army away in a series of hopeless attacks. That reserve is our rear guard. We need to withdraw."

"Fuentes, you are way out of line," Zeb said. "The authority of a political officer is policy and loyalty to New Terran direction. You have no command authority in the field."

"I have the authority to relieve you, General Mendenhall, and I am doing so now."

His hand went for his pistol, but it never reached the grip. He froze because Zeb's pistol was already out and aimed directly at his heart.

"Political Officer Fuentes, you are under arrest," Zeb said. "The charge is mutiny in the face of the enemy. Your court-martial will need to wait until we have addressed our immediate problem, but never fear, I will attend to it."

"You are a fool, Mendenhall. Persist in this and you will be hanged in Government Square in New Terra."

Zeb's response was to gesture to No Nonsense and one of the other messengers. "Tie him up and secure him in one of the other buildings. I want a guard on him at all times."

My pistol was out as well, on the chance that someone might disagree with Zeb. No one did.

Once Fuentes was trussed and removed, Zeb turned back to me. "All right, Leif, I think you and I have a little work to do."

.   .   .

That work involved assembling Merz's full reserve brigade at a safe distance behind our line and distributing the objectives by squad. I saw No Nonsense there with his squad. He would be one of the riflemen. The boy was intent on the briefing, focused and coiled like a spring ready to pop.

I could not help thinking that I was the one who had gotten him into exactly the sort of situation I had been determined to keep him out of.

When we were done with the troops, it was late in the day. The sun, to the extent it could be seen through the clouds, was low on the horizon and the light was growing dim. Zeb tapped me on the shoulder and waved for me to step aside with him, away from everyone else.

"I think," Zeb said, "once it is dark, it would be a good idea to reconnoiter up that hill and make sure the strongpoints and machine guns are where we think they are. If we have to change objectives, I would rather do it in advance than trust the squads to adjust to surprises. It's not that long a line up top of that hill. I'd like you to come with me and have a look."

Anytime you think you have seen and heard everything, trust me, you haven't. He did have one good point. With little time to prepare and no time at all to rehearse, being certain in advance of strong points to suppress and bypass and the weak points we could break through could make the difference between success and failure. This scheme, however, was cuckoo.

"Zeb, the last time I looked, you're the commanding general. You are not the person who should be skulking around enemy positions. That's my skill set, not yours."

Zeb smiled. "I'm sure you're right. However, I'm staking everything on this attack. I may deal with Fuentes, but the problem he represents will not go away. I will need to deal with that problem, and I can do that only with a clear victory. Further, I cannot keep the army out in the wild forever, nor can I bleed it white with one attack after another. I know these tactics we are going to use are familiar to you, but they are new to my troops and my officers. And to me. I want to know for myself."

"I give damned accurate reports." I noticed I had talked myself into doing the job. "What if you get shot? Or captured?"

Zeb shrugged. He was still smiling. "There *are* risks to participating in a battle. If I were to line the boys and girls up in close order, step in front of them, wave my hat, and lead the charge to inspire them, there would be some risk to that, wouldn't you say? I will charge you with making sure I am not captured."

I hate it when the person I'm arguing with is right.

CHAPTER THIRTY NINE

I met Zeb a little before midnight at what had been a fast-food burger place. Most of its plastic sign with red and yellow colors was still in its frame, which made it an easy-to-find meeting place even with only a lantern for light. Its windows were all smashed out; shards of glass could still be seen among leaves and other debris on the floor and around the building. In that sense it was no different from many other structures. Inside, seated at plastic tables as though waiting for their order, were Zeb and four of his staff. In uniform.

"No," I said. "Let me repeat, no. I agreed to do one stupid thing, but I am not compounding it by dragging a whole party of you along."

One of the staff officers started to speak, but I cut him off by drawing my hand across my throat.

"Don't start. I'm not listening," I said. "For what we're doing, numbers only increase the risk of detection. We're looking, not fighting. And Zeb, you need to look like me."

I was a walking pile of dirt. I had smeared my face with mud and grease to hide my skin. A black woolen cap, pulled down over my head, did the same for my hair. Maybe I looked like I had rolled in the mud. Well, I had.

"He is right, Thomas," Zeb said to the one who had tried to speak. "We are going to do this his way. Wait for us here. In the event I don't return, send out the orders in my name and, if anyone asks, say that I am ill."

I could see they didn't like it, but they obeyed. We spent a few minutes making Zeb as dirty as I was. Then we headed out.

With the cloud cover, it was a dark night. It was hard even to see where we were going until we reached the base of the hill, where the campfires of the Athenians beyond the crest provided some light against the clouds. I had a little advantage here. The bicentennial of the American Civil War had come while I was in the service during the Troubles. In addition to learning and singing almost every Union song, we had argued over nearly every minute of the Battle of Gettysburg. I knew that terrain—as it had been, anyway—and the location of every monument to unit or soldier. The area was more wooded than it had been hundreds of years ago, but the face of Cemetery Ridge was still open. The rail fence was long gone, naturally. The Copse of Trees was more like a grove now. Along the crest, though, the battle monuments to different units and states still stood out. They gave me as good a map of our location as I could ask for.

I made for a line of trees and bushes that grew up the hill to our right. With any luck, the two of us would be close to invisible. As long as we didn't trip over something and raise an alarm. We worked our way up the slope, as close to the ridgeline as I dared. This late at night, it was quiet in the enemy camp. They had done a good job of digging in, as far as trench and earthworks went. They would have good protection against shrapnel. Some places looked like we would have to drop a shell right on top of them to do anything with the artillery. That was okay. As long as we could make them keep their heads down, I was fine.

There were not as many machine gun posts as I expected. That could mean different things, anything from they were short on machine guns—good—to everyone had a light machine gun so they didn't need the strongpoints—bad. I moved along the slope, counting fires and trying to estimate the number of men along the ridge. Their line seemed thin. As a rule, they should have had troops back away from the line to counterattack against any breakthrough, but I couldn't see anything that looked like a second line of defense. Had they pulled troops from the ridge to reinforce their defenses to the north or south? That presented an interesting possibility. Did they believe the position was impregnable?

We moved south along the line where it ran into the woods. The defenses did not look as robust there. If they were used to troops attacking in close order, would they discount the woods because that would interfere with an attacking formation?

While I was considering that, I heard a snap next to me. Zeb had stepped on a branch. It shouldn't have broken like that, not with the rain and snowmelt, but it had. I froze. Tried to freeze my breath as well.

I heard an oath from the other side of the defense line. Damn it! Why couldn't the sentry have gone to sleep? I strained my eyes, trying to see if men were moving or aiming weapons. It was too dark and the night vision on my field was too poor. The crack and flash of a rifle discharge split the night. I heard the bullet whistle through the air, a gasp, and then the smack of the bullet into a tree to the right.

I heard another voice shout, "What the fuck are you shooting at?"

"Something out there."

"What was out there was your fucking bullet hitting a tree."

I heard other voices now, all angry at being woken. I heard someone moving in our direction but still behind the defenses.

Then I heard the one who had cursed first. "Nothing out there but your fucking imagination. Or maybe we'll find a dead feral in the morning. Or maybe it was your lucky starman and you just shot him. Idiot! Fire that thing off next to my ear again without a better reason, and I'll use you for target practice."

There were protests from the first man that he had heard something, that a shadow had shifted, that he heard a voice after he shot, that it was not his imagination. Those were to no avail. The night became quiet again. I decided we had seen what we needed to see. It was time to withdraw.

.   .   .

It was still dark when we returned to the burger place. A single lantern flickered on a table. Zeb's staff had remained there, a couple of them with their heads down on tables, but they all came alert as we walked through the entrance.

"General, what happened to you?" That came from two of them simultaneously.

I looked over at Zeb and saw he had his right hand pressed over his upper left arm.

"You were hit by that bullet," I said. "I heard almost nothing from you." My estimate of his self-control and composure went up several orders of magnitude.

"Grazed me only," Zeb said. "No more than a scratch. That was neither the time nor the place for noise. Anyway, I think my tongue is bloodier from where I bit down on it."

Everything else waited while we checked Zeb's wound. We crowded into an alcove where the burgers and fries had been made and where Zeb could be positioned close to hooks that were convenient for hanging lanterns. There, one of the staff officers lit two more of them.

By the light of multiple lanterns, Zeb's coat and shirtsleeve were bloody. He winced as we took the clothing layers off. Beneath was a gash in the outside of his triceps with a little tunnel at the back. It was a minor wound, as he had said. It looked a lot bloodier than it was.

An audible sigh of collective relief went up from his staff.

"I told you it was crazy for you to go," I said. "You were lucky."

"No," Zeb said. "For me, yes, it was lucky. An inch over and I would probably lose the arm. Another couple of inches and I'm probably dead." He shrugged, grimacing. "Maybe I had my lucky starman with me."

I was growing to hate that phrase.

"That's not the point," Zeb said. "Leif, you have an exaggerated idea of the importance of any individual. Plow any field, poke through any old building. Even today, you'll find bones. All of them were once people who probably thought they were important. But dead is dead, and the world goes on without any of them. I told you, the orders were set regardless of whether I was here. What is important is what we saw." He pointed at each one of his staff officers. "I can't say for sure if Leif's fire and maneuver tactics will work, but I am convinced that our usual tactics would fail. A giant, bloody failure. And I'm not sure how effective the artillery will be."

"Mostly valuable for making them keep their heads down so they can't shoot at us," I said. "The other thing we should do is shell that open slope before we start."

That brought protests from the staff. "All that will do is make it harder to cross the ground," Thomas said.

"Churning up that ground will actually provide us some cover on the way up," I said. "We're not trying to keep a straight line. Every squad goes on their own. Once you've done that with the artillery, blast the top of that hill and keep blasting it until our troops are almost there. Then stop. The defenders will have only a handful of seconds before we're on them."

"We have some flare rockets," Zeb said. "Give them to the squads going up. When they are close, they can set them off and we'll stop the shelling where they are."

"That assumes our troops will advance that close to where the shells are falling," Thomas said.

"Just don't drop short rounds into them," I said.

"Yes." Zeb stroked his beard with his good hand. "Have Howard get his men ready. The units that can still fight. They can follow the attack into the gaps, and they can take care of the strongpoints we bypass."

Thank you for thinking of that went through my mind. "Yes," I said. "And now, scratch or no scratch, that wound has to be cleaned up." In an era without antibiotics, any wound could be a game of roulette. I didn't want to put Zeb's philosophy of no individual importance to the test.

CHAPTER FORTY

Zeb did create a disruption, although it wasn't his fault. For all his asser-tion that the orders had been written and it would make no difference if he were killed, it was soon clear that none of his officers was doing any-thing, much less starting the assault, until he was attended to. So, we had to go wake up the chief surgeon. When that worthy realized his patient was General Zebulon Mendenhall, he turned into a stammering fumble-fingers. I told him I would be happy to take care of it myself, which made him indignant and cost us more time. Finally, he took Zeb inside the sur-gery tent to deal with the scratch while a crowd waited outside. I pushed into the tent and no one stopped me. Seen in better light, it was a lot more than a scratch and worse than I had thought by lantern light in the burger place. The bullet had cut a deep furrow across the muscle before tunneling under the skin and bursting out the back of the triceps. It did need atten-tion, and it left me even more impressed with Zeb's self-control. That was when the surgeon noticed my presence and ordered me out.

By the time the wound was attended to, it was fully light and we dis-covered that Political Officer Fuentes was gone. One of the guards outside the cabin he had been placed in was dead, knifed. The other guard was unaccounted for. Two other men from Howard's division were missing, as were four horses with packs. Again, everything ground to a halt while other men from that division were questioned. Naturally, no one knew anything. Zeb and his staff had a debate as to whether Howard's division could be relied on.

"I should have simply had him shot." Zeb's words came out of a face that could have just chewed horseradish. "I didn't do that, because I knew there would be repercussions in New Terra. Those would probably have come no matter what, and now he is loose."

"Do you think he has gone over to the Athenians?" I asked. "Would he betray our attack?"

"No." Zeb was definite on that. "He is running for New Terra as fast as his horse can carry him. Once there, he will set his revenge in motion, and there are plenty in the senate who will listen to him. Some things need to change. If we win this campaign, maybe . . . Leave that for now," he finished.

"I will have riders after him," Howard said. "We will catch him and finish this business."

"Riders, yes, General, but not from your division," said Thomas.

"What are you implying?" Howard's raised eyebrows framed his glare.

"Thomas is correct," Zeb said, "even if impertinent. If your riders did not bring him back, there would be talk. Kamper, send a detail from your troops."

I thought Zeb had framed the issue with Howard's men far more politely than Thomas had implied, or anybody else was thinking.

All of this chewed up more time. We decided it would be better to feed the troops and start the bombardment while they were eating.

I was sitting on the stoop of some collapsed house, trying to convince myself that weak pine needle tea was coffee and wondering why I didn't hear the guns, when No Nonsense came running up.

"Leif!" he yelled. "General Mendenhall needs you. We have a problem."

I wondered what would happen if, the next time someone said that to me, I said, *I don't give a fuck.* They would probably stand there the way No Nonsense was, with an expectant look on their face, like a puppy hoping for a treat.

"Do we know what the problem is?"

"We can't find Colonel Merz. He's not with his troops. That's why they held off starting the artillery. General Mendenhall said to get you." No Nonsense's posture said he wanted me to spring up and sprint back to HQ with him.

Well, the tea sucked anyway, and it wasn't going to magically make up for a night with no sleep. I pitched it and stood up. "Let's go."

By the time we reached the house Zeb had appropriated for his HQ, they had found Merz.

"In his tent." Zeb's voice dripped with disgust. "Dead drunk. It would be better if he had the grace to just be dead."

Naturally. I remembered Merz was inclined to drink and disinclined to combat.

"What difference does it make?" I said. "The squads and fire teams go on their own. It's not like we need the troops to line up with him in front waving a flag. That's the whole point. You can court-martial him afterward."

Zeb shifted his stance uncomfortably. I assumed his arm was bothering him. "They will go in that way," he said, "the way you trained them. But this is still new. It's important for their leader to be with them when they set out."

What was he getting at? "Okay, nice to have and we'll have to live without it. What do you need me for?"

He put his right hand on my shoulder and looked into my eyes. "Leif, I want you to take the boys and girls in."

My mouth dropped open. "Zeb, have you forgotten a couple of things? I'm not an officer, never was. I'm not even really in this army of yours."

Zeb smiled enough to show teeth. "Doesn't matter. You're the starman, Leif. They'll follow you."

. . .

It's an old military adage that no battle plan survives contact with the enemy. Ours hadn't even made it that far. We had planned to kick off the attack by the dawn's early light, but by the time we had Merz's brigade to the jump-off point, it was late afternoon. The one silver lining I could find was that the cloud cover had broken, so the westering sun would be in the defenders' eyes.

Leah met me as I left Zeb's HQ. She was carrying a rifle with a short bayonet fixed under the barrel, a plain helmet on her head, and, of all things, a grin on her face. "I told you I was willing to try this for real," she said. "I'll be on the left. It's good for morale that the girls and boys see their officers take the same risks. Especially when they see you."

Zeb and Leah were right. My appearance did bring a response from the troops. Wherever they saw me as I moved to the front, they raised a cheer for Starman Leif and shouted that they were with me. I thought they had gone insane. I walked over to where No Nonsense's squad was checking their equipment. He wouldn't have it any other way. One of the riflemen in the squad was a riflewoman whose name I didn't catch. She looked no older than No Nonsense, with a lock of stray brown hair that escaped from under her helmet and hung down across her cheek. I heard the whistle in the air that meant an incoming shell.

"Down!" I yelled, and dropped.

The shell hit short of our position and blasted into some rocks. After the rattle of flying fragments stopped, I stood up, along with the others in the vicinity. All except for the sergeant of No Nonsense's squad. A shard of rock had hit him in the chest, and he was down.

No Nonsense looked at me. "You lead us in his place, Leif," he said. "We all know you."

The girl with the stray brown hair brandished her rifle at me. Her eyes were wide and her knuckles white where she gripped the rifle. "I'll be with you all the way, Starman, and you'll see a girl shoot as straight as any man, or even you."

They were looking at me, looking *to* me. No Nonsense picked up the sergeant's rifle and cartridge box, brought them over, and gave them to me.

How do I get myself into these situations?

Any reply I might have made would have been lost in the roar because that was when our artillery began to shoot. I felt the ground tremor and heard the outgoing shells above flying toward their targets. I heard incoming, too—you can tell the difference—as the Athenian guns engaged in counterbattery fire. Our opening salvo blasted the slope in front of us, then all the batteries shifted to hit the defense line at the top of the ridge.

I felt the sickly-sweet cocktail of exhilaration and fear, both mixed with adrenaline, swirl through my veins the same as I had so many times before. I saw No Nonsense, the girl with the stray brown hair, and the rest of their squad. I saw Petey, Luke, Jamaal, and my old squad standing in the rain on Mindanao.

Whaddaya say, Sarge? Petey asked. *We gonna do this?*

I knew what to do.

"Time to go!" I yelled, and ran forward in a crouch, rifle at the ready. The fire team with No Nonsense and the girl with the stray brown hair followed me in a tight wedge.

Ours was a line that moved upslope, in the woods to the left, across the newly blasted face of the hill, and into the woods on the right, but it was an irregular one made up of small teams that moved on their own, each fixed on its own targets at the top. There was little fire coming down at us. The barrage was doing its job, forcing the defenders to keep their heads down or have them blown off.

We came to within twenty-five yards of the defensive line at the top, twenty-five yards from where our shells were blasting those defenses. I found a second for a prayer that none of our gunners would drop a round short and into our laps. One team leader fired a rocket to signal that we had reached that point. As if by magic, the shells stopped landing in front of us and shifted to a point farther back in the enemy position. I rushed at the enemy line, the squad with me.

We caught them as they were picking themselves up after the bombardment stopped. The few seconds between when the shells stopped coming down and when we hit them gave them no time to organize their defense. We shot down some and jumped into the earthworks and trench and took out the others hand to hand.

To my left was a jog in the trench wall. I couldn't see if the area past it was occupied. Our grenadier flipped a grenade into it. A helmet popped into the air with the explosion. I peeked around. Saw bodies. Saw a crew at a machine gun beyond the bodies. I burst around the corner, firing my rifle as fast as I could lever rounds into the chamber. The men at the machine gun dropped. More bodies in that section of trench. Good enough.

"Keep moving!" I yelled. "Next target is the guns. Move and fire! Fire and move!"

I was moving out of the trench and past it as I shouted. The rest of the squad was moving with me. Bypass resistance, penetrate deep, get the targets, leave the rest for the units behind us. That was the plan. Our enemy improvised a defense line before us. Sparks of muzzle flashes came from behind rocks and an overturned field piece, sending us to the ground. I risked picking my head up for a quick look. Our machine gunner was down in a pool of blood ten yards from me. The girl with the stray brown hair was on one knee, firing at the defenders. She gave me the opening I needed. I scrambled on hands and knees to the machine gunner's body, slung my rifle, and grabbed the machine gun. It was heavy and awkward compared to the M8 I had used, but it fired on automatic. I hosed down the position by the overturned artillery piece with a stream of bullets. The fire from that position ceased. Two men jumped up from their positions near it and ran back. We shot them down.

"To the guns!" I cried. "Get to their guns!" I ran forward, the air filled with the shrill whistle of bullets. "Rangers lead the way!" The words burst out.

Where had that come from?

We were into their artillery, far behind their initial front line. They tried to fight there at first, but as more men fell, they lost heart. They broke; they ran. Their guns fell silent.

Howard's men came up behind us and surged through the gaps we had made. They turned, some to the south, others to the north, to clasp the enemies there in a pincer. Our guns shifted to attack those positions. In the dying light of the day, the music of our artillery boomed out a symphony across the heavens while we danced to the staccato beat of machine guns.

Beyond my squad's position among the captured artillery was only open ground to the east. The enemy's position had been split through the middle. I was awash in adrenaline; it sparkled at every synapse in my body.

A little ahead of me was No Nonsense. He was leaning over, one hand supporting himself on a wheel of a 155 mm howitzer, the other holding his rifle by its barrel, stock upon the ground. He was vomiting over the wheel.

I turned around and saw the girl with the stray brown hair behind me. She lay on her back, sightless eyes turned up to the darkening sky.

Her left chest was soaked in blood, three bullet holes evident. I had never learned her name.

Glory has a price.

Always.

CHAPTER FORTY ONE

The Second Battle of Gettysburg was as complete a victory as I have ever heard of. For all intents and purposes, the Athenian Army in the east ceased to exist. Their troops, dead and wounded, lay on the field in the thousands. With the medical care available, I wasn't sure how many of those wounded would survive. Most of the rest were prisoners. A small number had escaped east toward the desolation of Bosnywash. We didn't worry about them.

The argument that raged in Zeb's HQ the next morning, once the scale of the victory was clear, was about what to do next and what to do with those prisoners. Nobody had anticipated the situation.

"Unless we are going to turn the army around and march back home, we can't send the Athenians to New Terra. It will be enough to send their wounded back with our own. For the rest, it would take too many men to guard them and too much of our supplies." Howard had his hands on the table that held the maps as though propping himself up.

"We can't build a camp for them and keep them here," Chopra said.

"We have plenty of machine gun bullets," Jorgenson said. "Simple and quick." From the smile on his face, I think he honestly liked that idea.

"No!" My fist hit the table hard enough and unexpectedly enough that some of the officers jumped. I no longer cared what my official position was. "They are prisoners of war. If you harm them, *I* will kill *you*."

I jabbed an index finger at Jorgenson's face. He blanched and backed up. I must have looked very crazy up top of that ridge. Soldiers will talk, and that talk spreads fast.

"It's all very well to sound noble like that," Howard said, "but you're not responsible for doing something with them. We can't send them back to New Terra, and we can't keep them with us and guard them. What would *you* do with them?"

I caught the emphasis on the word *you*.

"Let them go." I looked at each of the division commanders in turn, then turned toward Zeb. "Offer them parole if they agree never to fight against us again. If they take it, they leave without weapons and go home. If they're caught under arms again"—I shrugged—"then they're shot. They'll take it, the rank and file, anyway. Almost all of them, I'll bet, and I doubt there'll be many who violate it."

"I like it," Zeb said. "We're going to do that because this battle has given us an opportunity. We're going to march south and west into the heart of this land. The ammunition and guns we've taken here will keep us supplied. We've also taken enough horses, donkeys, and wagons for transport. We can forget the trucks. We'll send their troops home and have them tell their neighbors. If they give us food and supplies, we'll leave them in peace. Resist, and we'll burn everything to ashes. Athens won't have another army to oppose us, not coming from here. They'll have to pull troops from north and west when they hear what we're doing. That won't be easy, and it will take time to disengage them and bring them back. We can drive them to collapse and win this war."

A silence followed that little speech. Zeb was the commanding general but I think the audacity of the plan would have silenced everyone in the room anyway. The meeting broke up on that note.

One of the captains on Zeb's staff stopped me before I could get out of the room. I recognized him as the one named Thomas, who had spoken up before. I half expected another problem, but this time, his manner was diffident.

"Excuse me, Starman, I'm Captain Thomas D'Allessandro. You've seen me with the general, of course, but I know you don't know me. Could I ask you to look at something?"

He said the word *starman* as though it were a title, with a capital S, almost a patent of nobility. I realized I'd been hearing it that way from others since the battle.

"Sure," I said. "What is it? A wound?"

"No, no. I'm sorry. I should have been clear." I realized the man was sweating; I could see it on his face. "You see, I was there, Starman, when you took the lead of the troops. And you see, I sketch sometimes, and I wondered, well, what do you think of this?"

He pulled a heavy sheet of paper out of a breast pocket and unfolded it. On it, in charcoal, he had drawn me setting out at the head of that squad, rifle in hand, head and chin jutting forward. It was a decent rendering of me. On one side of me, also recognizable, was No Nonsense. The brown-haired girl was on the other side. Her face was clear, right down to the stray brown hair.

"It's good," I said. "You should keep it. If we win this, it may be worth something."

"Oh, I wouldn't sell it." His face colored under the sweat. "I wanted to know if you would sign it."

My first autograph.

.   .   .

Our army drove south without any pretense of a supply line. We lived off the land. Fortunately for us, that land grew richer as we went, and many of its denizens were perfectly happy to trade supplies for being left in peace. Others fled, and triggered more flight where they went. We helped ourselves to what they left behind. Almost no one took up arms against us. The prevailing attitude, as best I could tell, was that all governments were corrupt and bad; one was as good—or bad—as another. We found no organized resistance willing to give their lives for the Athenian government. I began to believe Zeb's idea that one army, storming through the back door and rampaging through the rear, could topple their government and end the war.

If I was growing more confident about Zeb's plan, I was feeling the opposite about the man. That arm bothered him more the farther we went. In fact, each day seemed worse than the one before it. I caught him several times supporting the arm with his other hand when he thought no one was looking. After two weeks on the march, when we were closing in on the ruins of Knoxville and not far from their capital of Athens, I saw red highlights on his cheeks. He looked feverish but would not discuss it with me.

A couple of days after that, D'Allesandro, with No Nonsense in tow, woke me in the early morning. The sky was red, the sun barely above the horizon. "Leif, General Mendenhall can't get out of his bed," No Nonsense said. "He won't let anyone near him, but he can't get up."

I didn't like the sound of that. I got up and rushed over to Zeb's tent. Fortunately, it was early enough that only a few of his staff were there. I wouldn't have to cope with the other generals. Not yet, anyway.

Inside, Zeb was lying on his camp bed. I could see him shiver from where I entered the tent. Beads of sweat stood out on his forehead. I crossed to his bedside and put a hand on his head. Hot.

"Do you think it's summer already, Ma?" he asked. "It seems hot today."

Fuck. This was not going in a good direction.

"I'm not your mother," I said. "I'm Leif. The starman."

Zeb shook his head. He looked at me and I could see him will himself to focus. Thank God for small favors.

"Leif," he said. "It's my arm. It's not . . . right."

"I need to look at it. You wouldn't talk to me about it a couple of days ago, but there's no choice now. I need to see it."

Zeb nodded. With me and No Nonsense helping him, we managed to get the clothes off his upper body. His left arm, where the bullet had struck, was massively swollen. In the center of the swelling was the fresh scar where the wound had been, along with evidence of the sutures our surgeon had put in. I put my hand on it. Felt heat and fluctuance. Around that area was pinkish skin that blanched when I pressed on it.

"I don't want the surgeon," Zeb said.

"Neither do I."

That idiot hadn't cleaned the wound adequately. It hadn't been a deep wound, but the bullet almost certainly drove pieces of clothing and dirt into Zeb's flesh. The surgeon, probably fearful of causing his commanding general pain, hadn't done a thorough job of cleaning it. And then he had sewn it closed.

"You've got an abscess in there," I said. "The infection is starting to spread."

"Do you need to take the arm off?" He was a lot calmer asking that question than I would have been.

"I don't think so. If the infection is past the point where we can deal with it by opening it, draining it, and cleaning it, well, I don't think amputation will solve it either."

I was practicing medicine without a license, but I didn't think I had a choice. We had no antibiotics. There was nothing we could do for Zeb that I couldn't have done for a soldier in the field. Anyway, the only license I would have given our doctors at that moment was as barbers. Maybe not even that.

"Don't put me to sleep," Zeb said. "I'll take the pain."

I wasn't going to argue. "Okay," I told him, "just understand that once I start, I'm not going to stop. I'll have your staff hold you down, if necessary, until you pass out."

"At least you're honest," he said.

It didn't take long to set up. His staff brought scalpels and dressings from the surgery tent. We made no pretense at a sterile field. I had alcohol for cleaning and as much sterilization as we could manage.

I made a long incision in the swelling on Zeb's arm. A mass of putrid yellow-green pus damn near exploded out through my cut. I heard gagging from the others in the tent. I extended the cut and got in there with some of the dressing material and alcohol to make sure I had every last bit of filth out. Zeb couldn't keep his jaws clenched. He let out a scream. Tried to sit up. No Nonsense and two others pinned him to the bed so I could continue working. I dug in there to break up any pockets that had formed. With the blood, and pus, and screams, it could have been a scene from a torture vid.

When I was convinced I had done what could be done, I packed the open incision with clean lint and a wick for drainage and wrapped a bandage around all of it. Time would tell if I had done enough. I hadn't seen any sign of one of those flesh-eating infections, so maybe we would be lucky.

What I wanted when I emerged from that tent was a place to wash up. Even a cup of that weak tea would have been welcome. Neither was going to happen right away. A crowd had gathered, Zeb's four generals prominent among them.

"Is he going to live?" was the question all of them asked, pretty much all at the same time and as soon as I showed my face.

"Maybe," I answered, satisfying no one. I searched among the faces in front of me and found the young captain whose sketch I had signed. "Set a guard on his tent, outside and inside. No one, and I mean no one, goes in without my say-so. If there's any change, have the guard get me. I don't care what time of day."

"Yes, Starman. I'll see to it."

No one questioned my right to give orders, not even the generals. The rank of starman had, somehow, become supreme.

The crowd dispersed when I gave no sign that I would say anything else. Only one man stayed between me and a hot drink. General Howard.

"A word, Starman, if you please." When I nodded, he continued. "By seniority, I am next in rank and should take command if General Mendenhall should die. However, General Jorgenson has said that command should devolve on him based on who his patrons in the senate are."

"Shit." All of a sudden, I was weary. If the grass wasn't still wet with morning dew, I would have sat down. "We are maybe a day's march from being in artillery range of Athens. This is not the time for a squabble over who is in command."

Howard smoothed down the curly beard he had grown during the campaign. "You heard Jorgenson about the prisoners at Gettysburg. He has said we should be leaving scorched earth behind us on the way here. Do you want him in command when we take Athens?"

It occurred to me that Zeb might be a brilliant strategist, but he had miserably underestimated the problems that would arise if he died. "What would you like me to do?" I asked. "Put a bullet in Jorgenson's head?"

Howard's eyebrows went up and his eyes widened. "No, no. Of course not. I just thought you should know the situation. I'm glad you set a guard."

That last sentence of his was enough of a warning that I moved into Zeb's tent. I couldn't do much more than I had done for the infection, but I would be a very effective guard against anything else happening to him.

CHAPTER FORTY TWO

Whether my presence made a difference I don't know, but Zeb was left alone. That incision drained copious amounts of pus for nearly two days and then dried up. His fever broke on the second day. Once that happened, we were able to have him sit up in bed and take some food. Zeb was going to recover.

He was still too weak the following day to dress himself. Walking without assistance, much less mounting his horse, was out of the question. He demanded that we dress him, however, and then, propped up in his bed, he had his officers brief him.

The army had come to a dead stop with his illness. We were, in fact, in a precarious position. We were deep in enemy territory, without a supply line, and with no hope of reinforcements. The carnage of the battle we fought had left us with two-thirds the strength we had when we marched out of Youngstown. Our security rested on our rapid march keeping the Athenians off-balance and in some terror because they had no army to put between us and their capital. The longer we sat in one place, however, the greater the chance they would recover their equilibrium and put a defense force together. We couldn't hang out by ourselves down there forever.

"The countryside here is picked clean," Howard said. "We have to send parties farther afield to find food. That weakens us, and it's a signal to the locals that we're vulnerable."

"Which is why we need to move on Athens now," Jorgenson said to Zeb. "I can take command of the divisions while you recuperate, and lead the attack."

"If you lead this attack like you advanced on Gettysburg, you'll miss the goddamn capital and go south of it," Kamper said. "We don't need a general whose greatest skill is counting senators."

Jorgenson flushed. "You go too far, Kamper. You will answer for this when we return to New Terra."

"I'll be happy to answer for it right now," Kamper shot back, "but I will answer for it with my pistol against yours, not whatever pack of lies your patrons put together."

"As if you would command a company without your patrons." Jorgenson's hand went for his pistol. "Outside now, and let's do it."

"Stop this," Zeb said. His voice was weak, though, and neither of them paid attention.

"Zeb said stop, and you will stop!" My roar could have blown away the tent. Maybe that's an exaggeration, but it got their attention the same way it would have frozen two privates arguing over a hand of poker. Back in basic, I had fantasies about yelling at senior officers and having them freeze the way I did in front of the DI. Now I had just done it.

"If you two want to have a duel and kill each other, do it when we get back. Right now we are in the field against an enemy, and you both have jobs to do."

No one questioned my right to say that. I thought I could get used to this.

"Well said," came from Zeb. "I want your divisions ready to move out. Tomorrow morning, whether I'm on a horse or in a cart, we advance on Athens."

That was when the tent flap burst open and an excited Captain D'Allesandro ran in, a sheet of paper clutched in his hand. He ran to Zeb's bed and gave it to him. Zeb read it, puzzlement fighting with a smile for control of his face.

"How did this happen?" he asked D'Allesandro.

"Luck!" D'Allesandro shouted. "Our luck! Emissaries rode in from Athens. In Athens, they thought we halted on purpose to give them a last chance before we attack the city and raze it. When the government wouldn't yield, the people revolted. There was blood in the streets. The emissaries told me about it. They ask for mercy on the city and want to negotiate a surrender."

Zeb's face had been reduced to hollows and skin stretched over his skull. When he broke into a broad smile, his face nearly split in two. "Tell them we would be glad to accommodate them. I will meet with them tomorrow to discuss the terms. I would assume, gentlemen," he said to the generals, "that you can bury your differences, rather than each other, and put on a suitable display."

.   .   .

The prospect of an unconditional surrender must be a tonic to a general's immune system, because Zeb was able to get up the next morning. His uniform was shabby from the long campaign, and the left arm of his coat was ripped where the bullet had gone through, but he was pleased with it for this purpose.

"It looks like it belongs on a fighting general," he said. "That's the appearance I want."

We found a mostly intact building in a small town whose name was lost to history. It had a usable table, if no remaining chairs, and the weather was sunny, so the fact that only part of the roof remained was not a problem.

A squad of men and women cleaned the debris out of the little house and swept the floor. The table that remained was one of those big heavy butcher-block types. It had held up well over the years while the rest of the interior furnishings disintegrated. We moved it to the front room so that people coming through the door would face it across the room. I thought the lack of chairs was useful. It would emphasize that any discussion would be brief.

I did worry that we would need to stake Zeb out behind the table like a scarecrow, even for a short meeting. Indeed, he didn't have much more substance left to him than a scarecrow with most of its stuffing knocked out. His clothes were more draped over him than worn. He said he could do it, however, and with a head that looked like a bearded skull, he thought he would make a good impression.

A delegation of six rode up to the house to meet with us, four men and two women. Five of them formed a nondescript group and gave their occupations as three shopkeepers, a clerk, and a teacher. Those five wore tired clothes that had seen a better day. The teacher wore a pair of glasses, the first I had seen in a long while. They were correctives, obviously, not chip-and-phone glasses. The last man was different. He wore a clean white cotton shirt tucked into denim pants. Atop that was a knee-length coat of linen, resplendent with embroidery. He stood apart from the others.

"I understand that you represent the government of Athens and have the authority to surrender in return for peace," Zeb said.

The teacher with the spectacles stepped forward to the table, cleared his throat, and gave his name as David Aguilera. "Actually, we are the government of Athens now," he said. "Yes, we have the authority."

At those words, I gave them a second look. Neither by occupation nor by appearances was this a crew of firebrand revolutionaries.

"How have you come to be in this position?" Zeb asked. Obviously, he was thinking the same as I was.

Aguilera shrugged. "The people are tired of wars. We are tired of tyrants. We have made an end of that and the ones who are left, we will give to you. We have brought gifts from the city." He turned and indicated the cart visible through the open door. "Those are an earnest of our good faith and our plea that you have mercy on our city and our people. All we ask is peace."

"The gifts you may leave here when you go," Zeb said. "What I require of you for peace is your surrender without conditions. That, and you instruct your other armies to cease fighting and lay down their arms. In return, I will grant peace. You may keep your lives and your property and New Terra will rule."

Aguilera bowed his head for an instant, then straightened up and squared his shoulders. "We can accept those terms. It was agreed before we came."

"There is one more thing," said the man in the fine coat.

His words drew sharp looks from the rest of the delegation. I had the feeling that they believed they had achieved what they needed, and now it was being put at risk by someone with a separate agenda.

"What is this other thing?" Zeb asked. He put his hands on the table and used his arms for support. He sounded tired. This could not go on much longer.

"I am Learned Hand McCabe, Chief Preacher of the Church of All Saints of the Apocalypse." He made it sound like a proclamation we were privileged to hear. "I ask as part of a peace that you agree to leave our church alone."

"Reapocalyptics," Zeb said. "You grow rich off your people. Why should we leave you with the wealth many would say is ill-gotten?"

Learned Hand stepped forward next to Aguilera at the table. "You need us to keep the peace. You must know that the postapocalyptics of your church buttress your government by telling people that they have been selected for Heaven and, therefore, should obey your government on Earth since the reward comes in Heaven. The top of your church is rewarded by your government for this, even if the preachers are not collecting money from the people."

Just what we needed. A religious faction fight to ruin everything at the last minute.

"I do not have time to argue reapocalyptics and postapocalyptics," Zeb said. "Why do I need you to keep the peace?"

"Because you bring a starman at the head of an army!" The chief preacher pointed at me. "Your existence is a problem."

My father used to say the same thing even when he was sober.

"Want to tell me why I am a problem?" I asked.

Learned Hand was six-two, and when he expanded his chest, he filled out that beautiful coat of his. I am sure he was impressive in front of churchgoers. His voice filled the old house. "The Twelve Saints came back from the stars to put the world right after the first apocalypse. They were murdered before they finished their work. That is why God said that He would make a second apocalypse and he would send twelve more saints back from the stars at the head of an army to select the few who will go to Heaven. At that time, He will make the world right for them. Children go to sleep at night praying for a starman to come back from the stars and grant their wishes before the final apocalypse comes. We have had plenty of fakes, but rumor is you are real. You are one and not twelve, but you do come with an army, and you know the saying, 'And a starman shall lead them.' Do you know what people who fled your army are saying?" he demanded of Zeb.

"No. What?"

"They claim"—Learned Hand pointed at me again—"at the last battle in the East, he drew the flaming sword that once guarded Eden, led the charge, and cut our army down like a scythe chops wheat."

Oh my God. I felt I was going to need the table to prop me up like Zeb.

"That's not what really happened," I said.

"What really happened doesn't matter," Learned Hand said. "It's what people believe happened that's important. This was the spark that set off our revolution. Be careful of what you have unleashed, General. You need us, unless you want mobs loose, creating their own final apocalypse."

Zeb studied the tabletop. Maybe he was running out of energy. Maybe he was looking for inspiration.

"I will make an agreement with you," Zeb said at last. "I will let your reapocalyptic preachers preach as they wish. I am not going to argue about religion or numbers of starmen, with or without an army. In return, your church will stop selling Selection Tickets. If you wish to believe that there will be a second selection of who will be taken to Heaven, that is fine with me, but no one can buy their assurance of selection to Heaven."

Learned Hand smiled. "So we will tell people they must earn their selection by their behavior. That is probably not a bad thing. I suspect that more than half the preachers pocket the money for the tickets anyway, and do not forward it to the church. We are agreed."

Zeb's knees buckled, and he would have fallen without his hands on the table. "Captain D'Allesandro," he said. "Please bring the documents for signature."

We agreed to no looting and no actions against the population. We also agreed to keep the army outside of the capital. They turned over the surviving members of the previous government to be our prisoners and sent family members of the new government to us as hostages. Messengers went out to their other armies in the north and west, telling them to cease fire and surrender. I crossed my fingers on that one, but Zeb was confident that, with the government having surrendered, the remaining armies would see no reason to keep fighting.

.   .   .

The day after we signed the agreement, half a dozen horsemen from New Terra rode into our camp.

"We've held them at the picket line as you ordered, sir," said the messenger who brought the news to Zeb.

I was seated by a cook fire with Zeb and his personal staff, having a cup of wretched tea after inspecting the artillery. Zeb had recovered to the point that he insisted on following his usual routine, but he was still weak and it showed. He took frequent short breaks.

"Did they state their purpose?" Zeb asked the messenger.

"No, sir. Only that they demand to meet with you privately."

Zeb gazed at the fire for a moment. "I am sure. Tell them that they can meet with me at my headquarters in thirty minutes. I am finishing with other business."

As the messenger left to carry that reply, Zeb levered himself upright. "Captain D'Allesandro, please bring four you trust to that building we used. Leif, please join us."

I stood as well and gathered up No Nonsense by eye. "You left orders," I said to Zeb. "You anticipated this."

"Of course," Zeb said. "Our former political officer, Fuentes, was never caught after he fled from Gettysburg. He would not need to go all the way to the city of New Terra to reach one of his patrons who is powerful enough to act independently, and to authorize the use of horses from the express posts in New Terran territory. That allows riders to change mounts and cover ground in a shorter time than you would expect. More than one group of riders, I would expect, to take into account some uncertainty about where the army is." Zeb stroked his beard. "On the fortunate side, to be sure, that is why we have a small group here and not a small army. We should prepare for this meeting." He started to go, then stopped and turned back to me. "Leif, do not hesitate if you need to shoot."

We stationed ourselves in the front room of the house we had used for the negotiations with the representatives from Athens. D'Allesandro left one of his men outside. He and his other men, along with No Nonsense, stationed themselves on one side of the front room. I stood behind the table, facing the door. Zeb was out of sight in what had been a kitchen. While the structure of the old house had gaps in places, it would not be obvious from the outside who was inside or where we were located.

It was only a short wait before we heard hoofbeats outside, followed by the sounds of boots hitting the ground and walking up to the door. The door opened and six men filed in, one of them carrying a rifle, the others with pistols on their belts. The expression on the leader's face said eloquently that he did not expect me to be the person at the table and he especially did not expect me to be holding a pistol aimed at him.

The leader licked his lips furtively. "I don't know who you are, but we are here to see General Mendenhall."

"And you will," said D'Allesandro, "as soon as we have all of your weapons."

The rifleman was an idiot. He tried to level his weapon at me. I shot him twice—killed him—and had the pistol aimed back at the leader before any of the others could even piss in their pants. No Nonsense laughed and ostentatiously chambered a round in his rifle. Hands went up in the air.

After D'Allesandro and his men had collected all their pistols and knives, plus the rifle from the man I shot, Zeb came around the partition to stand next to me.

"I am General Mendenhall, commanding the Army of the Northeast, as you probably know. Who are you and what is your business here?" His voice was hard and flat.

"My name is Always True Burkovina," said the leader of the men from New Terra. "I am a special envoy representing the senate and president of New Terra. You cannot treat me like this."

Zeb's smile did not touch his eyes. "We are not in New Terra. I command this army, and the government of Athens has surrendered to me, so I am the authority here. Do not speak of how you should be treated. Now, you have told me who you are, but not your business. You have about one minute to tell me."

Burkovina's eyes flicked from one weapon to another. "There is a paper in the pocket of my coat," he said.

"Don't even think of moving your hand there," I said.

"Do you know what it says?" Zeb asked. "Or do I need to have your clothing removed so we can find it?"

Burkovina licked his lips again. "It is a warrant for your arrest, General Mendenhall. You are ordered to accompany me back to New Terra to face charges of interference with the lawful duties of Political Officer Fuentes, who is assigned to this army."

Zeb said, "I refuse to be arrested."

"General, I would advise you to think about your situation and not make it worse than it is." Burkovina tried to put some hauteur into his words but failed. "You cannot think to go to war with New Terra. If you murder the senate's envoy, there will be no mercy. Do you think to stay here forever?"

"I doubt Political Officer Fuentes and his patrons have mercy in mind anyway," Zeb said. "As for what I am going to do, you are my prisoners. As long as you do not resist and keep your mouths shut, I will not shut them permanently. For whatever else I am going to do, that is no longer your business. D'Allesandro, get them out of here."

After D'Allesandro removed the prisoners and took his men with him, it was only me, Zeb, No Nonsense—and a body—in the house. The wind outside gusted hard enough to blow through the gaps in the walls and ruffle Zeb's beard. He leaned against the table and looked old.

"That was nicely done," I said, "but what comes next? Whatever you do with them doesn't solve the problem Fuentes created. Maybe it adds another one."

Zeb clenched and unclenched the hand of his wounded arm as though testing it. "That's always the big question, isn't it?" he said. "It's not what you do in the moment; it's what you have to do because of what you did. You always have to see at least one step farther down the road. Better if you can see three or four steps." He bowed his head so I was looking at his bald pate. "You could say this is the consequence of my not having shot Fuentes when I had the chance, but you could as easily say it's the consequence of my accepting this command knowing how the officers had been picked." He raised his face to me again. "Let me show you something, Leif."

Zeb walked over to the side wall of the room that was most intact. Several packs had been placed there, the gifts from Athens to its conqueror in a bid to buy favor or, at least, mercy. Zeb pulled a cloth package out of one of them and spread the contents on the table. I found myself looking at the Stars and Stripes.

"They said they made this for me as a symbol of unity. That we would have only one state on this continent again. We do have a chance to unify with the people here, but at the very moment we have that chance, it all comes unraveled in New Terra."

I was staring at the flag more than I was listening to him. "The flag is wrong, Zeb."

"What?" He studied it. "It's supposed to be right. White stars on blue at the upper left. Thirteen horizontal stripes of red and white."

"It has fifty-five stars, Zeb. The one I marched behind in 2055 had fifty-two."

"Hah." He shook his head. "Shows you, doesn't it, how badly our history has been twisted, and why no one believes much from the old records. Maybe three more were added before the Tribulation. Maybe this was based on a fake record. We'll probably never know."

I said nothing, tried to think. I had left Earth for High Noon in 2069, and there were fifty-two stars on the flag then. I hadn't been back for very long before I left again in 2098. I couldn't remember noticing a flag then, and thirty-nine years passed here after I flew to Heaven and before the apocalypse. The flag could have changed. It bothered me that Zeb was right. We might never know the truth.

"The number of stars isn't the point," Zeb said. "The flag is a symbol, and that's why I brought it out. We can change things, for the better I hope. But what is happening in New Terra may undo all of it. It's not just Fuentes and his revenge. It's the senators who will use that as one more piece in their games for power and wealth. It's a president who sees all of that and uses it for his own ends. Burkovina was right, of course. I can't stay here, nor should I. I do have supporters in the senate. Otherwise, I would not have been given this command. Nothing works for anyone without influence among the senators. But I need to mobilize that support and I cannot leave here. Not now. Not yet. I believe you know that Jorgenson would try to take command, and you can guess what will happen if he does. But if I march the whole army north, we will lose our hold on Athens."

"Zeb, you have an idea in mind. Would you like to let me in on it?"

He grinned at me. "I would like to send you as my representative. I will give you a list of my supporters in the senate. They will work to have these charges annulled. You have enough prestige to get to see them. I'll send Thomas D'Allesandro with you. An uncle of his is a senator. That will help with access. Take the 401st with you. After the fighting they have been through, they will do anything for you. That unit is big enough for a show of support, but not so big as to undermine our strength here or start a war there."

The 401st. Leah Samuel had survived the Second Battle of Gettysburg and ended up a legend to her troops. Zeb had promoted her to lieutenant colonel and sacked Merz. It made sense that he would send them with me.

Zeb had indeed been looking several steps down the road. Farther than I had, in fact. Because if the plan to quash Fuentes's charges failed, they would be able to take me out and shoot me while Zeb tried something else. That had been the whole point of the show with the flag. Because he knew I couldn't say no.

No Nonsense looked like he was going to laugh. If he did, it was going to be the sorriest day of his life.

"When do I start?" I asked.

CHAPTER FORTY THREE

The tourist map my chip projected on my field showed a route of 405 miles between Athens, Tennessee, and Terre Haute, Indiana. New Terra didn't exist when the map was created, but I figured it was close enough to where Terre Haute had been that the distance was nearly the same. My app told me to expect a drive of about seven hours but was unable to provide current traffic conditions. I chuckled carefully, and only to myself, while I supplied my own commentary in my head. *There is no traffic today*, I told myself, *but road conditions are not good, because the pavement is badly cracked, where you can find it at all*. None of that would matter to the horses, wagons, and feet. At the rate we were going, I estimated—without using the app, obviously—that we would be there in three weeks, give or take a couple of days.

What would our reception—my reception—be? I puzzled over that as we marched. A lot would depend on when this illustrious, corrupt government realized we were coming. I had gotten over my reflex of assuming that someone in a distant city would hear about events almost as soon as they happened. Communication went no faster than a horse. It would be best if I could figure out a way to appear at New Terra with no warning, but that would mean leaving the regiment and making it into the city alone. Since I knew neither the city nor any of the people, that seemed very high risk. Would marching toward the city give Fuentes and his backers warning, so that they could prepare trouble, or would it give Zeb's supporters time to organize? Which would be more important?

My musing on this came to an end as we were passing what was left of a speedway that touted ALL SELF-DRIVER RACE CARS in large red plastic letters. Captain D'Allesandro rode over to me while I was looking at the sign.

"Our scouts came in, Starman," he said. "There is an army up ahead of us, past this built-up area."

That pulled my attention away from the old speedway. "How big an army?"

"A division, at least," D'Allesandro said. "I know these scouts. They are good men and women, not prone to exaggeration."

"Any chance they are here for reasons that have nothing to do with us?"

D'Allesandro shrugged. "They cannot know about us in New Terra," he said. "Granted, if a man with a fast horse left Athens as soon as we made ready to go, yes, New Terra could know we are coming. But there would be no time to place an army here."

I searched around for signs to identify the place. Yes, by the speedway. This had been Bowling Green, Kentucky. I checked my tourist map. It had been home to eighty-nine thousand people in 2095, the last date my map had information. If D'Allesandro was wondering why I was looking off to the right, he said nothing. I had become so accustomed to seeing moldering piles of old buildings almost everyplace I looked that I no longer paid attention to them, but I considered the population number and thought this might be a tough ruinscape to fight through if they attacked us.

I brought my eyes back to the captain. "Send a messenger out with a white flag. Let's see if we can find out whether they're hostile."

"Have the messenger tell them there's a starman coming at the head of an army," said Leah Samuel, who had ridden up while I was conferring with D'Allesandro. "Can't hurt to play the myth for all it's worth and see what happens."

"I'll attend to that myself," he said. "If I'm not back in three hours, that's an answer."

.   .   .

D'Allesandro was back comfortably within his self-imposed time limit. His face, however, did not herald good news.

"It's the Fourteenth Division under General Morrell. I don't know who his patrons in the senate are, but he doesn't have a good reputation among men that I know. He told me himself that his division was assigned to watch for and block any troops led by, and I am quoting him, 'the traitor Zebulon Mendenhall.'"

"What happened when you gave him the fable about a lucky starman and an army?" I asked.

D'Allesandro laughed. "He said he was not impressed and that we should turn you over to his custody. He said he will send officers to take command of our regiment. He had his staff with him, though, when we spoke. I could see some of them talking when I left, but what they were saying, I don't know."

"They could have been talking about their rations, for all I care," said Leah Samuel. "If he's sending his officers here to take charge, we're going to give him a fight he'll never forget. I can guess what happens to us after he takes command."

Leah started giving orders to put the regiment into a defensive position. I could see she knew her business and was using the ruins effectively. If this General Morrell came after us, it was going to be a bloody business. The rule of thumb was that an attacker needed a four- or five-to-one advantage in street fighting in a city. So maybe we could send a whole division reeling back, but what would we do next?

Leah must have been thinking similarly, because she came back to me while the regiment was digging in.

"They will be quite occupied once the fighting starts," she said. "Take D'Allesandro and a couple of men with you then, Starman, and slip away. We are close to populated areas now. You should have a good chance to make it to New Terra."

"And what happens to you?" I asked. "What happens to our troops?"

"They won't break through us right away." She smiled, showing teeth that, in my day, would have been straightened. "They don't know the tactics you taught us. They will have to regroup after the first attack. When they do, we'll retreat south. With luck, we can rejoin General Mendenhall."

I know long shots when I hear them. Any objection I was going to raise, however, vanished from my mind as shouts rose from the area of our front line. But I didn't hear gunfire. An attack hadn't started.

After several minutes, I saw a knot of riders coming toward us, along with a group of our men on foot. One of the riders carried a white flag. When they caught sight of us, they dismounted and led their horses the rest of the way to our position.

Their leader carried the white flag. He was bareheaded, and from his cheekbones to his eyes to his short brown hair, he could have been a fraternal twin to Yang Yong. I liked him immediately.

"I am Major Cho Simon, now commanding the Fourteenth Division," he said. "We understand that these troops are under the command of Starman Leif Grettison. I want to meet with him."

"Lieutenant Colonel Leah Samuel is the one in command," I said, "but, yes, I'm Starman . . . Leif Grettison." I had to force myself to say it as a title. He seemed to expect it. "What do you mean that you are in command of the Fourteenth? What about General Morrell?"

Major Cho gave me a salute. I returned it automatically. All my mind could come up with was—WTF?

"The Twelve Saints of the Apocalypse were starmen and starwomen who came to serve the survivors of the Tribulation," Cho said. "They were murdered before completing their mission, and their killers are in Hell for eternity. We have replaced General Morrell and his senior officers so that does not happen again."

"You mutinied?" I was incredulous.

Cho smiled, the same tiny smile with lips together that Yong would have given me. "It is only mutiny if it fails."

I smiled in return. "Okay. And what are you planning to do next?"

"The saying is that the army is the state and the state is the army. The truth is that the army is its men and women, and we are tired of fighting and being used. Finish the work of the Saints, Starman," Cho said. "Go to New Terra and put things right. Make them rule fairly. We and the division are here to join you."

.   .   .

We marched north, a good twelve thousand strong, while I tried to figure out what I was going to do when we arrived. Leah had said to play on the reapocalyptic myth of a starman leading an army and see what happened. So far, it had brought me a division. If I had any questions about the expectations of the troops after I spoke to Major Cho, those vanished during the march. Rank and file, they cheered me when they saw me, and they expected me to lead a revolution. They were clear. We were going to march into New Terra, I would walk across Government Plaza to the Senate Building, and the senators would fall on their knees and beg forgiveness.

I had my doubts.

Spirits were high enough that the troops sang as they marched, day after long day. I'm fine with off-key—I can clear out a karaoke bar without even trying—but I didn't know any of the songs these men and women were singing. So, I taught them "Battle Hymn of the Republic." Of all the Union battle songs we had learned and sung during the bicentennial, that one had been my favorite. The troops I was with now probably didn't know the Civil War had happened. Even if they did, with the fucked-up state of history, they probably didn't know who had won. But they took to the "Battle Hymn." The trumpet that shall never call retreat sounded out with enthusiasm as we marched north past farms and through villages.

Word of what was happening got back to the government in New Terra. They sent two divisions to intercept us. No fighting occurred. As soon as they reached us, those divisions overthrew their senior officers and joined us as well.

The Rangers I had been with on Mindanao joked that we were the lightning from His terrible swift sword. Hearing the "Battle Hymn" sung by damned near forty thousand men and women marching on New Terra, the farmers and villagers who crowded by roads and stood on hills to watch the army go by must have thought we were His unsheathed sword and lightning come to Earth again.

Somehow, I had been turned into Joan of Arc. I remembered how that had ended the first time around.

New Terra was the first modern—that is, postapocalyptic—city I had seen. It was not impressive to someone who had grown up around twenty-first-century New York. As in Eastview, many of the structures had been built with rubble scavenged from preapocalypse buildings.

Others were of new brick laid in mostly straight lines. Few were more than five stories high. The streets were unpaved: packed dirt for most of them and cobblestones for the main thoroughfares. I saw garbage alongside and even in those streets. An odor that permeated the area told me that indoor plumbing was a rarity, if it existed at all.

New Terra had one grand and broad avenue named the Avenue of Glory, which bisected the city and led to the government center. We chose that for our march in. Word spread rapidly, and people lined the avenue to watch the army go by. When they saw the people packing the roadside to watch and cheer, the troops started the "Battle Hymn" again. People cheered. They tried to sing along with us. They threw flowers. The march turned into the parade of a conquering army.

The president, the senators, and their few loyal guards fled west.

.   .   .

The army filled the plaza in front of the senate building, which also held the offices of the president. That building looked like the government buildings I remembered from a school tour of Washington. Its front was made of six-foot-high whitish marble blocks that had been salvaged from some other building; the side walls that I could see were brick. Twelve shallow broad steps ran up to the front entrance.

We stopped at the bottom of the steps, where they adjoined the stones of the plaza. The singing stopped. For a moment, it was dead silent.

One half of the twelve-foot-high double front door of the building opened and a solitary man walked out. He was dressed in trousers and a shirt of wool twill dyed light blue, with a gray jacket. He stood on the top step and looked out at the plaza packed with troops, rifles at shoulder arms and battle flags flying. I could see him shiver. I'd probably shake at that sight too. Slowly, he walked down the stairs and came to a stop in front of where the senior officers and I had dismounted.

"My name is Proclaim Righteousness Lichtman," he said. "I am the Chief Clerk of New Terra." Up close, he was middle-aged with mild eyes, pink skin that showed little effect of sun, and a trim mustache on an otherwise clean-shaven face. His eyes flicked from one of us to another and came to rest on me. "Are you the starman—Starman Grettison?"

"I'm Leif Grettison," I said. "Yes, I'm a starman. It's not a title. Not a real one."

"That does not matter," Lichtman said. "I have come to tell you that almost all the clerks and administrators have remained at their posts and welcome you. As you may know, we are the apparatus of government and are the ones who communicate with all the regions and towns of New Terra. *We* are how the government works, even if we are not the government in name."

"Thank you for the explanation," I said. "Am I correct that you are saying the president and senators are no longer in control of the government?"

"They are gone." He said that with finality. "They do not have an army, and they do not have the apparatus of government."

"I've got it," I said. "What comes next?"

"Please tell us what to do," said Proclaim Righteousness. "The government is yours."

CHAPTER FORTY FOUR

I spent the next few hours in a state of shock. Proclaim Righteousness showed me the president's office and asked if I would like to use it. That office was opulent. The chairs had embroidered cushions. The desk, its top a large block of polished wood, had gilt finishings. Carpets covered the floors, and heavy drapes hung on the walls. I wanted no part of that office.

After a search, we came up with a small office in the part of the building where the clerks worked. It had a metal desk, a chair, and a door I could close to shut the rest of them out. Once I had closed that door and was alone, I sat down and tried to think. I had never run anything bigger than my section, except once when I had to take command of the whole platoon after the lieutenant was shot. I had no idea how to run a government, and I doubted a miracle was going to occur that would give me the knowledge. The old dictum of "fake it till you make it" didn't seem like a good idea in this situation. However, I couldn't sit there and do nothing. Like it or not, these people were looking to me. I didn't deserve that sort of position, but I had it. And not making any decisions would be, in fact, making a decision. A bad one. I pulled the door back open and shouted for my senior officers.

Sometimes it's important to know what you don't know.

The first step was easy. I told Leah, Simon, and the other division commanders to get their troops out of the city before we had an incident that would spoil the current good mood. I also told them to have their men and women take up defensive positions around the city, in case the former government could find units loyal to them and try to come back. No one thought that was likely, but they knew how to handle the troops and they followed my orders as though I had the right to give them.

Then I racked my brains for my next step. I knew that in the immediate aftermath of a revolution—and that is what had happened—there would be a brief window when something new could be built. Let too much time go by, and the old order would reassert itself. People have inertia and, left to themselves, will fall back into their old patterns because that is what they know. The problem was that I had no idea what to do.

All I could think of was that, not too long before by my biological time, I had been an American and an American soldier, and I had been proud of both. I had no illusions that my old country was perfect. Far from it. I had been taught about its flaws, and even more important, I knew it shared responsibility for the apocalypse and the world we were left with. I owned that responsibility, too, just as Yong had said. But there had been ideas and aspirations that had been good.

I have no originality.

I called for Proclaim Righteousness and told him we were going to have elections.

"What?" he said. If ever a man looked confused, that was him.

"Just what I said. Any office that rules anything, any position with power, whether it's mayor of a town or a representative of a region, a senator or your next damned president, people vote on who gets the job. Everybody over eighteen gets one vote. And the Athens state that we just conquered, they vote too. Make them fair elections, not rigged. One government for everybody."

"How am I supposed to do that?"

"Figure it out," I said. "You asked me to tell you what to do and I did. You figure out how to do it."

"Half the people can't even read," he said. "People won't know who will be able to do the jobs. They'll make mistakes."

"Worse than what you had?" I asked.

His eyes widened and he smiled. "Probably not."

"Right. And make sure everybody knows that if they screw up, they're responsible for the mess they make."

He turned to go, but I stopped him before he could get out the door.

"One more thing," I said. "Send a message to Zeb, General Mendenhall, at Athens. Tell him he needs to get up here and run for office."

Did I think a democracy was perfect and that we couldn't screw it up? No. What I did remember was Churchill's line that democracy was the worst form of government, with the exception of every other one people had tried. I knew I wasn't going to invent a better system.

.   .   .

It was another six weeks by the time Zeb rode into New Terra at the head of one of his divisions, and summer was in full swing. Howard's and Kamper's forces had been left in the south to keep control of that territory. The summer wasn't as hot as summers that I remembered, certainly not close to Miami, but it was sunny enough and warm enough for crops to grow and for people to shed the extra layers of clothing. I was concerned that as the weather warmed, the garbage in the city streets would add another dimension to the odor of city living, but on that, I was pleasantly surprised. The first elections were held in the city of New Terra, and the people voted in were ones who promised to clean up the city. They actually did it.

I was glad to hear about Zeb's arrival. Proclaim and the other administrators kept bringing me problems that needed decisions I was completely unqualified to make. I told them to figure it out when I could and tried not to screw it up when I had no choice but to make a call. One big decision I made I know was right. Again, I wasn't original. We didn't have a constitution in New Terra—and I wasn't about to write one—but I did say that everyone in the army had to take an oath to the people as a whole, not to whoever was president. That mirrored the oath I had sworn when I joined the army. That and no one in the army could hold any government office. I wasn't sure Zeb was going to like that, but I didn't intend to give him a choice. When he arrived at my cramped office, I told him what was happening. Then I told him I wanted him to be acting president, but he had to resign as general first.

Zeb spent a moment looking at me. "I owe you my life," he said at last. "I haven't forgotten that, and I won't. I'll do it the way you say, Leif.

I don't know if it's right, and I wonder if I'm going to regret it, but I'll do it. I will stand for president. And if I win it, I'll turn it over after my term. That's what you want, isn't it?"

"Yes. It did work before. Mostly. You said you thought we could have a better state."

Zeb laughed. "I did say that and I did mean it. We'll see what I can do. I won't give any guarantees beyond that."

"I understand," I said.

Zeb stroked his beard the way he did when he was thinking through a problem. "I've got a question for you, Leif, if you'll answer it."

I spread my hands wide. "Ask," I said.

"The way things happened, you're effectively the dictator. You could have kept it. You know that. Even my army might have mutinied if I had opposed you. Why didn't you do it? You're probably the only person in history to give up being a dictator."

It was my turn to laugh. "I don't want to be a dictator. And that's not an original thing. A Roman named Cincinnatus did it a long time ago."

"I don't know that name," Zeb said, "but there's a lot of history we don't know. But what are you going to do now?"

"Same thing Cincinnatus did. I'm going back to the farm."

CHAPTER FORTY FIVE

Zeb kept his word. He resigned his commission and became the acting president of New Terra. Based on his reputation and status as the conqueror of Athens, I figured he would have no difficulty winning election as president. Of course, we had no such thing as opinion polls, but I think it was a good bet. What would come after that, I didn't know. However, we hadn't done so well back when we thought we knew what we were doing either.

I went and found No Nonsense outside New Terra, where the 401st was stationed. He was sitting with a group of men and women playing cards.

"Losing again, No Nonsense?" I said when I came up.

"Yeah." He threw his cards in, stood up, and brushed off his pants. "Nothing else to do, though. No messengers needed. Never thought I'd miss a battle, but, God, I'm bored."

I looked at him as though I were seeing him for the first time. He had changed since we rode to Youngstown. His beard had grown in, thick and bushy. He had grown, too, now almost my height. His shoulders had broadened. He was no longer a boy.

"I'm going back to the farm," I said. "If you've had enough of soldiering, you might want to think of coming with me."

"Soldiering? Yeah, I've had enough of that. Question is, will they let me go?"

"They'll let you go," I said. "Technically, you're my aide and I'm gone from here. Even if you weren't, Zeb is going to shrink the army. The Formation Wars are over. If there's some other state beyond the plains and mountains, it's going to be some time before we come in contact. Maybe in that time, we'll figure out how to manage it without fighting. But back to you. You can muster out if you want to and come back with me."

No Nonsense turned shy all of a sudden and looked down at the ground. A switch clicked in my head. I had been seventeen once; why did I feel so old now?

"Did you find a girl here?" I asked. "Is that the issue?"

"No, no." He scuffed at the ground. "I'll ride back with you and see Ma. I'll stay there through the harvest for sure, maybe for the winter, too, if she needs help and has food enough for all of us. But then I'm going to go. You mentioned plains and mountains. Well, I've heard people here talk of the Empty Lands, and I hear there's a huge range of mountains beyond them. I want to see all of that. You can't argue now that I'm not grown enough to do it." He said the last almost as a challenge.

"No, I wouldn't say that." I clapped him on the shoulder. "I'll say that I'll be sorry to see you go, though. You're a good man, No Nonsense."

As we went about putting supplies together, our party expanded. Leah had taken up with a woman officer in the Fourteenth. They had heard there was good land for farming to the east and wanted to try their hands at it. Both of them were also done with army life.

"Join us," I said, adding to Leah, "If they still need a militia in Eastview, maybe you can run it."

It was a pleasant-enough summer ride. The weather cooperated and it only rained on us twice. We didn't push the pace and took almost a month to reach Eastview.

On the surface, life there hadn't changed from when we left. Guo was still the mayor, but this time he had been elected to the office. He had used that as leverage for a law that said you couldn't wear a gun while playing cards. That had cut down the number of gunfights, threatened or acted on—which was probably a good thing, since Hezekiah was still my deputy as marshal. He couldn't wait to give me back the star. Pressed it into my hand the moment he saw me, and declared he was going to get drunk and stay that way for three days.

I went to the church and saw Be Kind. He told me he had buried Tonya when the ground thawed and took me to the small cemetery to show me. Her grave was grassed over and neat but unmarked. I asked him to put up a stone and said I would pay whatever was necessary.

Then it was time for the last leg of our trip. That meant one more night camped in the open air. It was a far cry from when I had made that trip in the winter. The grass by the trail was thick and tall, and it smelled sweet when I lay down on my blanket. The air was alive with the buzz of insects and the chirping of birds. It happened to be a clear night and a new moon. The sky was black, speckled with a million twinkling stars. Lying there, it was hard to believe I had ever gone out to them.

I tried to look for where High Noon and Heaven were, but I couldn't pick out those stars by eye. I wondered if there were people now on those planets who looked up at their sky and wondered what was happening on Earth. I wondered what I was going to say to Charity tomorrow.

I wanted to talk with Yong about Charity. I guess I wanted Yong's permission for whatever I would say. But I couldn't hear her. Yong's voice did not come into my mind that night.

I looked up at that star-spangled sky and said, "I love you, Yang Yong, and I always will."

Two old soldiers, but one had died in their last action. The other had not. Before I fell asleep, I felt her hand on mine.

.   .   .

It was all so familiar when I rode down the lane to the farmhouse with No Nonsense. Doubting Thomas was playing out in the yard, much larger than I remembered him. He looked up at the approach of the horses, gave a shout, and ran into the house.

I had barely time to dismount before I was mobbed. Elvy was first out the door, flying to me at top speed. She had changed; I could see that. She was a young woman now, not a girl. She was the same Elvy, though. She hit me like a missile, damn near knocked the breath out of me, and grabbed me in a crushing hug that would never be suspected from one so tiny. Courtesy was right behind her and added to the hug, and then the younger ones were there, too, jumping on and around me. Truth walked out slowly and stood to the side with No Nonsense. And then Charity was in front of me, her eyes alight and a broad smile on her face.

"Charity," I said, "I'm home."

CODA

Fortune helps the brave.
Terence, *Phormio* (161 BC)

CHAPTER FORTY SIX

It was not that many weeks later that harvest time came, for the summers were short and the chill set in fast. It was hard work to bring it all in and have the food readied for the long winter. It was the hardest work I've ever done. I wasn't in town for that entire stretch. Fortunately, everyone else was working hard as well, which kept people from causing trouble. There's a lesson in that, I suppose.

When the bulk of the outdoor work was done, it was celebration time. I did need to be in town then. I was at Al's one of those evenings, along with No Nonsense. He was old enough to do as he wished, so he was there, a new pistol on his hip and—I hope—my words about thinking more and drinking less in his mind.

How had I turned out to be the one giving mature advice?

I was hoping he would meet a girl who would cure him of this itch to head out into the unknown. When had I become such a homebody?

I was musing about that when the door to the saloon was pushed open. Guo came in with a young man, a stranger, hard on his heels. Guo's eyes searched the room, found me. He pointed. The two of them pushed through the crowd to reach me.

"Leif," Guo said, "this man rode into town earlier today. Said he heard there was a starman here. Says he needs to talk to you. I offered him some food and rest, but he'd only eat a bit and wanted to find you right away, so I brought him here."

I looked over at the stranger, figured him for early twenties. He looked in need of a good meal—several, in actuality. His clothes hung on his frame. His slight brown beard covered but did not hide the hollows in his cheeks. Intense gray eyes framed a sharp nose, and a mop of hair that matched his beard flopped over the pale skin of his forehead. His clothes were travel-stained and worn. I could believe he had been riding on a trail for a long time.

"Are you a starman?" he asked without any preliminaries.

I had become accustomed to the sound of New Terran voices. His accent was odd. He was not trying to peer into my eyes. I had become accustomed enough to people's habit that the absence was striking. And he had asked about *a* starman.

"I am," I said.

"My name is Caleb Peterson," he said. "I'm from Earthbase."

That word dropped like a rock into a pool, and ripples of silence spread out from the source. Within a minute, all conversation in Al's had stopped. The sound of a chair scraping on the floor was loud.

I stared at this Caleb Peterson. Less than a year ago, I would have considered him a sign that I could complete my mission, such as it was. It would have meant everything to me. Now? He was an intrusion from the past.

"I know about Earthbase," I said. "At least, I know about it from long ago. What brings you to find me?"

"We know a starship came back. Never mind how, for the moment. Earthbase has sent messengers like me to find the starfolk and bring them to Earthbase."

His first sentence caught in my mind. I didn't pay much attention to the rest of what he said. They knew a starship had come back. I felt a thump in my chest. That had to mean Yong had made it to Earthbase. She *was* there. And I had spent a year not going there.

"Yang Yong is there! Correct?" I grabbed his jacket with both hands and pulled him close. "Yang Yong told you to find me! Right?"

His eyebrows arched up; his eyes went wide. He pulled his head back from me as best he could, and I could read both fear and surprise there.

"I don't know who that is," he managed to get out. "I don't know that name." He had his hands up and empty, as though he needed to show he wasn't going to fight.

As fast as my emotions had soared, they came crashing down. I shoved him away. I hurt worse in that moment than I had since the first night in Charity's barn.

Caleb felt for the front of his shirt, discovered it gaped open where a button had torn off when I grabbed him. He poked at the loose thread for a few seconds while we, and everyone else, were silent.

"My ship was the *Dauntless* and it came back to Earth over a year ago," I finally said. "If Yong isn't at Earthbase, I can tell you I'm the only one who survived. She would have been the only other. So, tell me why it's so important for you to find me—and it's only me—now? You've had a year. Why come now?"

He pulled his jacket closed over where his shirt had torn and looked up at me. "We've received a signal," he said.

"A signal?" I felt a tightness in my chest. "Another ship has come in? Is that what you are telling me? That can't be. There are no more."

"Not another ship. This signal came from a star, and not a star that Earth ever sent a ship to. It came from somewhere—from someone—else."

"Wait . . ." I stared at him.

Caleb said, "We need you."

DRAMATIS PERSONAE

CREW OF THE STARSHIP DAUNTLESS

Cristina Domínguez—senior ship systems engineer
Leif Grettison— exoplanetary scout
Anil Jenkins— junior ship systems engineer
Zoe Klein— junior nuclear systems engineer
Dev Likhar— senior nuclear systems engineer
Dr. Charles Osborne— senior ship physician
Yang Yong—pilot-in-command

THE FARM

Charity Blessed Montgomery

Amazing Grace Montgomery—age 8
Courtesy Always Montgomery—age 10
Doubting Thomas Montgomery—age 5
Elvy—age 12
Measure Carefully Montgomery—age 4
No Nonsense Johnson—age 16
Renounce Pride Montgomery—age 3
Truth Speaks Montgomery—age 14

TOWN OF EASTVIEW AND MILITIA

Constant Prudence Abernathy—militia
Be Kind Blanchette—preacher
Hezekiah Dobbins—former marshal and owner of the Golden Ass
Pride Goeth García —militia
Guo Fair Measure— mayor of Eastview and owner of the Bank of Eastview

Al Kowalski—owner of Al's Bar
Render Praise Martin—militia
James McSorley—barber and militia
Tonya Spurling—militia
Ethan Wyandotte—bank teller and militia

ARMY OF THE NORTHEAST

Major General Zebulon Mendenhall—commander of the Army of the Northeast

Brigadier General Sanjay Chopra—Twentieth Division commander
Captain Thomas D'Allesandro—General Mendenhall's staff
Political Officer Jesus Fuentes—assigned to the Army of the Northeast
Brigadier General Paul Howard—Twelfth Division commander
Brigadier General Amos Jorgenson—Eighth Division commander
Brigadier General Felix Kamper—Fourth Division commander
Colonel Ezra Merz—401st Regiment
Major Leah Samuel—401st Regiment

OTHER NOTABLES

David Aguilera—a teacher (Athens)
Always True Burkovina— special envoy (New Terra)
Major Cho Simon—Fourteenth Division (New Terra)
Proclaim Righteousness Lichtman— Chief Clerk of New Terra
Learned Hand McCabe—Chief Preacher (Athens)
Caleb Peterson—Earthbase

ABOUT THE AUTHOR

Colin Alexander is a writer of science fiction and fantasy. He has had a career as a physician, biochemist, and medical researcher. He now lives in Maine with his wife, where he also studies and teaches taekwondo.

The Lucky Starman is the third adventure of Leif the Lucky and follows directly on the events in *Murder Under Another Sun*. Colin is already hard at work on why Earthbase needs Leif.

Find Colin Alexander on the web at:
www.afictionado.com
www.facebook.com/ColinAlexanderAuthor
www.goodreads.com/colinalexander

Made in United States
Troutdale, OR
08/13/2023

12032719R00215